Cold Stone & Ivy

Book 1: The Ghost Club

H. Leighton Dickson

TO SUBBY

ACKNOWLEDGMENTS

Most of the news reports in this novel are taken from the actual accounts of the Ripper murders (albeit embellished and punkified) and the timelines are accurate. Many of the characters are historical but also, fictionalized (and punkified) and I challenge you to investigate them at your leisure.

I am exceptionally grateful to a large number of folks, whose encouragement got me started and, in fact, kept me going. Jules Vernes, HG Wells and A. Conan Doyle, to name a few. Amateur Latin expert and partner-in-crime Szabolcs Szterszky and editor/author Erica Orloff (aka ERICA), both of whom I owe many bottles of wine. And maybe some money.

And I have to thank House Calls, SpaceAnjJ, Purple Piggie, Castiello, PJaneL, Elodie Wolfe, Ebony 10 and so many others. You know who you are and why I love you.

Contents

Part 1: Lasingstoke

Part 2: London

Part 1: LASINGSTOKE

Chapter 1

Of Floating Arms, Blobs of Ink and a Murder in Manchester

September 11, 1888
Grosvenor Railway Bridge, London

It looked like a dead dog floating on the River.

Three boys had been sitting on the bank, counting the airships over the stacks of the Battersea Shipyards. It was dusk, and the lights of the yard turned the ships into dragons hovering over a land of smoke and volcanoes. For the boys, it was a magical sight and as they sat on the bank they imagined worlds where friends carried swords, not coal shovels and where enemies breathed fire, not steam.

When they spied the floater however, they scrambled to their feet.

"What is it, then?" called Sharpie. He was nine and all grown up. His name was Cyril Sharp, but you'd get a shiner if you called him anything but Sharpie.

"It's a dog." Martin Alcorn now, all of eight and tough as tack.

"It's not a dog, I tell ye," said Sharpie. "Dogs ain't pink now, are they?"

"Mrs. Tumblemorey's dog's pink."

They stared at him.

"It's got a disease."

"Maybe it's a snake…" Ronnie Shipley now, the quiet one, and the boys' eyes grew round at the thought of a snake. Not many snakes in Battersea. Dead ones were almost as much fun as the living.

"Can ye grab it, then?" asked Martin. "Pull it over! Let's get a look!"

Sharpie began to tug on the branch of a young sapling growing on the bank. The others joined him and within moments, the branch peeled away from the trunk into their hands.

Sharpie turned and slapped the switch into the water, trying to drag the snake-dog to shore. It was tangled in branches and floating timber, and as usual, the current of the Thames was strong.

"Get it! Get it!"

He dragged it in closer, and the dog rolled once, out from under the soggy brush.

Cyril Sharp screamed and dropped the switch, bolting up the bank as fast as he could. Martin Alcorn began to back away, tripped over his feet before turning and scrambling up after him. Ronnie Shipley watched them for a moment but he turned, picked up the switch and dragged the floater to shore.

"That's no dog," he whispered to himself.

It was an arm, tied off by a piece of string, floating down the river toward Whitechapel.

***

"You sir, are a fiend and a murderer," said Penny, and she turned to her father, Chief Inspector Charles Dreadful. "Arrest him, father. This man is your culprit."

"Bully for you, Penny," said her father. "I knew you'd jump this case. You're a crackerjack girl, you are."

She smiled at him, knowing it to be quite true.

He turned to his men, Penny's favourite boys in blue.

"Come along, chaps. Let's get this bludger into the claps!"

As they dragged off the nefarious Alphonse Lemeuix, Penny turned to her companions.

*"I always knew he was a villain," she said merrily. "He had a certain **sang-froid** about him!"*

They all laughed and lifted their claret by way of a toast.

And that is how Penny Dreadful, Girl Criminologist, not only caught the infamous Rue Buffon killer, but still had time to enjoy the new summer palette of French Chardonnay.

The Conclusion of A Murder in Pari ●

Ivy Savage growled as the slam of the front door caused ink to spurt from her fountain pen.

"Davis," she moaned, looking down at the glistening papers on her desk. She had envisioned ending her story—*Penny Dreadful and a Murder in Paris*—with a bang. Instead, it was ending with a rather large blob.

"There's been another one," called her brother from the foyer. "The coppers are out in full."

"Another one?" She sat up. "Where?"

"Dunno. Whitechapel, I expect. That's where the last one was."

She peered out through the rain-spattered window onto the streets. In a policeman's family, murder was a routine topic for conversation along with burglary, pick-pocketing and the treachery of four-wheeled steamcars. A killing in London's East End was nothing new but with the recent slayings in Whitechapel, even her father was reluctant to discuss them.

"There's a mob collecting at the stationhouse too," said Davis. He stepped into the room and peeled a soggy sweater over his head. "It's a bloody riot out there tonight."

"Did you see tad?"

"He's on his way. I think Remy's with him."

"It must be bad, then. Is it in the broadsheets?"

"Not yet." He dropped into a chair next to her desk, rainwater collecting in puddles at his feet. "So? Are you going to write it?"

"Davis, hush."

"Why? Mum can't hear you." He rolled his eyes. "She's as dead as the girls in Whitechapel."

"Hush!"

She glanced over at her mother sitting by the hearth, hands held limply in her lap. With dull eyes, gaunt cheeks and a black-collared dress, Catherine Savage looked dead. Truth be told, she'd looked that way for years. She couldn't feed herself, couldn't clothe or bathe or change herself. Those were duties left to Ivy, along with the raising of her brother. At the ripe age of eighteen, Ivy Savage had already been a mother for seven years.

She sighed. As dead as the girls in Whitechapel.

"C'mon Ivy, don't be such a 'good' girl," said Davis, green eyes gleaming. "The whole street's waiting for it."

She looked back at her brother.

"Tad'll kill me..."

"What else is new?"

"Right." She turned her chair to face him. "I'm calling it *'Penny Dreadful and the Terror of Whitechapel...'*

"Cor," her brother whistled. "I can't wait to start the sketches on that one..."

"I'm certain it will be very gruesome."

"Just the way I like it, blood splatters 'n all. I may need more ink."

She smiled now, despite herself. Davis was only three years younger than she, a talented artist and very clever with a rebellious streak as long as the Thames. He was set on the army, convinced his future lay in putting down rebellions in other parts of the world. But he was a boy. He couldn't see past his own heart.

The set of clocks chimed ten and as if on cue, the front door opened again, a gust of wind flickering the gaslight in the hall.

"Hallo, my girl," called her father and she could hear wet boots dropping to the floor. "Put on the tea! I've brought Remy with me."

Smiling under his moustache, Inspector Trevis Savage entered the small sitting room, followed by a well-dressed young man, top hat and town coat heavy with rain.

Ivy rose to her feet.

"Christien," she breathed.

"Found him with Bondie and the other surgeons at the station," said Savage. "Thought he might like a spot of tea with his fiancée."

"I couldn't refuse," said Christien. He flashed her a smile and Ivy felt her chest tighten. He didn't smile much for he was a very serious young man. With sleek, dark hair, clear blue eyes and skin like fine porcelain,

Christien Jeremie 'Remy' St. John de Lacey looked like he stepped off the pages of a French novel. One she could never write.

"But I can't stay long, Ivy. There's been another discovery."

"Ha!" yelped Davis. "Told ya."

"A murder?"

"Just an arm off the Railway Bridge," said her father. "The rest of her'll turn up sometime."

"I could help…"

"You're too busy with your mum."

"Well, I could."

Christien pulled the top hat from his head, gripped it in both hands.

"Ivy, I'm afraid I can't take you to the library this Friday."

"But it's Mr. Doyle. He's never come to the Whitechapel Library before."

"I have a meeting, Ivy. It's a very influential club in Pall Mall. They've been after me for months and Dr. Williams insists I go."

"But I thought you hated those sorts of things. You say they make your head ache."

"Ah, life with a police surgeon," said her father. "Get used to headaches, my girl."

"Perhaps we can go for tea on Thursday?" said Christien. "I have an exam until noon and then, rounds at Bethlem at six. We could fit it in between?"

She nodded, heart sinking like a stone. Doyle was one of her favourite authors. His latest novel had kept her up all night with the clues and plot twists and a fascinating protagonist. He had never come to the East End. No one ever did.

"I picked up the post," said Savage, pulling letters from the pockets of his waistcoat and tossing them onto the desk as he crossed the floor toward the fire. "Scribbles from your readers, my girl."

"All three of them," grinned Davis.

"Oh yes, and there was a parcel," said Christien. He rummaged through his town coat, pulled out a brown paper package wrapped in twine. "Apparently from someone named Jack."

He passed it into her hands.

"Jack? Jack who?"

"No last name, I'm afraid."

"You are the literary sensation of an illiterate neighbourhood," said her father. He knelt down beside his silent wife, took her hands in his. "Did she eat tonight?"

"Some soup." Ivy sighed. "Not much."

"Lonsdale could help with that," said Christien. "For a sanitarium it has a good reputation and Frankow is a fair psychiatrist. I wish you would consider my offer."

"I may have to, Remy." Savage rose to his feet, kissed his wife on the top of her head. "It'll be difficult for Ivy to care for her once she's married."

"Ivy can stay at Lasingstoke Hall while Catherine is being treated. My uncle won't mind and my brother is most often away." He looked down at her. "It will be like a holiday by the Bay."

His expression was earnest but she was disappointed and stubborn and cursed herself for it. They used to get on so very well, sharing stories of murder and medicine and the macabre world of policing. Then two months ago, he had surprised her with a ring and everything had changed.

"Your brother?" Davis grinned. "The Mad Lord of Lasingstoke? Don't he talk to ghosts?"

"He's a Baron, Davis," said Christien. "He sits in the House of Lords."

"Therefore he talks to stuffy old English politicians." Savage grinned and poked at the fire, causing it to rise in its bed.

"Still," said Christien. "It's a fine offer. You should both consider it."

"I might just do that, Remy," said Savage.

"Open the package, Ivy," said Davis.

"We don't need to consider it, tad," and she turned the brown wrapping over in her hand. Her name and address were written in red ink, with 'From Jack' in the top left corner. "My stories are selling and soon we may have enough to hire a nurse, care for her at home—"

"But once we're married you'll be with me at Hollbrook House," said Christien. "There are far too many stairs for her at Hollbrook."

"Open the package," urged Davis. "Maybe it's toffee. Or a pudding."

"But my stories—"

"You'll have duties as a surgeon's wife, Ivy. Mrs. Williams is always throwing elegant parties, arranging games of whist for the doctors' wives."

"I'll take care of her somehow." She began to work the twine over the paper. "Or we can postpone the wedding a few months. I've read in the broadsheets about a law school in Paris that opened its doors to women just last year. I could go, take some classes, work for the Met or Scotland Yard like tad."

"Hah!" Davis laughed. "A real life Girl Criminologist!"

"And who would care for your mother then, if you were in Paris?" asked Christien.

It was true. From the first light of morning to the last stroke of midnight, she was trapped in black collars and lace, bland soup and bleach. Her life was her mother, as surely as if bound with velvet chains.

"Then I'll keep writing." Slowly, she pulled the strings from the parcel as the paper began to unfurl in her hands. "Besides, I have an idea for a novel..."

"Oh no, you don't," growled her father. "Not *that* again. Don't you dare, my girl. Don't you dare even think about it."

"About what?" asked Christien. "Ivy?"

Davis waggled his brows. *"Penny Dreadful and the Terror of Whitechapel."*

"It's just a story, tad," said Ivy.

"Good Lord," her father grumbled. "You are a proud and stubborn girl. Why can't you just get married like other girls, have babies, start a new life? Be safe for once, spare your poor old tad some grief."

Out of the paper rolled an object, dark brown in colour, the size of a fist.

"Oh God," breathed Christien. "Ivy..."

Davis sprang to his feet. "What the bloody hell?"

"Ivy," hissed Trevis Savage. "Put it down. Put it down *now!"*

As for Ivy Savage, future Girl Criminologist and writer of Penny Dreadful serials, she was surprisingly speechless, for in her very hands was a human heart.

***

He stood outside the door of the row house, waiting for the frost. It would come, he knew it. It always did when they sent him. He had been standing there for hours, but he wouldn't act until there was frost.

The streetlamp cast shadows down the long, dark boulevard. Not a wealthy district in Manchester, but then again, far from poor. He'd been in better neighbourhoods and he'd been in worse. Murder was a knife that cut across all classes, an equalizer of the lowest kind. Victims, however, were mostly the same and he knew there was little he could do to change that.

A steamcab chugged through the fog and he pressed himself against the building, drawing his greatcoat close for protection. He wasn't afraid. No one would stop him. No one would even see him. They would make sure of it. They always did. Still, he reached behind his back, to the pistol he kept in his belt. It was a fine walnut musket-bore, with three clockwork chambers fully loaded. His was a simple pursuit. He rarely needed more than one shot.

Suddenly, his breath began to frost in front of his face. He could feel them behind him. Only three with this one, but three were too many. He preferred to stop them at one if he had the chance but the dead were poor communicators. It took him a long time to understand, although their pleas were always the same.

He stepped swiftly up the stair and rapped on the brass doorknocker, waited for a light or candle to spring to life inside. He rapped again to make sure someone would come and he prayed it wasn't an automaton. Those were a bugger to get around, especially the modern ones. Some of them even had security systems. Damn the technology that was allowing them to think.

A rattle at the knob and the black door swung open, revealing a short, stocky man in a dressing gown and nightcap. He wore a thick moustache and long muttonchops and appeared to be in his fifties. Rather typical, he thought. Looked like anyone's banker or solicitor or clerk. His wife was peering around his side. She had a puffy face, soft and bovine. He could not feel for her.

"What the devil do you want?" growled the man in a thick Manchester brogue. "It's bloody well past midnight."

"Alistair Byron Tup?"

"Yes, yes that's me. And I ask again, what the devil do you want, sir? Tell me now, or I'll raise the alarm."

He looked back over his shoulder. The three were there, standing on the walk. Their eyes were bulging, their throats red and swollen. They had been dead for months.

They nodded.

He turned back.

"Alistair Byron Tup, I have a message for you from Miss Abigail Charles, Miss Eliza Kerry and Mrs. Emmaline McKenna."

Tup's face fell.

As good as a confession.

"You are forgiven and the Crown has been served. May God have mercy on your soul."

He pulled the pistol from his side and fired.

***

The Steam Standard
September 13, 1888

The arm of a woman was found this week in the mud on the bank of the Thames, near Pimlico. Dr. Bond, Police Surgeon with the Metropolitan Police, decided that it had been cut off by some sharp instrument, but he did not express an opinion whether this was done by a professional anatomist or a murderer.

Met officials are not commenting on whether this case bears any connection to the notorious Whitechapel killings, although it most certainly smacks of the torso killing of last year. It is the opinion of Dr. Bond that the arm was not dissected for medical purposes nor as a prank on the part of medical students as is the common theory and he rigorously defends the practices of his apprentices as most professional. As for the arm, the doctor could not give a cause of death or show that a violent act had taken place, so the jury had no choice but to returned a verdict of "Found Dead."

Police continue to investigate.

Chapter 2

Of English Barons, French Castles and a Toxic Welcome to the Ghost Club

"Lancashire?" asked Penny, and she turned round to her father, a puzzled look upon her face. "Whyever are we going to Lancashire, father?"

"Capital question, my girl," guffawed her father, Chief Inspector Charles Dreadful. "I'm afraid there's been a rather scandalous robbery."

"A robbery, you say?" Penny sat up. "Is it the Clockwork Heart from Lancaster Castle?"

"Yes, by jove, it is the Clockwork Heart from the Castle!" Her father looked shocked. "How do you do that, my girl?"

"Oh father, the Clockwork Heart is a marvel of modern science. The Germans and the Americans are quite envious of our British engineering and would pay a pretty sum for it. And since it's stored in Lancaster Castle, I'm afraid it's quite an elementary deduction!"

"Bully for you, my girl! Bully for you!"

She smiled at him before turning to her wardrobe to choose a hat that would best suit a mystery in Lancashire.

Ivy sighed. It was a dreary start to a dreary story, for she had absolutely no idea what could possibly be mysterious in Lancashire. This was the northern heart of England, a vast green countryside with rolling hills, gray stone walls and sheep. Davis had not been helpful with story ideas for all his suggestions involved disemboweled livestock and beer.

She looked out the window, tried to still the bobbing of her head. She had spent days in this coach now, days of trotting horses, hills and sheep. Each night they had stopped at some inn with flea-infested mattresses, bland stew and potatoes for supper. Each morning they woke to the sounds of cockerels and cattle and the smells of fried pork. Lunch was bread, cheese and cold poulet wrapped in paper. She hadn't had a decent cup of tea since leaving London, and it had broken her heart to leave.

The road to Lonsdale Abbey, a sanitarium north of nowhere.

It had been coming for ages, she knew it now. The heart in the post had only served to set her on this road sooner rather than later. Her father was a good man, a modern man. He'd always indulged her writing—even supplying plots, clues and storylines on occasion, but the heart had done it for him. There was no way he would allow his only daughter to become the target of a killer, not for any story in the world.

But this time Christien had agreed, siding with her father and winning out in the end. Once a fellow intellect and kindred spirit, he was quickly stepping into the shoes of a protective husband and she was not sure she could ever forgive him for that simple fact. She was not a romantic girl, had never fallen for ideals of happy home and family and was certain Christien felt the same. Until of course, the ring. She twisted it on her finger, wondering if it would ever feel like home.

A dark shape blotted out the evening sun and she peered out the window again. It was an airship high above the hills, most likely heading to Lancaster. Airships were all the rage now in Europe and they routinely crossed the channel and back to London, making the crossing in less than an hour. By steamship, it still took the better part of a day.

She watched the large cylindrical shape until it disappeared from view.

"Perhaps it's not so bad up here after all, mum," she said, looking at her mother in the seat across. "We'll be staying in Lasingstoke Hall where Christien's brother lives. He's a Baron, you know. Sebastien Laurent St. John Lord de Lacey, Seventh Baron of Lasingstoke."

The carriage rattled as its wheels dug into then out of a rut in the road and it shook her in her seat. No cobblestones here. Just dirt.

"It's an old, old, *old* family and Sebastien sits in the House of Lords. When I marry Christien, we'll be related to the *Mad* Lord of Lasingstoke..."

She smiled to herself. Now that was a story worth writing. Christien rarely spoke of his brother save to say that he was strange and that he spent much of his time at Lonsdale Abbey, the very sanitarium to which she was taking her mother. He was a frequent target of the London tabloids and rumours abounded concerning him. He had a metal skull. He ran with wild horses. He died as a child and now talked to the dead. Christien had worked very hard to avoid notoriety but his brother, it seemed, was another story entirely.

And Ivy so loved her stories.

She sighed and sank back onto the coach seat. This was not what she wanted, not the story she would have written. But then again, she was only a girl in the *Empire of Steam*. Her father still ordered her entire life and soon, Christien would step into those shoes. It seemed the entire world rolled along on that particular road and she wondered if there was ever a woman who managed to live free of someone else's reins.

At every stop along their journey, people were oh-so-curious to see the old woman who lived like the dead and the novelist who was to marry the brother of the Mad Lord of Lasingstoke. She dreaded the sound of her life, boiled down like potatoes into one bleak sentence. Christien had assured her it wouldn't be so bad, but scandal, he told her, fed on lesser things.

Her heart was aching for just a taste of scandal.

There was a rap on the trap from above and she looked up to see a fearsome old face smiling down at her from the dickey. It was Castlewaite, the coachman. He was a wiry man with thin hair, a whirring copper eyepiece and an appalling lack of teeth.

"Lasingstoke 'all, miss."

Ivy peered out the window once again. It was twilight and the fading sun made everything hazy and dim.

"There, Ivy!" Davis shouted from the dickey. "Up there!"

She pressed her nose against the glass, making out a flash of sandstone in the distance.

"It's huge, Ivy!"

"Aye, Master Davis," she heard the coachman say. "She's grand."

She didn't realize it but she was holding her breath as Lasingstoke Hall played hide and seek between the trees.

"There," her brother cried. "Can you see it?"

Sandstone walls with high squared towers at the corners and at the far end, stacks billowing with smoke promised modern conveniences. Lasingstoke Hall was a French castle in the northern heart of England, but then again, 'de Lacey' was a very old French name with history dating back to the time of William the Iron Conqueror. Christien was proud of his French heritage, although she knew he took a ribbing from his friends. *The Industrial Republic of France* was the archrival of the *Empire of Steam* but she had to admit, it looked like it belonged in the hills and dales of Lancashire.

No – tall, regal and very French, Lasingstoke Hall was not at all the gothic ghost house of her imagination.

They had all but lost the sun as the coach finally rattled to a halt at the great arched doors of the Hall. She could hear the stomp and crunch as Davis sprang from the rig and onto the gravel. She growled silently to herself. Skirts were wicked terrible for jumping, so she sat waiting for Castlewaite to open the door. She took his hand and stepped out, breathing deeply the smell of wet grass and horses, dying roses and coal. Gaslight poured from lamps under the arches and she looked up, dwarfed by the sheer enormity of the place.

Lasingstoke Hall, Seat of the Barony of Lasingstoke, Lancashire.

She reached in to take her mother's hand when suddenly, the coach was surrounded by dogs—six large dogs barking and laughing and bumping around her legs, threatening to tip her to the ground. A voice bellowed out from the Hall.

"Get away, ye louts! Leave 'em be! Off now! Off! Away wi' ye!"

A woman appeared under the high stone doorway, broom threatening the many furred backsides but she froze at the sight of the coach.

"Castlewaite?" she hollered.

"Aye, Cookie," he called back. "We've guests!"

She was short, stout and scowling, with auburn hair pulled back in a tight knot and she stared for a long moment before turning back to the doorway.

"Guests!" she hollered. *"Here! Now!"*

People rushed out to stand at attention in the darkness. Servants, Ivy realized. Her father was not a wealthy man. They'd never been able to afford a housekeeper, let alone staff. She had only imagined this sort of life. She'd only written about it in Penny's adventures.

A small figure bobbed as it rolled under the doorway, gaslight reflecting from its metal surface. It was a very old automaton and she smiled to herself. Perhaps there was a story or two at Lasingstoke, after all.

As the bags began disappearing with the servants into the Hall, Castlewaite moved over to the woman. He spoke softly, wringing the cap in his hands.

"He did *wot?*" she growled. "Good Lord. As if we haven't enowt t'do 'round here."

Her eyes were sharp, like stones set in plaster, and she turned them first on Davis, then their mother, settling finally on Ivy.

"Savage. What sort 'o name is tha'?"

"Welsh, ma'am," said Ivy and she curtsied.

"The name's Cookie. Ah s'pose ye'll be wantin' supper, then?"

"We will indeed," grinned Davis. "What's on the menu?"

"Davis, hush!" Ivy swallowed. "We don't need much, ma'am."

"How ye 'spect t' run a Great House if ye don't eat, child?"

"I—"

"No wonder Mister Christien sent ye up here. Honestly, Ah don't have much to work with. There's nothin' to ye. Bony as a skinned cat."

"I—"

"Pork roast on Friday, with carrots and steamed sponge." She wiped her hands on her apron. "There might be sommat left, if the blasted dogs haven't got it all. Come this way, then…"

She turned and marched into the house. A girl with ginger hair and freckles smiled, curtsied and scurried in after her.

Castlewaite turned.

"Tha's Cookie, miss."

"Ah said, this way!"

Davis laughed out loud, but Ivy could find nothing amusing in it at all. She took a deep breath and followed, hoping that back in London,

Christien was making a better first impression then she.

***

It was Friday night and at the Whitechapel Library, noted author A.C. Doyle was reading the first chapter of his latest novel to the applause of delighted listeners. In a very different library in another part of London, Christien Jeremie St. John de Lacey had a headache and was trying very hard not to breathe.

Gas masks sat in a jumbled pile on a table by the fire, with the Pea Soup out in force tonight. London's toxic fog was a bane to city life, causing all good gentlemen to don masks for fear of infection. Christien remembered the first time he and the boys had dissected a cadaver to find the green slime coating the lungs. Some people lived for years with little impediment, others it killed within a fortnight. Tonight, smoke from pipes, cigars and cigarettes was creating an equally toxic cloud as it billowed under the library doors.

With a sigh, he popped a headache tablet onto his tongue and turned to study his face in the mirror. It was pointless to fuss, he knew, for his appearance mattered little to the group assembled behind the doors. They did not care a whit for how well a suit fell from his shoulders or whether his burns were long, squared, or fashionably scruffy. They cared not whether he was a physician studying under Dr. Thomas Bond, had several thousand a year in allowance or was brother to a baron, although he knew they'd have preferred his brother to him. In point of fact, they weren't interested in him at all, save for his pedigree. It was a rare group of men who didn't hear the name "de Lacey" and shudder.

No, he was here simply because he was his father's son and his brother had refused.

The halls of the Pall Mall rooms were lined in dark woods, gold-gilt paintings and busts of famous alumni. It was a fine location for the Club, sandwiched between other gentlemen's organizations like the Reform Club, the Jockey Club, the Carleton and the Athenaeum. It was a club for notable intellects and men of vision, and he had been sponsored by their very best. It was an honour, it was a milestone, and he dreaded the thought of being here.

And so he watched the smoke billow and creep under the doors, when like a cough, they swung open and his mentor stepped into the library. Dr. John Williams cut a formidable figure with his silver hair, intelligent eyes and an absence of burns or beard or moustache. Christien had always thought he needed something, for he had a very grim mouth.

"Are you ready, boy?" Williams asked. "They are an eager bunch. I can assure you that you have nothing to fear from them."

"I know that, sir," said Christien. "But I'm not certain I'm ready. Not for this."

The surgeon raised a brow.

"We've talked about this, Remy. If you want to make anything of yourself in London, this is the place to do it."

"I know that, sir, but my brother will surely kill me if he finds out."

"Tosh. You are embracing your heritage in joining this band of extraordinary gentlemen. Your father was a key player and you are honouring his legacy. Surely your brother cannot object."

"You've obviously never met him, sir."

"I have not, no." Williams smiled but without his eyes. He reached up to smooth the stiff lines of Christien's shoulders. "Regardless, your father would be proud. He was the very best of us. Have you brought the locket?"

Christien reached up to his collar, slipped a pendant out from his cravat. Dangling from a chain, he held it up to the gaslight.

It was a clockwork locket, fashioned from brass, copper, silver and gold, each tiny gear a different metal, spinning in connected but opposing directions like a watch. It was housed in a polished glass globe, again with brass, copper, silver and gold circlets ringing the globe. At the bottom apex, a pin.

It pulsed with a strange sweet light, like a heartbeat. Like a song.

"That..." breathed Williams. "Is exquisite. Does it work?"

"I don't know, sir. Bastien holds the key."

"And Sebastien won't join? You're certain of this?"

"Yes, sir." Christien slipped the locket back over his head, leaving it to swing across his waist-coated chest. "He's convinced the Club was responsible for Father's death. I believe he'd like nothing better than to

16

see it disbanded and all its members shot in the head."

The surgeon grunted.

"And you, Remy? Is that what you think?"

Christien's heart thudded.

"The Club was important to my father," he said carefully. "I think I need to find out why."

"Hmm. You are a clever one. The Club is Britain's best and brightest hope for the future, more important than ironclads or airships. Your father believed this with all his heart, as did Prince Albert, God rest his soul. As do Bertie and Eddy. You are in good company now, *royal* company. In fact..." Williams fished in his pocket, pulled out three small brass rings. He plucked one out, held it up to the light. "Eddy wants you to have this."

Prince Albert Victor, grandson to Victoria and second in line to the throne of the Empire, known as Eddy to friends and family.

"A ring?" Christien frowned. "But why?"

"You don't know?"

"I have never seen it before tonight."

"Fascinating," said Williams and he shrugged. "A mere trinket, then. Think of it as a token of your initiation."

The young physician stared for a moment before slipping it on the little finger of his left hand. At that moment, the locket sprang to life sending colours flashing across their faces. It chose the oddest times to activate, this little pendant, sometimes spinning, sometimes silent. Still, he had to admit was a very strange, sweet device.

The doors swung open once again and the Meeting Room echoed with thunderous applause. Christien felt his heart quicken in his chest.

"Welcome," said Dr. John Williams. "To the Ghost Club."

***

Manchester Standard

There has been murder most foul in our fair city. Yesterday morning at approximately two forty am, Davenport & Crabtree Bank clerk Mr. Alistair Byron Tup was shot dead at his front door by an unknown assailant. Tup was an acquaintance of Mrs. Emmaline McKenna of

Trowbridge St., whose murder last month is still listed as unsolved. Tup's widow has declined to comment to reporters but is rumored to have recently come into a large sum of money and is reported to be planning a trip to Blackpool to ease her troubled soul.

Police are continuing to investigate.

Chapter 3

Of Icy Windows, Toxic Fogs and the Beginnings of Strangeness

It was late and Ivy sat in a very dark room, writing by the light of a single candle and moonlight that fell in from the window.

September 14, 1888

My dear Christien,

I will not tell you of the trials that have beset us since leaving London, nor the utter unpreparedness of the staff for our arrival. But not to worry. Despite his appearance, Castlewaite is a resourceful fellow. I must admit I like him very much.

On the other hand, the housekeeper Cookie is quite fearsome. I'm certain she disapproves of our presence here, and I fear Davis will make mischief in order to pester her. He was quite taken with her steamed sponge, however, and has promised to spend his time working on the illustrations for Penny Dreadful and a Murder in Paris. *You know how talented he is in that regard. It may keep him occupied long enough to see us finished here and back in London within a fortnight.*

We have not met your brother, the Baron. Neither Cookie nor Castlewaite would speak of him during dinner, nor tell us when we might expect to make his acquaintance. You have told me so little about him and as you know, I am quite curious.

We head to Lonsdale Abbey in two days time. I am already dreading it and my heart is heavy and unsettled.

Have you made any headway with the heart or the arm?

With all fondness,
Your Ivy

She laid the fountain pen carefully down, desperate not to blob all over the letter. It was bad enough her stories were a mess. When her father had introduced them less than a year ago, she had inadvertently smeared ink on Christien's hands. She had been mortified, but he had merely smiled one of his rare smiles and said it was nowhere near as bad as the blood.

Odd, she thought, how she remembered that so fondly.

She sighed. Penny Dreadful herself had a fancy fiancé—a young barrister named Julian Terrence Hull. She had written the character into the storyline the week she had met Christien. Davis managed a decent likeness, although he frequently drew silly expressions or devil eyes or horns. Davis didn't much like Christien, but then again, Davis was only fifteen.

She looked down at the ring he had given her. It looked entirely out of place on such a common finger but there were few options for women even in these modern times. No school in all of Britain would take a girl in for Law, Criminology or even Psychology. Her writing was indulged as though it were something she would outgrow after marriage. She dreaded the thought that life spent throwing elegant parties might do just that.

There was a thump outside the door and she rose to her feet, opening it on the oldest automaton she'd ever seen. It was on wheels with a copper top hat, silver moustache and brass sorely in need of a polish. It had with it a tray covered by a shiny lid, which rose on a wire to reveal a small tea service and a lovely china cup.

"Evening tea," said the automaton, in a voice that sounded like a can of bolts rolling down a stair. "Compliments of Cookie."

"Thank you." She smiled. "What is your name?"

It paused as its AE batteries engaged, translating her speech into logarithmic patterns. "VINCE. *Very Intelligent Nickel-Coated Entity.*"

"I'm very grateful, VINCE. Thank you."

"You are welcome."

"And how long have you been here, VINCE?"

"Six years. Mr. Castlewaite bought me from Grimwalt in the town of…" He bobbed a little on his wheels. "Over Milling."

"How wonderful. What do you do?"

"I tend the sheep."

"But surely there are dogs, VINCE?"

"There are many dogs. But only one VINCE."

Ivy lifted the cup from the tray. "Well, thank you again, VINCE, and good night."

She moved to close the door, but the automaton lurched forward, bobbing on its wheels and stopping the door from closing. She wondered if it was about to finally fall apart.

"VINCE?" she asked.

The robot stared at her, it's eyepieces whirring and contracting like lenses.

"You are Ivy Savage, novelist?"

"Writer," she said. "Just writer."

"Would you sign my copper bottom?"

She blinked. "Your what?"

"Mr. Castlewaite is a fan of Penny Dreadful. He reads them to me at night to help with my language program. I would be most pleased if you would sign my copper bottom."

A brass plate slid aside to reveal cogs and gears and ticking mechanisms. A set of pincers slid out holding a very old copy of *Penny Dreadful and the Hounds of Haversham*, one of her first. At the bottom of the booklet was a copper plate, obviously meant to make holding the serial easier. The paper was notoriously flimsy—to keep production costs down, Alby Thistle had said. Many people invested in metal plates to keep the books from flopping over.

"Ah, your *copper bottom*…" She slipped back into the room to fetch her fountain pen. For once, she was grateful for the blobbing of the ink. She actually managed a reasonable smear across the metal.

"Thank you, miss. Enjoy your tea."

Both serial and tea tray retracted, VINCE spun on his wheels and bumped off down the hall. With the high ceilings, sprawling carpets and massive paintings adorning the walls, he soon looked very small. Not unlike herself, she thought and closed the door behind him.

She moved to the window, sipping her tea. There was a beautiful moon out tonight. By day, this land was ordinary and mundane but at night the moon came out to play. A mist hovered over the grass—the breath of ghosts, she imagined. The sighing of spirits. Branches looked like bony hands, reaching for the skies.

A fire glowed in the hearth but she felt cold without her mother nearby. For seven years, it had been this way as the rituals of Catherine's life played out like clockwork. Quiet, somber, private clockwork.

In the distant field, she spied a horse walking.

This *was* the north country, after all. Horses were still used in parts of the Empire where steamcars were as uncommon as automatons or airships. Every place had stables and hitching posts but out there, wandering alone in the field, it looked strange.

Through glimpses of moonlight, she could see its saddle, the swinging leathers that were its reins.

She pushed the window open for a better view and shivered as cold fell into the room. Yes, she was sure of it. Saddle and bridle but no rider. This horse was simply walking in a field at night.

There was a strange sound and she looked down to find her tea had frozen solid inside its cup. *Odd,* she thought as now her breath began to frost in front of her face. It was only September. In London, there was rarely frost in September.

She was about to close the pane when she noticed ice, crawling like a living thing up the glass. The trees outside waved their skeleton branches in a rush of wind, lifting leaves into the air when out of the mist, the figure of a man ambled into the moonlight. He was wearing a greatcoat and seemed to be following the horse the way a duckling follows its mother. He wasn't limping, so it was unlikely he had been thrown. Simply walking.

A crackle from the desk and she looked back to see the fountain pen splintered from within, shards of shiny black on the papers. She reached down to dab them with a finger, plucked one gingerly in her hand. *Ice,* she realized. Somehow, the ink in her pen had frozen solid. She looked back to the window, its glass entirely white now with frost.

Finally, the walking horse, then the walking man disappeared into the trees.

She crossed over to where her Penny Dreadful story sat drying. Slowly, she picked it up and crumpled it into a ball, tossing it into the fire as a new idea began to take shape in her mind.

Penny Dreadful and the Ghost of Lancashire...

And she stood there for a long time, waiting for the heat to return to the room.

***

Penny looked out over the fields of Lancashire. It was a beautiful night and quiet, and she had been mulling over the leads in the case. An accomplished thief, no doubt, and she wondered if he were still in the city, or had made his getaway by now.

She could see very far away in the distance, a lone man following a horse.

"Could this be a ghost, a thief or a madman?" she said to herself. "Or is he something altogether new? Why would a man be following a horse alone in the night? It is a strange business indeed."

Finally, both figures disappeared into the ghostly wood, and she could not see them come out. It piqued her curiosity, and she set her mind to follow their tracks in the morning. And when Penny Dreadful set her mind to anything, one could be sure it was bound to happen.

***

The Pea Soup fog was very thick, hovering over the ground like an eerie green blanket. Christien was grateful he had remembered a mask and now, it sat tight across his face, filtering his breath with charcoal and mesh and the faint scent of absinthe.

It was quiet on the path through Green Park. The only sound was the crunch of his shoes on gravel and the echo of his breath through the mask. Trees looked like charred bones and through them, he could see the lights of Buckingham Palace. By day, the park was filled with parliamentarians but at this late hour, he was very much alone. Club members had offered him rides in coach and carriage, some even in their six-wheeled steamcars, but he had respectfully declined. Hollbrook House was a short distance from Pall Mall and the walk would do him good. He needed to think and after the meeting tonight, there was much to think about.

They wanted his father back.

The Ghost Club, the first and foremost organization for scientific study into the realms of the paranormal, wanted his dead father back and they believed the locket was the key.

He sighed, feet moving steady as he ran through the night's events in his mind. He had shown them the locket but it had hung, as it was hanging now, quiet and coy around his neck. No show of lights, no flashing colours. They had questioned him on his beliefs next, his training, finally his family. Most of all, his family. His father's work, his life, his death. His brother next and it was apparent that even such esteemed members of London society were intrigued by the notion of the Mad Lord of Lasingstoke. How mad was he? Had he indeed died as a child? Did he indeed talk to the dead? Questions that ran from idle curiosity to wild fancy. He had certainly not expected that.

He touched the brass ring that Williams had given him. During the night, it had grown tight on his finger and he was sure he would need a dab of clove oil to remove it. Williams was an odd duck. Brilliant, hard yet socially-minded, it boggled Christien to think of such a man devoting so much time to the pursuit of the spiritual. Dr. Bond was not like that. Bond was a realist, devoting his life to the application of scientific principles and the study of the mind. Of his two mentors, Christien felt most at home with Dr. Bond, a man who lived to study the dead.

A hiss behind him and he glanced over his shoulder. The path was as dark, the trees darker. It wouldn't be hard for a villain to hide but he could see nothing other than the trees. There was no sound other than his breathing in the mask. He turned and resumed walking.

His life was such an odd thing, he thought, full of contrast and conflict. Gentleman surgeon with scandal for a family, skeletons in every closet and gold in lead boxes piled high in the cellar. French and English in equal measure, despised by both for that simple fact. He had had played with princes at Sandringham as a boy, danced with duchesses in Vienna and now was betrothed to a mystery writer from Stepney. Not two months after he had given her his mother's ring, she received a heart in the post. Blood and death, madness and ruin came with the name de Lacey.

Poor Ivy. What was he asking of her? Did he even know?

He wished he could leave it all behind and forge a life in the bright, new and unbiased world of science but he doubted very much that this Club would help him do that. In fact, the Ghost Club would threaten everything he held fast. It had been his father's passion, his life's work, his all-consuming pursuit and had driven him to the brink of insanity. His brother lived on that very road and it seemed they were all covered in blood.

Madness ran in the family. He knew he couldn't outrun it, but it remained to be seen whether or not he could outwit it. He would bring his scientific mind to the collective of the Ghost Club, show them there was indeed a better way. Perhaps in doing so, he might save his brother in the process. God knew his family needed the help.

Through the Memorial Gate now and he left the park, the familiar shape of the Wellington Arch towering above the fog. A row of white houses came into view, looking ghostly in the green mist. Hollbrook House boasted a prestigious address—Kensington-Knightsbridge no less, but he hated it almost as much as Lasingstoke Hall. As beautiful as it was, he was certain Hollbrook hid more secrets than any other house on the street.

There was a hiss again and he turned but could see no one. He pushed the mask onto his forehead.

"Hallo?" he called out, his voice echoing on the deserted road.

Behind him the Memorial Arch shone oddly luminescent as gaslight reflected off limestone and fog. Shadows moved across the arch, but they were the shadows of buildings in the moonlight and trees.

On his chest, the locket began to spin.

"Hallo?" he called again, wishing he had kept one of his surgical blades in his pocket, just in case. "Who's there?"

A whisper now in front and he whirled but there was no one, nothing but the street lamps, the fine houses and the fog. The street was entirely empty. Even the pigeons were asleep.

He shook his head. Histrionics. He was scaring himself with all this talk of blood and madness. The damned locket, however, was dancing up a storm, so he snatched it and tucked it under his collar, hiding it from view. The street grew quiet once again.

With a deep breath, he pulled the mask back onto his face and stepped onto the road.

***

Daily Steam
September 15, 1888
London Shocked Yet Again

Another shocking murder was perpetrated between five and six o'clock last Saturday morning, in Whitechapel. The scene of this crime was the yard of 29 Hanbury Street, and the murdered person, Annie Eliza Chapman nee Smith, was again a woman of low life and in the poorest circumstances. No clue to the murderer had up to last night been obtained. These repeated attacks in the Whitechapel district have produced an amount of alarm and anxiety in the neighbourhood bordering on panic. The inquest will be opened today, when evidence of the finding of the body and of the mutilations will be given.

Police are continuing to investigate.

Chapter 4

Of Servants, Sweepers and Very Fine Men

"Good morning, miss."

Reluctantly, Ivy opened her eyes.

"There's tea on the nightstand, miss."

"Oh, thank you," she mumbled. Arms and legs felt like lead as slowly, she pushed up to sitting, hair spilling across her face. "Very much needed this morning."

"Ah'd like to pull the curtains, miss. Mind yer eyes, now."

A great bank of fabric swished aside and Ivy blinked as morning light spilled into the most beautiful room she'd ever seen.

It was very grand, with high ceilings, elaborate crown moldings and wallpaper. The bed was high with walnut posts and a canopy of Oriental silk. The linens were crisp and clean and the mattress soft as down. Even the teacup was marvelous—white with pink roses and a gold guilt edge, and the tea.... She lifted it to her lips. The tea was as good as the best in all of London. She wiggled her toes in bliss.

Ivy studied the girl standing at the windows. It was the same girl she'd seen last night, the one with the ginger hair and the freckles.

"My name's Ivy," she said. "What's yours?"

"Lottie, miss."

"This is an impressive house, Lottie. It was difficult to see it all last night."

Ice at the window, tea frozen in the cup.

"Aye, Miss Ivy. Although Ah'd imagine London to be a fair bit grander with all its fine folk and steamcars."

"Oh I don't know. I'm certain there's no house in London as fine as this, except perhaps Buckingham or St. James."

"Ye should ask to see the stables then, miss," said Lottie. "They'll take yer breath away. His Lordship does like his Warmbloods."

"Warmbloods?"

"French Warmbloods, miss. It's a type of 'orse."

"French," grinned Ivy. "Of course."

"You must be used to fine things coming from London, miss—*Oh!*"

The girl had noticed the desk where the pen lay splintered, the ink dried like blood on dark wood. Ivy rolled out of bed.

"I'm sorry," she said. "It was so cold in here last night. There was ice everywhere, on the window, in my cup. I thought I got it all."

"Not to worry, miss," said Lottie. "We do get a chilly night from time to time."

"It was most unusual. And there was a man in one of the fields—"

"It's not haunted."

Ivy blinked. "What's that?"

"Lasingstoke 'all, miss. It's not haunted. At least, not like people say."

"Why?" Ivy's eyes gleamed. "What do people say?"

"They just like to talk." Lottie dabbed at the ink with the corner of her apron. "Just because the machines are old and the men are French. '*Oh, he's mad. Oh, there's ghosts.* Norman gold in the tower and Saxon bones in the cellar. Metal skulls and the Curse of Sebastien de Lacey.' Things like that. People can be so cruel, can't they? They talk but they don't know. This is a fine house, a very fine house. Ah'm very lucky to be here."

She looked up at Ivy and curtsied.

"But don't' mind me, miss. There's breakfast waitin' downstairs. Quickly, now or ye'll miss it."

Norman gold in the tower and Saxon bones in the cellar. She couldn't have written it better herself.

She rolled out of bed and reached for her clothes.

***

The Pea Soup had dissipated at some point and the houses gleamed gold in the early morning light. Christien trotted up the wrought-iron steps of Hollbrook House, pulling the mask from his face and breathing the sweet smell of fresh air, wet trees and chimney smoke. The row of white houses looked beautiful this morning, no trace of ghostly green, no eerie glow, and he had to admit life could have been far worse for him than to live here.

"Hallo, Remy!" called a voice and he turned slightly to see a man standing on the stair next door, holding a paper. He was small with thinning brown hair, neatly trimmed chops and a rather common face. "Not coming home from classes, are you?"

"Indeed I am, Dr. Jekyll," Christien lied. "You remember your qualifying year, surely."

"I do indeed, Remy. Hated every minute of it. If you managed four hours of sleep a night you were accorded an automatic failure."

"That sounds about right, sir. And I am due my four hours now in fact."

Jekyll was an odd neighbour. He was a medical man and his research into the human mind bordered on scandal. He conducted frequent experiments in the cellar of his home and Christien doubted they were sanctioned by any hospital or medical facility.

"And how is old Bondie doing with that Leather Apron character?" Jekyll held up the paper. "The News has an article. Has he put a finger on anyone yet?"

"Not yet, sir. It's all very unofficial at the moment. Dr. Bond is A-Division and these crimes are occurring in H."

"Ah, the life of a police surgeon. It must be very exciting, catching a killer and all that."

Christien held his tongue. The public lived for their scandals and the Whitechapel killer was selling more papers than the Royal Family.

"We don't 'catch' anyone, sir. We simply analyze the evidence. However it ends, I'm quite certain I will be the very last to know."

He turned to move into the house but Jekyll waved at him.

"And the headaches, Remy? Still giving you grief?"

"Yes, sir. But I can manage—"

"If you need any more of those tablets, son, just whistle. I do only live a wall away!"

"Yes, sir. Thank you sir."

"I've worked on a new potion that I think will do just the trick!"

"Thank you, sir. I'm sure I will be fine."

Jekyll disappeared into his door and Christien threw a glance around the street. Cabs out now, chimney sweeps heading to work, street girls selling flowers. No one following him, no villains or voices out of place. *Histrionics,* he thought again. Science and fact, those were the cure for an overactive imagination. He welcomed the challenge, knowing the Ghost Club would find him a hard nut to crack.

And with that, he stepped briskly up the last of the steps and pushed through the fine white door of Hollbrook House.

***

She followed Lottie down a long hallway, watching the sweepers whirring along the floors. They were all the rage in London, now. Small, round and mechanical, their spinning brushes polished the floors and beat the rugs. They detected changes in the surface of the floor, whether wood, carpet or stone and adjusted brushes accordingly. They were also designed to avoid both furniture and stairs and she could see tiny buttons glowing as the machines altered their courses at will.

At the end of the hall there was a grand staircase and one of the devices was humming toward it.

"Aren't these ingenious?" she said. "I'm quite amazed at how they navigate the stair."

The device hummed to the very edge of the first tread and paused, bobbing a little. She could see the lights along the top blink and flash, then turn green. Suddenly, the sweeper shot forward into the air, dropping top over tail from step to step to step with a series of thumps. It ended upside-down on one of the landings, whirring and humming happily but going nowhere.

"Perhaps that one is defective," said Ivy.

"They're all like that," said Lottie.

Ivy grinned and followed the girl down the stair.

Golden-framed portraits of great men and horses, fine ladies and dogs lined the walls. She shook her head, wondering if the great men placed the same value on the horses and dogs as the ladies.

"The Lords de Lacey," said Lottie. "Ye must be quite 'appy."

"I would be happier back in London."

"Honestly, miss?"

"I'm sorry, Lottie. Don't mind me. I'm not very good at restraining my tongue. It was a stubborn thing, growing up Savage."

"What's he like, then? Mr. Christien?"

"You've never met him?"

"Only once, miss. Ah've only begun working upstairs this past year."

"Oh, he's very clever and very serious. My tad likes him because he's rich but I like him because he's clever. He's so dashedly clever. He's studying to be a police surgeon, in fact, like his mentor, Dr. Bond. That's how we met. He was working with Bondie, met my father and came back for tea with the rest of the coppers. I'm hoping he'll let me help him on some of his cases. We would make such a grand team—Oh look! There he is!"

On the last landing, there was a large portrait of a gentleman standing by a curtain, dressed in fine clothes with a pair of dogs at his feet. As far as paintings went, it was only slightly exaggerated, but the dark hair, porcelain skin and delicate pouting mouth were unmistakable.

If any man could be called beautiful, it was Christien.

"Oh no, miss Ivy. That's Renaud Jacobe St. John Lord de Lacey, the sixth Baron of Lasingstoke." Lottie nodded. "*Yer* Christien's father."

"How remarkable." She tried to study the painting more closely, but it was a large canvas mounted high on the wall. "You can most certainly see the resemblance."

"He looks t'be right clever indeed, miss," said Lottie with a grin.

Ivy noticed the next and last painting in the line. It was also of a man in fine clothes, standing at a window. His back was to the painter, so that little could be seen of his face, and his hair was pulled back in a short cue. The rest of him was almost in silhouette.

"And who's that?" she asked.

"Ah, that is the seventh Lord de Lacey, miss. *Yer* Christien's brother."

Sebastien Laurent St. John de Lacey. The Mad Lord of Lasingstoke. Of his brother, Christien was notoriously silent. She honestly didn't know what to think.

"That's a strange portrait," she said. "Why can you not see his face?"

"He wasn't there, miss."

"What's that? He wasn't there?"

"Not for the sitting, miss. The painter came every week for four months, but each time, His Lordship was unavailable or away. A painter can only paint what he sees, miss, and the painter did not actually *see* His Lordship."

"What an odd story," Ivy mused under her breath, eyes glued to the figure in the painting. There seemed to be far more than two dogs at his feet. "You've met him, then?"

"Oh, yes, miss. Ah have."

"And? What is he like then?"

"Well, miss, he's, ah, he's…"

"I won't talk. Promise."

"He's kind, miss. He's very kind to me mother and Ah."

"Is he strange?"

"Of course he is, miss." The girl beamed at her. "As strange as can be."

And with that, she trotted down the last of the steps, and Ivy followed, but not without throwing one last look at the painting of the Mad Lord de Lacey, seventh Baron of Lasingstoke.

***

Davis had already enjoyed his breakfast in the dining room and he perked up at the sight of them.

"Hallo," he said, tugging the brim of his cap. "I'm Davis."

"Lottie, sir." She blushed and curtsied.

"Are you the lady of the house, then?"

"Oh no, sir!" she laughed. "Not me, sir. Ah'm just the maid."

"You're far too pretty to be 'just the maid', Miss Lottie." He leaned his elbows across the table. "Does Lottie stand for Charlotte?"

"It does, sir."

"Charlotte," he repeated, green eyes gleaming. "What a beautiful name."

Ivy kicked him under the table but Lottie seemed not to notice. She curtsied once more.

"Ah'll fetch me mum. She's trying to get the mop working. One of its gears keeps sticking."

And she ducked quickly through a doorway, Davis shoved a biscuit into his mouth and watched her as she went.

"Sweet," he grinned.

"Davis," she growled but leaned forward conspiratorially. "This house is haunted."

"I hope so. I'll go bloody batty sitting around counting the sheep."

"I'm serious."

"You're obsessed." Her brother turned his chair and straddled it beside her, tossing a newspaper down beside her plate. "Did you read this? There's been another one."

It was a newspaper, the *Lancaster Guardian,* and her eyes scanned for the article. It wasn't on the front page. The murder of a prostitute did not warrant the front page. In Whitechapel, things like that happened far too often to be considered news. But her father had seemed to think that this was different, this shadow man who killed with a stroke and dissected with skill. She began to read when a door pushed open and a woman bundled in.

'Here. That's not fit for breakfast readin'," growled Cookie. She carried a tray covered in breads and scones, jams and jellies and, of course, a pot of tea. "It's not fit for anytime, if ye ask me."

Ivy swallowed. The woman was as fearsome this morning as she had been last night. Her voice was musical however, with a lilting Cumbrian accent that was likely tempered by years working in a great house.

"It's just a newspaper, ma'am."

"Don't they teach ye nowt in London? Readin' at the table is bad manners."

Davis laughed. "Men do it all the time."

"As Ah said, boy," Cookie glared at his tweed cap. "Bad manners."

Davis grinned but, naturally, did not remove the cap.

"I suppose you're right," said Ivy. "But my father is one of the investigators. I already know far more than the papers will print."

"Yeah," said Davis. "It's one of the reasons we're here, ain't it? Ivy got herself a heart in the post!"

"A heart?" gasped Lottie from the door. In her hands was a mechanism that Ivy recognized as an automated mop. It was an awkward contraption with springs and levers to move the mop-head back and forth. They were all the rage in London and used the steam that powered them to scour the floors. It was supposed to be efficient. From the looks of it, it was anything but.

"It's true," said Davis. "Whitechapel's not fit for any woman lately. That's what tad said. Murders here, murders there. He said, 'there's not enough in the pot for the coppers and the crooks is running the streets.'"

"Davis, please," said Ivy.

"Well, he did."

"There's murders everywhere, lad," Cookie snorted. "Lancaster is a hell-hole for them. Murders 'n witches."

"Pelling, too," said Lottie. "Tilly Barton got herself cut into pieces at the Solstice this summer."

"Lottie!"

"But it's true, Mum. The peelers still haven't found her heart."

Ivy shuddered, remembering the feeling. Smooth, cold and rather sticky.

"She's your *mum?*" asked Davis.

"Oh! *Mum!*" Ivy gasped. She had completely forgotten her own mother. Cookie held up her hand.

"Not to worry. She had a good breakfast. Ate two bowls of me special pudding and toast and tea. Ah'll put some meat on that hen's bones."

"I'm so sorry, ma'am," moaned Ivy. "I didn't sleep much last night, with the ice and the cold and the stories in my head."

"Ah'm taking care, child. She'll be well with me." The woman sharpened her eyes. *"Ye* need to settle in like a proper young lady. Ye'll be married soon enough and to a gentleman to boot."

Ivy felt deflated. Like an airship, collapsing into a billowing mess of hot air and canvas. She had never forgotten her mum. Never.

"Thank you, ma'am," she said in a small voice.

"Not *ma'am,* child. Cookie."

"Yes. Of course. You're the cook. Hence, 'Cookie.'"

"Me name's Elizabeth Anne Cook, child. Hence, 'Cookie.'"

Deflating. Deflating. A billowing mess all over Piccadilly.

"Yes, Cookie. Thank you, Cookie."

"Lunch at one, here in this room. Dinner at seven in Midi."

And with that, Elizabeth Anne Cook hence Cookie left the room, taking most of the air with her.

Ivy dropped her head in her arms.

"I am a calamity."

"So, Miss Charlotte Cook," grinned Davis. *"Midi?"*

"The second dining hall, master Davis," said Lottie. "Lasingstoke has three."

"Cor. Three dining rooms. Let me guess—this is the little one."

"Exactly correct, Master Davis." Lottie beamed at him. "This is *la Petite.* Then there's *Midi* down the hall, then *Grande,* in First."

Ivy sighed and raised her head, just a little. "First?"

"First House, miss. First and Second make up the Hall. Third is where the servants live. It's attached to the stables. The others mark a square along the property."

Ivy shook her head, confounded by the sheer enormity of the estate. Honestly, most people did not live this way.

Lottie continued. "From Third, ye go east along the ponds. Ye can take a coach, but horse is best. Foot is good too, just mind the swans. They're nasty. Chase ye as soon as look at ye."

Davis' smile stretched from ear to ear, charmed.

Lottie went on, oblivious. "Fourth is on the southeast corner. Fifth is southwest. Sixth is northeast. All good cottages. Very warm. Very welcoming."

Davis leaned toward her. "And where do you stay, Lottie Cook?"

She blushed. Ivy had given up correcting him. Besides, the preserves were looking very good and the tea was steaming.

"I'm with me mum in Fourth."

"And your tad?"

"Tad?"

"It's Welsh. Means your father."

"Ah love yer accent," she said, in thickest Cumbrian.

"I love yors," he said in thickest Welsh.

"I thought there were seven houses," said Ivy before biting into her scone. She closed her eyes. The preserves were delicious.

"It's a grand property," answered Lottie.

"Where is Seventh?"

"Ehm, Northwest, miss," Lottie's eyes flicked downward. "But ye won't be going there. Not Seventh."

"Why not?"

"Ye'll pass by, surely enough. There's the church next to it, and the graveyard and the woods, which is a lovely walk. But Seventh, ye'll not be going. Not Seventh. Never Seventh."

Ivy exchanged glances with her brother.

"But why not?" she repeated. "Is that one haunted as well?"

"*Lottie!*" came a voice from outside the room, and the young woman snapped to attention.

"Ehm, Ah need to be fixin' this mop," she muttered, staring at the mass of copper piping in her hands. "Please excuse me, Miss Ivy, Master Davis."

And she curtsied once more before exiting the room. Davis folded his arms behind his head and leaned back in his chair.

"Well, I know what *I'll* be doing after I finish counting them sheep."

Ivy grinned and reached for the Guardian and the story not fit for reading.

***

London Steam Standard

September 15, 1888

Regarding the story ran on the arm found off the Grovesnor Railway Bridge, Police Surgeon Dr. Bond has concluded that the arm assuredly belonged to a tall young female with a history of comfort, but has declined to comment whether or not she was a victim of a murder or whether this is the work of the same Leather Apron who is stalking the women of Whitechapel.

Information of the discovery has been forwarded to all the metropolitan police stations, and it is expected that the Thames police will today renew their search for other portions of the body. In the meantime, it is impossible to form an opinion as to whether another revolting murder has been committed in London, or whether the arm has been placed in the water as a grim joke by some medical student.

Of both crimes, the police are continuing to investigate.

Chapter 5

Of Bond's Boys, French Warmbloods and the Mad Lord de Lacey

It was a puzzle, he realized. A puzzle of blood and limbs and tissue and bone and he had to put her together before the doors opened on the gentlemen of the Ghost Club. The smoke was heavy, the lab was hot, the locket was flashing merrily and it was very hard to know which body part went where. Both Williams and Bond were standing to the side, watching him with surgical blades in one hand, pocket watches in the other and very quickly, he realized that the body was Ivy's and that someone had stolen her heart—

There was a feather tickling his nose.

Christien opened his eyes.

"Dash it all, Rosie," he groaned and he sat up, pushing the lanky form of Ambrose Pickett onto the floor. "Get off my bed."

"You're so pretty when you sleep, you know that, Remy?" Pickett grinned wickedly, his moustache tugging up at one end. "Like a regular French girlie…"

"Bloody ass…"

"*Muddy* ass, old boy," came a voice and Christien saw Henry Bender sitting at his desk, dirty shoes up on the polished wood. Bender was built like a bulldog, with thick ginger hair, pale lashes and a wide jaw. He blew smoke out one side of his mouth and grinned. "It's a piss hole out there."

"And you decided to bring it all into my room?"

Christien rolled out of bed, grateful he was still wearing his trousers from the night before. He grabbed a freshly pressed shirt from his dressing stand.

"We did indeed, Remy boy," said Pickett. He slapped Bender's arm and was rewarded with a cigarette. "Your man *Pomfrites* was complaining of nothing to do!"

"Oh good heavens, sir…" moaned a voice from the doorway. "I just washed the linens yesterday, sir…"

Slim, prim and proper, houseman George Claudius Pomfrey still wore the satin breeches, buckled shoes and powdered wig of generations before him. Christien shook his head.

"I'll take care of this, Pomfrey."

"Oh no, sir. It is my duty but by all that is holy, sir—"

"But we're not holy, *Pomfrites,*" grinned Bender. He blew smoke in a thin stream. "In fact, we're very *un*-holy."

Pomfrey moaned again and disappeared down the hall of Hollbrook House.

"Honestly boys, that poor man."

"He loves us, Remy. You know it." Bender took a final drag on the cigarette and dropped it to the carpet, crushed it under his shoe. "Williams wants us in this morning."

"Why? Where's Lewie?"

Bender shrugged, dug about in his pocket for another cigarette. "Probably ducked off to gay *Pariee* with his little Marie."

"She ain't really French, is she?" asked Rosie. "I mean, she sounds like a Mick to me."

"She *is* a Mick, idiot," said Bender. "But she's pretty, mind. Almost as pretty as Remy's jewels…"

And he picked up the locket, dangled it from his stubby fingers.

"Ooh, Remy's locket," grinned Rosie. "Does it cuckoo in French?"

"Did you take it to your Club last night, Remy?"

"I did indeed," said Christien and he snatched the locket from Bender's hand, slipped it over his head. "They are a strange and passionate lot. I'm not certain I belong."

Bender raised his pale brows. "Not nearly strange or passionate enough, Remy?"

"Not by far," said Christien as his fingers began work on the knot of a necktie. "We're not scheduled for exams until tomorrow. Why does Williams want us now?"

"He's got a clinic at Bedlam," said Bender. "Another one of the patients got knocked up."

"Oh God," groaned Christien. "I hate those."

"You don't hate the clinics, Remy," said Henry. "You hate Bedlam. What d'you say? Madness runs in the family?"

"Bedlam reminds you of your brother, don't it, Remy?" said Rosie. "The Mad, *Mad* Lord of Lasingstoke…"

Christien ignored them, turned to study his appearance in the mirror, smoothed the lines of the waistcoat and necktie. The locket hung silent and sweet across his chest.

"You reading the papers, Remy?" Bender grinned. "The arm? Giving 'em all a bloody fright, it is."

"The papers is saying it's medical students playing pranks," said Rosie. "But we's a serious lot, ain't we, Dr. Bender?"

"We certainly are, Dr. Pickett. We most certainly are."

"You are idiots, both of you," said Christien but he smiled. It was impossible to stay angry with the boys. "Right, let's go. I don't want to keep Williams waiting."

"In Bedlam, Remy. St. Mary's Bloody Bedlam!"

"Lunatics, Remy. More bloody lunatics than you can shake a stick at."

"We can say hallo to your brother, we can!"

Christien snatched a town coat and left the room, two of the nefarious Bondie Boys at his heels.

***

The morning fog had lifted and the sun peered out from above the low clouds. Ivy found her mother in a tree-covered terrace on the South side of the Hall. The garden was lush but dying. Roses folding into dark hips, poppies going to seed, the ivy tipped red with frost. It was beautiful and sad and a fitting place for her mother, she thought. A stone angel in a forgotten cemetery.

She gave her mum a kiss and headed out under a massive arch.

At the very heart of Lasingstoke was a cobbled courtyard, bounded on all sides by stone walls. First, Second and Third, all built at different times but now connected to make the Hall. Small, dark windows peered like eyes in sandstone faces. From a far corner, two stacks towered above the roofs with smoke billowing up and onto the grounds. Black iron posts dotted the court and she wondered if they were for tethering horses. These 'French Warmbloods' would surely be fearsome creatures to warrant such fittings.

From the courtyard she could see it all—the Hall and its windows, archways, towers and rooflines. There was no greenery to be seen from the center of the court, only stone. Cobbled stone, hewn stone, walls and masonry, and she wrapped her arms around her ribs, feeling cold fingers run up her spine.

She was surrounded by old, cold stone.

The doors to the stable were open however so she crossed the large courtyard to slip inside.

Lottie had been right. The stables were finer than most London homes, with oak floors, cherry wainscoting and upper walls brilliantly whitewashed. Leaded windows allowed the precious English sunlight to pour into every stall, and the smell of pine, hay and leather filled the air. These were lucky horses, Ivy thought. Most people did not live this way.

She could hear voices down a long corridor and she followed them, approaching a trio of men around a dappled gray horse. She recognized Castlewaite immediately. He was holding a lead rope at the horse's head and she could hear the soft whirring of his eyepiece as he focused on first the horse, then the men. She felt a rush of warmth at the sight of him and marveled at the thought.

A second man was inspecting the iron shoes of the beast. He had fair hair, wore a rough linen shirt, tweed waistcoat and baggy trousers tucked into riding boots. Shabby, she thought, but likely work clothes. A farrier perhaps, or one of those newly-fashionable horse doctors. *Veterinarians* they were called. All the rage in London.

The third man was tall and lanky, with sleek black hair and a stubbled chin. He was also clad in waistcoat and riding boots, but he stood proudly, cut a finer figure. Her heart skipped a beat as she tried to recall the painting in the stairwell, that of the seventh Baron. There were six dogs laying around the floor—the very ones who had greeted her the night before. They raised their heads and wagged at her approach.

"Miss Ivy!" grinned Castlewaite. "Ah trust you had sweet dreams last night?"

"Vivid and dark, but those are my favourite kind." She smiled and thrust out her hand. "Good morning, sirs."

Hands on hips, the tall man turned and ran an appraising eye over her figure. His eyes were bluest blue and he looked like Christien, save for the hard lines at his forehead and mouth.

"Skirts have no place in a stable," he growled.

"Wonderful. I hate skirts. Perhaps I could wear breeches? Should we petition the Baron?"

He stepped toward her.

"You should petition the Baron before you do anything at all, miss. This is, after all, his estate."

She stepped toward him in the same manner.

"I would be delighted to do so, sir, but my mother, brother and I have been here for half a day, and I have yet to make his acquaintance. He seems a rather recalcitrant host."

The horseman grinned, his eyes dancing between her and the man and she thought absent-mindedly that he had a rather pleasant face for a farrier.

The tall man narrowed his eyes. "His Lordship is busy."

She narrowed her eyes. "Apparently so."

"What is your name, skirt?"

"Ivy Savage, sir."

"Oh God. The novelist."

"She signed VINCE's copper bottom last night, she did," offered Castlewaite. "You made him right happy, miss. He's quite a fan."

"What skill to entertain a robot," said the man.

Ivy felt her cheeks grow hot but she was determined to master it. She raised her chin.

"A sideline, sir. My primary occupation is the care of my mother and brother and soon-to-be husband."

"Congratulations are in order, then."

"It *is* called a pleasantry in polite circles."

The farrier laughed aloud and the tall man threw him a scowl. When he turned back to her, he placed a hand over his heart and bent low to the ground in the most formal of bows.

"Congratulations, to you, Miss Ivy Savage, novelist and fiancée of poor Christien Jeremie St. John de Lacey. May God bless you all the days of your married lives." He paused, ran his eyes along her form once again. "With a tongue like that, I fear your husband will need all the help he can get."

She raised her chin, uncertain how to respond but the man brushed past her in the direction she had entered.

"You know what to do, Laury?" he called over his shoulder.

"Aye," the horseman called back. "I do."

"*You* pick the mares this time. Three at most. Don't let him loose in the field like last time. It drives down the price."

"I know."

"Let me know when it's done. I have buyers ready."

"I will."

"And keep the skirts out of the stable."

And with that, the man disappeared out the doors and Ivy released a long-held breath. Her hands had curled into fists quite of their own accord.

She swung around to the remaining pair.

"Oh isn't he a terrible, horrible, mean-spirited man!"

"Aw now, miss," said Castlewaite and he smiled his gap-toothed smile. "He's not tha' bad."

"She has a point." The horseman straightened, dusted his hands on his trousers. "They call him the Scourge of Lasingstoke in the village."

"Is he always so rude?"

"Naw," said Castlewaite.

"Yes," said the horseman.

"I can certainly see why Christien prefers to stay in London. Fleas and potatoes and sheep and broken sweepers and broken pens and icy rooms and Cookie and, and now *him*... " She folded her arms across her chest. "I would still be in London if it hadn't been for that bloody heart."

"Heart?" asked the horseman.

"It's a long story."

"But ye're good at stories, miss," said Castlewaite and he winked at her before passing the lead rope into the younger man's hands. "Ah'm off to m'boilers then. Good day to ye, Miss Ivy."

Ivy watched his thin frame shuffle between the stalls, disappearing out of the stable entirely and leaving the two of them alone with the horses and the dogs.

The horseman stood quietly, running his hand along the horse's grey neck. The dogs looked up at him; those that had tails wagged them. There were at least six, not one of them smaller than a calf.

"Is your mother prepared for Lonsdale, Miss Savage?" he asked after a moment.

"Oh, Lonsdale," she sighed. "The sanitarium north of nowhere."

"That would be the one."

"I believe my mother is as well-prepared as she can be for Lonsdale. It's me who's having the difficulty."

"I'm sorry."

"No, *I'm* sorry," she said. "It has been a difficult journey, I am very tired and I don't know how to hold my tongue at the best of times."

"You'll fit in well here, then."

She smiled sadly. "I'm not sure what they can do for my mother at Lonsdale."

He said nothing, merely stroked the gray dappled neck.

"I don't think I want her to go. I mean they can care for her, surely. But they can't cure her. And they certainly can't love her. And that's important to me, silly as that sounds. She may be dead to everyone else but still, she needs to be loved. All people need to be loved by someone in their life, don't you think?"

He looked at the dogs. They wagged.

"My father doesn't really know what to do with her. He loves her so much, but there's no one inside. She's as dead as the girls in Whitechapel. He may as well be loving a ghost."

Her chin had begun to quiver so she steeled it, looked around the stable.

"I yearn for the day when she'll look up at me and smile in the way she used to, or laugh or enjoy a cup of tea or read one of my stories but if I'm honest with myself, I don't believe she ever will. But I can't give up on her, can I? I can't give up hope. I can't just run off to Paris and go to school and leave her to fend without me. She would surely die then, and so would my tad and after awhile, so would I. So, I'm trapped in a empty house in Stepney, watching the world go by with no way out, until Christien..."

Her knees were shaking now but she was stronger than her knees.

"He's so patient and perfect but if I marry him, I *will* be leaving her, won't I? Whether it's at home or at Lonsdale or throwing 'elegant parties' at Hollbrook, I will have to leave her and I know, I just know, that without me, she'll die and after all she's been through, all those little black coffins..."

Her throat was tightening but she was more stubborn than her throat.

"Well, that would just be wrong. That would mean defeat and a Savage can never admit defeat."

Her heart was aching but she was prouder than her heart.

"It's not that bad, really. I may never go to Paris, or study in a proper school or be a Criminologist or solve crimes or wear breeches or drink claret, but I will always write and as long as I can write, I feel alive. I may never be able to write my own story, but I know I will do my damnedest to finish hers."

She realized there were tears running down her cheeks. The horseman offered her a cloth.

"It's all I have," he said.

"Thank you." She wiped her cheeks, didn't care that it smelled of horse and leather and pine tar. "You are very kind."

"Well, not really. I used it to clean his hoofs. Now you have black marks down your face."

"Wh-what?"

"I'm not certain they will ever come off. Blast."

She blinked and blinked again but before she knew it, she began to laugh. She laughed until she cried all over again. The horse reached its head toward her, breathed on her with its great nostrils and and finally, she stopped her weeping, rubbed her cheeks with her palms and smiled.

"Better?"

"Not at all."

"Oh dear!"

"Indeed. We may need Cookie herself to clean things up."

"Please no!" and she surprised herself by laughing again. "I think I'll take my chances with the Scourge!"

"And there you go."

She looked at him. He had nice eyes. They were brown. Or maybe hazel. Or gray. She couldn't tell. Wide cheekbones, fair wavy hair. Too long to be fashionable in London, but it suited him. Very pastoral and earthy. Not at all beautiful like Christien.

And yet...

She tore her eyes away, concentrated on the animal standing so quietly under his hand.

"Is this one of the Mad Lord's French Warmbloods?"

"He is indeed. His registered name is *Montclaire's Ghyslain d'Auguste.*"

She raised her brows and he grinned.

"We call him Gus."

"Much better," she laughed and thrust out her hand. "Ivy."

He took it. "Sebastien."

"Seb what?...but..." She froze. "But I thought... But... He said..."

"Ah yes, just like Gus, Laury is my stable name. My 'registered' name is Sebastien Laurent St. John Lord de Lacey, Seventh Baron of Lasingstoke. See?"

And he rapped the back of his head and she could swear she heard the sound of metal.

"So, future-sister-in-law Ivy Savage, let's get this fellow out into the fields, shall we? He needs to breed some mares."

And he pushed past her with the horse and dogs in tow, and she could have sworn she saw a flash of silver under all his golden hair.

***

Alexandre Gavriel St. Jacques Lord Durand disappeared into the stable, and Penny felt a chill run up her spine. He was a villain, indeed—elusive and mysterious. To sit in the House of Lords and yet dress like a common farrier was confounding and, therefore, suspicious. Her instincts were always correct and she wondered if he, in fact, had stolen the Clockwork Heart from Lancaster Castle.

A gentleman thief, she thought to herself. Wouldn't be the first.

There was a knock on the door, and she was relieved to find Clarys, her best friend, with a basket of wine, cheese and biscuits. So the rest of the afternoon was spent in much merriment, and only a little sleuthing.

***

Wharcombe SteamPress

September 15, 1888

Charlie Fretts, 11 year-old son of fishmonger Reggie and Bernadette Fretts, was found dead in Wharcombe today.

Chapter 6

Of Live Women, Dead Boys and Horses at Midnight

She had seemed live enough.

At least, Castlewaite and Rupert had spoken with her, had interacted. All good clues, generally. And she had held her own with Rupert, which was never easy. His uncle was a cad. Brilliant with finances, with estates and horses, but not so good with people. He smiled, thinking the same could easily be said of himself.

She left quickly, however, once she'd uncovered his name. They all did. They either fawned and prattled or fled like a house on fire. But before she'd known, she had chatted. That was different than prattling. More natural. No, this little woman of Christien's had bared her soul, had laughed and even shed a tear. It had been sweet, almost normal and he'd learned to take normal whenever and wherever he could get it.

There was a loud squeal, and he turned his attention to the field where Gus was entertaining the new mares. He was prancing circles around a little bay, tossing his head and trying to impress. The mare was *not* impressed, however, and kept laying back her ears and snapping whenever he would dance too close. Sebastien shook his head. Five mares in a field, four willing but Gus would naturally choose the fifth. Life was curious that way.

He laid his arms across the fence rail, watching the dance of the horses, feeling the dogs wrestle and bump at his feet. The air was quiet and he knew there would be rain in two night's time. There was an enormous pile of posts on his desk at First, and he knew he needed to pass them over to Rupert. Cad though he may be, Rupert would never open a post not addressed to him. The man had scruples.

The dogs whined, and the air around him began to grow cold.

There was a boy watching him.

There was always someone watching. It was exhausting, and sometimes he found himself wishing for the solitary blackness of Lonsdale. Frankow was a good man. His laudanum was by far the best.

He turned to look at the boy.

Perhaps eleven he was, with dark hair matted on one side and a very pale face. They usually had pale faces. *If* they had faces at all. Large, dark eyes staring at him, blood and bruising at the right temple indicating a backhanded blow. Not a hand, however. The wound was too straight and deep for that. A poker perhaps, for there was soot on the boy's cheek.

"Where are you from?" he asked.

The boy didn't speak. The dead rarely did. Instead, he merely flicked his large eyes in the direction of the Bay.

"Dunbridge? Pelling? Wharcombe?" he asked, and at the name of the bayside town of Wharcombe, the boy nodded. "And did you die in Wharcombe as well?"

The boy said nothing. He was grateful it wasn't Manchester. Manchester was a long ride.

"Was it your father? Was he drinking or did you make him angry?"

Tears began welling behind those large eyes, and Sebastien looked away. Gus had found himself a willing mare, and he knew Rupert would be furious. Still, they were Warmbloods all. Any foal by Lasingstoke's Gus would bring a good price.

With a sigh, he looked back at the boy. "I'm sorry, lad. I'll see what I can do. Can you give me some time? My horse is rather busy."

The boy folded up and disappeared, and Sebastien ran a hand along his face. Once again he felt the rush of desire for Lonsdale, its dark rooms and darker laudanum.

At least the girl had seemed live enough.

***

There was a swing in the dying garden. It was late afternoon, and her heart was heavy and the swing took her back and forth, back and forth, as if the simple motion could rid her heart of the weight. The sun was struggling to come out, but the clouds were thick and low and winning. Catherine Savage still sat on the stone bench under the branches of an oak, staring but seeing nothing.

Tomorrow, thought Ivy. Tomorrow everything would change.

She had left the stables and the Mad Lord de Lacey, who had at that point seemed the most sensible character on the entire estate. He certainly did not look like her impression of a lord, let alone a mad one. With the gray horse and six dogs in tow, he had headed out straight away to the fields in direct defiance of "the Scourge." He apparently did have metal in his skull and he certainly liked his horses. She wondered how many more of the rumours were true. Life was becoming too strange for her. She didn't know what to think anymore.

She looked down at the newspaper in her hand, at the article in the *Lancaster Guardian.*

LONDON POLICE BAFFLED

The Latest Victim Discovered in Spitalfields Early Sunday Morning Shockingly Mutilated

LONDON, Sept. 10—The horribly mutilated body of a woman was found early yesterday morning in a yard attached to a common lodging house in Spitalfields. Her throat was cut from ear to ear, the body was ripped open, the bowels and heart were on the ground, a portion of the entrails were tied around the neck and the womb removed entirely from the scene. This is the fourth murder of a similar character that has been committed recently in this vicinity. All the victims were women of the lowest character. The author of the atrocities remains undiscovered, and the excitement in the immediate vicinity borders upon a panic.

Police are continuing to investigate.

She frowned. Leather Apron, the press had taken to calling him, but truth be told, it wasn't likely to be one man. At least that's what her father had insisted. People loved their conspiracies, he had said; would see devils in every lock and larder. The East End was a hard part of town, Whitechapel even more so. Women who worked their trade in dark alleys were easy to find.

Now Christien was involved for he was studying in the new field of forensic pathology. Dr. Thomas Bond had assembled himself a team of brilliant young physicians-in-training—Bondie's Boys, they were called. Christien, Henry Bender, Ambrose Pickett and Lewis Powell-Smith. When he was not with her, Bond or Dr. Williams, he was with the boys. They had been together for years.

It was an exciting pursuit, she thought, all for the advancement of the Empire of Steam. They were always dissecting something, analyzing something, cutting something apart. The other boys were hard as nails, but Christien was in it for the science. To see him working with Bond and the detectives of H-Division made her very proud. Not for the first time, she wondered what sort of wife she would make when she'd rather be in a morgue than a kitchen or a nursery.

She looked down at the article once again.

"Her heart was on the ground, mum," she said as she swung back and forth. "That's a terrible place to put a heart. Better than sending it to me in the post, I suppose, but still, I wonder what the devil was thinking..."

She shuddered, remembering the feel of the cold, sticky lump in her hands. It was as if Death was reaching for her from the pages of her stories. No, not Death. *Jack.* The heart had been 'From Jack'. Was that his real name? Had the heart been taken from a woman like in this article, from a scene just like this? Her chest tightened as the questions mounted.

"And why remove her womb, mum?" she asked. "That's strange isn't it and therefore, a very good clue."

Catherine Savage blinked but naturally, said nothing.

"Maybe he's a collector, or a scientist of some sort. You know, like how some men like to stuff dead birds or pin butterflies to cork. Maybe he works for collectors or scientists and needs to find new parts to keep his kids in taffy." She made a face as she swung higher and higher. "Maybe she was pregnant... Ooh, that would be bad, wouldn't it, mum? She *was* a working girl, after all. Dr. Williams says it happens all the time. He helps them with that, though we're not supposed to say. Hmm, I'll need to ask him when we're back in London."

And so she sat on the swing and went back and forth, going over the article in the Guardian until Lottie called them in for dinner.

***

The sun was setting over the waters of Wharcombe Bay and the smell of fish was strong on the wind. Trollers rose and fell with the waves and sea birds swooped low over the docks.

At the end of the road was the fishmonger's shop. It was small and boarded with clapping, with barrels and benches lining the stoop. Gaslight beamed from the lone window and the chimney curled with smoke. The shouting inside the thin walls had been going on for almost an hour, however. He dearly wished he could go in and put an end to it, but there were children and he had principles.

Besides, while the wind was biting, there was no frost.

The wailing had become unbearable when the door swung open and a man staggered out, a bottle in one hand, an iron poker in the other.

"Yor turn next, Dot!" the man roared and he struck the poker against the frame. It left splinters the size of a thumb. "You keep your gob shut or it's yor turn for sure!"

The door slammed shut and bolts slid home.

"Piss on 'em," the man grumbled. "Piss on 'em all."

And he turned toward the docks and the cold waters of Wharcombe Bay, striking the poker on the ground as he walked.

Sebastien de Lacey released a long breath, watching it as it frosted into a cloud in front of his face. He looked behind him. The boy with the sad eyes was there, leaning against the wall of the shanty. His cheeks had sunken in, his lips as gray as the Bay. He nodded.

de Lacey pulled the clockwork pistol from his belt, checked all three chambers for bullets and followed the man toward the docks.

***

September 15, 1888
Dear Tad,
I am happy to admit that our situation in Lancashire is beginning to

improve and I am beginning to believe that both Davis and I will settle in nicely. I have met both Rupert the Scourge – a miserable man who apparently is Christien's uncle, and the Mad Lord himself, who does not seem as mad as he is made out to be. However, I have only spoken with him once and then, our conversation was impeded by my weeping so I could be sorely mistaken.

We take Mum to Lonsdale Abbey tomorrow. I am still dreading it, although I know I cannot be both Christien's wife and Mum's caretaker. I do hope this Dr. Frankow is as kind as he is talented. Mum has been loved all her life. I fear that somehow, she will know that she has been abandoned and will fail to thrive under his care. That would be something I could not bear.

Regarding the woman found in Spitalfields, you might check with Dr. Williams on the possibility that she was pregnant. It's just a thought. He runs many clinics and his research in Obstetrics and Gynecology might prove helpful.

It is very late and I must be off to bed for it will be an early start tomorrow. Lonsdale is a good two-hour coach, and our appointment is for quarter of ten. Please give my regards to Mr. Beals and Ginny if you see them. I will give Mum a kiss from you.

Your girl,

Ivy

Lottie had found her a new fountain pen and Ivy laid it down on the desk, waiting for the ink to dry. It was late, but she was unsettled and found her mind spinning in many different directions. She wrapped the blanket around her shoulders and rose to stand by the window that only last night, had been covered in frost.

Funny how for six months of the year, it was the moon that was brightest, cast the most light. She had heard that in France, the sun was king. Cherries and winefields and steamcars and writers and dancers and bohemians, all in love with the regal French sun. But here in England, over the rolling, sweeping gray-green hills, painting everything in strokes of silver, the moon was queen. Like Victoria the clockwork Empress.

The squeal of a horse broke the stillness and then, an answering squeal. She peered out to see if it was the walking horse but could see nothing. Another squeal, louder this time and she grinned to herself. *Penny Dreadful and the Ghost of Lancashire* was a real life mystery. She exchanged the blanket for a woolen cardigan, slipped on a pair of Wellies and headed out the door and down the stair.

The air was cold so she tugged at the cardigan and hurried across the cobbles to the fields beyond. At the fence, several horses gathered, necks outstretched to a grey standing on the other side. As she neared, she realized two things. One, that it was the horse called Gus, the one that belonged to Sebastien de Lacey, and two, that it was fully tacked, with bridle, saddle and reins looped up on its withers.

She smiled to herself. Her father could not possibly have known the sort of story he had written her into.

Gus was blowing softly into the nostrils of a bay mare who was blowing back. She moved closer.

"Hello, Gus," she said softly, and he swung his head in her direction. She caught his bridle, making a point to run her free hand along his neck the way Sebastien had earlier. He was soft and warm.

"Where's your Lord, then?" she asked. "Did he fall off somewhere? You would be a naughty boy if you left him somewhere far, far away, now wouldn't you? That's right. Naughty, naughty boy."

The great horse turned back to face the mare, and the blowing ritual began all over again. With a hand still fixed to the bridle, she looked up and down the road for a sign.

She heard it first, the faint crunching of boots on gravel, but soon she could make out his shape, walking out of the shadows and into the moonlight. He was coming from the west, from the direction of Lancaster and wearing a greatcoat that billowed like a cloak. She clutched the cardigan tightly at her throat, wishing now that she had taken the time to lace up her country boots. Wellies suddenly seemed far too clumsy for her feet.

He said nothing until he was right upon her and still he did not pause, merely walked up to the fence and began to pull the saddle of the horse's back. She didn't know what to think, knew even less what he expected her to do so she stood, holding the bridle as he slid the saddle from the gray back and laid it across the rail. He then slipped the reins over the neck and began to work at the buckles of the headstall. She glanced at his face, lit on one side by the moon. There was mud on his cheek and hands. Or perhaps it was blood. She couldn't be certain and her heart thudded once in her chest.

Soon, the horse was completely undone, and still, without a word, he opened the gate. Gus trotted happily through.

He turned, swung the saddle off the rail and into her arms. She staggered under the weight but took it, too surprised to do anything else.

And throwing the bridle across his shoulder, he stepped back onto the path in the direction of the Hall.

All of this without a word.

At night, he runs with wild horses.

She stood in the moonlight and watched him go.

***

Wharcombe Steam Press

The body of local fishmonger Reggie Fretts was found off the shores of the Bay this morning. He was shot once with a bullet to the head. This is the second tragedy to strike the fishmonger's family, the first being the sudden death of his oldest son Charlie earlier this week. Upon interview, Mrs. Bernadette "Dottie" Fretts made mention that her husband was a terrible drunk and had gotten himself in low with the bookies. She has recently come into some money and made plans to leave Wharcombe with her four surviving children and move back to Surrey for a better life with her sister.

Police are now listing the Wharcombe/Milnethorpe bookmakers as prime suspects in this case and are continuing to investigate.

Chapter 7

Of Datamancery, Necroscopy and a Clockwork Man

Cookie set out an early breakfast but her brother had elected to stay behind at the Hall—helping Lottie with some of the cleaning machines, he had insisted. It didn't surprise her. He put on a good show of pretending his mother's state mattered little to him. She knew that deep in his heart he cared but still, it was up to Ivy once again, taking their mum on the road to Lonsdale.

And so for a little over two hours, the coach rolled along the dirt roadways of Lancashire. She had seen only one steamcar—an antique of the four-wheeled variety with a blonde woman at the helm. She was driving like a madwoman, great goggles covering her eyes and a long paisley scarf flowing in the wind. Ivy heard Castlewaite cursing from the dickey above and the horses snorted and reared as it roared past. While they were a common sight in London, they were fairly new contraptions. Built upon the same steam-powered principles as a locomotive, they were modern but noisy, their movements stilted and jerky. Ivy thought would need considerable improvements for people to abandon their coaches in favour of them.

She did not see a single airship. She did, however, see many sheep.

So, it was with such strange, trivial and unrelated thoughts running through her mind that she barely noticed Lonsdale Abbey come into view, perched like a tower over a stretch of gray water.

She sat forward, pressed her nose against the glass.

The Abbey sat on the hills above Wharcombe Bay. She loved the smell of the ocean. It always made her spirit leap with the promise of adventure. The Thames was not the same. The Thames smelled like rubbish. The Thames smelled like ashes and oil and the hulls of large ships. There was no promise of adventure in the Thames.

She threw a glance at her mother, head bobbing in time with the horses. Cookie had exchanged her bonnet for a cream mob although her dress was still deepest black. No matter what anyone did, she still looked dead.

Ivy felt her throat tighten, so she looked back out the window as finally the carriage rattled to a halt at a wrought-iron gate. There was no gateman. There was, however, an impressive set of gears set in a rusted archway over their heads. She watched as Castlewaite climbed down from the dickey to punch in a sequence of numbers on an antiquated set of hex-nut keys. She could hear the punch and click as each number was entered and she marveled at how a simple coachman could possibly know the code for such a place.

Suddenly, there was a shudder as the mechanism sprang to life. The articulating gears groaned overhead and wheels inside the gate lintel began to spin. Slowly, the wrought iron moved, swinging open to allow the carriage passage. Castlewaite urged the horses through and the wide black gate swung closed behind them.

Datamancery, she thought. What a remarkable science.

The grounds were vast enough to boast a small farm, residences for the staff and a chapel. As they neared the Abbey, she could see the weathered red brick with limestone over doors and windows. Three large stacks puffing smoke and steam into the gray sky. *This,* she thought, was the Gothic ghost house of her imagination. She dreaded what she might find inside.

The coach rattled to a halt, the door swung open and a hand was presented. With a deep breath, Ivy stepped outside and into the damp gray air of Wharcombe Bay.

Two men snapped heels at her approach. They looked like bellhops from fancy hotels. Two women dressed in nursing whites, their black cloaks and large winged caps reminded her of swooping birds.

"Miss Savage?" said one of the men. He was holding a wheeled chair. "We will take you to see Dr. Frankow presently. Would your mother care to sit?"

"I think that would be fine. Mum?"

Naturally, Catherine Savage did not respond but she moved when Ivy moved her and allowed herself to be seated. At once, the chair was spun and the man disappeared up and into the sanitarium.

The nurses followed.

"Ah'll wait here, miss," said Castlewaite. He sprang from the dickey, and began to help the second man with the bags.

Leaving Ivy to walk alone into the mouth of Lonsdale Abbey.

***

The surgical theatre was dark, illuminated only by a single gas lamp over the table. A sheet had been pulled across the body, the organs carefully replaced inside. Everyone else had gone home after the necroscopy, leaving him with the clean up. Christien didn't mind. The silence was good for thinking.

The lab smelled sharp and sweet, though not quite clean. In the mortuary of the London Royal Hospital, "clean" was a subjective concept. Carefully, he sprayed the last of the tools with the carbolic acid, began the slow, methodical process of wiping it clear of blood. It was the Lister knife, a fine piece of ebony and metalwork. It cut through both muscle and connective tissue with ease. Detail and precision—that was the name of the game in the police surgeon's department. He loved the lab. It was more a home than Lasingstoke or Hollbrook could ever be.

He was in the process of wiping the Lister and lost in thought when a man with a thick gray moustache entered the room.

"Remy?" said Dr. Thomas Bond. "I wasn't expecting you. I thought Rosie was on this morning."

"His mother's down with the Soup, sir," he lied, pulling his goggles under his chin.

"Ah damn," said Bond. "I do hope he's not drunk again."

"We have an exam later on today, sir. I'm sure he wouldn't drink before an exam."

Bond studied him for a long moment before moving to the body and lifting the sheet.

"Fine job, Remy. You've stitched her up nicely. Very neat."

"Thank you, sir."

"Terrible business, this. Are you certain you are fine with it?"

"I'm fine, sir," he said as he laid the blade on the cloth that held the bone saw, the chisel, the clamps and the scalpels. Set the threads back in their cases, dipped the needles in the acid, collecting his thoughts. "But I do have a question."

"Ask away, boy. It's our job to ask the hard questions."

"The blade that made those incisions…"

"Yes?"

"This is no butcher, sir. I fear this is a very different sort of character."

"Ah *ha*. Are you speaking of forensic pathology or psychology, boy?"

"Pathology, sir. I'm not nearly so skilled in psychology."

"Top of the class, I'm told."

"Motivated, sir," he smiled. "Madness runs in the family."

There was a twitch of Bond's thick gray moustache. It was unnerving, thought Christien, Bond's quiet, intrusive ways. Dr. Thomas Bond, Surgeon for the Metropolitan Police, was changing things with his character analyses and villain profiles, giving the Bottle a run for their money, making them work harder, think better. Bond was a brilliant man and Christien knew he was lucky to be here.

"Very well, Remy. Defend."

"There have been at least eight murders in the East End since April, sir, but with the exception of this one and the woman from Buck's Row, I can see no similarities in the acts, regardless of what the presses are reporting."

"The one from Buck's Row," Bond repeated. "Mary Ann Nichols?"

"Yes, sir. Called Polly on the streets. According to Dr. Llewellyn, the cuts on her throat were savage and deep, almost down to the vertebrae, just like these. Secondly, her abdominal mutilations were violent and concentrated in the lower regions. And thirdly, his report indicates a single, sharp, long-bladed knife, just like we see here."

"Have you spoken with Llewellyn, Christien?"

"No, sir. I have not. But I have read the reports as you asked us to. And those three elements are repeated here, in this unfortunate."

They both looked at the body under the sheet. Anne Chapman was her name, 'Dark Annie' to those who knew her. There was no need for the sheet, other than propriety and English manners. The boys would often joke that the French version of a necropsy involved suspending bodies on dartboards and tossing scalpels like darts.

"But why not a butcher, son? Or a craftsman? The papers are all calling him Leather Apron, you know. It's a catching title."

"They should be calling him the Surgeon, sir, or perhaps the Ripper. But not Leather Apron...."

"The Surgeon?" Bond raised a brow and Christien steeled his nerve. Bond was both baiting and encouraging at the same time, drawing him out and causing him to elaborate his thought process. It was an exhilarating, terrifying experience.

"Well, sir," Christien began. "The anatomy of a human woman is different from that of an ox or a pig. And the length of blade, being easily six to eight inches, is consistent with a surgical blade, not a tradesman's."

He reached down and selected a blade, held its long blade in both hands. "The Lister, for example, could remove the organs in one swift slice..."

"You think this Ripper is a medical man, Remy?"

"I think we should not be so quick to rule it out, sir."

Bond's gaze remained on him before his moustache quirked again. "You are a brave one, my boy. I have reported the very same to Anderson downtown."

Christien managed to keep rein on a smile. Understatement was a British life skill and Bond a master player.

"But remember, we are not official on this, Remy. It is Phillips' division. And Llewellyn—"

"—is not you, sir. Nor is Phillips."

"Nor are you," Bond said wryly. "Although one day you may very well surpass me if that bludger Williams doesn't snare you in his obstetrics traps."

"Not likely, sir."

He clapped a hand on the young physician's shoulder. "Come on, my boy. Scrub off and I'll buy you a pint. The Britannia is calling."

"Thank you, sir," said Christien as he turned back to the post-mortem kit, began wrapping it back in the cloths. "But I must warn you, Dr. Williams bought me dinner the other night at a club on Pall Mall. And he has promised me a weekend at Sandringham."

"Upping the ante, wot? Damn him to hell." Bond laughed and headed toward the door. "I'm just a lowly surgeon working for the Beak. My pockets aren't so deep."

"I'll meet you upstairs, sir," said Christien and he reached for the carbolic soap to clean his hands of the blood.

***

The foyer was enormous, with high ceilings arched in Gothic fashion. The walls were stained wood, the floor black and white tile, and elaborate lanterns hung from the ceiling, pouring gas-light down onto them from above. There were a few potted palms and a large marble fireplace was burning at the far end of the room. Halls and doorways led off deep into the Abbey like burrows.

There was no one else in sight. Not another nurse, not a doctor, not even a patient in the great arched foyer of Lonsdale. And, now that she'd come to think of it, she'd not seen a single soul on the grounds either. To make matters worse, the two men had immediately disappeared leaving Ivy and her mother in the company of the nurses. She turned to one, a stout, older woman with a shiny brass pin on her uniform. Amelia Dyer, it read. Ivy smiled.

"How long have you worked here at the Abbey, Mrs. Dyer?"

"Shhhh," said the woman and scowled at her.

Ivy closed her mouth, saying nothing more.

After a very long wait, she heard a sound, a very faint sound, as if from a long way away. It was tap, clank and hiss, tap, clank and hiss and growing louder. The sound echoed throughout the foyer and Ivy felt an irrational urge to flee. Soon, a figure appeared under one of the doorway arches and she swallowed.

It was a man of perhaps sixty years, with thinning hair, white beard and thick spectacles that made his eyes look huge. He was dressed in a fine wool three-piece suit under a laboratory smock. But her attention was drawn, most inadvertently, to his legs. They were clothed to the knee and ended there.

Shafts of copper made up his bones, cogs and gears were joints, pulleys of corded wire served as tendons. He moved slowly but deliberately across the tiled floor toward her, a cane tapping the ground as he came. She had heard of such amputees, had once seen a photochrome of Edward, Prince of Wales with his miraculous clockwork arm. And of course, there was Castlewaite with his mechanical eye, but this was truly a marvel of engineering.

He stopped immediately before her and she could smell ammonium and pipe smoke. His cane was black with a silver mallard's head for a grip.

"Miss Savage. Mrs. Savage. Welcome to Lonsdale."

German, Ivy thought, or Austrian or something European. She held out her hand.

"Dr. Frankow?"

He ignored her and immediately, his huge eyes darted to the woman in the chair. The spectacles had reticulating lenses, and she could see them slide over each other automatically as he focused.

"She has been like this for how long?"

"Seven years, sir. Since the death of my youngest brother."

"Ah. You have a letter from de Lacey?"

"A letter?" She blinked. "I have no letter. Christien simply told me to come."

"Not Christien de Lacey, child. Sebastien. He has seen her, yes?"

"Lord de Lacey?" She was confounded. "No sir, Lord de Lacey has not seen my mother. Why would Sebastien de Lacey need to see my mother?"

The huge eyes rolled back to her, held her captive in their intense, bug-eyed gaze. Then he sighed, shook his head and turned to walk away, the metal creaking and the cane echoing as it tapped along the stone.

"Wait," she called after him. "Dr. Frankow, I have come all the way from London to see you, on the urging of Christien de Lacey, brother of

His Lordship. He said nothing about a letter, just that I come. And the Baron, well the Baron has barely been home."

"You are wasting my time." And he waved a hand behind his back, dismissively.

"Please, Sir. Christien highly recommends you as does Dr. John Williams of the London College of Physicians."

He kept walking. She took several steps forward, suddenly angry.

"Are you telling me that, in this grand facility of yours, there is nothing you can do for my mother? Or is there perhaps, sir, nothing you *will* do?"

The doctor paused and she cursed her tongue. Honestly, she could never keep it in her head. Far too brash for a woman, her father had said, and she knew it was true. She wondered how Christien had put up with it for so long and if that too would have to change after marriage.

With a whir and a click, he turned. He seemed to study her now, not her mother and the lenses spun again, causing his eyes to grow larger and larger still. After a few very long moments, he tapped, clanked and hissed back again.

"Williams recommends me?"

"Yes, sir. He says you are a leader in your field."

"Interesting…" His mouth quirked and she thought it was a smile. A patronizing, condescending, self-righteous smile, but a smile nonetheless.

"I *can* do many things for your mother," he said finally. "But it may not be what you wish."

"Please, sir. Any help would be most welcome."

He studied her some more.

"You are engaged to the young one. Christien, yes?"

"We are to be married in the spring."

"And you love him?"

"Why would I marry him if I didn't love him?"

"It is just a question, Miss Savage. People do many strange things."

She raised her chin and the lenses whirred some more. With his metal legs, he almost seemed more automaton than human.

"I *will* do this," he said finally. "But I need Sebastien to come. Tell him that for me, Miss Savage, if you will."

He looked up, barked orders to the women, and turned one last time to cross the foyer's floor. One nurse scooped Catherine's bags, the other pushed on the chair, and suddenly, her mother was being wheeled away without even a kiss goodbye.

And Ivy was left very alone, standing in the haunting Gothic entrance of Lonsdale Abbey.

When the tears finally came, she whirled and fled in the direction of the carriage.

***

"This way, Penny," said her father and Penny followed him into the storage vaults deep beneath Lancaster Castle. It was a dark place, filled with dripping water and flickering gaslight and she wondered how something as marvelous as a Clockwork Heart could be stored in such a cold, inhospitable place.

First one door, then another wheeled open for her on great cogs overhead and the noise made Penny wonder how anyone could steal something from such a vault. The sound alone would surely trigger an alarm. Finally, they stopped in front of a wall of steel and a man in a laboratory smock turned toward them.

He was a clockwork man.

One side of his face was entirely metal, and both eyes were coiled copper. His lower jaw and teeth were likewise made of copper and white hair poked through his skull like cloves on an orange. His ribcage was iron, his left arm and leg comprised of gears and pulleys and wire.

He was the most fearsome thing Penny had ever seen.

"You must be the investigators from London," he said and Penny was certain he was of German descent. While she put little stock in nationalism, she took an instant dislike to this small, mechanical man.

"Yes, yes, we are," boomed her father and he thrust out his hand. "Charles Dreadful. This is my daughter, Penny."

"Dr. von Freud," said the man. "Siegfried von Freud."

"Please to meet you, sir," said Penny and she shook as well. "How could the Heart have been stolen from such a place as this?"

The doctor turned on her. His copper eyes whirred and clicked.

"That is the mystery, Miss Dreadful," he said after a moment. "It couldn't have. Only I have the key and the key is with me at all times."

"And where were you when it was stolen, sir?"

"You see, Miss Dreadful, it was the key that was stolen." He pulled a long brass key from his pocket, held it up so it caught the light. "But it was put back. And that perhaps of all things, is the greatest mystery..."

Penny looked at her father and smiled. This was proving to be better than she could have hoped.

Chapter 8

Of Newspapers, a Great Many Letters and the Threat of Scandal

Steam Times

LONDON, WEDNESDAY

The Thames police were engaged for several hours this afternoon in dragging the river between Pimlico Steamboat Pier and London and Brighton South Coast Railway Bridge, between which points the arm of a woman was found just days ago. A careful examination was also made of the timber rafts floating in the river, but no discovery of human remains was made. It is the opinion of the river police that the arm was dropped over the embankment, which at night is darker than most thoroughfares and little frequented. The arm is still in the mortuary, and will be further examined by surgical experts.

In regard to the theory that the arm might have been thrown on to the river by a medical student with a view to create a scare, our representative called at one of the chief London hospitals today. He was assured that the arm could not possibly have been removed by a student from any hospital dissecting room. Students are allowed to dissect only in the room set aside for that purpose. Under the Act of William IV, hospitals and medical schools are allowed to receive unclaimed bodies for the purposes of dissection, but 48 hours notice has to be given after death to the Inspector under the Act before the body can be removed from the place of decease, and then only after a certificate of death has been given. The bodies, after being dissected, must be buried in consecrated ground and within six weeks a certificate of burial must be forwarded to the Inspector. Under no circumstances are students allowed to take portions of bodies to their own homes; in fact they would be liable under the Act to heavy penalties for doing so.

Police are not saying whether or not they believe this incident to be connected to the ghastly events that are occurring in Whitechapel and are continuing to investigate.

***

The room was clean of all traces of ash and mud and Christien marveled at how Pomfrey could accomplish so much in such a short time. It rained again this morning, the streets were soggy and he had nipped home in a steamcab to fetch a new pair of shoes. He had not worn his spats and now his feet were paying the price for it. He hoped Pomfrey could get the shoes cleaned by the weekend. Williams had mentioned a Club meeting set for Friday and these new shoes did squeak something terrible.

The room was silent and not for the first time he found himself missing the little sparrow he had found in the spring. She had been mauled by a cat and he had nursed her to health, kept her in a wire cage on his dressing table. With all his books, globes, scopes and gadgets, she had been a welcome addition. He had found her dead at the bottom of the cage less than a week ago, and he missed her songs already.

The brass ring on his finger was tighter than ever and even the carbolic soap had not dislodged it. He was about to try a round of macassar oil when there was a rap on the door. Pomfrey stepped in.

"Mister Christien," he said. "The *boys* have asked me to tell you that they are waiting downstairs."

He said 'the boys' a certain way, and Christien pursed his lips. Pomfrey hated 'the boys' with every fibre of his very proper being. The boys were terrible to him.

"Yes, Pomfrey. I'm just changing my shoes."

"I do so wish Mr. Bender would not smoke in the house. He drops ash all over the floors."

"I'll speak to him about it, Pomfrey."

"They have dragged mud all over the carpets again and I only just washed them."

"They are nefarious boys, Pomfrey."

"Scallywags, sir. I will admit it. Complete and utter scallywags. What you see in their company I cannot fathom." He held out two letters. "The post has come early, sir."

Christien took the first. "It's from Ivy."

"Is it, sir? I couldn't tell. There were no ink splotches or sketches of dead bodies on the envelope."

"Pomfrey..."

"The letters from the Archduchess have no such scrawls. Indeed, I am quite certain they are penned in pure gold."

Christien shook his head.

"You still pine for her, sir. It is painfully obvious even to me and I am not a particularly observant man."

"You are dreaming, Pomfrey. Valerie has Princes and Dukes vying for her hand. She would be never be allowed a match with me." He turned the envelope over in his hands. "No, Ivy is a good girl. She is clever and modern and loves London. I could do worse."

"And you could do better. I know I have said this before but I believe she is all too common for a man of your station, sir."

"And that is where you're wrong, Pomfrey. I am not my brother. I'm to be a surgeon and if I'm lucky, a Police Surgeon. What could possibly be better than an investigator's daughter?"

"An Archduchess, sir." He held up the second letter. "Now, this one looks entirely more common even than the first. Are you certain you are not a-courting a barmaid on the side?"

Christien smiled.

"Is there tea, Pomfrey?"

"I shall make some straightaway. It will rain again today, sir. Do dress for it."

"You are a mother duck, Pomfrey. I would die without you."

"Indeed, sir. It is entirely possible."

And with that, the houseman exited the room.

Christien lifted the second envelope to the light of the window. The handwriting was small and scrawled in red ink.

"From Jack", it said.

***

Hands curled into fists, she marched toward the annex of the house known as First. It was the oldest part of the estate, having been built in the time of King George II and it had not been modernized along with the rest of the house. It was classical and cluttered, with photochromes of horses and dogs covering the walls. She would not stop however and kept on down the hallway toward the large corner office where de Lacey was apparently conducting his business.

She could make out the voice of Rupert St. John and she slowed her march. He frightened her. Just a little.

"By God, Laury, that's two this week! You could have been killed. Or worse, boy, worse, you could have been *caught.*"

She stopped next to the door, unsure of her next course. St. John was an imposing figure and she didn't know what to make of him. He had taken over the daily operation of the estate after the deaths of the sixth Baron and his wife fifteen years ago. She was not surprised Christien had left when he could.

"Are you listening to me, Laury? Not even Edward can protect you if you're caught."

"I prefer to stop them at one, Rupert."

"I prefer you not stop them at all, Laury."

"Well, he'll not do it again," the Mad Lord said quietly. "He has four other children and a wife. No, sir, he'll not do it again."

"Dammitall, Laury. That is not your concern. Old Vic is furious."

"What am I supposed to do, Rupert? What am I to tell them?"

She could hear the Scourge's boots on the floor.

"You tell them to go to hell, Laury. You tell them *all* to go to hell."

There was silence for a long moment before Rupert spoke again.

"Well, how much did you pay her?"

"Four thousand."

"And the last one? The one in Manchester?"

"Two."

"By God, Laury. You'll bankrupt us yet…"

"A woman should not have to lose everything simply because her husband is a cad."

"And any cad who's married has a fool for a wife. It's the way things are out there, Laury. It's just the way things are."

A dog whimpered and she remembered that wherever Sebastien de Lacey went, his dogs did also. She pushed herself off the wall, just as Rupert loomed in the doorway.

His nose wrinkled at the sight of her.

"Oh, it's the skirt," he growled. "What a tidy little spy you'd make. Cooking, mending and gossip. The veritable female trinity."

She felt the heat rush to her cheeks. "I wish to speak with Lord de Lacey, sir."

"He does not speak with skirts. He is preoccupied with affairs of the Barony."

"Such as forgetting letters of introduction and giving saddles to guests on the road after midnight?"

He scowled at her.

"I put it in the stable, sir, but I regret to inform you that I was wearing my nightdress at the time, not a skirt. I couldn't find breeches."

And she raised her chin, just a little.

"Ah damn," came Sebastien's voice. "Let her in."

"Very well, Laury," Rupert growled. "But I expect to continue this later."

"I expect so, Uncle."

St. John nodded stiffly and moved aside, making his way down the hall with long, ground-covering strides. Ivy took a deep breath and stepped into the room.

It was not so much an office as a study. There was a settee and two wing chairs beside a fireplace, bookshelves lining the walls and the floors covered with Persian rugs. But the furniture was almost invisible beneath the piles of books, broadsheets, newspapers and envelopes. From the floor, the dogs looked up at her and wagged what they could.

Sebastien de Lacey was sitting at a desk overflowing with papers, letters and envelopes, some with Victoria's seal. She almost did not recognize him, for he was wearing spectacles with thick dark rims, and his fair hair was uncombed and wild. There was a red line across his cheekbone that was in the ripe stage of bruising. She had been right last night by the fence. It had not been mud on his face.

"Please, sit."

She raised her chin. "I have no need for sitting, sir. Of all the things I have experienced at Lasingstoke, comfort is not one of them."

"That is regrettable."

"I don't believe you regret it at all."

"Oh, but I do." He pulled the spectacles from his face and dropped them onto the pile of papers in front of him. He seemed far too young to be a Baron. "You were a bit of a shock. We don't get many guests at Lasingstoke."

A fact that did not surprise her.

"Did you not receive a letter from Christien?"

"Two, actually." He rifled through the envelopes, finally held up a pair of letters. "But I have only just opened them this morning. You required a letter of introduction for Frankow? That's odd."

"He didn't want to help her," she began. "He insisted that you needed to see her before he could do anything."

The Baron frowned, leaned back in his chair. The dogs lifted their heads at the movement then dropped them again.

"Hm. Christien doesn't mention that in his letters. Did he tell you why?"

She sighed now, feeling the fury draining away like cold tea.

"Not a word, sir. This is very disturbing for me. I've never been this far from her since Tobias died. And I would be with her still, if not for that blasted heart."

"Again this heart. And who is this Tobias? Take a chair, please. You are shipwrecking my thoughts."

She looked around for a chair that wasn't hidden under a tower of paper. Spied a heavy wooden stool in a corner of the room but it took her several minutes to unload it and drag it over to the desk. All the while he sat in his chair and did not move to help.

She placed it and sat. He rose to his feet.

"No sitting. Stand up."

She stood.

He moved around the desk to stand in front of her. He was dressed in much the same way as yesterday, presentable but shabby, with a pocket watch tucked into his vest. She noticed his hair had much more curl to it than Christien's. Christien's was straight, sleek and very dark. This, this looked like a rolling field of wheat and she wondered if it was to hide the metal in his skull.

"Give me your hands. Tobias?"

He reached out his hands.

She stared at them. The knuckles were bruised and as bloody as his face. But his fingers were clean, the nails polished and trimmed, and she did not know what to think. Besides, he was not her fiancé. She should not be holding his hands.

"Tobias?" he repeated and presented them yet again.

She took them and he closed his eyes.

"Tobias was my youngest brother," she said tentatively. "My mother loved him very much."

"Hm. She lost many children, yes?"

Little black coffins, each a chapter of her childhood.

"Five stillborn. Only myself, Davis and Tobias survived."

With eyes still closed, he began turning her palms over in his hands. She swallowed, suddenly understanding the very real potential of scandal in anything this man did. She would have to be very, very careful.

"Tobias was unexpected," he muttered. "Very young when she was old, and therefore, precious. He died...drowned in the Thames...she could not save him."

"Yes," in a small voice. "She could not swim."

"She watched him die." He opened his eyes. "And has been dead ever since."

Tears were stinging once again and she wished to pull her hands away but didn't. Far too proud, she knew it. Far too stubborn.

"It was seven years ago," she said. "She never wanted to come out of her room, slept all the time. Then she stopped eating, drinking, bathing..."

"Hmm."

"How did you know? Did Christien—"

"*Aah....*"

He paused as his fingers brushed the ring around her finger. Christien had given it to her two months ago and she had been flabbergasted. It was a single pearl set in a delicate golden band, two diamonds on either side.

"My mother's ring," he said softly.

Now he slid his hands around her thumbs, then up to her wrists. And he held her there a moment, seemed to be puzzling over something. This was a very intimate contact. Even Christien, ever the gentleman, had never touched her like this. But she would not pull away. Not now. She was a proud, stubborn girl and he a very unusual man.

Finally, he released her and stepped back with a deep breath. Then he smiled, a smile as bright as the regal French sun and it occurred to her that he was rather handsome.

"Why on *earth* are you marrying my brother?"

She blinked in surprise.

"I, I beg your pardon? What sort of question is that?"

"Forgive me, Miss Savage. I did not mean to confound, although I suppose I do confound more than most." He folded his arms and leaned against the desk. "Your father is a crimes investigator, yes? Metropolitan Police?"

"What of it?"

"He has seen much in his profession. Far too much of the darkness in the human soul. Do you believe in the soul, Miss Savage?"

"What has that got to do with—"

"Christien does not. He is a man of science. I fear your father does not, either. And nor I think, do you."

"Faith is a personal thing, sir. Hardly something that should dictate the suitability of a marriage partner."

"Entirely the thing. Think it through. You have a father with a gruesome profession, a fiancé with an even more gruesome one. A dead brother and a dying mother. You write murderous stories, have your living brother illustrate them and yet you are shocked when you receive a heart in the post. You yearn for a vibrant and fascinating career in Crimes, but you set yourself up to be the wife of a city doctor. It is a conflict, in my estimation."

"Christien is to be a Police Surgeon," she countered. "Hardly a mere 'city doctor'."

"Ah. And you are to assist him in his investigations, then? And would that be before or after the elegant parties?"

Now the heat rushed to her cheeks.

"You are bold, sir!"

"It's just a question, Miss Savage. Is that the life you want for yourself?"

"I...I..."

"Be honest, now," he said.

"I have no realistic alternative," she snapped. "A man could not possibly understand."

"Oh, I understand completely. It is the most realistic course."

"You are mocking me."

"I'm not, Miss Savage. Sincerely. But I see in you so much more than what you see yourself."

"You don't know me, sir."

"But I do know my brother. It is Christien who wishes for a quiet, normal and 'realistic' life. He is pulled towards the arcane as much as me, but masks it under the guise of science. He denies this and in doing so, he denies himself. He deeply wishes for respect and approval, for vindication from his peers in London. He'll get it, I'll wager, but it will come at the expense of his brilliant mind and extraordinary talents. Our family's history has set him on that course. Understandable, I suppose. But you, Miss Savage, you are quite the opposite. You come from an ordinary home yet you yearn for the fantastical and are fascinated by the macabre. More than that, you have a quick mind, a vivid imagination and are fairly bursting with the need for a challenge."

"And you can tell all that in the holding of my hands?"

"Indeed."

She raised her chin.

"The 'fantastical' is quite beyond my reach, sir."

"Reach a little higher, then. Else buy yourself some very fine boots."

They remained that way for some time, he with his arms folded, observing, and she standing with her chin held high, being observed. Frankly, she did not know what she should be doing, or what was allowed in the presence of a Baron.

"You will write a letter of introduction for Dr. Frankow?"

"Certainly. Although I suspect that is not what he is wanting from me." He pushed off the desk and moved around it, preparing to take his seat once again. "No, I will need to pay a trip to the Abbey myself. I was planning to do it anyway. Now I simply have an excellent reason. Thank you, Miss Savage."

"When will you go?"

"I'm not certain. Sometime, I expect."

She didn't know what to say to that.

He sat, slipped the spectacles back onto his nose, slit open the Victoria letters with a penknife. Peered up at her over the thick dark rims.

"Is there anything else, Miss Savage?"

"Nothing, sir. Good day to you, then."

"Every day spent living is a good day."

She stared at him.

And he bent back to his papers, dismissing her with that simple act. She stood for a moment longer before turning and slipping out of the room. Only the dogs watched her go.

***

She reined in her Thoroughbred, Marlborough, next to the man on the French Warmblood. He was wearing a mask that covered his eyes and made him appear entirely villainous.

"You, sir? What is your name?"

The man smiled at her and she thought to herself that even with the mask, he was surprisingly handsome, and most likely a thief.

"Why should I tell you? You are a girl wearing breeches."

"And you are a man wearing a mask."

"Aren't we a scandalous pair?"

"I do not live my life afraid of a little scandal, sir. I am a modern woman."

"I see. Then I shall tell you my name if you tell me yours."

"Agreed."

"Alexander Dunn," said the man. "And yours?"

"Penny Dreadful."

"Ah. The Investigator's daughter." His horse was prancing, ready to bolt at a moment's notice. *"A Girl Criminologist. How rare."*

"Are you mocking me, sir?"

"Not at all. Have you found the stolen Heart?"

"I have my leads," she said defiantly.

"The thief is clever, surely."

"Not as clever as he thinks, sir."

"Or as clever as you think."

"I do not think a man clever who has to steal to make a living."

"What about a man who doesn't have to steal, but simply chooses to?"

"Then he is a rogue, sir, and a cad. Do you know anyone like that?"

His grin widened. *"Is your horse as quick as your tongue, Penny Dreadful?"*

"Quicker."

"Then catch me and I'll tell you."

And he wheeled his horse and galloped off the common. Penny spurred Marlborough in the flank and set off in pursuit.

Chapter 9

Of Brass Rings, More Letters and a Woman named Annie

Christien looked around the chaos that was the Stationhouse. The floor was packed with officers. Those that had desks were at them, others milled about with papers and reports. He could tell the plainclothesmen from the clerks at a glance. There were several bobbies in uniform and a few reporters as well, and the entire building had the smell of old coffee and pistol grease. It was the Leman Street Station— the heart of the Metropolitan Police's H-Division, Whitechapel.

Automatons wheeled and clanked through the crowd, doing the menial work of filing and fetching, delivering and recording. They were adept at navigating the chaos with a minimum of bruised shins and Christien wondered how long it would be before the Surgeon's department had robots doing simple procedures. As he watched them carry on with their tasks, he envied them their singular lack of emotion. It would make his job so much easier.

"This way, Remy," called Trevis Savage as he appeared amid the crowds of coppers. "I've passed it on to the boys in Analysis. They seem to think the ink was the same and they have an automaton running tests on the paper now. It's a low quality, likely something used in a butcher shop to wrap meat."

Christien fell in at his side as they moved down a narrow hall.

"He's not a butcher, sir."

"And so you keep saying. The post mark is the same as Ivy's parcel."

"London E."

"Yes, by jove, it is. Good observation." And Savage smiled at him. "I knew Ivy had met her match in you."

The investigator pushed open a door into a room painted a sickly yellow with a window so high up that it was little more than a grey rectangle. Photochromes lined the walls, maps pinned and dotted with red. An automaton worked in a corner, punch cards moving in and out of its mouth like a tongue and the room smelled of burnt wire. Sitting at a table covered in documents, a small man with thinning dark hair and great handlebar moustache looked up.

"Freddie," said Savage. "Here's Remy – I mean *Dr.* de Lacey. He's the one who received the note."

"Inspector Frederick Abberline." The man reached out his hand and the pair shook. For a small man, his grip was strong and he glanced down at the automaton in the corner. "And this is PAUL. *Police Automaton Under Law.*"

PAUL's optic plates flashed twice.

"Just a few questions for you, Dr. de Lacey," asked Abberline and he indicated the chairs. "If you don't mind?"

Christien and Savage took seats and the detective pulled a slip of paper from the rest.

"The 'bot downstairs is running some tests on the original, but we've made a transcript here. Can you read it for me, please?"

Christien took the paper, took a deep breath.

"Ha ha, my son. Nevr giv a woman yor hart. They will not keep it hole.

Next ones for you.

This is yor fathr, back from the ded.

Call me, Jack"

He laid the letter back on the table, looked up at the man. Abberline steepled his fingers beneath his chin.

"You work with Bondie, yes?"

"I'm in my last semester now."

"The letter. What do you think it means?"

"I couldn't tell you, sir. I would think it a joke from the boys had it not been for the heart Ivy received in the post."

"Miss Ivy Savage of Stepney," rang the tinny voice of PAUL, the automaton. "Daughter of Detective Trevis Savage, Metropolitan Police H-Divison, formerly of A."

"Thank you, PAUL," said Abberline. "The 'boys'?"

"My fellows, sir. But they didn't do this."

Savage grunted and Abberline noticed.

"You're certain of it, then."

"Quite, sir."

He folded his hands across the table.

"Interesting letter, isn't it?" said Abberline. "What's your first impression?"

"Atrocious spelling, sir."

"Meaning?"

"I am particular, sir."

"Take a guess."

Christien blinked slowly. This man would never be a match for Bond. "Intentional, perhaps? To throw us off the trail?"

"Us?"

"The police, sir."

"So you think the villain intelligent?"

"He could be. There must be a reason he has eluded capture."

"You have assisted in these cases, have you?"

"Only the post-mortems, sir. I am very good at stitching, or so I'm told."

"And what do you make of them?"

"They are very gruesome. I can't fathom it."

"Bond tells me you have a theory."

"I have no theory, sir. I simply stitch and dissect."

"Hm." Abberline rose to his feet and began to move around the little office, PAUL's optic plates following him as he went. "What do you think it means, 'this is yor fathr, back from the ded'?"

"I have no idea, sir. That is why I am here."

"Your father has been dead for how many years?"

"Fifteen," said Christien.

"Renaud Jacobe St. John de Lacey, Sixth Baron of Lasingstoke, dies in 1873 AD," said PAUL. "Many tragic events occur in that year, including the sinking of the *SS Northfleet,* the Economic Panic of

Europe and the—"

"Thank you, PAUL." Abberline looked up. "Did your father write this note?"

"Not likely, sir, being dead."

"Did *you* write this note, doctor?"

Chess, thought Christien. Even in the police branch when they should be studying the evidence, it was all about games. Smoke and mirrors and chess.

"Emphatically not, sir. I would not."

Abberline narrowed his eyes. "You would be surprised at how many false notes we get. People do love notoriety, in all its forms."

"Not me, sir." Christien raised a brow. "I avoid notoriety like the Soup."

"The Pea Soup," said PAUL. "Toxic fog that settles over industrialized cities—"

"Had enough of it in your family, wot? Notoriety, that is?"

"Indeed. Had I thought it a fraud, I would have disposed of it at once and spared myself the indignation."

"Forgive me, then, if I have caused any." Abberline sat back. "But you can breathe easier, good doctor. It is indeed a fraud."

Christien glanced at Savage, then back at Abberline. "How can you be certain?"

"Because your father is dead, isn't he? Shot his own head off with a three-chambered pistol, if I recall correctly..." And he held up a police report. "You were, what? Five?"

"Six," said the automaton.

"Someone is playing a jape upon you, sir. One of your 'boys', most likely and it is a very cruel jape indeed. But alas, that is the reputation of medical students, isn't it? Arms, legs, what's a heart or two between colleagues?"

And he smiled again but it wasn't a pleasant thing.

"One last question, Doctor. Your ring. Did one of your 'boys' give that to you?"

"This?" He glanced down at the little brass ring. "No, sir."

"A family heirloom, then?"

"Not at all, sir. It was given to me by Dr. Williams to commemorate a special event. Why?"

"Dr. John Williams of St. Mary's Bethlem?"

"And the London Royal Teaching Hospital and University College Hospital along with Kensington, Buckingham and Sandringham, sir. Why do you ask?"

"Three small brass rings were removed from the dead body of Dark Annie Chapman, or so the story goes. It's just a coincidence then, that you have a matching one."

Christien's heart thudded in his chest but he kept his face a porcelain mask.

"They are cheap rings, sir. You can buy twelve for a penny at Billingsgate."

"Of course. I know that."

And Abberline smiled at him one last time.

"Well thank you for coming in, Doctor. And do say hello to Bondie for me."

"I will do, sir. Thank you sir."

He rose to his feet, his mind racing in many different directions, not the least of them being the innocuous brass ring making a home on his finger.

***

My dear Ivy,

There has been another killing in Whitechapel. You will likely have read about it in the papers and I am so grateful that you are not around to see the growing panic in the streets. This time, the woman's body was so terribly mutilated that I feared it would be too much for me. Upon close investigation, it is clear that the villain has some medical skill. Your father fears this will not be the last, and I feel inclined to believe him.

I have been getting head aches of late. I suppose it is to be expected during these last six months of my internship but Dr. Williams has insisted I try a tincture of laudanum next time and will consult his fellows. If anyone can secure treatment of these accursed episodes, it will be him.

My exams amid-terms have gone well, and Bondie has granted me and the boys leave for a few days, given the trying circumstances of our apprenticeships. I will attempt to visit you at Lasingstoke. Perhaps I will take an airship. They run fair regular from London to Lancaster, and I am eager to try my hand at this very modern mode of travel.

Did I mention that my brother has an airship?

I am looking forward to seeing your sweet face again. I miss you already.

Yours,

Christien

Ivy laid the note carefully on the table and reached for her tea. The post had been late and Castlewaite had just given her the letter after lunch. Cookie frowned as she had torn it open, ignoring the penknife in front of her, but Ivy didn't care. After her strange conversations with Arvin Frankow and Sebastien de Lacey, a letter from Christien was a welcomed thing.

"He's coming," she said and Davis looked up at her from his soup.

"Who's coming?"

"Christien. Christien is coming to Lasingstoke."

He slurped and from her post polishing the silver, Cookie glowered at him. He grinned and slurped some more.

"Don't he live here?" he slurped.

"Only sometimes," she said. "He came back for a brief visit this June, but he's been in London for years now. His schooling, you know."

"Ye should take some schooling, young Davis," grumbled Cookie from the hutch. "Ye've done mighty fine on tha' mop. Works like a charm, it does."

"Really?" Davis sat up. "Like a charm?"

"That's what Ah said, weren't it?"

"Is there anything else in need of fixing?" He popped a crust of bread in his mouth. "I could take a look…"

"Hmph. Ah'll send ye t'Over Milling."

"Over Milling?"

"The wee town o'er the hill," she said, turning back to the silver. "Ye can get parts at Grimwalts."

Davis sat straighter, and Ivy marveled at his attention. Davis never paid attention like that.

"That'd be grand," he said.

"Ye'll go in the morn, ken?" And with a sour glance, she marched out of *la Petite,* disappearing entirely.

Davis looked back at his sister.

"D'you hear that, Ivy? She'll see what she can do. The mop works like a charm, she said. Just needed a bit of tinkering. One of the gears was too tight. Buggered up the pulley mechanism."

"Well, I'm glad you fixed it Davis. You have a talent. I have several chapters of *'The Ghost of Lancashire'* finished. Would you care to furnish it with illustrations again?"

"If I have time between the mops and the sweepers and trying to find that bloody Seventh house. I've only got as far as the church."

"I wonder when Christien will come." She sank back into her chair and looked down at the letter in her hand. It wasn't dated, but still, she wondered how long it would take to journey north in an airship. Perhaps, there were connections to be made. Perhaps he wasn't able to leave on time. Perhaps the airships were filled.

She frowned.

Did I mention that my brother has an airship?

Why wouldn't he take his brother's airship? Surely, it would be available for him had he the need? And where was it stationed, this de Lacey airship? In the Lancaster dockyards? Here at Lasingstoke?

Reach a little higher, he had said. *Else buy yourself some very fine boots.*

She sat back, scowling. The Mad Lord was as odd as people said and deserved every word of his tabloid reputation. She understood now why Christien never spoke of him or of Rupert or even Lasingstoke for that matter. And yet, Sebastien had been surprisingly astute in his observations and she wondered how he could have guessed so much simply by the holding of her hands.

Metal in his skull. Runs with horses. Died as a child, now speaks with the dead.

Two rumours confirmed. One to go.

"I think I'll go with you to Over Milling, Davis," she announced, pushing back her chair.

"Yeah? Why?"

"I need to find myself a pair of boots."

***

Sebastien reached down a hand to touch the grizzled gray coat. He could walk blindfolded knowing Fergis the wolfhound would be there, watching for stumps, pot holes and ruts in the road. Clancy was next, a fine retriever with a flaxen coat and a good nose for grouse. He grinned at the others bumbling all around him, some ranging out in front, some lagging behind. Jo the English Setter; the collie Birdie; a Springer Spaniel by name of Tag and a scruffy tailless mongrel called Dickey. The best family he could ever ask for. The best of friends. His pack.

He'd completely forgotten about Gus. He'd left the horse behind in the pasture with the mares. He hadn't even noticed the girl but she had surely noticed him. He could see it in her eyes as she had studied his cheek. But to his surprise and to her credit, she had said nothing, had even indulged him while he read her like a book. She was a spirited little creature, highly-strung and emotional but then again, he had no experience with the fairer sex. Maybe they were all like that. Truth be told, when his human company was overlord uncles, brilliant psychiatrists, dead people and Cookie, an emotional woman was an earthly delight.

He could see the fence up ahead flanked by elms, could make out the horses grazing in the fields. Sebastien smiled to himself. That would be a fine colt if the bay mare caught. He had hopes to keep it, train it himself if he lived long enough. If Seventh didn't kill him first.

He reached the fence, ran a hand along it as he walked its length. Wood, dogs, horses, stone. No shadow in those, no vice. No fear of death, no fear of life. Even cold stone was warmer than most people.

Gus nickered and trotted to meet him. He laid a hand on the gray nose, ran it up along the cheek to the neck, down to the deep chest and there he gave him a sound pat.

"Did you have a good night, my lad? She's a fine thing, I know it."

He turned to lean against the fence, pulled a letter from his pocket.

Sebastien,

We do not need to tell you of the pressing incidents occurring in Whitechapel. We know you and Rupert keep abreast of the tabloids where the scandalous details are out for all to see. The French anarchists are paying close attention as well, and we have it on good account that there are those who are already planting the seeds for riot if the crimes continue. Such villains will use anything as fodder to undermine the solidarity of our Empire. This is something we shall never allow.

Bertie has informed me that you have refused him once again. We will remind you that you are an English citizen and a gentleman and have responsibilities to the Crown. Lonsdale exists because of our good pleasure, sufferance and purse.

We trust that we will not need to remind you again.

Victoria RI

He crumpled the letter into a ball and tossed it onto the road. Dickey fetched it like a stick and the others bounded after him in the game. Sebastien turned back to the fence where Gus was waiting, pushed the gate opwn.

Suddenly, the horses squealed and bolted for the far end of the pasture.

Fergis whined and the air around him grew deathly cold. He refused to look behind him. He knew what would be standing there.

"Go home," he growled, and his breath frosted in front of his face. "I've told you, stay at Seventh. You'll do no good out here."

He cursed his luck. The horses would never come if *she* stayed at the gate. Animals were sensitive that way.

"I said, go home!"

But the cold remained, so he turned and immediately wished he hadn't. It was the woman, the one with her intestines around her neck. It had made him sick when she'd first shown up and he wasn't certain he was getting used to it now. She still shook him to the very core.

"Where are you from?" he asked again, but still she said nothing. The dead rarely did. But unlike the boy from Wharcombe, this one would not even nod. It was impossible to help those who would not help themselves.

"Are you Annie from Whitechapel? Annie Chapman? Tell me. I can't help you otherwise."

She had died quickly, it seemed. The gashes in her throat were deep and he could see the white tendons beneath the skin. Her clothes were tattered and separated from her torso in a bloody mass. Her hair was brown, her eyes blue and very sad. She held up her hand, extended a finger.

"You've shewed me this before." He shook his head. "I don't understand."

She gestured again but he closed his eyes and turned away.

"Please," he moaned. "Go back to Seventh."

She stared at him for a long time until, like the boy from Wharcombe, she folded up on herself and faded away. He stood very still, as if the very act of moving would bring her back. Finally, he released a long breath. There was no frost, there was no cold. He simply breathed again and again and again. Just the filling of his chest reminded him that he was still alive. Any day spent living was a good day. The air was sweet with rain and life.

The dogs gazed up at him adoringly.

He looked around. The gate was wide open, and the paddock was empty. He could see the shapes of horses thundering down the path toward the road.

"Ah blast," he groaned, closed the gate, and set off to fetch them.

Chapter 10

Of Clandestine Visits, Very Fine Boots and the Clairvoyant Properties of Tea

Three brass rings. Three brass rings. Christien could think of nothing but those three brass rings.

He knocked on the door, waited for a moment before stepping into the Doctors' Room of St. Mary's Bethlem Hospital and Lunatic Asylum. It was a fine room, with wide windows, walls of books and lounge chairs of studded leather. It was frequently used by Dr. John Williams and at the moment, was completely deserted.

He closed the door behind him and breathed deeply, trying to steel his racing heart. Three brass rings. Dark Annie Chapman had owned three brass rings. The night of the Ghost Club meeting, Williams had pulled three brass rings from his pocket, given him one. He had been able to think of nothing else since the meeting with Abberline but those three damned rings.

Large mullioned windows cast light across the desk and the young surgeon crossed the floor to stand behind it. There was a tea service with two china cups, a stack of letters and a series of notebooks lined against a lamp.

He glanced around the room again.

Paranoia, he told himself. There was no one here, Williams wasn't due until tomorrow and the boys were off on three days leave. No one would question him. No one would even care.

He picked up one of the notebooks, recognized it instantly as a physician's log. There were at least twelve so he went through each until he found one with Williams' distinctive handwriting. Flipped it open on dates and places of clinics, patient names, diagnoses, prescriptions and procedures. It was a record of Williams' clinical files dating back over three years and Christien understood immediately the importance of what he was holding in his hands. Many of the procedures held at the clinics were abortions and at the moment they were illegal, the topic still hotly debated in parliament.

His eyes scanned the lists, looking for any variation of Annie Eliza Chapman he could find. To his surprise, he found another—Mary Ann Nichols. The name of the woman found dead in Buck's Row, the one he had spoken to Bond about that morning in the mortuary, had been Mary Ann 'Polly' Nichols. According to the journal, she had been given a 'procedure' for an unwanted pregnancy and it had gone terribly wrong.

Pregnancy was a complicated marvel, Williams had always said, *but never a guaranteed joy.*

His eyes ran over the list of names, searching but not finding Annie Eliza Chapman, or Elizabeth Ann Chapman, or any variation of it, but then again, these women changed their names as often as men changed their socks. He was grateful that Ivy was made of more constant stock. He wondered how she was doing, hoped she was enjoying the fine country air.

A familiar name caught his attention, but he was diverted by a rattle at the door.

He placed the notebook down as John Williams entered the room.

***

The morning started out gray with clouds hanging heavy over the skies but by nine o'clock, the sun had reappeared as the coach rolled into the tiny town of Over Milling. Ivy liked the look of it at once.

According to Cookie, Over Milling had a population of twelve hundred people, but it served an area of close to five thousand. Many of the streets were cobbled, others were dirt, and they rose and fell with the land. Most of the small houses were fashioned from limestone, sandstone or slate and once again, it served to reinforce her image of the north country. The gray and the green. The cold stone and the ivy.

Davis leapt from the cab and stretched. Cookie had given him a list of machine parts for apparently, there were many, many machines in need of repair at Lasingstoke. She had also given him a sizable purse and made him promise to bring back the rest. He had crossed his heart and sworn to die and the look on Cookie's face made Ivy wonder if she intended to take that literally. Lottie had smiled sweetly and disappeared with the jams.

"Well, Castlewaite, where should I start?" Davis called up as the coachman began dismounting the dickey.

"Well, lad. Farnun's is over yonder. They'll 'ave much of wha' on yer list. And, if'n they don't..." He hitched his trousers up a notch. Being a thin man, his trousers frequently sagged. "Ye could always talk to Grimwalt. Tha's Andy Grimwalt over at the fact'ry. They makes pistons for motorcars and Victoria's *sous*-boats, they do."

"*Sous*-boats," said Ivy. "Do you mean the submersibles?"

"Aye, miss. But Grims calls 'em '*sous*-boats.' Fer the French."

"*Cor,*" Davis grinned. "Submersibles. Brilliant."

And he darted down into the cobbled street toward the factory.

"Be back by noon, mind," called the coachman. "Cookie's 'olding lunch fer us back at the 'all."

Davis waved over his shoulder and was gone.

The coachman turned back to Ivy.

"And wha's on yer map today, miss?"

"Boots." She raised her chin. "A pair of very fine boots."

"Well, good luck wi' that." He winked. "Just be back by—"

"By noon, yes. I most certainly will."

He grinned his gap-toothed grin, and Ivy wondered how he could afford an artificial copper eye but no teeth. As he led the horses toward the post, she turned and surveyed the town square.

They were at the feet of a terribly old Sentinel, a huge automaton made entirely of metal. This one was perhaps the oldest she had ever seen and she wondered if he had been a part of the original fleet, manufactured and sent out to every town across the country as a part of Prince Albert's Great Steam Exhibition of 1851. A little park had been built around it, with flowers and pigeons and vines that climbed his clockwork legs. But he was a fearsome sight nonetheless, standing guard over the town as a symbol of imperial majesty and might.

Black iron posts circled the Sentinel, to which a few horses were tethered, as well as three dogs and a toddler. There was also a badly parked steamcar on the side of the road and she briefly wondered if it belonged to the same blonde woman who had driven so madly on the road to Lonsdale.

She could see shops in the buildings nearest the square and she cast her eyes across their fronts for a promising venue. *Benny's Books*, read one placard. *Verne's Clocks*, read another. *Simon's Smokes & Fine Tobaccoes*. The *Lancashire Fishmonger* and *Oldtown Cloth and Feed*. *Peter's Pork Pies, Salisbury Sausages* and finally, *London Shoes*.

Her heart leapt within her and she made for it straightaway.

Within minutes, she stood at the door with the promising title. It was locked so she tried the bell to no avail. Higher up, a sign posted on the glass read:

Closed by Order of His Lordship
Due to Scurrilous Rats, Ghosts and Other Vermin
April 17, 1884

The heart that had leapt so happily only moments ago began to sink like a stone and on that stone, only one name was carved.

Sebastien de Lacey.

"Oh, Franny, look. A new girl," said a voice behind her.

"Yes, Fanny, a new girl," echoed a second and Ivy turned to see two young women, dressed in fine, if dated, clothes. They were standing very close to her and she felt the need to step back to avoid bumping noses.

"What is your name, new girl?" asked the first. She was perhaps Ivy's age, tall and thin with dark hair piled high under a feathery cap. Her face was long, her eyes small, and her teeth reminded Ivy of a horse. Before Ivy could respond and she thrust out a gloved hand.

"I'm Fanny Helmsly-Wimpoll," she said. "And this is my sister, Franny."

Franny was very different from her sister, being shorter, stouter, fairer and less equine. Although perhaps, more bovine. Her hat looked like a flowerpot and she sported a set of goggles round her neck. Ivy recognized her immediately as the mad-driving woman in the steamcar on the way to Lonsdale. She also held out a gloved hand.

Ivy looked at the hands, took one in each of hers.

"Ivy Savage," she said, shaking politely. "I'm very pleased to meet you both."

The women's eyes grew very round.

"*The* Ivy Savage?" said Fanny. "Writer of the '*Penny Dreadful, Girl Criminologist*' serials?"

"I love Penny Dreadful," said Franny.

"Franny has an entire shelf full of them, don't you, Franny?"

"I love Girl Criminologists…"

Ivy smiled. "I had honestly thought them a fancy only in Stepney. It surprises me to hear they've left the city, let alone the county."

Fanny leaned back, placed a hand theatrically on her chest, sniffed. "Got 'em from my mother's sister's cousin's chemist's chimney-sweep's uncle, Alby Thistle."

"Alby Thistle," echoed Fanny.

Ivy grinned. Alby, her agent, publisher and merchant all in one. He ran a parlour press on Bruley Gate that produced everything from flyers and tracts to broadsheets and the penny serials that gave her a few shillings a month. He insisted that he lost money on them but would tear a strip off her if ever a chapter were late.

"We're almost family, you know. You and we."

"Really?" Ivy cocked her head. "How so?"

"My mother's sister's husband's sister's cousin's daughter. She knows your fiancé."

"My fiancé?"

Fanny pulled her close, leaned into her so that they were indeed nose-to-nose. "Why, you *are* engaged to Christien Jeremie St. John de Lacey, aren't you?"

And she sniffed.

"Ooh, Christien Jeremie," sniffed Franny. "He's sweet."

"Very sweet, dearest," sniffed Fanny. "And he's yours, Ivy. How adorable."

"How adorable," sniffed Franny. And both women released her hands to study her.

"Thank you," said Ivy. "I think."

"Oh, that's not to say that his brother isn't sweet, now is it Franny?"

"Not saying that at all," said Franny.

"But Sebastien Laurent is very different than Christien Jeremie, don't you think?"

"Very, very different," said Franny.

"He has a metal skull, after all."

"All metal."

"And well, of course, he's mad."

"Completely mad."

"You aren't looking for ghosts, are you?" asked Fanny, suddenly serious. "Or vermin?"

"*Scurrilous* vermin?"

"Ah, no. Just some very fine boots, I'm afraid," said Ivy.

Fanny laid a hand upon her heart. "All the way from London, in need of some very fine boots."

"Alas." Franny lowered her eyes. "No boots."

"Oh, we can show you where to buy boots, dearest Ivy," sniffed Fanny. "But not very fine ones. For very fine boots, Lancaster is the place."

"The only place," sniffed Franny.

"Have you been to Lancaster, dearest?" asked Fanny.

"No," said Ivy.

"Well then," exclaimed Fanny. "We must go!"

"To Lancaster, we must go!" sang Franny.

Fanny snagged her hand, pulled her close once more. "But not *today*, you impetuous thing, you! What *ever* were you thinking?" And she laughed merrily.

Franny laughed merrily.

"No," said Ivy. "Not today, I'm afraid."

"But later this week, surely."

"Yes, later. Surely," said Franny.

"Surely," said Ivy.

"But tea… Now tea is something we can do today, surely!"

"Oh yes, surely!" echoed Franny.

Ivy smiled.

"Tea would be lovely."

"There are no lovely tea shops in Over Milling, dearest, but there is *a* tea shop in Over Milling…"

"*A* tea shop," echoed Franny.

And before she knew it, they grabbed her by the arms and pulled her down the road in search of tea.

***

"I'm surprised to see you here today, Christien," said Williams and he stepped into the Doctors' Room of St. Mary's Bethlem Hospital and Lunatic Asylum. "I thought Bondie had given you boys a few days off. "

Christien slipped his hands behind his back. "Yes, sir. But I wanted to check up on that young woman we attended last week."

"Oh well done, boy. I'm proud of you for doing so, especially since it was extracurricular business." He moved his stocky body around to the desk and lowered himself into the chair. "And? How is she?"

"Doing well, sir," said Christien. "I was just coming to take some tea before leaving."

And he held up a one of the tea cups. Cold leaves were stuck to the china like bark. Good luck, that.

"The other boys didn't see fit to check, did they, Remy?"

"I believe the boys have gone home for the break,"

"They are not in the same league as you."

"They are 'the boys', sir. Friends, regardless."

"Hm. Very diplomatic. Let me tell you what I think, as their teacher and your mentor."

Christien waited, saying nothing.

"Henry's a stout fellow. Always up for a challenge. He'll do fair in life but he'll never be a success. Powell-Smith, the bastard, has avoided clinical for three weeks now. He always has the most damnable excuses but I can't fault him when his father is in Bertie's bend pocket. Hospitals will line up for him no matter what his grade. And Pickett, well, he tries but he is no means gifted. How he has lasted this long in Bondie's company is quite beyond me."

"Perhaps he helps Dr. Bond with 'extracurricular business', sir?"

Williams lit a cigarette, blew the smoke out into the air.

"By God, you're a cheeky thing." He studied the young surgeon for a long moment. "Well, I think we can both agree that there are certain facets to Obstetrics that might not be suitable for you."

"Yes, sir. I know that, sir."

"It's not the morality of it, is it? The things we need to do for these poor unfortunates?"

"No, sir."

"It's an occupational hazard. The girls do what they can, but they can't afford to keep the little bastards. They'd pop one out every nine months if Mother Nature had her way."

"Yes, sir. I know that, sir."

"Even the bloody parliament can't make up its mind. A capital crime one sitting, our civil responsibility the next."

Christien nodded. The legality of abortions was hotly debated in Parliament, with the government swinging back and forth like a pendulum. Williams called it his 'extracurricular business' — research for his Obstetrics Foundation. He was very skilled, very discreet and a very busy man.

"Does it remind you of your mother, Remy? The night she died?"

"It must, sir, although I cannot say why. I don't remember it at all."

"It stands to reason." Williams tightened his grim mouth. "Nonetheless, I'm sorry. I am a thoughtless lout."

"No, sir. It's not your fault. It was a very long time ago."

"You were six?"

"Yes, sir."

"Damn your father."

"I have tried, sir. Believe me."

He stared into the empty cup, the thin leaves stranded across the china. There were people who could read such leaves, he remembered. Gypsies and fortunetellers, mystics and clairvoyants. People like his brother. Sometimes he hated them all.

Williams continued to study him, the cigarette held aloft in one skilled hand.

"You are brave in joining the Club then, Christien. They want your father back."

"I know, sir."

"They think the locket is the key."

"It's just a locket, sir."

"Do you keep it on you, boy?"

Christien kept his expression passive, like porcelain. John Williams. Personal physician to the Queen and all the ladies of the Royal Family. He was friend to Edward, Prince of Wales and Albert Victor, Duke of Clarence and Avon. He was, like Victoria's dead husband, a member in good standing of the Ghost Club of Cambridge and London.

"No," he lied. "It is in a safe at Lloyds."

"Pity," said Williams. "It's a fascinating piece, eh wot? What do you think it does?"

"I couldn't tell you, sir. Without the key, it is simply a bauble."

"Hm. Bring it again on Friday night, will you? Crookes will be there. He's itching to get that thing into his laboratory."

"I will do that very thing, sir. Good day, sir."

"Good day, Remy. And Remy?"

"Sir?"

"You don't need to tell anyone about the girls you visit in here. You know that, yes?"

"Yes sir. I know that, sir."

The man blew out a thin stream of smoke. It drifted up and over his head.

"We'll see you on Friday at eight."

"Friday, sir."

Williams was still watching as he closed the door behind him.

***

The tea shop was tucked into a small house at the corner of a street at the bottom of a hill. It was called, strangely enough "A Tea Shop", with a very large "A" painted in Red. It didn't take long to realize that the sisters Helmsly-Wimpoll were not only odd but terribly clever, and she enjoyed their company immediately. It was a refreshing change from all the sobriety of Lasingstoke.

The sisters had been born and raised in Over Milling, had spent some time in Newcastle with wealthy relatives upon their coming out into society, but had eventually ended back in Over Milling when, oddly enough, no offers of marriage were presented. But their spirits were not dampened, and they were the socialites of the town, knowing everyone's business and, naturally, everyone's secrets.

Fanny laid a gloved hand across Ivy's sleeve. "And how is your mother, dearest? Have you really sent her to Lonsdale, like they say? You know it is a dreadful place, Lonsdale is."

"Simply dreadful," echoed Franny and she popped an entire scone in her mouth. She had picked it clean of currants and they sat like little flies on her plate.

"I...I'm afraid I did." Ivy looked from one to the other. "Christien said Dr. Frankow was the best in the country..."

"Well then. I'm sure that he is." Fanny sniffed, looked off dramatically. "He must be worth something then."

"Muffming," said Franny, with her mouth full of scone.

"He's Edward's mortal enemy, you know."

"Mortal enemy?" asked Ivy. "Of Edward, Prince of Wales, Edward? That Edward?"

"The very one, dearest. Old Mechanical Bertie."

"Mechanical Bertie," said Franny after the scone.

Ivy frowned. 'Mechanical Bertie' was one of the nicknames for Edward, Prince of Wales. He had survived an attempt on his life during a tour of India, which required the amputation of his right arm. Of course, being the Heir Apparent to the English Throne, Edward had at his disposal the very best in medical treatment. His arm, elbow and hand had been replaced by an artificial clockwork limb. It was fully operational, but left much room for wild speculation. It was often said that inside that mechanical arm were torpedoes, cannons, the crown jewels and cigarettes.

"But why would a psychiatrist be the mortal enemy of the Prince of Wales?"

"There was a problem with the War Office, dearest," said Fanny. "He was working on opening up new areas of the mind. What was it called, Franny?"

"Hypersensory Mental Acuity, Spiritualism and Communion with the Realm of Departed Souls," said Franny

Ivy stared at her.

"For the wars, you know," said Fanny. "For the progress of the Empire. And science is all about progress, isn't it dearest?"

"Do you believe that?"

"That science is about progress?" asked Fanny. "Of course it is."

"No, sorry. About Frankow being an enemy?"

"Well, not at first," said Fanny. "Frankow was the engineer of Mechanical Bertie's arm, you know. But there was some problem years later and he was exiled up north. To Lonsdale."

"But, but why?" asked Ivy, completely bewildered now.

"Oh dearest. You couldn't have such a man running around performing horrific experiments on upstanding British citizens, now could you?"

"Experiments?"

"Don't fret, dearest," said Fanny, laying a hand across Ivy's. "I'm certain he's learned his lesson by now. Otherwise he would have been deported."

"Bye bye," said Franny.

"Deported?" said Ivy.

"To Slovakia," said Fanny. "Dr. Frankow is a Czech, after all."

"Oh yes," Franny nodded. "Quite Czech."

"They make them that way, in Slovakia, I've heard. Almost everyone there is automated. You've seen him, surely. All cogs and gears and metal shafts."

"Oh my," said Ivy.

"No, no dear. No Czech machine-man can be experimenting on any Englishman. Not under Victoria's watchful eye. Not under any circumstances. Not anymore..."

"Whatever do you mean, not anymore?" asked Ivy.

"Why dearest, look what he did to de Lacey."

"Poor de Lacey."

"de Lacey? Which de Lacey? Christien or Sebastien?"

"Why Sebastien Laurent, of course. Christien Jeremie is quite sane, is he not?"

"Is he sane?" asked Franny.

"Yes, but," Ivy cocked her head. "What did Dr. Frankow do to Sebastien de Lacey?"

The sisters exchanged glances, becoming strangely reticent in their conversation.

"Please tell me," Ivy said.

Fanny suddenly looked young and frail. "You do love your Christien Jeremy, yes?"

"I *am* engaged to marry him," said Ivy, wondering again why the question should keep coming up in conversations.

"And you are completely honest with each other?"

"Of course."

"And has he told you how his parents died?"

"I…I never thought to ask."

Oddly, Franny said nothing, merely began picking the currants out of another scone.

Like a very old friend, Fanny took Ivy's hand. "Perhaps you should, dearest."

"Oh you should," echoed Franny, laying her hand now on top of Ivy's.

They sat that way for a very long moment.

"But a wedding!" sang Fanny, breaking the spell. "Have you picked out your dress, dearest? We can help you with that, can't we, Franny?"

"Oh yes, Fanny. We can help."

"We have the best eye for fashion in the county." Fanny sniffed. "Lancaster has good dresses. Preston even better. But if you're in mind for a bit of a romp, I would suggest Chester."

"Oh Chester," cooed Franny.

"Franny can drive, you know. She has her very own steamcar. It's an antique, you know! Quite the little roadster!"

And the rest of the afternoon was spent in idle chitchat, with a goodly amount of gossip thrown in. When the tower in the center of town chimed noon, Ivy Savage climbed into the coach, with more than one clockwork conspiracy on her mind.

Chapter 11

Of Anarchy, Library and a Murder in Lancaster

September 16, 1888
My dear Christien,

Over Milling is a charming town, almost entirely what I expected. I met two sisters — perhaps you know them. Fanny and Franny Helmsly-Wimpoll. I think we shall become fast friends. With caring for my mother, I haven't had a friend in a very long time who wasn't a copper.

I am feeling most dreadful strange after these past few days. I thought perhaps our luck was changing but after your dreaded Frankow and now, a hint of that aforementioned 'scandal,' I do fear I will be taxed to remain much longer. I have half a mind to return to Lonsdale and retrieve my mother and see how I can manage as both daughter and wife. Please, consider it, Christien. I am sincerely torn.

You have not come as you promised. I understand the nature of your studies, but surely Dr. Bond and the boys can manage for a few days without you. If only you could petition for the use of your brother's airship. Surely you could be here and back before you were even missed.

I do not know what to make of your brother. At times, he seems a fair and hearty fellow but at others, I find myself unnerved and apprehensive. Rupert is prickly. I understand he was as a father to you, but still, he leaves much to the imagination.

The day has been heavy and I believe it will rain. Perhaps that will wash away my fears and leave me renewed.

I miss you, Christien.

Your Ivy.

***

Exhausted, Christien dropped into a wing chair by the fire in the study of Hollbrook House. The fact that there was no fire didn't even occur to him and he was asleep before it could register in his mind.

Very soon however, someone was pulling a blanket over his legs and he cracked an eye.

"Pomfrey," he smiled.

"Sir, would you like me to start a fire, sir?"

Christien glanced at the black hearth. "God, yes, Pomfrey. That would be wonderful."

"And some tea, sir?"

"Please."

"And biscuits, berries and clotted cream, sir?

Christien closed his eyes. "No, Pomfrey. Just the fire and the tea."

The prim man studied him for a long moment. "Are you well, sir? Do you want me to call that horrible doctor fellow from next door?"

"Intern's hours, Pomfrey. I'm quite convinced that it doesn't matter your marks, simply whether or not you survive to the end to become a surgeon nowadays."

Pomfrey straightened. "Modern times are confounding to me, sir. What with these airships and steamcars and auto-men. I shall never employ an auto-man in the service of this house, sir."

Christien smiled, eyes still closed.

"Furthermore, I am convinced that if a man were meant to fly, God would have given him wings, not balloons. And oh my, don't get me started on those contraptions they call steamcars..."

"Oh dear," said Christien.

"Such noisy, malodorous inventions I could never imagine. A blight on the good name of the Empire. They do clog up the streets so. Terrify the horses and the good women. Why the chaos in the markets yesterday, all because a four-wheeled steamcar tipped over onto a booth of radishes. Gulls swooped down in the thousands, sir, and then the street dogs set about chasing the gulls, the shopkeeps set about chasing the dogs..."

"Pomfrey?"

"It was anarchy, sir."

"Tea?"

"Yes, sir. Of course, sir. And a fire, sir. At once, sir."

And the man immediately turned to start the fire, had it roaring in good time and quietly left the study for the kitchen.

Christien sighed, slipped the locket from his pocket, let it dangle from his fingers. As it spun on its chain, he marveled at how each of the metal gears caught the light in a different way. The glass that housed the tiny instrument was in need of a polish and he was certain that his pocket was not the best place for it. Still, the way Williams and his strange Club had looked at it, he felt much safer with it on him than in any room of Hollbrook House.

Perhaps he *should* take out a safe at Lloyds.

As it twirled at the end of its chain, he ran his mind over the discoveries of the last few days. Annie Chapman was rumored to have three brass rings, which were removed after her murder. John Williams was in possession of three brass rings, one of which had grown very tight his little finger. Williams ran clinics for the street girls of the East End, and abortions were by far the most common procedures during the clinics. He had seen the name of Mary Anne Nichols in Williams' book, along with a mention of a procedure gone wrong. Abortions often went wrong, Christien had discovered. Women went septic, some died. He and the boys spent hours covering up for Williams in that regard but he was beginning to wonder how far or how deep this problem went.

The locket was still in his fingers when he slipped off to sleep.

***

"Oh no, dearest," said Merryl Dewhurst-Smythe, and she laid a hand over Penny's. "It's not at all what you think."

"Not at all," repeated her sister Berryl Dewhurst-Smythe.

"No?" asked Penny. "But then, why would the Crown employ a German scientist to guard British national secrets? It simply does not make sense. We British are a sensible people."

"But darling," said Merryl. "Dr. von Freud engineered the heart, not for Victoria firstly but for Durand."

"Durand?" Penny frowned. "Alexandre Gavriel St. Jacques Lord Durand?"

"The very one, dearest."

"The very one," said Berryl.

Merryl leaned forward. "He lost his heart, you know. As a boy."

"As a boy."

"And since von Freud was a friend of the family, he simply engineered one. Put it in himself."

"Himself."

Penny sat back, deep in thought. "So this elusive Baron, this Mad Lord of Graystoke, has no heart?"

"Not since Queen Regina Imperiatrix needed one. von Freud used the same design on Regina Imperiatrix as Durand, but the War Office thought it too dangerous. Someone could simply kidnap or kill the Lord, steal his heart and find a way to sabotage our dear Regina Imperiatrix the same way."

"The very same way," said Berryl.

"So then, Lord Durand..."

"Precisely, darling," said Merryl. "Alexandre Gavriel St. Jacques Lord Durand... has no heart..."

"No heart..."

"No heart," said Penny and she set her mind to finally speak to this man, and we all know that once our plucky heroine sets her mind to something, it invariably happens.

***

The rain started just after dinner.

In fact, it seemed the skies were falling, and she had to admit that she was trapped inside Lasingstoke Hall. And so with VINCE and his teapot next to her, she sat in a window seat of the Library at Second, writing and watching the raindrops run down the glass.

She missed her mother terribly.

She missed her frail, bird-like hands, her empty eyes, her tight drawn lips. Whenever she was tending her, Ivy would talk. She would describe the sights, the weather, the time of day. She would sing songs, tell stories or read letters that had been sent from distant relatives. Her mother had been a loving woman before Tobias's death. Deep down, Ivy knew that she was still in there somewhere. It was impossible to think otherwise.

What was it about love that caused so much pain? Did she love Christien enough to be his wife or was it friendship that had taken a turn somewhere? He was a very good prospect for a girl like her but was that all she was looking for in life? Was she settling for less because she couldn't imagine better? *Is that the life you want for yourself,* Sebastien had asked. Could he have possibly been right in any of his observations? If so, what did that say about her to give up her dreams so easily?

And if he was right, what on earth did that say about him?

She looked at VINCE. He seemed happy to simply sit, her teacup balancing perfectly atop his squared head.

"VINCE?"

"Yes."

"Do you love?"

"Love. An intense feeling of deep emotion. Love." His eyepieces whirred a moment as his logarithms engaged. "Conversation. Castlewaite. Lasingstoke. Sheep. Yes. To the fullest extent of my programming, I love."

He inclined his head and she watched the teacup slide, just a little. "Do you love, Ivy Savage?"

She smiled sadly. "I do, VINCE. Very much. I love my mother and father. I love my crazy brother. I think I still love Tobias, even though he's dead. Is it mad to love a dead person?"

"No," said VINCE. "Just sad."

"Mm. I love writing. Yes, I love writing very much. And I do love Christien. He's so very perfect..."

"Sheep are not perfect," said VINCE. "But I love them. Their imperfections make them lovable."

"Hmm," she said. "You are very wise for a robot."

"I know," said VINCE.

She sighed, watching the trees bend in the gales, and she thought of Dr. Frankow. *"He's part machine,"* Fanny had said. *"All cogs and gears and metal shafts."* Could her mother be treated by such a man?

Could she be loved?

"No Czech machine-man should be experimenting on any Englishman."

What had she done?

She leaned her forehead against the windowsill, sleepy, melancholic and waiting for the morning to come. Once again, she thought of Sebastien de Lacey, remembered how he stroked the gray horse, how he talked to the air and held her wrists. The large dark spectacles, the painting in silhouette, the blood on his cheek.

"Hypersensory Mental Acuity, Spiritualism and Communion with the Realm of Departed Souls," Franny had said. Spiritualism was all the rage in London.

But they were a far cry from London.

What had Frankow done to him?

She closed her eyes and slept, waiting for a break in the rain.

***

It is raining in Lancaster, and she tucks into a doorway to keep dry. She has not made much tonight. The rain keeps most away. It's hard to make a living when there is always rain.

A shape moves past, slowly in the darkness. He is well dressed, she can tell. It serves her well if she can tell. The gents expect a little more and if she's smart, she gives it to them. They pay her well for the illusion.

She is hungry, but she hates the rain, so she slides her skirts up to her thigh, slips her leg out into the lamplight. If he's looking, he'll see. If not, she stays dry. Either would be fine tonight.

He pauses, turns back as if thinking. His felt hat is effective for keeping the water off his face, and his collar is turned up against the gales. Slowly, he moves back toward her and she is on, performing like a stage actress calling the spotlight.

"Hello, luv," she coos. "It's a cold night. Spare a bob an' I'll keep ye warm."

She can't make out his face, but reaches for the wool coat, pulling him closer. There is an understanding in her trade. Most men abide by it.

It is the way of the world. He strokes her face with the back of a gloved hand and she sees his eyes, light and clear like a summer day. She likes the light eyes. They are so very pretty.

He turns her away from him, so that he is hugging her from behind. She arches her back, pressing into him. They like that. His hands are moving along her waist, her bodice, her neck. She leans her head back so she can smell him and it is the scent of clean laundry and steam and brandy. This one could be good, she thinks. This one likes his pleasures, takes his time, knows his women—

Sharp jerk at her throat. Heat. A second jerk and she is gone.

Chapter 12

Of Lost Loves, Wet Dogs and a Very Strange Wallpaper

Tap, clank, hiss. Tap, clank, hiss. Large eyes looming, whirring, clicking. Straps and buckles, chains and locks. Tap, clank, hiss.

It was still storming when she awoke, and she lay for a while, eyes closed, listening to the sound of rain pelting the windows. The floors would be cold, so she drew her blankets up a little higher, wishing for just a few more minutes in the comfort of her bed.

But she could hear the crackle of a healthy fire, could smell the sharp, bitter scent of a cigarette, and it suddenly occurred to her that she wasn't in her bed. In fact, she wasn't in her room at all.

She opened her eyes and realized with horror that she was still in the Library of Second. She must have fallen asleep at the window. Somehow, sometime, she had moved or had *been* moved to the settee, and the thought filled her with dread.

She hiked the blanket higher and sat up. VINCE was gone, and there was a man sitting, reading a newspaper. It was Rupert. He was drinking coffee, not tea, and she wasn't surprised. Many men who liked the sharp, bitter taste of cigarettes also liked the sharp bitter taste of coffee. It made her wonder at their taste in women.

He glanced her way, took a long drag of the cigarette. Blew it out slowly as he studied her. Finally, he smirked.

"Good morning, skirt."

"Good morning, sir."

"Nip into the wine cellar, last night, did we?"

All she could think to say was "No."

"Has anyone ever told you that you look terrible in the morning? I'll wager Remy has never seen you like this."

"I can assure you, sir, that I frequently look worse."

He grinned at that, and she thought he looked rather less fearsome when he smiled.

He indicated a second wing chair by the fire. "Come, sit. I'm quite certain I can bear your terribleness a while longer."

And so, bundling up the blanket, Ivy removed herself from the settee and shuffled across the room to sit in the chair. Strands of hair fell into her face, and she was sure he was telling the truth about her appearance.

He held up the silver urn. "Coffee?"

"Is there tea?"

"I'll call Cookie."

"Coffee is perfect."

He grinned again, and she thought that when he did, he looked like a lazy cat. Big teeth, cunning eyes. She wasn't surprised he had claws. He reached for the coffee urn and began to pour. It was a full setting, with cream, sugar, silver spoons and two china cups. Some fashionable folk refused to refill a once-used cup. Rupert did not seem the type to care. He passed one her way.

She lifted the coffee to her lips, knowing it would not likely have nearly enough cream or sugar, but she drank anyway, needing the heat to warm her blood. It was very strong and she gagged as it went down.

"By God, you're a charmer," he said, shaking his head and going back to the paper.

She glanced out the window. It was black outside and gusting and she was very grateful she was indoors. There was a sweeper humming along the floor of the Library, under the chair legs, over the carpets.

She looked at Rupert. With him sitting like this engrossed in his news, she could imagine now what Christien would look like in twenty years or so. Truthfully, with the exception of the foul disposition, it wasn't such a bad thought.

The sweeper hummed along around his feet and he gave it a kick, sending it whirring out of the Library, bumping into everything as it passed.

"No wonder they're all broken," she said.

He harrumphed, bent back to his paper. She continued to study him and finally, he peered at her from the corner of his eye.

"Why are you staring at me, skirt?"

"You look like Christien."

He blinked slowly.

"What was he like as a boy?"

"Remy?" He seemed to consider this and she thought he might snort again, but instead folded his paper and leaned back in his chair. The cigarette was still in his fingers, spilling ash upon the carpet. From the looks of it, he sat here often.

"Remy was a quiet boy," he began. "Thoughtful. Too thoughtful, if you ask me. Very intense, very self-controlled. He did well in his studies. Of the two of them, Remy is most like his father."

"His father, the sixth Lord of Lasingstoke. He was your brother?"

"We were twins. Which explains the likeness to Remy I expect. Ren was much the same. Very intense and self-controlled. He was exceptionally clever as well, just like Remy. He could figure anything out. Would run rings around the servants and rob 'em blind. If Ren wanted something, Ren would get it, come hell or high water. Money, land, horses, it didn't matter. He always got what he wanted."

He paused, took a long drag of the cigarette, let the smoke roll in his mouth before exhaling.

"One day, he set his sights on Jane."

She smiled now. "Jane. Their mother?"

"The prettiest girl in all Lancashire. Blonde, like Sebastien. The sweetest, fairest flower in a wildflower meadow."

His words trailed off and he stared into the fire, a sad smile on his face. Ivy watched him with new eyes now, wondering how Christien would look confessing the name of the woman he loved.

"Forgive me for asking, sir, but..."

"You want to know they died?"

"Yes, sir. I believe I do."

He studied her for a long moment, blew a stream of smoke out through tight lips.

"Violently, skirt. They died violently."

"I'm sorry, sir. I didn't mean to pry."

"Of course you did. It's a way of living for you, isn't it? A vicarious adventure. Simply another line in someone else's story."

"I didn't mean—"

"I would expect nothing less from an East Ender like yourself." He raised his cup, almost a toast. "A skirt needs some skills to survive in this world unless she has beauty and God knows you have little of that."

She took another sip of the coffee, marveled now as the bitter taste had suddenly found a home on her tongue.

"So you raised them both then, after their parents died?"

"I raised Remy. Laury spent most of his time away."

"Away?"

"At Lonsdale."

It took a moment, but only a moment. She sat quietly as his words began to sink in.

No Czech machine-man should be experimenting on any Englishman...

"Is he a good doctor, this Dr. Frankow?"

Rupert snorted, flicked the cigarette into the fire and reached for his paper.

"You've heard the rumours."

"I have."

"They're all true."

"What?" She sat up. "But I thought... but Christien said..."

"Oh stop fretting," he grumbled. "I thought you were made of tougher stuff."

"But my mother—"

"Is in capable hands. I don't like Frankow and he doesn't like me, but not many people like either of us, so it's not surprising is it? We both have a history and history is rarely pretty. Let's end it there, shall we, little skirt? Women bring such melodrama into the house. Can't imagine what Remy was thinking, sending you here just because you found a bloody heart..."

And he snapped up the paper once more, bringing an end to the conversation.

The strange white-bearded man with the reticulating spectacles, the tap, clank and hiss of his walking.

Look what he did to de Lacey...

She drew the blankets a little higher, suddenly very cold.

They sat that way for a very long time. Rupert would rise, nudge the fire with an iron poker, sit back down again to read. She let her coffee grow cold, thinking about the sadness that seemed to plague most families. She wondered if there was ever a family without its own particular grief.

And so she sat lost in thought when barking, bootfall and the bellowing of voices rose from down the hall.

"No sir! No wet dogs in the 'ouse! The mop is only just fixed and they're leavin' muck all over the floors."

"But once they've dried by the fires, they won't be wet anymore. I'm sure of it."

Suddenly Sebastien de Lacey emerged through the library's double doors, a soggy package in his arms and pack of wet dogs at his heels. He himself was drenched from head to toe and when he spun to face Cookie, the motion sent water spraying across the room.

"Do you have any more of the raspberry tarts?" he asked. "I would dearly love a raspberry tart for breakfast!"

"Raspberry tarts are for pudding, not breakfast."

"Well, I missed the pudding last night, so I will have the tart now, then I will have pork at lunch, soup at dinner and eggs before bed." And he smiled at her. "The entire day shall be backwards. Perhaps even Cookie will be sweet."

Cookie scowled and swept her stony eyes across the room. Ivy swallowed, tried to sit up a little straighter but it was no use. Cookie shook her head and flashed a glare at Rupert.

"You're getting the ash all over the Turkish carpet again," she growled.

Rupert glanced down, then back up. "I don't know where that came from."

She shook her head, turned back to her Lord. "Raspberry tart, is it?"

"And tea, please." He leaned forward and kissed her cheek. "And don't forget the dogs."

With a huff, she turned on her heel and stormed out of the library, six happy wet dogs in tow. Sebastien watched her go, creating a puddle from the rainwater dripping off him. He sighed and turned back into the room.

"Morning, Rupert, Miss Savage—*Oh!* Your hair…"

She felt the heat rush to her cheeks, reached a hand up to attempt to smooth things into place.

Rupert waved a hand. "She fell asleep on the window seat. Sit, Laury. Why the hell are you so wet? Were you out riding in all this?"

"Yes, as a matter of fact, I was." Sebastien snagged a leather footstool and dragged it into the warmth of the fire. He peeled off his greatcoat, heavy with rainwater, and tossed it to the floor. Began to work on the buttons of his riding jacket next. "I got in just now."

Rupert arched a brow. "From where, Laury?"

"Lancaster." He tossed his jacket on the same pile, loosened the cravat at his throat and began to mop his face with it. "I thought Christien was coming in on a commercial airship. I was hoping to meet him at the platform, but he wasn't there."

"Christien?" Ivy sat forward. "He said in a letter he'd come."

"Well, he didn't. His name was on the docket, so I waited for the next and then the next. Do you have any idea how many airships make the trip daily from London to Lancaster and back again?"

Ivy pouted. "I have no idea."

"Neither do I. I waited for hours."

Rupert eyed him strangely. "You rode to Lancaster last evening, spent the night on an airship platform, and then proceeded to ride back this morning?"

"Yes." He smiled like the sun.

"Did this trip… *cost* us anything?"

"Nothing substantial, Uncle."

"Hmph. And Gus?"

"In his stall at this very moment, sleeping on soft sweet straw, with a belly full of mash."

"That's a long ride," Rupert scowled. "You had better check him in a few hours."

"I will. Surely." He looked at Ivy and smiled again. His eyes were brown, she realized. Most definitely brown, and she wondered why she could ever have thought otherwise. At this moment, he was as different from Christien as the sun from the moon. "I have something for you."

"For... for me?"

He reached down, grabbed the package that was as soaked as he was. Passed it into her waiting hands.

"I figured if I couldn't bring you Christien, I would bring you something else. Something more practical although considerably less romantic."

"I'm not a romantic girl," she said.

Rupert snorted, rolled his eyes.

"But thank you." She turned the package over in her hands. "I don't know what to say..."

"Well, open it and see what comes."

The strings were tight with dampness, and she needed to work them over the wrapping in one long, knotted twist. The paper unfurled of its own accord, opening to a bolt of tan cloth.

She glanced up at him. "I don't understand?"

"No no," he leaned forward. "Take them out. Take them out."

She did, lifting the fabric high to reveal legs like the paper cut-out dolls she had made as a child. Trousers, in fact, but slim fitting trousers, with what appeared to be suede leather inseams and a brass button at each ankle.

"Breeches!" she exclaimed. "You found breeches! Are they fitted?"

"They're boys', actually. I couldn't find breeches made for women. Perhaps they don't make them. Honestly, I don't see why you all prefer skirts. At any rate, I had to guess at your size. I do hope you don't mind."

"I don't mind at all." She beamed at him. "I think they're wonderful!"

Rupert rolled his eyes once more.

Sebastien leaned forward. "I picked out a mare for you as well, a spirited little bay. I think you'll like her. Her name is *Rouen Delfina d'Arc en Ciel.*"

"And her stable name?"

"Rue."

"Thank you ever so much."

Lottie appeared at the door.

"Breakfast is ready," she said and she curtsied. "Tea and tarts, in Midi."

***

Breakfast was, as requested, simply tea with raspberry tarts. It seemed almost decadent to have the sweets and nothing more, but Cookie had loaded the table with them, so they ate until Ivy was certain she would never eat another raspberry tart again in her life. Rupert had disappeared immediately afterward, apparently to attend to some financial matters for the Barony. Cookie had disappeared, apparently to begin cooking the pork that was now on the menu for lunch. Lottie had disappeared, apparently to steam the linens in the laundry. Davis had disappeared, apparently to the workshop where Cookie had projects awaiting him, and Ivy thought she had rarely seen her brother so happy.

The Mad Lord himself had simply disappeared.

And so Ivy made it a point to pin up her hair as not to frighten any more gentlemen, and began to explore the other rooms of Lasingstoke. More specifically, to explore First.

She had only been there once after her disturbing interview with Dr. Frankow so now she took her time, admiring the construction of a dwelling well over a hundred years old. The ceilings were high and sculpted, the windows large, rectangular and orderly. The walls were painted in creams and pinks, blues and greens, and it felt like an entirely different house than Second. Even today on the darkest of stormy days, First was lovely.

She slowed as passed Sebastien's office, peered inside. It was empty so with a deep breath, she stepped into the room.

It was as disorganized as the day before and she honestly couldn't imagine doing any sort of work in a place like this. The letters from Victoria were gone from his desk and she shook her head. Of course, if he were a Baron then he would have a seat in the House of Lords. She found it difficult to imagine him running Lasingstoke without Rupert or Cookie, let alone having a say in the running of the Empire of Steam.

Her eyes swept over the stacks of books, finding little of interest. Bound editions of *Peoples of the British Empire: a Census, The*

Manchester Birth Registry, A History of English Surnames and other similar titles made her yawn with boredom. Other books had more fanciful titles. *Spiritualism: The Next Age, An Illustrated Encyclopedia of Psychical Phenomena, The Ghost Club: Charter Members 1862–present,* to mention a few. There were Bibles in various translations, some of them apparently very old, and other volumes of a similar nature, but differing languages. Books of faith, she reckoned, from distant lands.

Other titles were more disturbing. *Occultism: Seeing in the Dark* by Charles Livy. *Dancing with the Dead* by Ernst Stroud. *Angels and Daemons: A Clairvoyant's Guide through the Seven Levels*, by Siliistro. She shivered as she walked past. Perhaps there were some things about this man that she did not wish to know.

And then, there were the papers. Newspapers and journals, tabloids and broadsheets. In fact, as she surveyed the room, she realized that of all the clutter in the room, by far the greatest was due to newspapers. Every horizontal surface had some form of newsprint, and not only the horizontal surfaces for she noticed clippings posted to the far wall. In fact, she had originally thought it to be wallpaper. With a quick glance at the door, she slipped over to see what they were about.

Her chest began to tighten.

Whitechapel Horror, read one headline. *London Startled Yet Again,* read another. *The Butcher of London* a third. Names were circled in ink, and she could make out a man's handwriting and the words "At Seventh." She frowned. Mary Ann 'Polly' Nichols—At Seventh. Annie Chapman—At Seventh. But there were others.

Matilda 'Tilly' Barton—At Seventh
Martha Tabram—At Seventh.
Annie Millwood—At Seventh
Ada Wilson—Gone
Abigail Charles—R'leased
Eliza Kerry—R'leased
Emmaline McKenna—R'leased
Charlie Fretts—R'leased
Clarissa Agatha Polkey—at Sevemth
Sarah Ann Polkey—at Seventh

The list went on.

Some of the names were familiar, others were not, and she realized that it was not only clippings from the Whitechapel murders on the wall but from all parts of the county. Manchester, Blackpool, Preston and York. The entire section of wall was covered in news articles on missing children and gruesome deaths and fiendish murders and she found her head spinning with thoughts. What interest could a Baron of a northern county possibly have with such horrible events?

Her heart thudded in her chest now. She needed to get out, to get to Second and the company of Cookie and Lottie and Davis. Or better yet, as far away as she could from the strange mysteries of Lasingstoke. She whirled, took a step and froze.

The Mad Lord stood in the doorway, a pack of dogs at his heel.

Chapter 13

Of Old Books, Older Photochromes and a History of the Ghost Club

London's Butcher Opens Shop in Lancaster
Prostitute Found Murdered, Eviscerated near the Col. Springs Airships Platforms

Clara Clements, of 33 Maudgate Rd, was found murdered in an alleyway behind the Ticket Platform of the Col. Springs Airships Field. Her throat had been cut twice, her bowels removed from their cavity and several organs moved or removed from the scene. It is believed to have taken place between 9:00 pm and 4:00 am this morning. Her husband, Oliver Sloan Clements insists that despite her profession, his wife was a woman of good character and did not deserve to be treated in such a low manner. The murder bears a shocking resemblance to the killings in London's Whitechapel district and already there are calls for Imperial intervention.

There are no witnesses, and police are currently investigating several leads. Anyone with any information regarding this heinous crime is asked to come forward to the police.

***

"Miss Savage?"

She curtsied. Again, she didn't know if it was good form. It just seemed the proper thing to do. "Your Lordship."

The Mad Lord of Lasingstoke moved into the room, the dogs following like shadows. They were all dry now, dogs and lord alike, and he moved to where she was standing beside the papered wall. His eyes—hazel now, most definitely hazel—flicked to the clippings, then back to her. He raised his brows.

"Are you looking for...a book?"

Relief flooded her from her head to her boots.

"A book!" she gasped. "Yes! I had seen one the other day that looked, um, interesting."

"Indeed. Which one?"

"Ah, well..." She turned, swallowed, stepped over to the shelves. "This one! This looks most intriguing!"

She pulled a book from the shelf.

His gaze flicked down at the spine, then back up. *"The Manchester Birth Registry?"*

Damn.

"Silly me," she said. "Grabbed the wrong one. I meant this one."

And she pulled out *The Ghost Club: Charter Members 1862— present.*

"It sounds like a wonderful mystery novel. I do love a good mystery—it helps when I'm writing my Penny Dreadfuls to have a brain full of mysteries."

"It's non-fiction, I'm afraid," he said. "The Ghost Club is an active organization for gentlemen, clergymen and scholars interested in paranormal phenomena. They consult for the Empire, the War Office and the Home Secretary of Defense."

Ivy blinked several times. The words of the sisters Helmsly-Wimpoll ran immediately through her head.

"In what regard, sir?"

"I wouldn't know. I'm not a member."

"But you *are* a gentleman and you *are* interested in paranormal phenomena. Clearly."

"A family pastime." He smiled at her. "My father was a founding member."

"But not you."

"Not me. Never."

"Why not then?"

"It's a complicated thing."

"I love complicated things. I am bursting with the need for a challenge, or so I've been told." Her heart was racing and she clutched the book to her chest. "Why do you have those newspaper posts on your wall?"

He frowned at her and she bit her tongue, for once again, it had gotten the better of her. And if she looked very closely, she could have sworn his eyes were changing colour.

"The world is an unpredictable, terrible, fantastical place."

"So I'm beginning to discover. You haven't answered my question, sir."

"That may take some time. I will need to show you around the rest of First first."

"It's raining outside. First is entirely more pleasant."

"I think perhaps," he began. "You have decided to reach a little?"

"I couldn't find any boots."

He turned away. But she noticed he was smiling, and that it was a very pleasant sight.

She stepped out with him and the dogs, *The Ghost Club* clutched tightly to her chest.

***

It was a time device. It had to be.

He had fallen asleep with it in his hand in the study of Hollbrook House. And now, he was waking in his own bed without any knowledge of getting there. He stretched, wondering if he had missed any classes in the interim. He was only supposed to sneak in a nap, but looking out through the crack in the drapes, it seemed closing in on supper.

He wondered if either Bond or Williams would fail him for missing a shift.

He rolled to sitting on the edge of the bed, slipped a hand into his waistcoat for the fob. Five o'clock. He had honestly slept from eleven this morning to five. It felt remarkably good and he sprang from the bed, feeling he could work now for twenty-four hours or more.

He trotted down the steps, the smell of lamb stew urging him onwards.

"Pomfrey!" he called. "Pomfrey, I have time for a quick bite if it's ready!"

The wigged man appeared at the foot of the stair. He blinked several times.

"Welcome back, sir. Are you sitting for dinner?"

"Welcome back? You mean, welcome down."

"Well, yes, sir. If that is what you prefer."

Christien sighed. Pomfrey was an odd duck. He'd attended Hollbrook House for years now, since the death of his father.

"I shall make some tea, sir. And oh yes, the paper is in the study…"

"I've already read it, Pomfrey. Before I fell asleep."

"No, sir. I meant today's paper. The Times, sir."

"Well yes, the very one."

"Oh very good, sir. They must have an earlier run for you medical types…"

And he turned in the direction of the kitchens, disappeared down a long hallway, leaving Christien confounded but used to it, and so he turned in the direction of the study. The aforementioned newspaper was folded like new and he shook his head. Pomfrey was an odd duck indeed, and he picked it up with idle curiosity, scanning the headline.

Steam Times (London)

September 17, 1888

The Whitechapel Murders

The detective officers continued their investigations, but up to a late hour last night, no arrest had been made, neither is there any prospect of an arrest being effected. The public of the neighbourhood continue to make statements, which are committed to writing at Commercial Street station, and in several instances the police have been made cognisant of what the informants consider to be suspicious movements of individuals whose appearance is supposed to tall with that of the man wanted. Every clue given by the public in their zeal to assist the police has been followed up but without success, and the lapse of time, it is feared, will lessen the chances of discovering the perpetrator of the crime.

The article went on, but his eyes had ceased reading. In fact, they were stuck, quite simply, on the date.

September 17.

He barely heard Pomfrey slip in to the study, place the tea cup on the table beside his chair.

"Is that not today's paper, sir?" asked the houseman.

"What is the date today, Pomfrey?"

"The seventeenth, sir."

"It is not the sixteenth?"

"No, sir."

"Not Sunday, the sixteenth?"

"Well, no sir. Today dawned Monday, September 17, last I checked."

Christien swallowed. "Of course. Thank you, Pomfrey."

"Are you quite all right, sir?"

"Yes, thank you."

"For you do not look well, to my eyes."

"I'm quite fine, thank you. Just needing some food. Lunch?"

"Dinner, sir. It is, after all, five o'clock, sir. In the evening. Of Monday, September 17."

He sighed, sank back into the chair. Pomfrey waited a moment.

"There is a steam car in the mews, sir."

"A *what?*"

"A steamcar. Shewed up this morning sometime. Ghastly thing. All metal and gears and steambricks."

"A steamcar..." Christien ran a hand through his hair. "When the bloody hell did I buy a steamcar?"

"I would suspect either Sunday September 16 or Monday September 17, sir. Unless there are more days of which I am unaware."

Christien blinked slowly.

"Is there anything else, sir?"

"No, Pomfrey. Thank you."

Pomfrey left the study as Christien sank deeper into his chair.

He had lost an entire day. His last recollection was of the clockwork locket, and he pulled it out from his pocket. Its gears were ticking merrily like a watch. It was cold in his hand.

He didn't even touch the tea that had been brought for him.

***

The photochromes on the walls were amazing.

"And this is my father with his first Warmblood. *Rouen Jardin Bleu de Mer.*"

She grinned. "And his stable name?"

He grinned back. "Blue."

She watched him, *had* been watching him the entire afternoon as they strolled about the large wing known as First. He was very different from Christien, at times awkward, at other times animated and she had no sense of why this man would be so fascinated with the Whitechapel killings, or any killings for that matter. He did not seem such a man. Still, she had enjoyed a lovely afternoon and was finding herself growing strangely comfortable in his company.

She wondered why he was not married.

On the third floor now and the last hallway leading to a large padlocked door. The walls were lined with photochromes of a personal nature, featuring both he and Christien as very young boys along with their parents. Physically, Renaud and Jane were as dissimilar as Christien and Sebastien. Renaud was the spitting image of Rupert, but with perhaps more hard lines across his face. All the chromes with him were stiff, posed, as if he was always aware of the presence of a camera and acted accordingly. He was a handsome, fine-figured man, and he knew it. His wife, Jane, was entirely different.

Ivy could see the likeness of Sebastien in her, the fair wavy hair, the animated expressions and sunny smiles. And the dogs. There was not a chrome of Jane without dogs. It was clear she adored them and Ivy wondered if she had shared that love with her oldest son. It would explain much.

She was about to ask the reason for the padlock at the end of the hall, when her eyes were diverted by a chrome high on the wall. It was a group of men in dark suits. There was one in particular who seemed familiar, with a high forehead, piercing eyes, muttonchops and small moustache. She narrowed her eyes.

"Is that Prince Albert?" she asked.

"Yes," said Sebastien. "Just before his death in '61."

"Impressive connections, sir," she grinned. "Is this a gentlemen's club?"

"And there you are. This is what I wanted to show you," he said, nodding at the book still clutched in her hands. "It is the Ghost Club."

"Seriously?"

"Seriously. There were many influential people involved in its founding. Edward is still a member."

She stared at him for a long moment, before turning back to the chrome. This was not the first time Edward Prince of Wales had cropped up in the family history. She remembered the newspapers after he had been shot in India, and his first public appearances with his clockwork arm. Suddenly, the use of prosthetics amongst the general public increased one-hundred fold.

She wondered if Frankow actually did design it. The world was an unpredictable, terrible, fantastical, place.

"This,' she said as she studied the chrome further. "This looks like Dr. Williams…"

"Hm," said Sebastien. He pulled thick spectacles from a waistcoat pocket, slipped them over his nose and peered up at the chrome. "Dr. John Williams, yes. I believe it was his first year in London. Got snatched up by the Club straightaway."

"But I know Dr. Williams. He's a friend of my father's from Swansea. He and his wife have dined at our home and we at theirs. He's not a member of some paranormal club, sir. I can assure you of that."

"I shan't argue," Sebastien shrugged. "I don't know the man. Although, according to the books, he's on the registry as an active member. I would shoot the lot of them if I had my druthers but that would be hard to justify, even if they did conspire to drive my father mad."

"Did you just say you'd shoot them?"

"Yes. And I have the perfect pistol with which to do it."

She stared at him but he did not seem to notice.

"It would be poetic justice but in all honesty, madness runs in the family. The Club just capitalized on my father's expertise and gave him enough rope to hang himself. So to speak. He used a bullet. I'm so glad Christien has escaped their attention all his years in London. They would want to corrupt his innocence and I would hate to see him burdened with even more loathsome cadavers."

She was certain her mouth was hanging open.

"Cadavers?"

"Yes, they are simply too much for me. Can't stand the sight of them. And Christien brings trunkloads of cadavers whenever he visits. It's difficult for us to be in the same room. Hollbrook House is hell for both of us."

"Trunkloads?" She blinked. "Of, of cadavers?"

"Well, not literally 'trunkloads'. Although for me, it is the same. They want me to shoot him, but he's my brother so I refuse. They are quite a persistent lot."

She stared at him now, as "animated" slid a ways past "awkward," deep, deep into the territory of "bizarre.'"

"Gads, I've done it again, haven't I?" And he shoved his hands into his pockets to stare at the floor. "Do forgive me, Miss Savage. I often forget myself when in the company of the living."

"But why, why would you want to shoot Christien?"

"No, no, you misunderstand. I love my brother. Rest assured I will never lift a finger to harm him, no matter what the women say." He shook his head, his eyes appearing distorted and currently very blue behind the lenses. "Never."

And then he smiled like the sun.

What had Frankow done to him?

Her heart was racing as quickly as her mind. Could any of this possibly be fact or was it all simply a glimpse into the addled mind of the Mad Lord of Lasingstoke? She tore her eyes away but they came to rest once again on the chrome of the Ghost Club.

There was a man with thinning brown hair, a neatly trimmed beard and spectacles.

"Wait," she murmured. "This fellow…he's familiar as well… Who is he?"

Sebastien peered closer, then straightened.

"Ah," he said. "That is a photo of a very young Dr. Arvin Frankow. You've met him, I believe."

A cold fist gripped Ivy's heart, and she turned back to the image. Sure enough, along with Dr. John Williams, Renaud Jacobe St. John Lord de Lacey and Albert of Saxe-Coburg and Gotha, stood a much younger Dr. Arvin Frankow. A Charter Member of the Ghost Club.

And he had both his legs.

Chapter 14

Of Mad Women, Machine-Men and a Locket Filled with Angels

Sebastien stared out the dark window as the hilly county of Lancashire rolled past. Across from him, Ivy Savage sat staring out the window on the other side. She had insisted on returning to Lonsdale immediately after seeing the photochrome of Arvin Frankow and the Ghost Club. Had he been alone, he would have ridden but he was certain the woman was soft from life in London. Instead, he summoned Castlewaite and the coach had set out in the rain.

They said nothing to each other on the ride.

Fergis sat on the bench beside him, Tag next to Ivy. The other dogs lay on the floor of the cab and he had to give the woman credit. The coach smelled of wet dog and she had yet to complain. Quite a resilient creature, all things considered, if more than just a little highly strung.

He wondered what she thought. Coming to Lasingstoke was a plucky thing for a girl to do, even on the urging of a father and a fiancé. Lonsdale was a fearsome place and Frankow a formidable man. It was obvious that she loved her mother and it was commendable. Christien was lucky to have her.

Finally, the gray bay of Wharcombe and the Gothic rooflines of the Abbey came into view and he felt the cold descend on him like a blanket. Through the gate now and the codes spun through his mind like leaves. He knew them all by heart. Along the drive that still filled him with dread and finally the lurch as Castlewaite stopped the carriage at the doors.

They were met by uniformed men, Vickers and Toewes. He knew them well. They nodded as he stepped out of the carriage along with the dogs and he held out a hand for Miss Savage. Two nurses as well, one familiar, one not, but Ivy bundled past them all into the foyer of the Abbey.

He turned to the dogs and held up a finger. "Stay. Do you understand? Dickey? Tag? I mean you too."

Neither Tag nor Dickey had tails, so they wagged their back ends vigorously.

Sebastien turned and bounded up the steps but as he passed the nurses, the cold rose up all around him. He paused, turned back to study them. Agnes Tidy was the first. He'd known her for years, but the other scowled at him and he stepped closer.

Gagging, choking, silent as night

He narrowed his eyes at her. She stiffened, raised her brows in defiance.

Barely a whimper, Godfrey's Cordial, dressmaker's tape

In a smooth, swift motion, he reached behind his back to pull a clockwork pistol, leveling it between her eyes. He cocked the hammer.

"Leave," he growled under his breath. "Leave before I put a bullet in your brain."

Tidy gasped, but the woman whose pin read "Amelia Dyer" did not. She scowled one last time before spinning and quitting the foyer. He waited until the sound of her shoes had died away, then pocketed the pistol and threw a look at Tidy, smiling like the sun.

"Hello, Tidy. How's the children?"

He didn't wait for an answer before turning to follow Ivy into the sanitarium.

***

Dr. John Williams looked up from his desk, his grim mouth splitting into a smile at the sight in the doorway.

"Remy, my boy! Come in, come in!"

The young physician did so, slipping into the office and closing the door behind him.

"Take a seat, man!"

Christien pulled up a chair, dropping into it as if he were carrying a great weight. Williams laced his hands across his desk.

"What's up, boy? And don't give me any cock 'n bull story about interns' hours. Tell me the truth. Are you missing your little Ivy, or is this Whitechapel business wearing down your nerve?"

"Yes on both counts, but that is not why I'm here." Christien reached a hand into his pocket, tossed the locket onto the blotter on Williams' desk. "What the devil *is* this, sir?"

Williams' gray eyes grew sharp as he glanced first at the locket, then at Christien.

"You honestly don't know?"

"No, sir. I don't. I know it belonged to my father and to his father and perhaps even his father's father. I know that it was engineered by a French metallurgist who worked for our family back in Normandy, but for what purpose, I can only suppose. I know that it is kept in a lead-lined box and that we must change the box every year for it turns the lead into gold, which we keep under the beds and in the cellar. I know it was given to me after my father's death and Sebastien was left the key, although what he has done with it, I have no knowledge. And I know that when I wear it, I experience headaches and now a loss of time. It is most disconcerting, sir."

"Interesting." Williams cocked his head. "A loss of time, you say?"

"I lost an entire day, sir. More than twenty-four hours. So pray tell me, what is this thing and why does the Ghost Club want it so?"

The doctor reached a hand toward the locket, hesitated a moment.

"May I?"

Williams plucked it up, holding it in his fingers as if it were made of eggshells. The pendant caught the light, flashed colours across the walls, across the desk, across their faces.

"It is not alchemy, nor pure metallurgy, although it may be a combination of both. It is perhaps the most perfect example of metaphysics you will ever see—a clockwork device that needs no winding nor in fact any key, so what, precisely, your brother holds is beyond me. These gears are not silver or gold, copper or brass, but elements we are only beginning to discover now. You have read

127

Crookes's works, no doubt?"

"I have not, sir."

"Well, see that you do. He is a founding member, Remy. His work in both the applied physics and metaphysics fields are quite astronomical, if you pardon the pun."

Christien blinked slowly.

"Ahem. Crookes believes that it is fashioned out of elements such as uranium, selenium, antimonium and zinc. Fascinating materials, quite fascinating. That is why he wants to study it in his laboratory in Kensington. You see, Remy, it powers itself."

"But that's impossible, sir. A machine cannot power itself." He reached for the locket.

Williams passed it back. "There is still much in the scientific world that we do not understand, Remy. If this little trinket does indeed contain antimony, it may well be powered by angels."

Antimonium. The Philosopher's Stone. The stuff of childhood myth and legend.

"Angels…" Christien tucked the locket back into his pocket. He raised his blue eyes, his face becoming porcelain once again. "I can see why the Club wanted my brother."

"We may have him yet, Remy. But right now, we have you." And he leaned across the desk, patted Christien's hand. "We have you."

"But why would it give me headaches?"

"I can't say, boy. We should get it into Crookes' laboratory. See what we can find."

"Thank you, sir." Christien rose to his feet, turned toward the door. "This has been most illuminating."

"I wouldn't wear it if I were you," Williams called after him. "I would hate to lose you to the angels."

"Good day, sir," said Christien, and he closed the door behind him.

***

Once through the arch, Lonsdale Abbey changed before her very eyes. Where the foyer had been dark and somber, the corridor was marvelous with brightly-coloured paneling and a low ceiling that looked like it had been dabbed with a hundred different paints. There were stripes and flowers, zigzags and swirls. It was as if the dim light was caught, reflected, magnified and distorted to create a surreal palette. It was a distinctly different atmosphere from the foyer.

Sebastien had caught up with her and she wondered what he thought. According to both Christien and Rupert, he had spent much of his youth here. She wondered if a place like this could ever truly feel like home.

They rounded a corner and her breath caught in her throat. A dining hall as large as any she'd ever seen, with raftered ceilings easily four stories high. Again, the colours—almost a different colour in every panel, with lilies and roses, butterflies and bumblebees, suns, moons and stars. Paintings of princes and clowns, ponies and dragons. Everywhere she looked, it was madness. Beautiful, terrifying, childlike madness.

She looked at him and he smiled.

"Tea?"

"My mother."

"Right. This way."

And he led her out of the dining room and down another hall towards a large wooden door. The brass nameplate read *"Dr. A. Frankow, MMBS, FRCS, MRCP"* but underneath the plate, the long handle of an axe protruded from the wood. On a stool next to the door, a young woman sat reading. She had dark hair piled on top of her head, a tiny mouth and rather round cheeks. She looked up as they approached.

"Hallo," she said. "Who are you?"

"Laury," Sebastien answered slowly. He seemed to be studying her. "This is my companion, Ivy Savage."

"Hallo, Laury. My name's Lizzie!"

Ivy stepped forward, rapped on the door.

"I'm going to the Americas." Lizzie clapped her hands. "Fall River, Massachusetts. I'm terribly excited."

Sebastien seemed spellbound. He was staring at the woman, cocking his head like one of his many dogs.

"Dr. Frankow?" Ivy called and rapped again.

"You're jealous of me," said Lizzie. "Because I'm going to Fall River."

From behind the door, Ivy heard the tap, clank and hiss that had begun to invade her dreams. The door creaked open onto the shiny shaft of the mallard cane, then the metal of his legs, and finally, the glare of the reticulating spectacles. He eyed her until he noticed the axe.

"Lizzie?" he said slowly. "What did we decide about your temper?"

"That girl is a greedy girl," Lizzie snapped. "She's jealous of me."

"You must keep your axe in the pigeon coop."

"The Russian scares them! He jumps off the roof and scares them every time! I hate him!"

"No pudding for supper tonight, I'm afraid," said Frankow.

"I hate him and will chop off his head!"

"Girls who chop off heads do not get pudding."

With a growl, the girl sprang to her feet, yanked the axe out of the door and stormed off down the hall. Slowly, the doctor turned back to them.

"Miss Savage, how kind of you to visit," he said with the ghost of a smile. "And Sebastien, what is this? I hear you are dismissing my nurses."

"Didn't want to waste a bullet," he muttered. "That woman. You're not releasing her?"

"Who? Miss Borden? Oh yes. She is quite cured."

Sebastien raised his brows.

"I am convinced, at any rate, that there is nothing more we can do for her here." Frankow looked at him, and the lenses circled in. "Why? Would you care to try?"

The Mad Lord shook his head and sighed.

"Miss Savage is concerned for the well-being of her mother. Would we be able to conduct a short visit to ease her mind?"

"Her mother is in the Baths, now. Perhaps later."

"I will not leave without seeing her," Ivy said.

"Then I suppose you will be staying the night." Frankow asked and his tone filled Ivy with dread. "Would you like your old room, Sebastien? You may share the bed with Miss Savage. She seems small enough. We haven't changed a thing, you know."

"Is Mumford there?"

"He is. He has commenced a treatise on the care of fine woolens but is currently suffering from what he calls 'writer's block. He has not left the room for months."

There was a long and awkward silence when suddenly, Sebastien began to laugh.

And even more suddenly, the two men embraced like old friends.

"Please," Ivy moaned. "Tell me what in the heavens is going on!"

With an arm draped across the doctor's shoulders, Sebastien grinned at her.

"He's been having a jape on you, Miss Savage," he said happily. "Frankow is a good man. A middling doctor, I'll admit, but a good man."

"But my mother... When can I see my mother?"

"My dear young woman," Frankow began. "Your mother is indeed in the Baths. But she will be done within the hour. Please, come into my office. It is a dreadful night and I have some fine port warming by the fire. They will notify us when she is ready."

They followed him in and Ivy dropped into a large chair, too confounded to be amazed at anything anymore. Which was saying something, considering the office of Dr. Arvin Frankow was amazing.

It was was a marvel of engineering, with windows rising at least three stories in height, the many panes of leaded glass bending and folding the weak English sun. Above their heads, great cogs wheeled in slow motion, creating a low hum and generating sparks that leapt in lanterns higher up. It gave her the impression of a factory and she thought it fitting for the machine-man from Slovakia.

As Sebastien and Frankow chatted like old friends, she sank deeper into the leather chair. This man, this machine-man, was treating her mother. He was a founding member of some wretched Ghost Club, along with Dr. Williams and Sebastien's dead father. For the first time in her life there was entirely too much mystery for her.

"But the woman is unstable, clearly," said the Mad Lord as he lifted the port to his lips. "I can't believe you will declare her cured."

"With the exception of her little outburst tonight, Miss Borden has been an exemplary patient, Sebastien," countered Frankow. "Her father and stepmother wish to start a new life abroad. There is no clinical reason to detain her."

"I see no good in her future. Violence and death at the end of that axe. Notoriety. Infamy..." He sighed, swirling the port in his glass. "And pigeons."

"And pigeons," Frankow grinned and his lenses whirred. "And how is your Christien doing in London, Miss Savage? Oh, one moment—"

He rose to his feet at the whoosh and thump of pneumatic pipes and she watched him clank over to a brass wall plate, slide open a hatch and remove a large capsule. Inside was a letter and she understood. Pneumatic pipes were all the rage in London. Could send posts speedily and efficiently throughout buildings and, if some reports were to be believed, throughout cities as well.

The lenses whirred and clicked and Frankow looked up, his eyes as large as moons. "Your mother has retired from her baths. We may see her now."

"Thank you, sir," she snapped and she rose from the chair. "You don't need to accompany me. Just point me in the general direct—"

Ivy's breath frosted in front of her face and she gasped as the temperature drastically plummeted. Above her head the gears groaned and sparks leapt between the lanterns across the ceiling. Her attention was drawn to the window. The rain that pelted the glass was quickly becoming hail. Pane by pane, the ice crawled its way up the glass, crackling in a crystalline wave just like that first night at Lasingstoke.

"What's happening?"

Suddenly, the fire roared in the hearth. It just as suddenly died and the office was plunged into darkness, save the eerie crackling sparks above them.

"Mulieres mortuae iratae ..."

It was a strange voice, hollow and echoing and in a language she didn't understand. Slowly, Ivy turned to look.

Sitting deep in his leather chair, the Mad Lord was completely still, his eyes bluer than a country morning and fixed on something no one else could see.

"Mulieres mortuae iratae ..."

"Sebastien?" said Frankow slowly. "What is it?"

"Mulieres mortuae iratae...Mulieres mortuae iratae..."

"Is that Latin?" Ivy shivered, wrapped her arms around her chest.

"Dead Women," said Frankow as he laid the capsule on his desk.

"Very Angry Dead Women… Sebastien, speak to me now."

"There is someone in Seventh," Sebastien announced in English but his voice was strange, as if narrating a tale on a theatrical stage. "A boy… in the windows… the women…"

Frankow moved to the chair where the Mad Lord was sitting.

"Sebastien, is this present or future?" His breath fogged, created tiny icicles on the hairs of his beard.

"Present. Now. A boy…the boy…" He closed his eyes as if trying to recall a name or a face. *"Puer insipiens… Mulieres mortuae iratae… occident te… saevus… saevus…"*

"Saevus…" Frankow looked at her, his eyes made huge by the spectacles. "That is Latin for 'savage'…"

"Davis," she gasped. "Davis kept saying he would find a way to Seventh. Is it Davis, Sebastien?"

"Davis Saevus," said Sebastien. "Davis Savage. The women are going to kill him."

"Women?" She dropped to her knees beside the chair. "What women, Sebastien? Please tell me what is going on!"

"They are very angry, and they will kill him."

"Who will— *Oh!"*

Suddenly, the port glass shattered in his grip. Blood dripped from his palm onto the floor.

Frankow moved slowly, surprising her by removing the glass and taking the Mad Lord's hands in his.

"Sebastien…Sebastien, look at me. Look now at me… yes, that's right. That's good…"

Slowly, Sebastien did as he was asked, blinking as if surfacing from deep and dangerous waters. Frankow nodded and continued.

"You need to get home, Sebastien. Take this young woman and crack the whip on your horses. I will have Karl send a telegraph to the Scourge. But you, get home as quickly as you can. Do not forget your training. You may yet be able to save him."

"There are too many women," he whispered. "It's so cold. I can barely even look at them."

"There are always too many women, Sebastien. Do not forget your training. Use the frost. Harness it. Rise above it. Now go."

"Please, sirs," wailed Ivy. "Tell me what is happening to my brother!"

Sebastien rose to his feet, grabbed her hand and bolted out the door.

Chapter 15

Of Bad Boys, Good Samaritans and the Seventh House of Lasingstoke

The Good Samaritan was a public house on the corner of Turner Street and Stepney Way. Tucked in behind the London Royal Hospital, it was a favourite for doctors, patients and medical students alike because of its proximity to the Royal and because of the local ales on tap. It was a favourite of Bondie's boys as well and they could often be found at a round table in the corner. They had carved their names into the wood when they had first started studying together. The table was near the dartboard and it was well known that Henry Bender was a crackerjack with a dart.

Christien sat now with Ambrose Pickett while Bender gathered his darts. Rosie had a wall of empty glasses in front of him and he looked up over it as Henry dropped down onto the bench.

"Won my drinks for the week," he grinned, stabbing his darts in a row into the wood.

"Ours too?" asked Rosie.

"Dream on, you git." Henry raised his beer to his lips. "My darts, my money."

"Damn," grumbled Rosie.

"Where's Lewie?"

"Late," said Christien. "As usual."

"Typical. He should've been a lawyer."

The pub was loud and they had already gone through two pints before Lewis Powell-Smith shewed up with a young woman tucked under his arm. He was a trim fellow, dapper in tan pinstripes and tweed. Like Rosie, he was mustachioed, with a bolt of blond hair that fell across his forehead. The woman on his arm was young and quite beautiful, and when she smiled, she shewed great dimples in her cheeks. Upon closer inspection, it was clear that her clothes were old and the red shawl over her shoulders was threadbare and patchy. But her hair was a mass of strawberry blonde curls, and the fact that she was not hiding it with a hat caused very few to pay attention to the state of her clothes.

"Marie," said Bender. He sat up a little straighter at her approach.

"Henry," and she winked at him, the dimples giving her the look of an impish little girl.

The pair dropped into seats at the table and their beers were brought and left. Immediately, Powell-Smith raised his glass and downed a good third before dropping his mug to the table with a thump.

"Damn that Bond," he growled and he tossed his head. "He made me work overtime tonight. There was a bloody accident with another steamcar."

"How many?" asked Bender.

"Four, naturally. A woman got her head crushed under the wheel. It was putrid. He made me do the autopsy for the lawsuit."

The boys grinned. Lawsuits against four-wheeled steamcars were all the rage in London now, fueled, it was said, by the makers of the six-wheeled variety.

"He's also asking about that Jane Doe. About why she got shipped from Bedlam to us."

"Oh God," groaned Bender. "She's still bagged, yeh?"

"Yeh, he didn't look."

"Yet."

Christien raised his glass to his lips. "And what did you tell him, Lewie?"

"Nothing. I told him I didn't know nothing."

"Well, it's not unheard of for Bedlam to send us cadavers."

"Yeah," moaned Rosie. "Happens all the time."

"Not without the papers," groaned Powell-Smith. "And with the Bottle on his ass about that arm, we've got a very, very short chain."

"Indeed." Christien sipped his ale slowly before lowering the mug to the table. "We're medical students. The public would love nothing more than to see us trotted out as villains here. We must be very, very careful in this particular climate, boys."

"Yeah," grunted Bender. "No mistakes."

"No *more* mistakes," said Christien. "We have six months until we're done and I want to finish free and clear."

"So's you can get married," said Marie and she smiled at him, her eyes roaming over his fine face, his perfect lips, his smart suit. "How's yer moll, then, Remy? You missin' her somethin' awful like?"

Powell-Smith didn't care. He had paid for her so she was his tonight. Marie Kelly was a favourite of the boys. She would go with whomever had the coin but she was a good-hearted girl and very pretty. She had acted on the stage in Paris, or so she said. She had worked in Kensington-Knightsbridge with a French matron who had shown her the ropes. She was a friend to John Williams, and it had been her name Christien had seen in the book at Bethlem. Mary Jane 'Marie' Kelly with an abortion at Bethlam.

"Yes," he said evenly. "I am missing her."

"I can help with that."

She bit her lip coyly and raised the gin to her lips. He noticed she was wearing a brass ring on her middle finger. It was a simple loop of stamped brass and was identical to the one on his little finger.

"Your ring... Where did you get that?"

"Oh this?" She held it out as if to study it and grinned. "My John. *Gan fy* John."

"John Williams gave you the ring?"

She dropped her chin onto her palm.

"He's takin' me back to Paris next month. He's a dear man, is my John. A smart, sweet, *very* generous man."

"Looks like your ring, Remy," grinned Powell-Smith. "You going with Jackie to Paree next, you Frenchie dog, you?"

Suddenly, the room grew cold.

"I luv Paris," said Marie. "I been three times."

"I never been to Paris," moaned Rosie.

Inexplicably cold, and his finger throbbed where the ring lived.

"Paris is for whores," snorted Powell-Smith and he swigged his beer.

"Old men and whores and Remy."

"What the hell's wrong with you, Remy?" laughed Bender. "You're all blue!"

"I'm not a whore," said Marie under her breath.

"Course you are, luv," grinned Powell-Smith. "And you're very good at it."

And he began to kiss her neck, in spite of the fact that she was scowling.

It was all he could think of, the cold shooting up his hand, stabbing like tiny needles into his chest.

"Remy?" asked Bender. "Remy, you all right?"

"Damn, but it's cold in here."

The boys looked at each other.

"It's not cold in here, Remy," said Powell-Smith, leaning across the table. "It's a bloody Turkish bath."

Suddenly, Christien bolted to his feet, patting his waistcoat and pulling out the locket. It was spinning madly at the end of its chain, its rings creating sparks as it did so. The air around it began to frost and to his utter surprise, snowflakes floated to the table like Christmas morning. They turned immediately to tiny droplets of water on the wood.

"What the bloody hell is that?" asked Bender.

"That's beautiful, that is," cooed Marie, spellbound as colours flashed across her pretty face.

Powell-Smith leaned in. "By God, Remy, has your precious Club seen this?"

"Not like this," said Christien as he stared at the locket, eyes larger than almost anything in the room. "It's never been like this."

Quickly, he shoved it back in his waistcoat, ignoring the shock of cold as the locket touched the ring. He turned and pushed his way through the crowd and out the door of the Good Samaritan public house.

***

The carriage thundered along the muddy roads, without even a moon to guide them. Ivy sat in the seat, clutching first one railing then another as she was lurched from side to side, and it was purely good fortune, better driving and the best horses in Lancashire that kept the wheels on the road. French Warmbloods. She would never forget them now.

The dogs lay in a wet pile on the floor of the coach, huddled and dejected.

Sebastien sat opposite to her, eyes fixed to the window, but she was certain that he was seeing nothing of the world. His lips were moving but in a language she did not understand. Latin, Frankow had said. It sounded just like the high masses said at important holidays. The windows were frosted and she could see her breath in the cab.

This was not a world she knew. This was not a world she had ever heard of, this world of madness and ice and she felt herself growing numb to it. Sitting here in a racing coach through the cold wild heart of England, she was turning to stone. Soon all that would be left of her would be pebbles and dust.

What had Frankow done to him?

"'old on down there!" called Castlewaite from above and the coach veered sharply around a bend in the road. She grabbed the railing, held for dear life. They had passed through Over Milling earlier and were on the last stretch toward Lasingstoke. Her head was spinning but her mind was slowing, and she had no idea what she should be thinking, or if in fact, she would ever think again.

Her brother had gone to Seventh. She knew it in her heart of hearts. He had told her he would. She had promised him ghosts and tonight, it seemed, he had found them. She couldn't imagine how or why but she knew beyond a shadow of a doubt that the world had shifted and would never be the same.

Suddenly, the coach skidded to a halt and Sebastien and the dogs were out like a shot, leaving the door open. But she was a shadow, out and onto the wet grass at his heels.

They were near a church and as they raced past, a tall figure came out of the trees. It was Rupert, grim-faced, an axe in his hand.

"I can't get him," he said. "They seal it up as soon as I split a board."

Sebastien nodded and together, the three of them continued deeper into the forest. The dogs had gone on ahead and Ivy could hear barking over the howling of the wind. They were moving through a graveyard now, with young trees growing like daisies over most of the plots. Dying ivy covering everything.

The men were but silhouettes when she spied a flash of stone deeper in. All but hidden from view, Seventh was as dark as the night sky. Dark stone, dark lintels, dark glass on the windows. Dark trees that formed a canopy above and around, dropping rainwater on their heads, turning the path into mud under their boots. Even in such darkness, she could see the blows made by the axe in the wood of the door.

"Davis!" she cried and pushed past the Scourge, heading for the door. "Davis, please! Open the door!"

Suddenly, an arm was around her waist, pulling her backwards in the muck.

"No skirt," growled Rupert in her ear. "This is no place for you now."

"But Davis—"

Sebastien moved around them, his greatcoat billowing as he laid his hands against the splintered wood. The howling of the wind became the scream of nightmares, the wail of a thousand banshees, the hiss of angry trees and earth and stone and voices and Ivy struggled in Rupert's grip as the door began to move.

Not inward, not outward, but both at once, rippling like waves on a shore and she could see lights flashing from within. As if in the distance, she could hear a voice, Sebastien's voice speaking in Latin, hollow and echoing and very strange. He drew on the door with the tip of a finger and ice began to crawl up the stone, up the windows, up to the roof, until the entire house was shining like glass. The cold descended like a blanket so that even Rupert's arms could not warm her.

Suddenly, everything grew deathly still.

"Damn," Rupert whispered behind her.

She didn't know but she knew.

"No," she gasped. "No! No! NO!"

And she began to thrash in his grip.

"Davis!" she wailed. *"Davis!"*

The Scourge of Lasingstoke dragged her away from the door as Sebastien picked up the axe and swung. It was like a thunderclap as the house struck back and they were all lifted off their feet and sent flying backwards into the trees and the blackness.

"Skirt."

The trees and the blackness

"Skirt."

Her head was spinning in the blackness

A wet nose nudged her and she reached a hand into the soft golden coat of the retriever.

"Get up, skirt."

She pushed herself up from the forest floor. It was raining now and both leaves and mud came up on her cheek. She looked up to see Rupert standing over her, surrounded by the dogs of Lasingstoke. There was a ribbon of blood along his forehead and there seemed considerable effort in simply standing. He was holding something in his arms.

"Davis..."

She felt the world shift around her at the sight of his body, cradled like a baby, arms and legs hanging, limp and unmoving.

Ivy scrambled to her feet to follow as St. John stepped onto the path that led back to the church. She could see her brother's face and the world shifted yet again.

So many cuts. So many cuts.

"Skirt! Now, if you please!"

Numbly, she followed, but she did throw one last glance at the house known as Seventh. The door was shut and there was not even a sliver to show for the axe.

Of the Mad Lord, there was no sign.

Chapter 16

Of Steamcars, Airships and Princes of the House Saxe-Coburg and Gotha

"Wake up, Ivy."

Someone was stroking her forehead.

"Wake up, my Ivy. I've some tea for you."

It was like a dream. A strange, wonderful dream in which she was back in London and everything was perfectly happy and normal. There were no murders. There was no madness. There was only tea and a soft bed and the strange warm scent of a man.

"Sebastien?" she mumbled.

She felt the weight shift and opened her eyes.

"Christien?" She smiled. *"Christien!"*

She sat upright far too quickly and the room reeled like a night after too many brandies. He reached a hand to steady her, put a finger to his lips.

She looked down. She was on Davis's bed at Lasingstoke and her brother was asleep on the pillow. His young cheek was pink, his breathing regular. There wasn't a single cut on him. Not one cut, not one scratch. Nothing.

"I don't understand. His face, the wounds. Oh, Christien, it's been terrible."

For two nights she had stayed at his side. She had eaten at his side, read at his side, slept. When she'd closed her eyes last night, his breathing had been laboured and his face livid with cuts. Now, all of those wounds were gone without even the hint of a scar. He was breathing like a fifteen-year-old boy. In fact, she could have sworn he was snoring.

"Come," he said, taking her hand. "I have tea downstairs."

She allowed herself to be raised from the bed and with one last glance, she followed Christien out into the hallway and down the stair into the sitting room of Second. It was morning, a fire was crackling, and she tucked herself into Rupert's wing-backed chair, trying to recall the events of the past days.

"Tea, Miss Ivy?" It was Lottie, smiling in her shy way.

"Thank you, Lottie. Thank you so much for everything."

"And Master Davis?" She wrung her hands like damp dishcloths, seemed to be holding her breath. "How's he doin', then?"

"I think he'll be fine, Lottie."

She could see tears brimming behind the ginger lashes and Ivy felt a rush of warmth that had nothing to do with the fire

"Well, that's good, then. Very good, indeed. Ah... Ah'll let me mum know yer up. And Mr. Rupert. He'll be wantin' t'know."

"Thank you, Lottie. You've been such a good friend to both of us."

The young woman smiled through her tears, quickly curtsied and rushed from the room. Ivy looked at the tea cup, noticed the slight tremor in her holding. She felt her own eyes begin to sting.

And suddenly, Christien was at her side, removing the cup and gathering her in his arms. And she sank into him, feeling his strength and wetting his shoulders with her tears.

***

Side by side, they strolled through the courtyard. He had offered her his arm and she had taken it. It was her first time outdoors since that terrible night and she marveled at how fine the estate looked when not beaten down by rain. The sun was shining, puddles were drying. There were birds flitting through the branches, sheep and horses grazing in the fields. The lawns looked lush and green and she filled her chest with sweet damp air. Everything looked so normal and she found herself wondering if the last few weeks had happened at all.

They had managed almost a full circuit of the Hall when they came upon a crowd of servants gathered around a shape on the drive. Castlewaite turned as they approached, his copper eyepiece clicking like a shutter.

"Ah suppose it'll do," he said. "If ye like that sort o' thing."

She glanced at Christien. "Is that a steamcar?"

"It is," he said.

"You bought a *steam*car?"

"It beats waiting in those blasted queues for an airship ticket. You know how I hate to wait for things."

"*"ere!"* hollered Cookie from a doorway. "Get t' work, the lot o' ye!"

The crowd of servants, including Castlewaite, quickly drained away into the estate, leaving the two of them in the company of the steamcar.

"Do you like it?" And he smiled at her.

She looked up at him and she marveled once again at how fine he looked when he smiled. His lashes were envied by women everywhere and his eyes were as blue as a French sky. Not an English one. No, that was more his brother. Sebastien had gray eyes. Or were they brown? She realized she hadn't seen the Mad Lord for days and wondered if he was still in that sinister house called Seventh.

"I'd been thinking about it for some time," Christien continued. "So when Rupert sent the telegraph, I couldn't stomach the thought of taking an airship then renting a coach for the drive to Lasingstoke, so I simply... bought a steamcar."

"Six wheels?"

"Naturally," he said. "Four wheels are notoriously unstable. You see the bloody things tipped all over the streets back home. It's said that Edward has one with eight."

She looked back at the car.

"Can we go for a drive?"

"What? Now?"

"Yes. Now. I'd love to go for a drive."

"Ivy?" He studied her for a long moment. "What on earth are you thinking?"

"I need to go somewhere."

"You are incorrigible, you know that?"

But he held open the door, helping her up onto the high tufted seat before moving around to the rear of the car.

She watched as he slipped on goggles, then a set of heavy leather gloves and raised the boot of the car. She watched him rummage around the firebox and pull out a block of coal. She sat a little higher, twisting in her seat to see the flash of a copper boiler as the coal disappeared into the furnace with a slap of a plate. He closed the boot and flashed her another smile before climbing up behind the driving levers. He passed her a set of goggles and she remembered the sight of Franny, her blonde hair and goggles, her wild scarf flapping in the wind.

With a dramatic flourish, he held up a beautiful golden key, set it into the lock, rotated it three times, and punched a hex-key painted in green. It took but a moment for the engine to catch, and suddenly, the vehicle begin puffing and chugging like a locomotive. She threw a nervous glance at her fiancé.

"Just warming up," he purred. And with a deft motion, he released the clutch, hauled off the brake lever and the steamcar bounced forward, and forward again.

Ivy yelped as the steamcar puffed and chugged, puffed and chugged down the drive that led away from Lasingstoke Hall.

***

"This was a bad idea, Ivy."

They stood by the graves near the little church at Lasingstoke, having left the steamcar by the side of the road. It was called "All Souls Christchapel" and had served the estate and surrounding area for centuries. There was no minister, no parson or priest as the de Lacey family had historically refused to incorporate English rites into their charter. According to Christien, marriages, christenings or funerals were to be conducted by the resident Baron in either Latin or French.

Headstones dating back over six hundred years sank beneath statues blackened with age, wooden crosses splintered and tipping. Barely visible was a mound of new earth with name carved into a hazel branch. 'Charlie Fretts, 1877 -1888,' it read.

"I would just like to see it," she said.

"It's just an abandoned old house."

"Come on."

Without waiting for his answer, she turned and set off down the path. The imprints of boots were still visible, drying like mortar in the mud.

"I'm sorry this has happened," said Christien as he reluctantly followed. "But going there will only fuel your fears, not cool them."

"But how could a thing like that happen, Christien?" she asked. "You should have seen his face."

"Superficial wounds, Ivy," he said. "He likely fell out of a tree and scratched it on the holly. Look at this. It's worse than thistle in this forest."

"They looked like claw marks," she countered. "Some were very deep."

"But if they were so very deep, how could they heal in two nights?"

"Your brother did something at the church. That's what Rupert said."

"Rupert is not a medical doctor."

"Your brother knew that Davis was heading into Seventh."

"My brother knew because we were once boys too, Ivy."

She said nothing more for some time. The forest was dark and damp and there was no trace of birdsong this deep in. She was growing winded hiking over the uneven terrain and looked at down her city boots, the hem of her skirt swishing and snagging on the branches. She wondered what the breeches would feel like on her legs.

And then she saw it, the place that almost killed her brother. Tall, dark and all but hidden by the ivy that worked to consume it, the Seventh House of Lasingstoke was made of stone. There were black sashes over the windows and rusted locks over the doors. It was empty and run down, but there was no blood, there were no axes, no cobwebs or spiders or anything remotely sinister.

It was just a house.

Christien moved around to stand beside her and his face was neutral, skin like fine porcelain. A lock of dark hair fell across his forehead. It looked out of place.

"Bastien used to always say this was where the bad things went."

"Here? To Seventh?"

"Yes. Father used to scare us all the time with tales of Seventh.

Entire families murdered in this house, he would say, since before the de Laceys staked the claim back in the Iron Conqueror's time. Sometimes Father would bring him here when he was being bad, which was quite often. I'm not surprised he's made up an entire mythology around this place."

She couldn't tear her eyes away. It was just an abandoned house.

"After our parents died, Bastien spent years at Lonsdale. *Years*, Ivy. Even Frankow couldn't take the voices away, despite all his treatments. He still can't bear to be in the same room as me. Says the cadavers are too much for him."

"But Rupert—"

"Rupert indulges him. He protects him, shelters him and treats him like a child. Which, I suppose, he still is."

There was only a faint breeze drying the leaves that remained on the trees, preparing everything for winter. It would be cold soon. They both continued to stare at the house a long while before Christien spoke again.

"Bond insists we learn the new theories for our psychology course. He says it will be instrumental in understanding the criminal mind. Naturally, because of Bastien, it has a special interest for me. The monographs of Drs. Freud, Bleuler and Schneider have opened my eyes to my brother's illness."

Ivy covered two sides of the house, already turning red with the first touches of frost. She remembered it had been an evening of ice and frost.

"They're calling it 'schizophrenia.' It's from the Greek, meaning 'to split the mind.' He sees things no one sees. He hears things no one else hears. Frankow is a pioneer in such conditions and has pharmacological compounds available to help dull the symptoms but Bastien refuses to take anything. It's a terrible syndrome and I am certain there is no cure."

She sighed.

"So there is nothing 'fantastical' left in the world…"

"Not in my world," he sighed. "There can't be. There are only facts and evidence and unexplained science."

The large spectacles, the blood on his cheek, the words in Latin.

"Are you disappointed?"

"I'm sorry, Christien. I'm afraid I don't know what to believe anymore."

"No, Ivy. *I'm* sorry. I shouldn't have sent you here. To be honest, I didn't expect Bastien to be here at all. He rarely is."

He took her hand in his, gave it a squeeze. She looked down. Long elegant fingers, neatly trimmed and polished nails, no blood or bruising. There was a brass ring on his little finger. She had never seen it there before.

He smiled a thin smile. "Can we go back now? I hate this place."

"Wait—" She paused, glanced up at the sky above the house. "Can you hear that?"

"Oh Ivy, please…"

"No, Christien, it's like a heartbeat. Listen…"

Once again the trees began to move and moan and soon, a sound very much like the beating of a heart, growing louder and stronger by the moment. Not a thud, thud, thud, rather a thwup thwup thwup. That and the rustle of the dry leaves in the trees. Thwup thwup thwup went her heart and the rustling trees were beginning to sound like the humming of a very large engine and she thought it nothing at all like the howling and roaring of that rainy night.

A huge dark shadow fell across them and they both looked up as the vast underbelly of an airship came into view over the Seventh House of Lasingstoke.

***

With the steamcar running on full throttle, they managed to beat the airship back to Lasingstoke Hall and watched from the courtyard as the massive vessel slowed in mid-air, preparing to dock. Servants she had never seen before flooded out of the Hall to attend it and when she looked up, she saw four other ships in the sky high above Lasingstoke. The hum and thwup of propellers was almost deafening and the sunlight danced in beams from the sky. Painted in gilt across her bow, the name *"HMAS Royal Carolina."*

She was a grand airship with a large cylindrical balloon of black and gold canvas, brass scalloped fins and copper rudders, with rings of aluminium and girders of polished steel. Beneath it, the cabin was as ornate as a royal frigate, her hull painted a gleaming white, with ebony and gold fittings. The bowsprit figurehead was a woman of solid gold and on her stern — gold and silver mer-people frolicked in ivory waves.

She was flying the colours of the House Saxe-Cobourg and Gotha.

Ivy clutched Christien's arm.

"The Prince of Wales?"

He turned to her and she thought she had never seen him smile so.

"This is a surprise." He looked back, shaded his eyes against the flying debris for a better look. "I wonder if Eddy's here too?"

The gondola hovered scarcely ten feet from the ground, and she could see faces in the saloon of the cabin. The crew shouted orders, cables were dropped and servants rushed to catch them. From the cabin, uniformed men dropped to the ground and suddenly Ivy understood the reason for the black iron posts in the courtyard. They secured an airship to the ground much the same way a ship was secured at a dock.

More shouting now, and Rupert's tall form appeared from one of the court's many doorways, hands on hips as a metallic stair unfurled from the deck like a sea-faring gangplank. A bosun's whistle blew all to attention.

First, several goggled men in naval dress but soon, a stout figure in breeches, riding boots and town coat stepped onto to stair. Albert Edward, Prince of Wales, kept one hand on his top hat to keep it on his head. His other hand was gloved and tucked across his belly, and she knew it was the mechanical one hidden in the sleeve. He was bearded and she thought he rather looked like a bear. A fine, intelligent, decorated bear.

Directly behind him followed another man, much younger, perhaps the same age as Christien and once again, she knew him. Albert Victor Christian Edward, Duke of Clarence and Avon, eldest son of the Prince of Wales and grandson to Victoria. Scandal followed at his heels like flies after a butcher's cart. He was taller than his father and slimmer, and his dress was much finer, with a pale gray waistcoat, red silk cravat and yellow carnation in his lapel. But the likeness was undeniable, down to the upturned moustache and he followed stiffly down the stair. His disinterested gaze swept over everything.

The Prince of Wales and Duke of Clarence stood, goggles toffed, awaiting a formal greeting so both Rupert and Christien strode across the square to oblige. Ivy stayed near the archway however, as they exchanged greetings, handshakes, claps on the shoulder as men were wont to do. But Christien waved her over and before she knew it, she was standing before the heir apparent to the English throne and his son.

She curtsied, keeping her eyes low.

"And this is Ivy Savage, Your Royal Highness," said Christien. "My fiancée."

"Enchanted." The bear man thrust out his gloved hand and she was obliged to take it. It felt odd, stiff, and the fingers closed about hers with a series of clicks. "A bit of a wild thing, isn't she? 'Savage,' you say? Common Welshie name, wot? Are you a child of the Red Dragon, girl?"

"Yes, Your Highness." She felt her cheeks redden. "I grew up in Swansea, sir."

"She knows Williams," said Christien. "From the same town, in fact."

"Ah, Jack! Capital fellow!" Edward guffawed. "*Y Ddraig Goch ddyry gychwyn,* and all that, wot, little *Cymry!*"

"Indeed, sir," she grinned. His pronunciation was atrocious but, she had to admit, fluent.

"You don't have the lilt, girl."

"No, sir. My father moved to London many years ago."

"Splendid, splendid. Good catch, I'd say. A Prince of Wales must love the Welsh! And I do, girl! I most certainly do! Eddy, say hello to the little *Cymry.*"

Ivy swallowed as Albert Victor stepped forward, took her hand in a formal, if unremarkable, grip.

"Enchanted," he said and she could feel his disinterested eyes sweep over her figure. And, Ivy thought, over Christien's as well.

"Eddy has made captain," the Prince of Wales bellowed, obviously proud of his son. "He will be commanding the new Royal Corps of Airships in the New Year."

Albert Victor released her hand and as he did, a ring brushed against her finger. It was small and brass and remarkably similar to Christien's, but before she could think too much on it, the Prince of Wales turned to

Rupert.

"And where is that damned nephew of yours? Our mother is not amused, you know. Not amused at all."

Rupert inclined his head as if thinking. "Laury is... laid up at the moment. Hunting accident. He's been bedridden for days now. Was he expecting you?"

"Hunting accident, you say? Blast it all, no one can sit a horse like Laury."

"Took a fence badly and landed in a patch of thorns. But he'll live, Bertie. Never fear."

Ivy threw a glance at Christien. He patted her hand and said nothing.

"But can he walk, man? Can he walk? We've come to fetch him off to Balmoral for the week. War Office business, old man. War Office business."

"He can walk," Rupert smiled. "I shall fetch him presently. But Bertie, we were about to sit for lunch. Cookie's prepared a ham. Would you and the Duke care to share our table? It would be honour upon Lasingstoke if you did."

"Ham, you say? Can't remember the last time I had a good ham. We shall accept your invitation, old man." The Prince dropped a meaty hand on Christien's shoulder. "And we can chat with the Club's newest member over port, wot? It's about time we got another de Lacey on the roll."

Ivy's heart thudded in her chest and she noticed the flash of Rupert's eyes.

"Club?" she asked, certain her voice was no more than a squeak. "What Club is that, sir?"

"Why, the Ghost Club of course! Now, I say, where is that ham?"

Chapter 17

Of Clockwork Arms, Bloody Faces and a Dead Man on the Books

Cookie had outdone herself with the ham, and they had even indulged in wine with lunch. After all, it wasn't every day that the Prince of Wales and the Duke of Clarence came to call.

They sat now in a small drawing room, drinking port and smoking. There were Persian carpets, crushed velvet sofas, a large marble fireplace and in the center of it all a piano, the size of which she had never seen rivaled. But she could appreciate none of it and she sat like a stone as once again, the Ghost Club cast its shadow over the Hall.

Edward had removed his town coat and the mechanical arm was visible for all to see. It was as remarkable as Frankow's legs, she thought, a mass of intertwining cables and shafts, belts and pulleys. The hand was holding the cigarette and every time he moved, gears whirred softly. She marveled at how a Czech psychiatrist had been able to duplicate the remarkable engineering of God.

Albert Victor, the Duke of Clarence, sat stiffly as if balancing his head on his rather long neck. He was absentmindedly fiddling with the ring on his little finger and she wondered if it was significant to the Ghost Club. She had also noticed his eyes, for the most part dull and disinterested, would occasionally dart to the piano and she wondered if he played.

He sat next to his father, poised and unmoving, while Edward held forth on the merits and perils of the House of Lords. Rupert sat opposite and had not taken his eyes off his nephew the entire afternoon. For his part, Christien had refused to look at him and had seemed preoccupied with the etchings in the port crystal. It had been, in Ivy's estimation, a most uncomfortable meal.

"Williams has great plans for our Remy, he has!" boomed the Prince. "Both in the Club and in the Obstetrics Room, wot! That man's a master player! Beats me fair regular at whist! Ah ha, ah ha!"

"Remy never mentioned he'd joined the Club," said Rupert and he took a long drag on his cigarette. "Why was that, Remy?"

"It was rather a spontaneous thing," said Christien.

"Tosh!" said the Prince. "Williams has been after him for years. The Club is not the same without a de Lacey on the books!"

"If I remember correctly," said Rupert. "You still have a de Lacey on the books."

"Quite right, old man, quite right," said the Prince. "A member is never removed. It would be bad form."

"Which de Lacey, sir?" Ivy sat forward. "Sebastien has insisted that he is not a member. Is it you, Mr. St. John?"

The Scourge of Lasingstoke blew a thin stream of smoke through his lips.

"We've tried, dash it all," boomed the Prince. "But Sinjin won't join! Far too stodgy for religion or politics! In fact, I can't remember the last time he set foot in London or Cambridge! Ah ha, ah ha!"

Ivy glanced between them both as Edward puffed happily on his cigarette.

"No, no. I was referring to Renaud, child. Renaud de Lacey, the sixth Lord of Lasingstoke."

There was silence in the drawing room

"Forgive me, sir, but…" She glanced from face to face. "But isn't he dead?"

"A mere inconvenience. No reason to be removed from the books, wot?" The Prince tapped his elbow and yet another cigarette slid out from the copper shaft. "It *is* the Ghost Club we're talking about, after all."

Rupert slid his eyes over to her, rolling the smoke around in his mouth before exhaling. She swallowed and looked away.

"You can't blame 'em," Edward continued. "It's what Mummie

wants. And when Mummie wants a de Lacey, Mummie gets a de Lacey. No one says no to Mummie! Isn't that right, Eddy?"

"That is what you keep saying, father."

The bear man leaned forward and slapped his son's knee. "Such a card you are, my boy. Such a card! A regular Ace of Clubs!"

Ivy took a deep breath. 'Mummie' was Victoria, make no mistake. There were more rumours floating around about Victoria than all the other Royals combined. It was said that, over the years, she'd worn out three mechanical hearts and had already commissioned a fourth. That she kept her dead husband's head in a bedroom wardrobe to speak with when she grew lonely. That she'd had her uterus surgically removed to prevent any more unwanted pregnancies and that she had donated it to Dr. Williams Obstetrics Foundation for preservation, complete with royal foetus if he ever felt the urge to grow it.

Suddenly, with all this talk of the Ghost Club, Ivy found the rumours a little easier to believe.

"And Mummie wants her de Lacey now," said Edward and he raised the cigarette with clicking fingers. "That's why we're here, to fetch that elusive Laury! Where the deuce is that boy? You sent that little ginger girl to fetch him hours ago! Ah *wot—*"

For suddenly, there were dogs everywhere, skittering and wagging and laughing in the way only dogs can laugh. The room had grown strangely cold and she wasn't surprised to see the Mad Lord standing in the doorway.

She gasped at the sight, covered her mouth.

"Forgive my lateness, Your Highness," he said. "I was praying in the chapel and I heard someone call."

"By *God,* Laury," boomed Edward and he rose to grip Sebastien's hand in his mechanical one. "That was some hell of a fall!"

Sebastien's face, neck and hands were—like Davis' for two nights running—littered with cuts. Long ones, short ones, some shallow, some deep. They were beginning to close up and scab over but it was difficult to look at him without feeling the need to look away.

"I fear you make too much of my skills, Bertie. A man unhorsed has wounded his pride more than his body. Welcome to Lasingstoke." He turned and bowed to the Duke of Clarence. "And hello to you too,

Eddy."

"Laury," said Albert Victor but he did not move to rise.

Sebastien studied him until the duke looked away. With a quirk of his head, the seventh Lord of Lasingstoke glanced around the room and his eyes fell upon Ivy. They were blue now like a summer sky.

"It's good to see you again, Miss Savage," and he smiled. "How is your brother?"

"He is well," she breathed. She could not imagine what had happened to him, what he had done to earn those cuts. Whatever it was, she was so very grateful. "Very well, indeed. Thank you for asking."

"Good. Good." She could have sworn his cheeks had reddened. "Very good."

Christien rose to his feet.

"Hello, Bastien."

"Gads, you brought them all with you again." The Mad Lord turned away, a hand clapped over his eyes. "I can't…I just can't. I won't."

"I know, Bastien. I'm sorry."

"No, no, Christien. It's not you. It's all those cadavers. They are simply too much for me. Ah damn, damn, *damn* them all to hell!"

He released a deep breath, then another.

"Someone called me…some*thing* called me…"

"Well," said Edward. "We did send the little ginger girl."

"Latin? Was it in Latin? Is she dead?"

There was another awkward silence before the Mad Lord sighed and turned to Edward, deliberately keeping his back to his brother. "Forgive me. I'm a trifle addled. I'm told we're off to Balmoral?"

"Yes, Balmoral it is! In the *Carolina*, no less!"

"I'm afraid I've lost my spectacles," said Sebastien. "Will I need to read?"

"Not at all, my boy! Unless you need 'em to shoot a stag or two! Mummie wishes to have a word with you about our little…*ahem*… problem in London. If you're up to it, that is?"

"Yes," he said. "I'm up to it. Please may we bring the dogs?"

They looked up at him adoringly, wagged.

"Don't see why not? Can they behave in an airship? Would hate to lose one over the side, eh wot? A little spaniel splatter over Pitlochrie just won't do. Say Eddy, do you think your grandmum would object to a few more dogs?"

Albert Victor shrugged. "As long as they refrain from urinating on every post and pillar of the airship, they should be fine. Urine does rust the frame so."

"True, enough, Eddy. True enough. Right, then, off we go and all that. Sinjin, old man," he turned and extended his mechanical hand. "Don't be a stranger. I know a Duchess or two who would be happy to make an honest man of you yet."

"I've had quite enough of skirts, if you ask me, Bertie," and Rupert smiled his lazy cat smile. "Give me a pipe and a paper and I'm a happy man."

"You'd be happier with a 'skirt' of your own. And Remy..." A firm if noisy handshake. "You've got a fine little woman, there. Keep her happy or you'll have hell to pay. The Welsh are like that."

"Yes, sir. That is my aim."

"Perhaps we'll see you at the next meeting?"

"Of course, sir."

"Miss Savage..." The Prince executed a most formal bow. "*Hen Wlad fy Nhadau*, and all that."

She curtsied. Pronunciation still atrocious. "It has been an honour, Your Highness."

"Eddy. Come!"

And with that, Edward of Saxe-Coburg and Gotha, Prince of Wales, whirled and stormed out of the sitting room, Albert Victor a slim quiet shadow at his heels.

Sebastien looked back to the others and Ivy could have sworn she saw his breath frost in the room.

"Christien, I'm so terribly sorry..."

"I know," said his brother. "I understand."

"Miss Savage, take care of your brother. We *will* see your mother at Lonsdale, I promise you."

"Sometime, I expect."

And she smiled at him.

"Sometime." He smiled back at her.

And for a moment, all time seemed to stop in the room.

Christien noticed.

Finally, Sebastien turned to St. John.

"Rupert…"

"Bugger off, Laury."

"Right." And he was gone, just like that, with six dogs happily trotting behind.

Very quickly, heat returned to the sitting room.

Christien sank to the sofa while Rupert lit another cigarette. He puffed a few good puffs, eyes flicking from nephew to fiancée and back again. He shook his head and left the room.

Ivy stood for a while longer, unsure of what had just happened but sure it was not all good.

***

The courtyard was quiet once again and she was lost to her thoughts as he led her out under the stone arches toward the steamcar. But he caught her hand, turned her toward him and she found she could look nowhere but the perfect blue of his eyes.

"Ivy, I must go back tonight."

"What? But Christien, why? You only just got here."

"I know. But the heat is on to find this Whitechapel villain and things have become rather complicated."

"Complicated? How so?"

"Nothing. There is simply so much work."

"Christien…" Her heart thudded in her chest. "Why didn't you tell me that you've joined the Ghost Club?"

A furrow appeared between his brows.

"And when did you learn about the Ghost Club, Ivy? It's a part of my family's history, not yours."

"Sebastien told me."

"Well, that makes sense then, doesn't it?"

"Christien, please. I wish we could talk about these things. We used to talk about everything, remember?"

"We still can."

"Not if you think you need to protect me from ideas. I don't want that kind of marriage."

He pulled her close and she could smell cigarettes, sweet brandy and coal.

"I know you're right, Ivy. I do. But these are dangerous times and I have no idea where this Ghost Club may lead. In fact, it's probably nothing, simply a Pall Mall club for gentlemen with scads of money and far too much imagination."

"And if it's not?"

"I don't know. I just…"

His shoulders sagged and she looked up at him, wondering at his sudden need to touch her. He was not normally a vulnerable man and she certainly not a fawning girl. This was an altogether different side to him, unexpected and rather sad. She placed her hands on his waist-coated chest, could feel his heart beat beneath her palm.

"Is it true your father was a member?"

"A founding member, yes. And it drove him mad. I need to find out why."

"But Dr. Williams—"

"It's become so very complicated, Ivy." He blinked slowly, brushed a strand of dark hair from her brow. "There are bad things happening with the boys in the lab and in Bethlem and the papers are on us hard. John's involved somehow but I don't know how. They're all keeping secrets from me and then there was the letter—"

He cut his words short, as if saying too much.

"Letter? Secrets? Christien, tell me, please."

He is pulled towards the arcane as much as me, Sebastien had said, *but masks it under the guise of science.* She could see it happening before her very eyes. Pushing everything deep, deep inside, locking it all in place under a fine porcelain mask.

"It's not important. What is important is for you to be safe up here, up north and away from all of the intrigue in London."

"But I want to help, Christien. I'm strong that way."

He took her hands and she couldn't help but look. His fingers so clean and elegant, so very different from his brother's. His grip skilled and sure. Sebastien's moved like water, like earth and wind and trees.

"Ivy please, for the first time in years, you don't have to care for someone else. Take up the piano. Learn to embroider. Write poetry. Go shopping with those Wimpolls you wrote about. Something. Anything. You can help me the best simply by staying safe."

Is that the life you want for yourself?

Was it?

"I can't," she sighed. "Not anymore. Christien, something is wrong and I don't like it. I don't like what it's doing to you. How long has the Ghost Club been after you and why?"

"Ivy…"

"And what if you do find out what drove your father mad? What then? What if it drives you mad too?"

"It won't."

"But Sebastien said—"

"Sebastien doesn't know anything about the life of civilized men, Ivy, let alone mine." He pulled his hands away. "Did you hear him in the parlour? Too many damned cadavers for him."

She sighed.

"You don't know what it's been like living in his shadow, Ivy, what I've lost because of him, how hard I've had to work to make my own way. One time, he shewed up at to take his seat at the House of Lords with a blanket over his head. He wouldn't take it off and he was ejected from the House. The papers were after me for weeks…"

"I'm sorry, Christien," she said. "I know it had to be hard. I'm so sorry for the both of you."

"It doesn't matter," he said quickly. "I'm sorry too, Ivy. I'm tired and I miss you and I do miss the way we used to be. I wish this damned case were over and I didn't have to go back tonight, so I'm feeling a bit childish, I suppose."

"No," she said. "I'm the one who thinks everything is a mystery story waiting to be written."

"A very gruesome mystery story," he said, smiling with his eyes. "With altogether too much blood and gore."

She grinned and leaned into him, not wanting this moment to end.

"Here, I give you a mystery, then." He reached a hand into his waistcoat pocket and pulled something up to the light. It was a locket, dangling from a long serpentine chain. "Science, spiritualism and alchemy all rolled into one little bauble."

It pulsed and danced like the music of a star.

"It's beautiful," she whispered.

"It's been in the family for years," he said. "The Ghost Club is interested in it but I find it a distraction."

"Interested? How so?"

"They are a curious lot. I think they want to take it apart, discover how it works."

"You can't let them," she said. "It's too beautiful."

He slipped it over her head and it nestled in the curve between her breasts. She looked up at him.

"You want me to have it?"

"I can't think of a better, safer, more clever place to hide it."

"Christien, I don't know what to say."

"Now that is a first." He kissed her forehead. "I'll write again soon."

She closed her eyes, breathing him in for a long moment before he slipped on his goggles and climbed back into the steamcar. She watched the turn of the key and soon the vehicle chugged out of the courtyard and down the gravel drive, leaving puffs of black smoke in its wake.

With one hand on the locket, she watched until it had all but disappeared, but she couldn't help but spare a moment to search the skies for the sight of an airship and the Mad Lord of Lasingstoke.

***

And so Penny planted a kiss on the cheek of both the Prince of Wales and the Duke of Clarence and bid them Adieu as they trotted up the gangplank of their fine airship, the HMAS Royal Dalton. She turned to her father, Charles Dreadful.

"Father," she cried, holding on to her touring hat as the airship exchanged ground for sky. "Would you be a dear and check whether or not Alexandre Gavriel St. Jacques Lord Durand has his own airship, and if so, where it was moored on the night of the theft?"

"Capital idea, my girl!" her father boomed and he left her in the courtyard of Lancaster Castle.

Penny watched the royal airship until it was little more than a speck in the clouds.

"I believe I must get myself one of those," she muttered to herself, before turning and heading to the vaults.

Chapter 18

Of Steamcars in Lancaster, Royals in Balmoral and Whispers on Hanbury Street

"Hold on to your hat, dearest!" cried Fanny Helmsly-Wimpoll and the four-wheeled steamcar took the corner on two. Ivy let out a yelp and did indeed grab her hat. While they were safely inside the cab, the sensation was pulling at her stomach like the downward swoop of a very high swing.

Franny laughed madly from her perch in the dickey. Her steamcar was several years old and already antiquated. It was shaped entirely like a coach with the boiler stack in the boot and puffs of steam trailed behind them like clouds. While her passengers sat inside the cab in relative comfort, Franny rode the gears and levers from outside in much the same way a coachman would ride the rein. She had left the trap open, however, and Ivy could see the scarf flapping in the wind.

"Don't you think it's magnificent how Franny's scarf flaps so?" barked Fanny over the noise. "I've suggested longer, dearest. It would be ever so dramatic, don't you think?"

"Oh," yelped Ivy, gripping the seat for her life. "I think the one she has is perfectly fine."

"Tosh," sniffed Fanny loudly. "One can never be too young, too rich or have too long a scarf. That's what I've told my dear Yankee friend Isadora. By the way, darling, did you see those airships the other day? I heard they were ferrying the Prince of Wales to Balmoral!"

"Yes, I heard," shouted Ivy, her bottom flying from the seat as the steamcar roared over a stone bridge. Normally, by coach it would take four hours. In a steam car, it would take just under three.

At the rate Franny Helmsly-Wimpoll was driving, they would be there in less than two.

"And your hat, dearest! What *scandal!* Is it yours? Did you steal it? Is it all the rage in London?"

Ivy rolled her eyes up to the black brim. It had been days since both Sebastien and Christien had left – one for the north, one for the south – and the estate had grown quiet in their absence. So one night, as Davis was sitting up in bed happily slurping cock-a-leekie soup and remembering nothing of his experience, he, she and Rupert engaged in a friendly game of whist. She had cleaned Rupert of all the change in his pockets and settled on his hat instead.

She had won it fair and square, along with his pocket watch and a cigar. She had both tucked away in her waistcoat pocket, along with ten pounds for a pair of 'very fine' boots and dinner. She needed answers and of all the people she had met since coming north, the sisters Helmsly-Wimpoll would be happy to provide them.

"Perhaps, we'll take a tour of the castle, dearest!" yelled Fanny. "Have you ever been?"

"Never!" Ivy shouted back.

"It's old, dripping and dilapidated. And the ghosts! The place is as haunted as a graveyard. And the witches! More witches in Lancaster than sheep. But we don't need to fear. We're brave and modern women, fearing nothing, not even men!"

Ivy swallowed and held on to her hat, as they rounded yet another corner on the way into Lancaster.

***

"Thank you, Remy," grinned Rosie. "You're a good friend."

"You're drunk," said Christien and he hiked his friend under his arm. "I hope Bondie doesn't catch on."

"He can't even catch the Ripper. 'ow's he gonna catch little ol' me?"

They pushed their way out of the public house known as The Ten Bells. On the corner of Commercial and Fournier and across from the Gothic Christchurch, Spitalfields, the Bells was always full of patrons.

For his part, Christien was happy to be leaving the noise and smoke behind. Besides, it was a rare sunny day and he was very glad to be back in London.

"Come on. I'll fetch you a cab."

"I ain't got no money, Remy. I spent it all on the gin!"

"I'll pay for the cab, Rosie."

"Does Bondie want me for something, Remy? Izzat why you're here, t'fetch me?"

"I'll take care of it, Rosie."

"I can work…"

"He'll sack you if he sees you like this. Go home. Sleep it off. You can take my shift tomorrow. How's that?"

"You're a good friend, Remy. A right good friend," and Rosie slapped his friend's chest once, twice, three times. His breath smelled of sour potatoes. "Bugger you're so damn French…"

The street bustled with hansoms, broughams and even a pair of noisy, chugging steamcabs. Christien had no trouble flagging one down and bundling the sloppy form of Ambrose Pickett inside. He slipped the driver two shillings, along with Rosie's home address and the cab rattled off, quickly disappearing in the crush of black along the street.

He stood for a long moment, wondering what on earth he was to tell Bond. The Police Surgeon had requested Pickett specifically for a necropsy on a vagrant and had refused to let Christien stand in for him. Rosie's grades were slipping and Christien hated to see him fail. But try as he might, there was only so much one could do for a friend like Rosie.

"You lookin' for it, luv?" came a voice from behind and he turned to see a woman dressed in cheap clothing. She had thinning hair and pockmarked skin and Christien could tell her occupation at a glance.

"No, thank you," he said stiffly. "I have to get back—"

"You want to see it. I know you do."

"I'm afraid I don't know what you mean."

"Really?" She arched a brow. "All the flash gents wants to see where Dark Annie got snuffed. It's just round the corner, there…"

Dark Annie. One of the many nicknames of Annie Chapman, the second victim of the London Ripper.

He twisted the ring on his little finger.

"See?" the woman grinned, leaning into him. "I knews you did. Ten pence gives you a peak in the yard. Blood's still on the fence, it is…"

He pulled a pocketwatch from his waistcoat, checked the time. The necropsy was scheduled for two. That gave him an hour to hail another cab and get back to the hospital. He would make Rosie's excuses, do the necropsy, save his friend from failing yet again. He had time, he knew it. He had time.

"Ten pence it is. But I warn you. I work with the Met. Any trouble and I'll have you in irons. Do you understand?"

"Oh, I understand, luv. I do indeed. This way, then." She turned away, marching down Commercial with a swish of her tattered skirts. Christien steeled his nerve to follow.

***

"We are not amused."

Sebastien stared at the tartan carpet under his feet. Balmoral was a study in tartan. There were tartan curtains, tartan chair-covers, tartan blankets and even tartan linoleums. There was the Balmoral Tartan (designed by dear deceased Albert) and the Victoria Tartan and of course, the Royal Stuart. By her own admission, Victoria RI was an ardent Jacobite.

"So you are blatantly refusing the Crown, boy. That is a capital offense."

"I'm sorry, Your Majesty," he said. "But I will not assist the Ghost Club. Not now, not ever."

"Not even to serve your monarch in her time of grief?"

Twenty years of grief, he thought grimly.

"Not even then."

She arched a brow, small eyes boring holes into his forehead. Her mechanical heart beat like a drum, and the DE program that ran it ticktocked in its gearbox like a clock. She had mechanically-assisted lungs as well which created a sound like that of a bellows stoking a fire. But the most unusual of her prosthetics was the wheeled brass crinoline that carted her around. Victoria had severe rheumatism and the crinoline served to take the weight from her legs and distribute it to a set of wheels, allowing her both mobility and modesty. Her black skirts covered it completely, but like the heart and the lungs, the sound of the device was a dead giveaway.

Other than the crackling of the fire and the clockwork Empress, there was no sound in the room. The tension however, was as thick as the smoke in the air. Edward had consumed at least seven cigarettes this evening and it seemed his mechanical arm went through the motions of its own accord. Sebastien wondered if perhaps there were a small difference engine running a specific "smoking" program and if it could be programmed differently for cigarettes, cigars and pipes.

Albert Victor sat quietly and Sebastien was certain he was holding the same cigarette as when he'd entered. The brass ring on his little finger was attracting an apparition however. He couldn't make out her face. Someone had painted the *ligaturae spiritus* over the doors so it was impressive she had made it through at all. She hovered around the Duke, so likely he had some involvement in her death but then again, these were Royals. Death was historically at their disposal.

"The Club has not been able to help us speak to our dear Albert since he passed," said Victoria. "They insist that is something only you can do."

"The dead contact me, Your Majesty," said Sebastien. "I do not, nor would not, contact them. In fact, I wish they would stop."

"You belong to the War Office, boy. Never forget that. Your father died, taking his secrets with him and leaving the Club with one hell of a mess. And while we still wait to speak to our dear Albert, we foot the bill for Frankow and his failed experiments. Is that all you are, boy? A failed experiment?"

He continued his study of the floor.

"If you could shoot some of the hoodlums in London, then perhaps we could justify funding Lonsdale to the War Office. And yet you insist on skulking round the countryside, ridding the world of Lancashire's ne'er-do wells, but leave London to rot like a slab of moldy cheese."

"Perhaps you *should* come to London," offered Edward as he lit his eighth cigarette of the evening. "Perhaps the proximity of the crimes would do something for you."

"I hate London and would happily shoot all the hoodlums I could find," he muttered. "But there are only so many hours in a day and a finite number of bullets."

An absurd giggle escaped Albert Victor's mouth before he composed himself once again, lifted the cigarette to his lips.

"Insolence! We have half a mind to give you over to the Ghost Club on that alone. Both Williams and Gull has been after us for months. They could draw it out of you with their experiments and science. What do you have to say to that?"

"I would shoot myself then if they dared try."

Victoria snorted and wheeled back to face the fire, hands folded against her black skirts. The ticking of her clockwork heart accentuated the long silence that followed. Finally, the monarch of the Empire of Steam took a deep wheezing breath.

"There have been eleven such murders now in Whitechapel, did you know that, boy? Damned Frenchies are already claiming that civil unrest is at the root of such crimes and the Anarchists are calling for riots until the villain is caught."

Edward leaned forward to rest on his cane, eyes bright under the bushy brows.

"Can you, or can you not, catch this villain, Laury?"

"I am trying, Your Highness," said Sebastien. "But there are so many dead at Seventh besides the women from London. Two young siblings drowned in sacks with rocks. A man hanged wrongly in Furness. A mother and daughter poisoned by a cad in Milnethorpe. And then there are the torsos…"

"Torsos?"

He pinched the bridge of his nose.

"The torsos are the worst. Dismembered bodies. They hover together but separate. I want to claw out my eyes when I see them..."

At least Edward was distressed. Victoria was colder, however, than the breath of the dead.

"Take something for it, boy. Surely, Frankow can give you the lithium."

"The lithium stops everything, Your Majesty."

"Well. Opium, cocaine, something else, then. We don't really care."

Laudenum, he thought. *Deep, dark, quiet laudanum.*

"Good *God*, boy," she snorted. "Do not look at us with such a face. It is ghastly to behold. You shall make us toss our kippers."

Quickly, he looked back down at the floor.

"Forgive me, Your Majesty. The women of Seventh are very angry."

"And they can do this to you, then? Spectres, ghouls and apparitions can rend flesh and bone? Is that what you would have us to believe?"

"When the spirits are willing, the flesh is weak. Even in this room, there is a woman trying to communicate but she's a vapour, a shadow and I would be hard pressed to learn more."

"Here?" said Edward. "In this room? But the Latin—"

"The *ligaturae spiritus* keeps most out, yes. This one is attracted by Eddy's ring. Jewelry is a powerful magnet."

The Duke looked up. The smoke curling around him looked very sophisticated.

"But you see how difficult this would be," Sebastien continued. "The dead might lead me to shoot Eddy whom I'm sure has never harmed a soul in his life, simply because he's wearing a peculiar ring."

Edward glared at his son but Albert Victor merely blinked his heavy-lidded eyes and covered the ring with his other hand.

"Jewelry a powerful magnet, you say?" said Edward after a long moment. "What about lockets?"

"Lockets, cameos, charms, rings." Sebastien shrugged. "They are all the same to the dead."

"Williams has a locket," said Edward. "To which he insists you have the key."

"Me?" said Sebastien. He shoved his hands into his pockets. "I don't even have a key to the Hall. I get locked out most nights and frequently sleep in the stables."

"Do you deny it, then?"

"I know of no locket, so yes, I do deny it. What is this locket?"

"Some blasted locket that can open doors to other worlds, or some such rot. The Club wants it badly. Williams says it belonged to your father."

Sebastien glanced over.

"My father? How would the Club come into possession of something that belonged to my father?"

"From Christien, boy!" exclaimed the Prince. "Wot? Don't you know?"

The world lurched beneath his feet.

"Know what?" he asked thinly. He barely had words.

"That Remy's a Clubber! Williams recruited him weeks ago!"

Sebastien had to force his legs to hold. They were shaking like a newborn colt's.

"Why, they've already had success and Gull is certain he will step into your father's shoes presently."

"I would like to go home, please."

"You will come to London?" asked Victoria. It was not a question.

"Yes," he said. "I will come."

Every sight distorted, every sound magnified.

"Ah capital, man!" boomed Edward. "Capital! I'll let the Club know to expect you! Williams will be thrilled!"

"He can meet Erica," said the Duke.

"Tosh," snorted Victoria. "Erica is useless. Worse than useless. She is in league with Schlaumann and the German Intelligencia. No, after Sebastien shoots this Whitechapel villain, he will come to Sandringham where he shall contact my Albert."

"Mummie," said Edward.

"We keep his head in our wardrobe. That should prove a sufficiently powerful magnet, yes?"

Sebastien felt ill.

"It *is* me they want, yes? Not Christien. Me."

"Well yes, they've always wanted you. But *dashitall,* if two de Laceys ain't better than one, wot! Ah ha, ah ha!" Edward slapped his son on the knee. "Eddy, sport this good man and his pack of hounds to the Airships Port Tower at Westminster—"

"Lasingstoke, please?" asked Sebastien. "I, I must attend to one matter before I leave."

And he held his breath when Edward waited on his mother, little more than a shadow in black lace and crinoline as she stood silhouetted by the fire.

She nodded and the Duke rose to his feet, flicking his cigarette into the flames.

"Come along, Laury. The *Carysfort* is riding high and ready to sail."

"And *don't* shoot our grandson, boy," said Victoria from the fire. "You'd get the gallows and we'd drop the trap ourselves."

Sebastien nodded, grateful to finally leave the fireside room to the tartan, the smoke and the Clockwork Empress.

***

This part of town was unknown to him. The Ten Bells was *not* the Good Samaritan and was a fair walk from the Royal. He was not intimidated but he was also not naïve and once again he wished he had kept at least one of the surgical blades on him. The East End was a hard part of town. Anyone could be rolled for their cap, let alone their coin.

"Was Annie wearing any jewelry?" he asked as the woman led him deeper into the maze of dark buildings and black cabs. The smell of rotting garbage was overwhelming but he resisted the urge to cover his nose with his handkerchief.

"Rings," she said. "Like the one yor wearin', luv."

And she grinned at him over her shoulder, shook her head.

"She said she got 'em from the king, she did! That's Dark Annie for ye. Full o' piss 'n vinegar. She gave it up for the king and 'is three bloody brass rings..."

They slipped between warehouses to a lane in the back. It was everything he had imagined—the shadows cast by the buildings, the odor of garbage, the whispers of violence, the promise of blood.

She paused, jerking her head toward a rickety fence bordering the yard.

"In here," she said. "Froat slit open like a gutted fish. If you look real close, you can see it on the rails…"

He couldn't bring himself to look. The ring was constricting his finger and he could feel the pulsing of blood in the vein.

"Aww, it's always the flash ones ain't got no stomach. Not to worry, luv. It's all over for Annie, it is. She's feelin' no pain, now I can tell you."

His heart was racing in his chest and he struggled for some measure of self-control. He was a forensic surgeon. Death and bodies, blood and violence—these were a part of his life but this was different somehow. He could see it all in his mind—the throat, the intestines on the shoulder, the heart on the ground. He had sewn her up, nice and tight but for some reason, he just couldn't bring himself to look.

Quite unexpectedly, the woman took his hand.

"Come on, luv. Just a quick peek. You'll see…"

And like a mother leading a child, she took him step by step to the fence, placed his hand on the edge, nodded with each movement. He took a deep breath and turned his face to the yard.

It was just a step, an awning, some dried yellow grass.

"There. See? If you look real close…"

He exhaled, sagged against the fence, ran a hand along his face.

"Gads, you're a softie, ain't you?" The woman clucked her tongue at him, patted him on the cheek. "So, luv… That ten pence?"

He rummaged through his pockets, pulled out a coin, pressed it into her palm.

"You can finds yer way home, right luv? 'Cause I got customers an' all…"

And with that, she was gone, leaving Christien alone with the whispers of Hanbury Street.

Chapter 19

Of Riding Boots, Crown Princes and Scandals on All Fronts

Annie's Apparel was apparently one of the 'very fine' shoe shops in Lancaster. It was low and dark with an old Tudor ambiance but Ivy had to admit, very good leather. She could hear the hiss of the boiler as it puffed steam into the air, keeping the apparel soft and supple. The smell reminded her of wet horse and that made her think of Sebastien.

"Really, Ivy darling? Riding boots?" Fanny turned to her with eyes fairly gleaming with delight. "Whatever will Christien Jeremie say?"

"Ooh, Christien Jeremie…" echoed Franny. "What will he say?"

"Christien…is in London…" She twirled, liking the way her skirts draped across the leather. It was a well-cut boot of ox-blood brown, laced up mid-calf and continuing up to her knee. The heel was copper, the toe pointed and somehow, they made her feel strong, confident, and perhaps, just a little taller.

"Hah!" she said under her breath. "Take *that*, Sebastien…"

"They do look dashing with your waistcoat and bowler, darling," said Fanny. "And a pocket watch to boot! Why, if it weren't for the skirts, you'd look like a regular boy!"

"Like a regular boy!"

"And, of course, with your new trinket a-spinning around your neck!"

"A-spinning away!"

"Did Christien Jeremie give that to you, dearest?"

"Did he?"

She paused to stroke the locket with her fingers. It purred like a cat.

"Yes," she said fondly. "It's been in his family for years."

"Is it a clock?" asked Fanny.

"A timepiece?" asked Franny. "A radiometer? A spinthariscope?"

"I have no idea…" It spun happily on its own. She had not needed to wind it at all.

"And what about Sebastien Laurent then, dearest?" asked Fanny. "Will he approve of your riding boots? After all, he *does* love his horses…"

"He loves horses…"

"Well, *actually…* " Ivy bit her lip.

Fanny gasped.

"Out with it, darling!"

"Out! Out!"

"Sebastien did offer me the use of one of his horses."

"One of his horses? Not the French Warmbloods?"

"The Warmbloods?"

"Yes. A fine bay mare named something something *de la* something. I call her Rue."

"Rue! That's lovely, dearest! It's simply wonderful when a gentleman offers you the use of a fine French Warmblood! Have you ridden her? Have you been riding with him? With Sebastien Laurent? Have you fallen off?"

"Have you fallen?"

"Not yet." She sat and began to unlace the boots. "But he bought me breeches to wear when I ride."

There was silence.

"They're quite fine cloth with leather inseams and brass buttons. He bought them here in Lancaster. I'm certain they'll fit rather well."

Still nothing.

Ivy looked up. She had never seen such an expression on the faces of the sisters Helmsly-Wimpoll. In fact, with their eyes wide and their mouths hanging open, they looked extraordinarily equine and bovine. All they needed was some hay.

"Is something wrong?" she asked.

"Sebastien Laurent bought you breeches?" said Fanny.

"Breeches?" echoed Franny.

"Why?" She pulled first one, then the other boot from her leg. "Is that strange?"

"Of course, it's strange, dearest. It's very, very strange. Just like him." Fanny cocked her head as if thinking. "It's utterly strange, utterly odd…"

"Utterly romantic," sighed Franny.

Fanny grabbed Ivy's shoulders, hauled her to her feet, drew her close.

"It's completely and utterly romantic, dearest Ivy! Do you love him? Doe he love you? Is he mad with love for you?"

"Mad with love," sighed Franny.

"No!" Ivy protested. "Not at all!"

"But of course he is! Why would one man buy another man's fiancée breeches? It's unheard of! Christien Jeremie does not ride, does he dearest?"

"Does he ride?"

Ivy blinked, for in fact, she had never seen Christien astride a horse.

Fanny pushed her away. "You're simply playing with us, you tease, you! Imagine that, both de Lacey boys smitten with the same new girl! How romantic!"

"Utterly romantic," sighed Franny.

A clerk waited nearby, a small, round woman with a large red plume in her hair. She watched them with keen interest and Ivy cursed the turn of events. Scandal, Christien had said, fed on lesser things.

"Well, *I* am not romantic and it's not at all what you think. Penny Dreadful wears breeches." She fished the boots from the floor, turned them over in her hands. "I can wear these with skirts, you know…"

"Oh yes," said Fanny. "They look simply smashing with skirts."

"So smashing."

"And the land around the Hall is quite hilly, so boots are in order…"

"Oh, yes, darling. Boots are capital for rough country."

"Capital. Capital."

She could feel the expectant gazes of the sisters, the scandalous stare of the shop clerk.

"But I would hate to give anyone the wrong idea so, I think I must decline." She handed the boots back to the clerk, whose expression fell like a stone. "Thank you, though. They are very fine. I'm sure I could reach quite high in them."

She turned to the sisters.

"Is there a place we can go for dinner? I have some delicate questions I need to ask."

"Ah, dinner and delicate questions! What a delightfully delicious duo!"

Fanny took Ivy by one arm whilst Franny took the other and together they bustled out the door of *Annie's Apparel*, leaving the very fine boots behind with the scandal.

***

The airship glided over the landscape of the northern counties like a ghost, its propellers designed into silence by the Royal Academy Corps of Airships Engineers. It was not the *Royal Carolina*. No, she was a simple Royal Airship Frigate with the name *HMAS Carysfort*. She was a thirty-two guns Comus-class Corsair cruiser, one of the four that covered the *Carolina* and her canvas was black and gold. Against the darkening sky, she looked like an orca.

They leaned over the railing of the ship's forecastle, breathing in deeply the evening sky. It was cold but not raining, perfect for enjoying a gentlemanly smoke and a drink. But neither were smokers so they more than made up for it in drink and the conversation had wandered from the state of the German military to career paths, from the ethical dilemma of fox hunting to family dynamics. Of all the topics, that of family was the most unsettling.

"Well, yes, I suppose I will write May but honestly, I quite enjoy the company of Helene. Have you met Helene, Laury?"

"No, I'm afraid I have not."

"She is a fine girl, altogether fine." The Duke sighed, reached a long white hand far out over the railing as if trying to catch a cloud. "And I'm quite certain I could do worse. But after watching my parents bobble back and forth all these years, I would be quite satisfied never to marry at all."

"Women are a riddle that I am in no great hurry to solve." Sebastien raised a glass to his lips. "By the way, you still have one hovering over you like a black cloud."

"She's dead, the woman I gave this to," said the Duke, twisting the brass ring on his finger. "I met her at a brothel in Whitechapel. I treated her kindly and paid her well but I didn't kill her, Laury, I swear. I do hope she doesn't hold me responsible."

"If she did, I'd see her clearly and then I'd be forced to push you over the side of the airship. I'd get the gallows for sure."

"Grandmummie's justice all around…"

They were quiet for a while longer, content with the cold air and the warm Scotch.

"How much do you know about the Ghost Club, Laury?"

"I try to keep myself dissociated."

"This is a messy complicated business that Remy has got himself into, what with Williams and the boys and the girls and then there's all the chaos at Bedlam. Damn parliament, I say. Damn all politics, wot?" The Duke looked at him from the corner of his eye. "Are you certain you want to wade into it? You won't come out clean, you know. *If* you come out at all."

Sebastien sighed, studied the lights far below.

"The Club was my father's business and I've tried to steer as clear as I possibly could. I had hoped Christien would do as well. But in all honesty, it's my fault so it should be me who deals with them, not Christien."

"Remy's a clever fellow. He'll do what needs be done." The Duke sighed. "What do you think of his little woman?"

"I don't know a bloody thing about women so I'm afraid I can't comment." He lifted the Scotch to his lips. "If she were a horse, a dog or a spirit, it would be a different story."

"Have you never been to a brothel, Laury?"

"No, Eddy. Can't say as I have."

"Well then, I'm quite certain you will need to after Sandringham." The Duke grinned a lazy grin. "I must admit I find them very exciting places. They are like theatre— the singing and the drama, the laughter, the music. The sheer crush of humanity—men and women together searching desperately for the promise, the illusion, of love. Yes, I must admit I like them very much, indeed."

He turned his heavy-lidded eyes toward Sebastien, blinked slowly.

"Is that so terribly scandalous?"

"Well, for a man of your station, I would think so, yes."

"My entire life is a scandal, Laury. I fear there is nothing I can do that would be acceptable either to my family or to the British people."

"Responsibility is a bugger, Eddy."

The Duke sighed, leaned back over the railing. Lights were visible far below, from a city or large town. They were over Keilber Forest now, had spied glimpses of Hadrian's Wall, so likely it was the city of Carlisle. They were too far west for it to be Newcastle and the smell of many factories filled the air.

"You must meet my Erica, Laury. You will like her, no matter what Grandmummie says."

"Is she another one of your bawdyhouse women, Eddy?"

"No, no! She is the Club's Analytical Engine. *Engine for Rational Input, Computation and Analysis.* ERICA. I could watch the mathematicians work for hours, punching in the data, hearing her shuttles hum and fly. I believe I could truly be happy if I could work there for the rest of my life."

"And who would be king?"

"Why George, naturally. He would make a splendid king. The people would love him and leave me well enough alone. I would enjoy myself at the Club during the day and in brothels at night. What a blissful thought."

"Life is wondrous strange," said Sebastien.

The Duke raised his glass. "To Life."

He did the same. "To Life."

And they drank down the last of the fine Macallan Scotch, dropped the glasses over the side and took their conversations inside the cabin for the rest of the night.

***

The Cumbrian Steam Quarterly
September 24, 1888

Mr. Yancy Greengrass of 21 Grovenshire Road was driving home from a drink with his mates when something shattered on the top of his four-wheeled steamcar. According to witnesses, Mr. Greengrass shrieked and flung his arms in the air, leading the steamcar to swerve, teeter and ultimately tip over into the gutter of Penninewalk Way.

He was not injured but his nerves sustained a fright, and the steamcar itself sustained considerable damage. There is a call to look into the compatibility of four-wheeled steamcars and our northern roads. Of the object which caused the unfortunate Mr. Greengrass to swerve, there is no evidence, although police are suspecting debris from a German airship that was reported seen doing reconnaissance over the district.

The War Office has declined to comment, and police are continuing to investigate.

***

The *Lancaster Mews* was not quite pub, not quite tea room, and they picked for themselves a table with a view of the castle lights through the window. Ivy dined on chicken pie with leeks, Fanny on pork tart and beans, and Franny had tucked into something called "lasagna." It was apparently Italian and rather like a tomato casserole. Ivy watched with fascination as the woman put away the entire dish and still had room for gooseberry crumble.

There were very few patrons in the establishment, and so they sat drinking tea as Fanny held forth on fashion, footwear and, of course, family.

"And so, I simply had to tell the poor boy, Ninny, my dear—his name is Ninian, you know. Ninian Liddell. I called him 'Liddell Ninny!'" She sniffed. "So I said, Ninny dear boy, never would any good Helmsly-Wimpoll woman consent to giving her hand to such an union, so I bid him adieu."

She sniffed once more, and raised her tea. "He still pines for me, I fear. Such is the effect of a Helmsly-Wimpoll woman. I do drop him a letter from time to time, however. It is the socially acceptable thing to do…"

"More crumble!" called Franny.

"I'm quite certain that if he could find himself some occupation more suitable to my disposition, I would perhaps entertain the thought…"

Ivy smiled. "And what is his occupation, Fanny?"

"Mathematician. More precisely, a logarithm writer for the Newcastle A.E. Society."

"Well then, he must be very intelligent. Analytical Engines are all the rage in London."

"But darling," she sniffed. "There is simply no future in computing machines. No future at all."

"Hmm," said Ivy.

"So, what are these 'delicate' questions?" Fanny leaned forward, dropped a hand on Ivy's sleeve. "Have you reconsidered about your mother, dearest? Do you know what the Czech has been doing to her?"

Ivy took a deep breath. That night had been almost a week ago. It was hard to know what was real and what had been imagined. Sebastien had been gone for days now, and she realized that Lasingstoke without the Mad Lord and his pack of happy dogs was a quiet place indeed.

"We did go up last week, but I didn't get the chance to see her…"

"We, dearest?"

"Nasty Czech," said Franny.

Fanny looked Ivy in the eye. *"We, dearest darling?"*

"Sebastien and I," she said carefully. "We took a carriage to the Abbey, but we were called back before we could see her."

"Were you wearing your breeches?"

"No!" Ivy laughed. "No, I've not worn them yet. I…I've not been riding…"

Fanny sat back.

"There is more that you are not telling me, dearest. But never worry. I never pry into the affairs of the heart."

She sipped her tea, gazed out the dark window, and Franny happily began working on a second dish of crumble.

Ivy glanced around the tea shop. It was late, the place was almost empty and the questions had been eating at her like the crumble on Franny's plate. Her heart thudded in her chest.

"Fanny…"

"Dearest?"

"You know everything about the families in the district, yes?"

"Absolutely everything, dearest." Her eye flashed. "You haven't asked, have you?"

"Well, I tried…" Ivy sighed. "Honestly, I'm afraid to ask. Christien has gone back to London, Sebastien's gone off to Balmoral—"

Fanny slapped a hand on the table, causing the serving girl to jump and Franny to fling a spoonful of crumble into her tea.

"I knew it! I knew it! I was right, wasn't I, Franny?"

"You're always right, Fanny. About what?"

"Why, about the airships!" She leaned forward. "Edward Prince of Wales *did* bring his airship by Lasingstoke, didn't he dearest? Sebastien de Lacey's gone to Balmoral with Victoria!"

"With Victoria Imperatrix?"

Ivy sighed. *Honestly, why could she never keep her mouth shut?*

"Yes, Fanny. You are quite right. The de Lacey family is on friendly terms with the Royals."

"Mm*Hm,*" said Fanny with triumph. "A Helmsly-Wimpoll woman has a nose for such things."

And suddenly, she leaned in so close that she almost touched Ivy's forehead with her own.

"He killed her, dearest. Cut her into a hundred pieces in their very bed."

"Who did?" whispered Ivy. "Who killed her? Who 'her'?"

"Jane Penteny of Eccelston, dearest. Christien and Sebastien's mother. It was rumoured she was having a love affair with another man and in fact, that she was pregnant with his child. So Renaud Jacobe killed her with a hunting knife and cut out her womb and her heart. He was a member of the Ghost Club, you know. A ghost hunter. Drove him mad."

"Quite mad," said Franny.

"It's the curse, dearest. Renaud Jacobe killed his wife, because his father killed *his* wife, because his father killed **his** wife. No one wants to marry poor Sebastien because of the curse." She gazed out the window. "And of course, because he's mad…"

"That, that's terrible," said Ivy. "Is this common knowledge?"

"That he's mad? Of course it is, dearest."

"No, no, Fanny. The way his parents died. How do you know this?"

"My mother is friend to the cook of the Hasting family's farrier's aunt. I have it on good authority, and a Helmsly-Wimpoll woman is never wrong."

"Oh my…"

"But that's not all, dearest," said Fanny.

"There's more?" whimpered Ivy.

"The boys saw it all, they did. They had been fighting. Apparently, Sebastien Laurent was a terrible ruffian and little Christien Jeremie was running in to tattle and they saw their mother in a bloody bed, her heart in their father's hand."

Ivy felt sick inside.

"But there's *more,*" continued Fanny. "Sebastien Laurent, being the ruffian that he was, tried to stop his father. He rushed him, trying to hit him with his little fists. Renaud Jacobe would have absolutely none of it, but Sebastien Laurent wouldn't stop, so Renaud picked the boy up and threw him from the third-story window. Right out the window! He was dead to the world for weeks."

She sniffed, looked out at the castle. "He was at Lonsdale for a good year, I believe, before he even uttered a word. He was, what Franny? Ten? Eleven?"

"Ten."

Ivy sat, dazed and senseless. It was worse that she could have imagined. Worse than anyone could imagine. Fanny continued.

"When Renaud Jacobe came to his senses and saw what he'd done, he killed himself. Blew his head right off in front of young Christien Jeremie. It's quite amazing that your Christien is as sane as he is. Sweet, sweet boy."

"So sweet."

"At least," sniffed Fanny. "That's the tale from mother's friend's cook's farrier's aunt. But why wouldn't it be true? No one would lie about something like that, would they?"

They spent the rest of the evening, drinking tea, making small talk before heading back to *Annie's Apparel* just before closing, where Ivy Savage bought herself a pair of very fine boots in spite of the potential for scandal.

They left the ghosts of the castle for another visit

Chapter 20

Of Radioactivity, a Clockwork Pistol and Broken Spectacles in Church

"You what?"

Christien sighed. "I gave it to Ivy, sir, when I went up to visit."

Williams glared at him, tightened his grim mouth. "That was not a wise thing to do, boy. She is an impetuous girl."

"All I know is that I have not had a headache in days, sir. I am convinced that thing is detrimental to my health."

"And so you gave it to your fiancée?" came another voice, and they turned to see the figure of Dr. William Crookes, chemist and physicist with the Royal College of Chemistry. His hair and beard were snowy white and his eyes shone like stars from under bushy brows. "A radioactive device that gives you headaches and causes you to lose entire days at a time, you decide to give to the woman who will one day bear your children? What a colossal act of love and chivalry."

"Radioactive?" gasped Christien.

"Oh most certainly," said Crookes. "What did you think it was, my boy? A pocket watch?"

"I didn't know what it was, sir. All my attempts to discover its nature were met with deflection."

"As good a response as any, under the circumstances. It is a powder keg of atomical and parapsychical energy. I sincerely hope she does not explode."

"Explode?"

183

"A joke, boy. Sit down, sit down. You are far to pretty too fret."

They were in one of Crookes' many laboratories at his home in Kensington. It was a conservatory almost entirely made of paned glass and containing hundreds of species of tropical plants. There were scientific instruments amongst the greenery, pots of rich black earth spilled over magnifying lenses and microscopes. Small birds flitted between potted palms and telescopes. The greenhouse lab was humid and it smelled of oranges. As Christien sank into a wicker chair, he wished he could drip away like the condensation streaking down the windows.

"My concern," began Williams. "Is what will happen once Sebastien de Lacey sees the device at Lasingstoke? Will he know what it is? Will he take it to the War Office? God forbid it fall into the hands of Arvin Frankow!"

"*We* don't even know how to use it, Jack. Frankow will not either. No, I am by far the one most suited to uncover its atomical and parapsychical properties. My lab upstairs is equipped to both investigate and contain, if necessary."

Christien sat forward now. "But what does it do, sir? And if it is so damned important, why did my father leave it to me? Why not will it to the Club and be done with it?"

Both Williams and Crookes exchanged glances. Crookes leaned back in his chair.

"Your father hoarded his treasures like a dragon hordes gold. From what we can gather, it was one of three lockets manufactured two hundred years ago, by some damned metallurgical Frenchie hired by Ashmole. You've heard of Elias Ashmole, certainly?"

"No, sir, I have not."

Crookes sighed now. "Jack, you have been terrible lax in this boy's education. How could he possibly be voted in for Club membership when he has absolutely no understanding of who we are or what we do?"

"He's a de Lacey, Bookie. His pedigree speaks for itself."

"True enough. Look him up, boy. Elias Ashmole. He was a queer duck but brilliant. *Ahem.* To continue, the lockets were apparently constructed based on designs by the Danish alchemist, Tycho Brahe.

Have you heard of *him*, boy? No? Oh dear me, dear me. They have names, you know, these lockets, although where the names come from is still a mystery."

"Names?"

"Ghostlight, Arclight and Lostlight, or the French equivalent. Yours was Ghostlight."

"Ghostlight…"

"At any rate, they were intended to be a channel for angelic forces to enter and exit our world, a sort of 'ghost door' to other worlds and planes of existence that we are only beginning to understand now. All my work in chemistry and physics springs from this fundamental hypothesis. You see, I firmly believe that solid matter is neither solid nor matter, but rather collections of particles moving at great speeds through the vacuum of space, and that we are little more that a conglomeration of universal forces held together every second of every day by every word that proceeds from the mouth of God… "

He paused, eyes darting from Christien to Williams and back again. He looked down at his tea, sipped a moment before continuing.

"Ahem. Needless to say, only Ghostlight is left and your father used it to hunt and dispatch ghosts."

Christien frowned. He did not know what to make of any of this, especially in light of the incident at Seventh.

"Is that what Sebastien thinks he's doing up North?"

"Likely a form of it," said Crookes. "Although without the locket, I'm not entirely sure what he's able to accomplish."

Williams leaned forward. "And you said your father left you the locket, Remy?"

"Yes, sir."

"Are you sure about that, boy?"

"Well, yes."

"And how *exactly* did he leave it to you?"

"He…I…" Christien blinked, blinked some more. "No. He didn't. I found it in his room when I was twelve. How odd. I'd completely forgotten…"

He cocked his head and sank back in the wicker chair, a furrow appearing between his brows.

"After they died, Rupert and Cookie kept the room locked up. I'd never been allowed in, not ever, but Cookie would go in once a month to dust. One day, I slipped in behind her. She didn't know I was there and when she left, I spent the entire day going through my things…"

"Your things?"

"*His* things…" Christien struggled to recall as the memories rippled like water. "I found the locket in a chest of drawers. It had turned the inside solid gold. I've had it ever since."

"Did you start wearing it then, Remy?" asked Williams.

"No, not then. I kept it, however. Went through several lead boxes to keep it contained." He raised his brows. "You should see the wall of little gold boxes I have at Hollbrook. Worth more than the bloody house…"

The two men glanced at each other. Williams cleared his throat.

"When *did* you start wearing it?"

"On and off for years but regularly last spring."

"March? When you started with Bondie and I?"

"Yes, sir. The dissections were trying on my nerve and for some reason, the abortions reminded me of my mother."

"Abortions?" asked Crookes but Williams waved a hand, dismissively.

"And that's when your headaches started, am I correct?"

Christien nodded now but distractedly, in a world of his own.

"It could be a form of atomical poisoning," offered Crookes. "The parapsychical waves these elements give off are quite remarkable."

"No no, it's working," said Williams and he leaned forward now. "Do you hear anything, Remy? When the headaches come, do you hear voices?"

"Yes…"

"What do they say?"

"I don't remember…"

Williams turned to his fellow.

"It could be angels."

"Quite so. This the proof we've always wanted, Jackie. What the Club was founded to discover."

"Indeed. We all know it to be true, the existence of the spirit world, but to prove it using scientific methods—"

"To *consistently* prove it, Jackie. To remove all skepticism and doubt." Crookes leaned back in his chair. "These are trying times, Jackie. God is testing us. We will not let Him down."

Christien looked up. "So is there a key, sirs, and if not, why have I not been able to open it?"

The two men glanced at each other once again.

"There is a key, Christien," said Crookes.

"And Bastien holds it, then?" said Christien. "I have never seen him with a key so small. Does he know how to use it? Would he?"

"Your brother does not *hold* the key, my boy," said Crookes and he set his cup quietly down on a glass table. "Your brother *is* the key."

***

He turned up the gaslight only enough to see what he was doing, for what he was doing was best done in the shadow. The pistol was a fine musket-bore walnut and steel officer's piece, with carved ivory laid in the grip. It had been his father's weapon, commissioned by Albert's favourite gunsmith, William Westley Richards. It had three barrels that rotated due to very delicate interlocking clockwork gears. It could fire three balls in sequence although he rarely needed to use more than one. He was a crackerjack shot. It was a marvelous pistol.

It had taken his father's head off in one go.

The dogs began to thump their tails and he looked up. In a woolen smoking jacket, Rupert was silhouetted in the light from the doorway.

"Laury."

Sebastien turned his back and continued loading the pistol.

"Hello, Uncle. Sorry to wake you."

"You didn't and you're not. How's Old Vic?"

"Terrifying."

"Good to know." He could feel Rupert's eyes on him, knew instinctively what the man was thinking. "Are three bullets enough to take down London's Ripper?"

"I don't mean to be taking down London's Ripper. Not tonight, at any rate."

"Oh God, Laury. How much are you planning on dropping then? I can spare you two thousand, no more."

"It depends." He slipped the pistol in his belt and moved around the desk toward the wall with the clippings. "I may have to kill the wife too."

"Lovely. Wonderful. That's very economical of you. Saves the estate a fair bit of money if you can do that for me."

Sebastien sighed. Now he did look up at the silhouette in the doorway. "Where is Christien staying?"

"He's gone, Laury. Left the same day he came."

"Why?"

"Didn't ask."

"And the boy, Davis?"

"Right as rain. Doesn't remember a bloody thing."

He nodded, pulled several clippings and a set of addresses from the wall and studied them. Milnethorpe. Thankfully not far. There were still so many names.

"Right. I should be back by morning."

"Be careful, Laury. Be careful and be right."

"I will." He turned back to the dogs and raised a finger. "Stay."

They lowered their heads onto the carpets, all wagging ceased.

And he slipped past his uncle and out the door, in the direction of the stables.

***

The sisters Helmsly-Wimpoll dropped her off and headed back to Over Milling. It was very late and she met no servants as she rushed up the stairs and into Davis' room. There was a note saying he was at Fourth, taking tea with Lottie. He was obviously well enough to travel and she silently gave thanks to God and to Sebastien. Of the two, she didn't know who was the most confounding.

Her own room was cold, but she was colder, so she started a fire and curled up on a wingback chair. *The Ghost Club* was sitting on the arm as if waiting for her. It had been sheer chance that she had chosen this one. She could have just as likely pulled something on dog training or horsemanship or the history of the Royals at Kensington.

She opened the page.

Be Born. Work. Die. Be Born.

Herein is a recounting of the Charter Members of The Ghost Club 1862, a Gentlemen's Society dedicated to the serious and impartial investigation, study and discussion of subjects not fully understood or yet accepted by science, especially psychical and parapsychical phenomenon. All members are such until they are disbarred. Death of any member is no requisite for removal from list, and therefore all will continue being recounted on roster along with their living compatriots. If they do not put in an appearance by November 2 of each year, they will be listed as inactive.

Honourable mention to Francis Albert Augustus Charles Emannuel, Prince Consort of the United Kingdom, founder and departed member, 1861

Albert Edward of Saxe-Coburg and Gotha, Prince of Wales

Benson, E.W.; Archbishop of Canterbury, Kent

Balfour, A.; First Earl of Balfour

Barrett, W.; FRS, FRSE, FRDS

Crookes, W.; OM, FRS

de Lacey ,R.; Sixth Baron of Lasingstoke

Dickens, C.; Author and Humanitarian

Eastwicke, E.; Earl of Dunwarden

Frankow, A.; MMBS, FRCS, MRCP

Gordon, A.; Hon. Lieutenant-Governor of New Brunswick

And the list went on and on. She found herself looking for and finding *Williams, J, MRCS MB MD*, just as Sebastien had said, and for some reason, it filled her with dread.

He was a member of the Ghost Club, you know. A ghost hunter. Drove him mad.

What in the world was a ghost hunter? And how would such a profession drive one mad? She pressed on.

It was like a census, she realized, a book of names and dates and occupations. Some of the names were familiar, belonging to politicians, aristocrats and highly ranked clergymen and two chapters alone were devoted to the roster of membership, living and dead. The next several chapters included case studies of hauntings in churches, castles, halls, museums, pubs, inns and even royal residences.

Mediums, spiritualists, Egyptian magic, second sight, poltergeists. She read these terms with growing alarm. What had caused Davis's strange injuries? Her brother had no recollection of even entering Seventh, so he had no idea as to what or whom had been his attacker. And why was Seventh a forbidden house? What was hiding in there that should cause such horrors?

What had Frankow done to him?

She remembered the cold, the ice, the phrases in Latin. She remembered the face of her brother, how Rupert had carried him like a dead man, how Sebastien had shown up with the same injuries the very morning her brother had lost his. *Not Seventh*, Lottie had said. *Never Seventh.*

What in the world was going on at Seventh?

She closed up the book and stared out the window. It was growing dark but she knew the roads well enough now. She rose to her feet, stepped out of her skirts and into the breeches Sebastien had bought for her. They fit like a glove and she marveled at the freedom that they allowed. She pulled her new boots up to her knees, carefully tied the laces. Tucked her dark hair under the bowler, threw on her brother's woolen peacoat and dashed down the stair toward the stables.

She found tack and carried it out to the pasture. Rue, the bay mare let out a nicker as Ivy tacked her up in the last of the evening's light. The other horses watched as she led the mare out of the paddock, slipped her foot in the stirrup and in a heartbeat she was up. It was a strange sensation, breeches, and she felt remarkably free and unfettered.

Somehow, she knew the sisters Helsmly-Wimpoll would approve.

There was only a crescent moon now and it seemed odd that she had barely been here a fortnight. She couldn't remember much of her old life in London. But then again, her life had mostly been her mother and with her mother gone, there was simply nothing to fill the gap. Her old life had been one of duty and responsibility and mundane chores. She did not know whom she would have been if life had gone differently and Tobias had lived.

The Penny Dreadful serials were her life, she realized this too, the life she wished she had. Penny was bright, clever and independent. Ivy was bright, clever, but alas, in the real world, independence for a woman was not a thing freely given nor easily won.

She needed to fight for it.

She wheeled the mare down the drive toward the chapel and the house called Seventh. Neither was visible from the road, but she had passed them so many times on the way to Over Milling, Lonsdale and Lancaster. And of course, there had been *that* night. *That* night would be etched in her memory forever.

It was very dark but she had never been afraid of the dark. It was night but she had never been afraid of the night. In fact, she had never been afraid of anything at all. She was the daughter of a crimes investigator, she told herself as she rode. She sat at the feet of men who put their lives on the line every day and every night. From their tales, it wasn't the dark to be feared, or the night, but the men and women who inhabited it, used it like a cloak to cover their nefarious deeds. Someone had tried to kill her brother and somehow, Sebastien had known. She could never rest knowing that there was a real life mystery living—or dying— right here at Seventh.

When she reached the northwest corner of the estate, she dismounted and led the mare off the road toward the church. She could see the graveyard stones and statues but little other than trees blowing in the wind. When she reached the steps, she stood for a moment patting the horse's long nose and steadying her racing heart. With a deep breath, she headed up, pulled the door open and stepped inside.

It was as dark as a tomb but suddenly, there was a glow all around her like a halo in a Renaissance painting.

Beneath the first button of her waistcoat, the locket was glowing.

Science, spiritualism and alchemy, Christien had said. It certainly seemed to be living up to its reputation.

It was deadly quiet as she moved slowly along the pews. She wasn't entirely sure what she was even doing but she felt sure there would be clues somewhere in this little church. She saw the glint of moonlight in the presbytery, spied a large brass candelabrum on the step. She headed toward it but paused as something crunched under her boot.

She glanced down. To her relief, she saw matches, along with broken glass and something that looked like chalk. She scooped the matches, lit the candelabrum and instantly, the chapel glowed with gleaming wood. She dropped her eyes to the floor. Sebastien's large, black-rimmed spectacles lay broken under her very fine boot. She bent to pick them up, slipped them into her waistcoat. There was chalk and candle wax and something else smeared across the stone. Once again, she had the distinct impression it was not mud.

She turned the candelabrum in a wide arc, feeling her chest tighten at the sight. Strange symbols, some written in chalk, others in what she knew to be blood, on the walls, pews, windows and floor.

The thin glow of light from the locket was pulsing now, like a heartbeat.

Yes, very much like a heartbeat and she remembered the words of Fanny in the Lancaster Mews.

He killed her with a hunting knife, cut out her heart and her womb

Slowly, the odd rings on the locket began to spin. Very slowly at first around the glass ball in the center and she could see the occasional spark thrown off from their orbit. She had never wound the thing, had never used a key to keep the tiny gears moving. It was as if they worked of their own accord.

They saw their mother in a bloody bed, her heart in their father's hand.

She began to shake. She had to leave, that was all she knew. She had to leave this God-forsaken place. She blew out the candles and headed once again, through the pews in near darkness. She pushed open the door, breathed in the cold night air, grateful that the mare was still there and very much alive.

He was a member of the Ghost Club, you know. A ghost hunter. Drove him mad.

As all light and movement from the locket died away, she tucked it into her waistcoat and leaned on the door of the church, waiting for her own heartbeat to return to normal. She feared it never would.

Rue made a rumbling noise and Ivy looked up. Far off on the road, heading away from the Hall toward Over Milling, was a gray horse and she knew without a doubt that the Mad Lord of Lasingstoke was back.

She waited until he was quite a long way off, before mounting up the little bay mare and following.

***

"Oh, bugger," groaned Penny as she waited in the dark. Her trap had been set for hours and still, not a trace of either von Freud, Durand or Dunn, her three suspects. Her horse, Marlborough nickered softly and she stroked his long nose. "Just a little longer, Marley, I'm sure of it."

And when she felt herself about to nod off, she spied a masked man riding toward the Castle on a steel gray horse. She couldn't see much, nor make out whether he was entirely human, so she slipped from the shadows cast by the wall to follow."

Chapter 21

Of Trained Horses, Screwsmanship and a Disconcerting Situation

The road was dirt for the majority of the ride and he was grateful. Cobbles and stone were hard on a horse's feet, even with iron shoes. Dirt and grass were far more forgiving.

It was after ten and the streets were for the most part dark but street lamps burned at intersections and along high-end avenues. Where Sebastien was going was affluent. There was money in Milnethorpe now.

Up until recently, the town of Milnethorpe had been precisely that—a town. But in the last decade since the explosion in demand for steamcars, factories had sprung up like mushrooms on a decaying tree trunk. In the moonlight, he could see smoke from the stacks that skirted the town, and lights from factories that never slept. Shifts worked round the clock to make the cogs and gears for the car companies. Both Imperial Steam and Bentley United had plants here.

Down Coggins Rd and a left at Dorchester. These were fine houses now, with even finer farther along and the road had become one of cobbles, not dirt. Hooves made a clopping sound on the stone. There were many steamcars puffing along the streets, but there were a few horse-drawn coaches as well, so a man on horseback was not a sore thumb. There were no pubs in this neighbourhood; coffee shops were all the rage, where good British gentlemen went to read the news and argue politics and discuss wars and rumours of wars and smoke. He spied one on a corner, where steamcars and carriages were parked alongside hitched horses. It was perfect.

He dismounted, led Gus up to a post and raised a finger.

"Stay."

He pulled the address from his coat pocket.

1011-A West Pinchon Street.

Quietly, he moved to the window, cast a quick glance inside. Men, smoke, cards, coffee. Stacks of newspapers and broadsheets and bulletins. These gentlemen loved their issues. He was about to leave when he did a double take—Easterton Fredrick Crumb. The villain in question, dressed entirely in black, drinking coffee and being consoled by a veritable stable of gents.

Such a normal sight. Such an abominable man.

The glass at the window began to frost.

"No," he growled. "Not yet."

And he set off down the walk on Dorchester. He had only gone three blocks and had not met another soul on the street. Of course he wouldn't. At this hour, all respectable folk were settled down for the night. With Crumb in the coffee house, it would serve him well, but his wife presented another matter entirely. He hated frightening women. They were by far the fairer sex but they killed too, as often and savagely as men.

He was being followed.

He had known it for a while. The rider on the dark horse had not known to keep to the grass to muffle the sound of the hooves. He did not know to follow at inconsistent distances, or how to remove the bowler and exchange it for another hat by way of disguise. And when he'd dismounted, he'd tied his nag at the same shop. No, this was an inexperienced thief, most likely hoping to roll him for his coin or his coat.

He could see the turn for Pinchon Street and the grove of trees that served as a boulevard. It cast very dark shadows across the already dark street. Perfect for cover. He continued to walk straight into that blackness, then ducked into the mews between the houses and pulled the pistol to wait.

Step, step, step, step.

A light step. Not a big man by any means. Step, step, step, step. Just as the fellow was about to pass by, he lunged out of the mews, snagged the man's arm and forced it up between the shoulder blades. Without slowing, he swung the man face first into the brick of the wall and brought the pistol up to the back of the head.

Cocked the hammer and leaned in close.

"Why are you following me, sir? Answer me true, or I'll shoot your head off."

"I'm sorry, sir. So, so sorry…"

It was a woman's voice. Most unexpected.

"Miss Savage?"

"Yes, sir. Please don't shoot my head off!"

He stepped back, lowered the pistol, utterly confounded.

"Miss Savage, what? Why?"

"May I turn around, sir?"

"Of course, woman! Turn, turn."

Slowly, she did and he could make out her face in the darkness, strands of her dark hair escaping from under the bowler. He stepped back again, and yet again. Peacoat, breeches, riding boots, derby. She had entirely passed for a young man.

Except for the fact that her breasts were glowing.

"I…I saw you riding," she moaned. "I was so very curious. Everything has been so strange, with you and Seventh and the sisters Helmsly-Wimpoll. And I know it was wrong…"

She looked about to cry.

"Wrong?" he snapped. "It was bloody dangerous! I could have shot you just now!"

"I know," she wailed. "I'm so sorry…"

And suddenly, the tears spilled from her lashes. She bit her lip and turned away, hugging her ribs. He waited a moment, confounded even more. Her glowing breasts were a puzzle, but now, a strange voice was beginning to whisper in his ear. He didn't understand any of it. It was like something he should know, a scrap of memory from childhood but he needed to push it from his mind. He had one thing and one thing alone to do tonight.

"Listen," he said. "Things are about to get a little sketchy. I need you to stay here. Do you understand, Miss Savage? Ivy? Please, will you stay here?"

She sniffed some more before turning around. Her eyes were wet and shining like an ocean and she tried to smile. Dash it all if his knees didn't suddenly feel weak.

"No, sir," she sniffed. "I'll not stay here. I'm coming with you."

"No, Miss Savage, you most certainly are not."

"Yes, I am. And if you refuse, I'll..." She looked around the mews. Sniffed. "I'll..." She looked back at him, raised her chin. "I'll scream."

She was serious, he could tell but it was difficult to look anywhere but her breasts. The whispers were becoming a voice inside his head. It was a puzzle.

He held up one finger. "If you come, you will say nothing. You will do nothing. Do you understand?"

"Yes, I most certainly do."

"And when I say, look away, you will look away. Understood?"

"I will most certainly look away."

"Right." And without any further discussion, he grabbed her wrist and dragged her out of the mews and back out into the street.

***

"Alexander Dunn, I apprehend you, Sir, in the name of the Crown!"

She pulled the mask from the rogue's face and let out a startled yelp.

It was none other than Alexandre Gavriel St. Jacques Lord Durand. They were one and the same man.

"That is a lovely pearl necklace you are wearing, Penny," he said.

He smiled, raised his pistol and that was the last Penny remembered for some time.

***

They stared up the steps of 1011-A West Pinchon Street.

Gaslight lit the front door and stair. He had released her wrist earlier when she had complained that his grip was causing her discomfort and he cursed his weakness. Rupert had been right. Women were a complicated, messy business. Better to stay disentangled. This one was like a bloody thornbush, always catching on things and drawing blood.

And the damned voices were singing a very old song in his head.

"What are we waiting for?" she whispered. She smelled good, like rose hips and fine leather. A most unusual mix.

"The frost," he whispered back.

"Ah," she said and thankfully nothing more.

There was no frost. There was no cold. It was confounding. Perhaps the woman had thrown them off. Perhaps the singing was a problem. Perhaps there was more that he needed to do.

He turned to her and raised a finger.

"Stay," he said and proceeded up the steps to rap on the doorknocker. He could feel her warmth on his back. Disobedient she was. Like Tag. Disobedient and needy.

There was no cold, only the singing of a very old song. He rapped again. Nothing. No answer. No cold. He reached for the knob. Locked. Turned back to the woman.

"Look away."

To her credit, she did. He fished from his pocket a file and pick, bent low and set to work.

"Oh look! The Mad Lord de Lacey is a regular screwsman!"

"Louder please," he muttered. "I don't think they heard you back in Milling."

"You are truly Alexander Dunn, sir, Penny's favourite jewel thief. Do you have a clockwork heart?"

There was a click and he straightened, turned the knob with his hand. The door opened with a very loud creak and he cursed the bane of rusty hinges.

She leaned into him.

"Louder please," she purred. "I don't think they heard you back in Milling."

He began revisiting his decision not to shoot her.

The house was empty. It was well furnished and comfortable and he thanked God once again that there were no automatons. It was an older home, with low ceilings and plank floors. Imitation Turkish rugs were everywhere.

"What are we looking for?" she asked in a whisper that could not hide her grin. Damned creature thought this was a game.

"Henbane," he answered. "He's poisoned his mother- and sister-in-law. I need to prove it."

"Are you a police detective, sir?

"If I were, I wouldn't need to be skulking around in the dark, now would I? Hush, I need to ask."

"Ask who? There's no one home."

Yes, seriously revisiting his decision not to shoot her.

He closed his eyes, turned his palms to the ceiling and the cold descended like a blanket over the room.

He could feel them, their voices like whispers in the night, needed to sift them out to find the ones who wanted him here. But the singing was a distraction. It was most definitely coming from the woman, but not *from* her and it didn't belong here on this street in Milnethrorpe. It was the same voice that had summoned him from the Chapel on the day the airships had arrived. It was like an echo of something he should know, something from a lifetime ago, from a lifetime, from his childhood...

The voice of angels...

"Oh," he heard Ivy say and slowly he turned to look at her.

For the first time since he'd met her, there was a shadow flickering in and around Miss Ivy Savage.

"What the devil...?"

She frowned, reached under her collar and pulled it out to dangle it from her fingers. It was spinning quietly, flashing light in all directions.

He approached her. "Where in heaven or on earth did you get that?"

"Christien gave it to me..."

He raised his hands toward the locket. It began to move at the end of the chain as if pulled by some great magnet, whirring and humming like clockwork. He cupped it in his palms, not touching it but keeping it taut at the end of its chain by some unseen force.

"What are you doing, sir?"

The voice of angels...

He could barely hear her. The spinning was calling, locking, binding."

"Sebastien, your eyes are changing colour..."

199

"Voces," he whispered, engrossed. *"Voces angelorum...* the voice of angels..."

In the sitting room, the air began to thicken like mist or fog and the casings of the doors and windows had grown inexplicably white.

He turned now toward the middle of the room where the air was so frosty that it seemed to be taking shape. He followed it, moving stiffly and leaving her standing in the foyer. For its part, the locket merely continued to whir and hum.

"Here?" he glanced around as ice began to crawl up the walls, creating a plume with every breath. *"Hic? Ostendite mihi..."*

He looked around at the writing desks and bookshelves and settees. He began to open drawers and dressers, ran his hands along the surfaces of the desks. He felt Ivy watching him.

"Why are you speaking in Latin, sir? And what in the name of heaven is going on with this locket?"

It was still spinning at the end of its chain, now hovering at a right angle to the floor. Her eyes were wide and they darted from him to the locket and then back again.

"What sort of detective are you?"

"Servio ab arbitrio maiestatis eius."

"English?"

He blinked, trying to reenter the conversation.

"I slouží u potěšení z jejího majestátu."

"What?"

Damn. He shook his head. The locket was throwing him off.

"I serve at the pleasure of Her Majesty."

"Her Majesty?" She stepped into the room. "You mean Queen Victoria?"

"The very one. Listen, we both have far too many questions. Right now, we need to find that henbane and get this done."

"But I don't understand!"

The frost had not moved and he began lifting cushions from the settees, running his fingers between the seats. "I will explain what I can later. Please, either help me find the accursed stash or go back to the corner where you left your horse. One or the other."

Out of the corner of his eye, he could see her chin rise, just a little.

"Very well. What sort of henbane?"

"What do you mean?"

"Well, what form? Liquid, powder, leaf, roll? It would help to know."

He frowned. It was a good question. "I don't have an inkling, Miss Savage."

"Well then, I – I would think the kitchens, unless..."

She put her hands on her hips and in the locket's glowing light, he noticed that the breeches fit her rather well. In fact, he thought he had never seen a woman look so very good.

He swallowed.

"Unless..." She bit her lip, thinking.

"Unless? Unless what?" *Damn her.* She and her accursed locket were a distraction.

"Wait!" she exclaimed and stomped into the room toward him, taking great pains to make as much noise with her boots as she could.

"Hush," he hissed. "You'll wake the dead."

"I thought that was your job. Ah *ha!*" And she beamed at him. "Did you hear that?"

"In fact I did. Do it again."

She stomped back. Over one area of the floor, the thump of her boots produced a rather hollow sound. She turned and smiled again and the locket flashed light across her face.

"Sometimes I forget that I am the daughter of a Metropolitan Police Crimes Investigator!"

He began to shoulder the settees out of the way. The carpets next, and he grabbed one end and rolled. It was stiff and bristly under his fingers and wrinkled his nose at the cheapness of the fibre. "Turkish" carpets made in Birmingham, most likely. Or Italy.

She hovered over him as he dropped to hands and knees. He could feel the locket purring now as though it were a part of him—his heart, maybe or his soul and he wondered how Christien could have come into possession of such a thing. He ran his fingers along the floorboards. Old wood, worn smooth by time. He could feel the knots, the nails, and finally, one loose board. He pried it up and the cold hit him like a fist.

"Oh," she yelped. "Snowflakes! Sebastien, this locket is making snowflakes!"

Sure enough, it was snowing in the sitting room of Easterton Frederick Crumb.

He flattened now onto his belly, reached his arm down into the crevasse between the boards. His fingers brushed tins and boxes, letters and papers. He worried if this might be a simple hiding place for family treasures but he was committed now so he pulled up a frosty tin and passed it over to Ivy.

"Oh my," she gasped. She tossed it from hand to hand, the locket flashing light like a beacon. "What on earth is going on?"

"On earth as it is in heaven," he said. "Open it, please. Open it."

She did, smelled the contents. "Mm-hm. Henbane."

He waited.

He looked about the room, waited.

He sighed, frowned, shook his head. "*Non est completum...*"

"English, please."

"Ah, it's not finished. We're not done here..." It was like the holding of a breath and he lay back down on the floor, stretched his arm under the boards once again. He closed his eyes.

"*Adiuvate me,*" he whispered. "*Auxiliate me cum hoc...*"

One of the boxes crackled under his fingertips, so he pulled it up to sit cross-legged on the floor. He could feel her lean over his shoulder, felt both the cold of the locket and the warmth of her breath on his neck. It was an unusual experience for him and a distracting one.

"What's in there?" she breathed.

"Proof..."

He blew his own warm breath across the latch, saw it thaw and crack as he lifted the lid. A pearl necklace and a cameo brooch. His breath frosted in front of him as he released it.

"Sebastien, what does that mean?"

"Guilty."

Suddenly, there was the rattle of a key in the lock, and the loud creak of a front door opening as Easterton Frederick Crumb and his wife returned home for the night.

Chapter 22

Of Murder, Mayhem and a Revisiting of the Four-Wheel/Six-Wheel Controversy

Ivy's heart leapt into her throat.

The front door of 1011-A West Pinchon Street swung open and she could hear two sets of boots stomp into the hall. She dared not budge while Sebastien remained crosslegged on the floor beneath her. She felt his shoulder move, an arm draw back, but the movement was so smooth, so quiet, that she wondered if in fact, she imagined it.

"Oy, Celia, what's this, then? You stupid haybag! D'you leave a window 'jar?"

"'ere, Eastie. I didn't leave no window 'jar! What's all this ice?"

And the large shape of Easterton Frederick Crumb reached to turn up the gas.

Ivy had never been so afraid in her life.

Gaslight hissed, and Crumb and his wife literally leaped back at the sight of two strange people in their disassembled sitting room. First, they leaped then they slipped as ice lay in slicks across the floor. And before she knew it, Sebastien was on his feet, tucking her behind him with a sweep of his arm.

Finally, she could see the man whose estate they had just jumped. In his late thirties, with dark hair and a pockmarked face, it was clear Crumb was trying for a handlebar moustache but seemed to have purchased the incorrect wax. He was very swift in regaining his balance however and with one hand on the frame of the doorway, he brought a pistol to bear with the other.

"Who the bloody hell are you?" he growled, and cocked the hammer. His wife, a small, wiry creature, peered out from behind his back.

Around Ivy's neck, the locket was spinning and bit by bit, snowflakes were being replaced by sparks.

Sebastien had grown very still now and the cold began to crackle in the sitting room.

"Easterton Frederick Crumb?"

"Answer me question, mate. Or I'll pop ya between yer eyes. You first, then yer missus."

"I have a message for you from Clarissa Agatha Polkey and Sarah Ann Polkey."

His left hand moved slowly, dangling the pearls and cameo from his fingers.

Mrs. Crumb let out a wail. Mr. Crumb's face crunched up in fury.

"You got no right being in my house. You got no right goin' through my gear." He wagged his piece. "Drop 'em and get out now, er I'll pop you, I swear!"

"Ivy," said Sebastien in a very low voice. "Look away now."

Unfortunately, she was unable to comply. The locket had begun spinning in the opposite direction.

Ivy watched Sebastien slowly throw a look over his shoulder and just as slowly, looked back at the man holding the pistol.

"You are forgiven and the Crown has been served. May God have mercy on your soul."

And in one swift motion, he swung his right arm up and pistol fire shattered the frost like ice on a lake. It had happened so quickly, and Ivy ducked instinctively, deafened by the blast but she could have sworn there had been two shots not one. There was the sound of iron clattering to the floor and Celia Crumb began to scream.

Hands over her ears, Ivy looked up. There was a very large, elaborate pistol in de Lacey's outstretched hand, smoke curling from it like a serpent. Standing in the eerie gaslight of the foyer, Crumb wavered a bit as he stood, a small dark hole in the centre of his forehead. He wavered some more and crumpled to the planks.

Ivy could not breathe. She could not move. She could not think.

"Murder!" cried Celia.

The gears rotated the chamber and the pistol angled several degrees towards her.

"Hush, woman. You may yet live to see the morning."

Her cries faded to whimpers and she dropped to her knees.

"Sebastien, what are you doing?" Ivy whispered. She had no voice; it had frozen inside like her blood.

"I said look away." He was fixed on the woman. "What is your involvement in the murder of your mother and your sister?"

"I don't know nothing about that! I don't know nothing of what he does, my Eastie. He's a hard man. He has wants. He has needs. I'm just his woman, and he does what he pleases! Don't kill me, good sir! Please don't kill me."

He looked over his shoulder again.

He sees things no one else sees. He hears things no one else hears.

There was nothing over his shoulder. There was no one else in the room.

A splitting of the mind.

He looked back to Celia Crumb, his expression as dead as her late husband.

Whom he had just murdered.

The Mad Lord de Lacey.

And the locket was spinning merrily.

"Sebastien, stop."

"Celia Bess Polkey Crumb?"

The woman wailed loudly, shrunk back into the stairs.

"Sebastien, *no.*"

"You are forgiven and the Crown is served. May God have mercy on your so—"

Ivy leaped forward, grabbing the pistol as it fired and Celia screamed once again. A sudden wind picked up, throwing ice around the room like daggers. There was a sound as well—the wail of a hundred voices and Ivy clapped her hands over her ears once again. The wind whipped her hair and clothing, buffeting them all as if in a storm and arcs of electricity leapt from the locket to every metallic surface in the room. Celia saw her chance and bolted across the slick floor for the door.

"Damnation, Ivy!" Sebastien shouted over the gale. "You've left me with only one shot!"

He scrambled after her and out into the night with Ivy at his heels. Celia was already onto the street with her screams of 'Murder', waving at a set of approaching headlights. It was a steamcab, ferrying drunken passengers to their homes on affluent Pinchon Street.

"Don't shoot her," Ivy begged, her voice raised to be heard over the wailing of the winds. "Please, Sebastien. Please, don't shoot her!"

He stared at her for a long moment, the locket flashing eerie lights across his face, before he raised the pistol and took aim across the street.

"Please."

He pulled the trigger.

There was the roar of the pistol, the pop of a tire and squeal of brakes as the cab began to fishtail over the cobbled road. Celia had the time to shriek one last time before cab struck her and the impact sent her tumbling onto the stone. Screams could be heard from within when like a leaf on the wind, the steam cab flipped over onto its side and continued down the road before slowing spinning to a halt.

Four wheels, thought Ivy with a strange detached sort of thought. Much more tippy than six.

The gale within the house died as suddenly as it came and Sebastien released a deep breath, lowered the pistol to his side. He stood as still as stone, face pale in the gaslight, watching it all from the steps.

For its part, the locket lay silent now, a simple adornment around her neck.

Ivy stared at him. He was mad, that much was certain. He was a murderer and that a surprise. She was a good girl, the daughter of a crimes investigator with the Metropolitan Police. She knew she should run back to the coffeehouse, grab the mare and flee now, before he had the mind to kill her. She knew she should take her mother from Lonsdale and return to Christien and some semblance of normal life in London. She knew she should turn the Mad Lord in and leave him to his fate. She was certain it would be far worse than Lonsdale Abbey.

But he hadn't shot the woman, she realized. He hadn't shot her.

People poured out of the cab, shouting and wailing and running to the side of the downed Celia Crumb.

Against everything good and sensible and normal and respectable,

Ivy grabbed his hand and ran.

***

They ran for what seemed like hours but Ivy knew it was only a matter of minutes before the sound of a siren pierced the night sky. Then she slowed, reckoning that a couple walking from the scene of a murder might look less suspicious than a couple fleeing. Sebastien was unresponsive but, like her dear mother, he slowed when she pulled him back and walked beside her. She was certain that at this moment, his eyes saw nothing.

The police vehicle, a squat wide six-wheeler, barreled along Dorchester, its steam engine straining the need for ballast against the need for speed. She watched it pass, watched the red-tinted lanterns swing off into the distance. They neared the coffeeshop and she could make out patrons, milling outside the door speculating about the mayhem down the street.

Gus nickered at their approach and left his post and Ivy marveled that the horse hadn't been tied. He had stayed where he had been all night. Her own mare looked over at them but, being tied, could not move.

"You shouldn't tie her," said Sebastien, his first words since the house. His eyes were glassy still and of indeterminate colour. "She's well trained and she'll come when you whistle in case you need to make a getaway of it."

"Please don't say anything," she whispered, gathering the rein from the post. "We need to look as if we're just leaving the coffeehouse and returning to our neat little rowhouse by the factory."

"I would never live in a neat little rowhouse by a factory."

"You, sir, are a madman and a murderer," she hissed under her breath.

"Louder please. I don't think they heard you back in Milling."

In fact, no one was paying them any mind. A second police car barreled down the street, its six wheels gripping the cobbles like rails. She stared at him in the light of the coffeehouse lamps, before slipping a boot in the iron and mounting up.

He leaned onto the shoulder of her mare. "If you could, remember to take a left at Dairy Castle Road, not a right."

"Lasingstoke is right."

"We're not going to Lasingstoke. Not tonight."

"Oh? And where are we going then? Do you have some else in mind to murder?"

He smiled at her and she marveled at how swiftly and easily he moved from killer to country lord. Christien had been utterly right in his assessments.

"Many, actually. But not tonight. You see, I've been shot, and I don't think I'll make it to Lasingstoke. Lonsdale is only an hour's ride north, and right now, Frankow's infirmary promises the best chance of surviving the night. Besides, you could visit your mother, see what the good doctor has in mind for her, and if I do happen to live, then I could see if there is anything I can do for her myself. After that, you are completely free to go wherever your high-strung nature dictates."

He nudged her knee.

"So, Miss Savage? Does that sound reasonable? Ivy?"

She blinked several times at him. Truth be told, she hadn't heard a word since "I've been shot."

"Yes, of course. Left." She nodded woodenly, suddenly feeling as cold as Crumb's sitting room. Sebastien mounted his horse.

"We're just leaving," he announced to the group of patrons. "Returning to our neat little rowhouse by the factory."

Patrons stared at them now as together they pulled the rein and the horses moved out onto the street.

***

It was almost dawn before she saw the wrought-iron gate and familiar geared archway. What Sebastien had described as 'an hour's ride north' took the better part of the night, as the Mad Lord began to fade and his horse had adjusted its pace accordingly. His cravat had grown dark as the night wore on and she found herself talking, singing and telling stories in effort to keep him awake.

At last, the hex-nut keyed plate gleamed in the early morning light and she slipped from her mare to stand beside it. Up close, she could see a wide key beneath it all, and several buttons above. She pressed the wide key with a click.

"Enter code," said a grinding mechanical voice.

"I don't know the code," she spoke into it. "Please, I need help."

"Unknown response. Enter code."

"What's the code, Sebastien?" she called up, loudly now so he could hear.

His eyes were closed.

"Sebastien? I need the code? Do you know the code?"

"Yes," he murmured.

"Please, Sebastien, tell me the code."

"Mm. It has sevens in it."

She glanced through the iron, could see the Abbey far, far up the drive. It could be an ocean away if they couldn't get through the gate. She pressed the wide key again.

"Enter code."

"Can you hear me? Is there anyone there?"

"Naturally there is someone here," droned the voice. "You are speaking with someone."

"Please, sir. I have Sebastien de Lacey here. He is injured and needs to see Dr. Frankow."

"Welcome, Sebastien de Lacey. Please enter de Lacey code."

"I don't know his code. We need help! Please!"

"Unknown response. Enter code."

She growled and slammed both fists into the keys.

"Unknown response. Initiating intruder protocols."

Lights flared suddenly along the posts and the iron fence shuddered. With the hum of what sounded like a thousand bees, wide spikes began to emerge from its capstones and in the distance she could hear the wailing of an alarm.

"Ivy, I don't feel well."

He began to dismount his horse. It was more a controlled fall than a dismount and she caught him before he hit the ground. He was heavier than she could manage, however, and she was forced to lower him to the grass beside the wall. She could feel the blood now, wetting his shirt and staining his waistcoat red.

"No!" she growled. "No, I need the code! Sebastien, what is the code?"

"Hmm." He smiled at her, eyes still closed. "That's a special code, the one for me. Mumford made it up. Something about sevens."

And then he was still.

She sat back, cold and numb but undefeated. She was the daughter of a crimes investigator and a writer of crackerjack mysteries. She had survived all manner of strangeness since coming to Lasingstoke. Surely a little datamancery was not beyond her. Something about sevens. Seventh House. Seventh Lord. She took a deep breath, pushed herself to her feet and stepped to the panel.

She punched seven once. Twice. Thrice. Seven times she punched the number seven.

The lights above the panel turned green.

"Welcome home, Sebastien de Lacey," droned the mechanical voice and suddenly, the gears above the gate whirred and groaned and the iron began to swing open. It was impossible to move him, however, and so she sat with him on the grass as the first rays of dawn broke over Wharcombe Bay.

***

The Milnethorpe Press

Mayhem in the Streets

One unfortunate Milnethorpe family has once again been struck with tragedy. Only weeks after the shocking and untimely deaths of Clarissa Agatha Polkey and Sarah Ann Polkey of 1011-A Pinchon Street, Mrs. Celia Bess Crumb nee Polkey was killed in an unfortunate steamcab accident late last night. Several passengers of Roach's Steamcab (license 33752) were injured and sent to Saint Margaret of the High Street Infirmary and released. The ensuing investigation revealed yet another shocker – the murder of Crumb's husband Easterton Frederick Crumb in the family home. The sitting room was disassembled and several planks in the floor removed, revealing a stash of jewels, notes and bonds from several suspicious deaths in the county. Police

Constable Terrence Tartworthy believes that, at some point during the evening, Celia Crumb discovered the stash and confronted her husband. A scuffle apparently occurred, during which the villain Crumb was shot cleanly between the eyes. "A crackerjack shot" said Tartworthy and he confirmed that Celia had been well known for her marksmanship with pots, pans and other kitchen sundries.

Passengers of the steamcab report hearing the sound of a tire blowing, once again raising the issue of the safety of four-wheeled steamcars as opposed to six. Roach's Steamcab Company has declined to comment.

Police are continuing to investigate.

Chapter 23

Of Metal Works, Morgues and the Peculiar Tale of a Skull

"Would you like tea, miss?"

Arms wrapped around her ribs, Ivy swung around to the doorway. There was a nurse standing there, her winged cap looking stark in the gaslight.

"No, thank you."

The woman disappeared and Ivy resumed her pacing. She was outside an operating theatre and it was very different from the rest of Lonsdale. Whereas the Abbey proper was either dark and gothic or brightly coloured and surreal, this ward of the sanitarium was – simply put – terrifying.

They had wheeled a gurney carrying Sebastien de Lacey down a spiraling ramp deep underground. As they went down and further down, they seemed to leave all colour behind to enter a world made entirely of metal. Doors were not the 'open and shut' variety but rather great wide panels that slid on tracks, or double panels that swung in and out, or heavy reinforced iron doors that were moved by massive gears. Almost entirely, the ceilings were low with pipes that ran the length of the subterranean construct. Floors were grated and they clanked underfoot. She could imagine worms, rats and madmen living beneath her boots.

Frankow himself had appeared down the ramp. There were wheels clipped to the mechanisms that served as his feet and he sent her a somber look before rolling into the theatre. For a brief moment, she could see inside. It was gruesome with drills, saws, drips and all manner of macabre devices suspended from coils on the ceiling. In the center of the room was Sebastien, unmoving under a stained white sheet. Blood was dripping into a pan beneath him. But then the doors had closed and she had been relieved of the sight.

The room outside was cool, smelled of ammonium and rust. There were no chairs so she stood, arms wrapped around her waistcoat, waiting for hour after hour after hour.

She could not even think, so strange her life had become in only a matter of weeks. She had lived more strangely in these past weeks than in all her life but she had lived. She had driven with wild women in steamcars. She had dined with royals and their airships. She had been witness to murder and mayhem and mysteries that defied explanation. She realized the moment he had shot the tire and not the woman that she was hooked like a trout, somehow affixed to the life of Sebastien Laurent St. John de Lacey, the Mad Lord of Lasingstoke.

She had lived more in these past weeks than she had lived in her entire life.

Sometime later, Dr. Frankow emerged from surgery, his smock spotted with blood. He motioned for her to follow and together, they moved up the long winding spiral ramp toward the daylight.

***

Here at a sanitarium north of nowhere, the china was beautiful and the tea surprisingly good.

She stood now at the large windows of his office and she could see how in daylight, each individual pane turned to catch and reflect the sun. The panes hummed and she felt the heat radiating off them; tiny connector wires ran to grids likely hidden somewhere deep within the Abbey. He had said that the sun powered much of Lonsdale. She could believe it now.

Frankow was seated at a large chair by the fire. He had changed out of his operating smock into a neat suit of pinstripe gray. His reticulating spectacles sat idle on his forehead and if she didn't look at his legs, he looked almost normal.

"You have questions," he said.

She turned now, placed the cup in the saucer and set both on his desk. She was still in her breeches and she realized they made her feel strong in many ways. Curious. She wondered if the suffragettes had thought of this.

"Many," she said. "A world of questions."

He grinned his patronizing grin. "There are only so many hours in the day."

"I have no engagements pressing."

"Ask your questions, Miss Savage. I will answer what I can, short of treason."

"What did you do to Sebastien de Lacey?"

"That..." He laid his cup down. "Is a complicated question."

"It's a simple question, actually. I suspect it's the that answer proves complicated."

"Yes. You are quite right."

She arched a brow and waited.

"What did I do to Sebastien de Lacey? Hm. Let me think. I repaired his broken skull. I waited for him to speak. I trained him in his vocation. I introduced him to a world in need of his skills. I loved him like a son." He smiled again. "Which of these would you like me to account?"

"All of them, sir. In sequence."

"Ah. A policeman's daughter, yes?"

"Hm."

"When I first met Sebastien, he was a little boy and very naughty. He was constantly pushing the boundaries of his parents' rules and the limits of their affections. I was not surprised to hear he had fought his father the night they died. He was a stubborn, willful child ..."

He trailed off, remembering. Ivy gave him that.

"They tried everything for him, those 'physicians' of Lancashire. He should have died that night, but didn't. As I said, he was a very stubborn boy. But his skull was fractured here..." he made a motion over the back of his head. "And here..." Another motion. "The brain had swollen and pushed the *meninges* through the boney matter. He did not die, but neither did he awaken. The things they did I can only imagine. It borders on butchery. So after three weeks, they bring him to me. They think he will be this way for the rest of his life and so, where else do you bring the vegetables, the refuse of humanity, but to the sanitarium. Keep them alive but away from society. Unseen, unheard, invisible."

He could be speaking of her mother, she thought. He could be speaking of her very life.

"So, I start with his brain. The surgeons had been trying to keep it together so I do not. I remove large parts of the skull, allow the tissue to swell without constraint. Naturally, it does, and after a few days, it shrinks back, satisfied. So, I leave it. I know I can repair the plate with aluminium later. I must let the brain do what the brain needs to do. For the most part, he sleeps. For weeks, he sleeps, but soon, his skin is pink again not gray, and I know he will live. But he doesn't wake. I know I need to stimulate the brain, so I insert wires into the tissue and run small electric charges into the parietal and occipital lobes."

"You sent electrical charges into a little boy's brain?"

"Compared to what the other physicians did, Miss Savage, it was a blessing."

She set her jaw but said nothing.

"So, finally, after several treatments, he wakes. He wakes, but he doesn't speak. He doesn't blink. He just looks. Looks here, looks there, looks right through you. He looks at you the same way he looks at a stick or a chair or a wall. Nothing registers. Nothing matters. Nothing except Mumford. Now Mumford is different. He looks at Mumford, and I know this is special."

"Who is Mumford, sir?"

"Mumford is a toy, Miss Savage. A knitted dog made for him by his mother at his birth. I wanted something from his old life for his new one here and Mumford was the thing I was given. He would go nowhere without Mumford, and when he finally did begin to speak, it was to Mumford. And it was in Latin."

"Latin? You taught him Latin?"

"I did not teach him Latin, Miss Savage. I taught him English. Well, Czech first, but then English. It was almost a year before he began to speak and when he did, it was Latin."

"How did he know Latin?"

"I believe that is the language Mumford speaks."

"Mumford. The knitted dog Mumford."

"The very one."

She blinked several times.

"Oh yes, I do know how this sounds. But I am telling you the truth. I patched up his skull with large plates of aluminium, stretched the scalp as much as possible for the hair to cover it. I wanted him to have at least a chance of looking somewhat normal, but he was a very different boy then, Miss Savage. Very different."

"How so?"

"Excuse me." The man reached forward to the china service on the ottoman, poured himself a second cup. He sat back, sipped thoughtfully.

"Yes, he was different. Everyone could see that. A bright, articulate but strange little boy." He smiled again. "And he has been that way ever since. But he is happy, for the most part. And that, I think, is good."

"Do you not think him mad, sir? Christien is quite engaged in the study of the brain, and he insists his brother is… is…"

"Schizophrenic?"

"Yes," she said. "That was term. A splitting of the mind."

He smiled, but the thin, patronizing grin as before. "Have you ever seen a cat watch something that was not there, watch it so intently that you were convinced it was seeing something?"

She had to admit she had seen it, although she did not have a particular fondness for cats.

"It was said cats could see spirits, Miss Savage. For the longest time, they were thought to be magical animals, in touch with a realm few humans could see. Of course, now with our understanding of the scientific world, we know this to be impossible. And yet, how many of us can see with the eyes of a cat?"

"What are you saying, sir?"

"I'm saying that it is impossible to see like a cat if one is not a cat. For whatever reason, now and ever since the trauma, Sebastien sees with the eyes of a cat. He sees things no one else can see. Terrifying things. Otherworldly things. Spirit things."

"But how can he see this, sir? He has the same eyes he had before, undoubtedly."

"Ah yes. A skeptic. But that is a very good question. I don't know, Miss Savage, why Sebastien sees the things he does. Up to this point, he has not given me permission to dissect his eyes. Insists he needs them still."

She could well imagine Frankow dissecting someone's eyeballs and wondered if Castlewaite had ever paid a visit.

"And the cold? The frost?"

"I cannot say, Miss Savage. When he is in communion with these 'spirits,' all manner of strange things may happen."

"Communion with the Realm of Departed Souls," she said, looking at the fire for a moment before looking back. "You were a founding member of the Ghost Club, yes?"

"Ah, you know this too. You are a good detective, Miss Savage." He sat back in his chair but did not cross his legs. She wondered if he could. "Yes, I was a founding member of the Ghost Club."

"But no longer."

"No longer, no."

"And why did you leave?"

"That is a long story." There was the familiar whoosh-thump sound of the pneumatic pipes. He smiled at her. "For another time, perhaps."

And he rose from his chair, the gears and pulleys in his legs moving like pistons. He retrieved the capsule, pulled the spectacles down onto his face and read.

He turned to her and his eyes loomed larger than life.

"He is stabilized and has been moved in the recovery theatre. Would you like to see him now?"

It sounded so personal, as though she were a wife or a lover, that she should be invested in this man somehow. But she could not stop the rush of her heart.

"Yes," she said quietly. "Yes, I would."

He stared at her for a long moment. "You are a brave girl to be following him on his adventures."

She lowered her eyes, wondered if he could read her thoughts. "Not brave, sir. Merely stubborn."

"It is the same."

She watched him as he stepped first one foot then the other into the flat plate of wheels. They clipped over his feet with a snap. He whirred toward the door and went through without even a backward glance. She sighed and followed, closing the door behind her.

Chapter 24

Of Mumford, a Levitating Man and a Kiss in the Infirmary

Despite the name "Recovery Theatre," Ivy was hard pressed to determine why anyone might elect to recover there. Like the rest of the infirmary, it was entirely metal and green kaleidoscoping lights did little to improve the mood. In fact, the lighting was curious, and as she moved closer, she realized that these were not ordinary gas lamps. They were the work of a glass blower and she thought they belonged upstairs, not in the dungeon-like confines of the infirmary. She could feel Frankow's large, bespectacled eyes on her, so she turned by way of asking.

"It is a Geissler tube," he said. "And you are quite right, Miss Savage. It is simply a piece of beautifully blown glass. However, if you coat the inner surface with mercury and run an electrical charge through it, it creates the most beautiful display of lights. Soothing, yes?"

Frankow wheeled towards a pair of steel doors where a uniformed man was sitting at a desk. His brass pin read Karl Feigenbaum and he was tapping out a message on a telegraph. It was curious and she wondered what a hospital orderly would be doing that warranted a telegraph. He did not look up at them, but punched a code into a hex-key panel on the wall behind his desk. The double doors shuddered and swung inward.

She was surprised to hear music playing through grilles in the ceiling. It was the sound of a carnival organ grinder, pleasant-sounding at first, but oddly disturbing and she looked at Frankow again.

"Music is therapy for the soul, Miss Savage. It helps our patients recover so much more quickly."

He smiled proudly and she shook her head. Green kaleidoscopic lights and carnie music. Frankow had strange ideas for therapy.

Beds were lined up along the copper wall and it made her stomach churn to see the Mad Lord on one of them. He was clothed only from the waist down, and there was a brass brace holding his right arm across his chest. Tubes ran into and out of his body, and red and clear fluids in bell jars were suspended from the ceiling. His mouth and nose were covered in a silver respirator and she could see his breath fog the glass plate. The respirator was attached to a large cylindrical tank and gas hissed as it flowed into the mask.

At the foot of the bed was an automaton—the first she'd seen here. It was attached at the base of the bed via a lever that allowed it to access all sides. Now, it sat at the foot, watching. In the shadow of the robot lay a brown knitted dog. It had long floppy ears, understuffed legs and wooden buttons for eyes. It was well worn, had been patched repeatedly and was the most human thing in the room.

The infamous Mumford.

Frankow had moved to Sebastien's side and began to move his fingers across the bandaging, lifting, tugging, checking.

"The projectile went in here, just under the clavicle and lodged at the scapula in his back. It was a clean shot, all things considered but took some of the waistcoat and shirt into the wound. I must say wool and linens are tricky to remove. They have long fibres that get caught in the tissues and quickly turn septic. He is a lucky fellow to have had you to help him."

Despite the man's clinical exterior, she could see his eyes, grossly magnified through the spectacles. He was staring at Sebastien as a father might stare at his own child.

"He has never been shot before," he said softly.

She lowered her eyes, not wanting to tell him that he might not have been shot at all had she not been in the room.

"But he will be fine, yes?"

"Yes. He will be fine."

"Can you fix these?"

She reached into her vest pocket, pulled out the black-rimmed spectacles.

"I, I stepped on them earlier..."

He took them, looked up at her over the rim of his lenses.

"You, Miss Savage, are a calamity."

He pulled a pocket watch from his vest. "Would you like to see your mother now? It is currently one forty. We shall find her outside."

One forty in the afternoon. So strange. She had lost all track of time.

"Yes, thank you. I would like that very much."

He looked at the automaton. "Otto, notify Karl once he awakens."

Green lights flashed across the faceplate. "Yes, Doctor."

"And then, we can arrange a coach to take Miss Savage back to Lasingstoke." He began to wheel out of the room toward the double doors.

"Oh, no, sir. I mean to stay."

The doors swung outwards, but he slowed then stopped. He did not look back.

"You mean to stay...here? At Lonsdale?"

"Yes, sir. That is precisely what I mean."

"But your brother?" He spun around on his wheels to face her. "Doesn't he need you?"

"Davis is a very independent boy. He spends most of his time in the company of Cookie's daughter."

"He will not be making any more explorations of forbidden houses?"

"No, sir. He remembers nothing of the incidents, but I am quite certain he will not be going back. I am not needed at Lasingstoke."

He moved closer.

"He could have died, you know."

"Yes, sir."

And closer.

"And for Sebastien to have helped him the way he did... He could have died as well."

She swallowed. "Yes sir."

"The women of Seventh are very angry."

He was so close now that he reminded her of the sisters Helmsly-

Wimpoll, and his eyes were the largest things in the room. She could only imagine what he was thinking, but she raised her chin a little, determined to bear up under his scrutiny.

"You will need a change of clothes…"

"I'm fine wi—"

"We have a wardrobe room upstairs. You are welcome to anything that might fit you. We also have many, many sleeping rooms. Again, you are welcome to any of them. I will have Agnes Tidy will show you the way."

"Thank you, sir."

"I will also have Karl send a telegraph to Rupert at Lasingstoke. They may be growing worried." His eyes flashed over her again, taking in her now wild hair, boy's breeches and muddy riding boots. "Then again, they may not."

She did not know what to say to that.

With that, he whirled and rolled toward the door, pointing a finger to the sky.

"Back up to the sun, Miss Savage! Up, up, up! Once more into the breach…"

And then he was gone out the double doors. Ivy stayed a moment longer before following.

***

There was a grey fog that had settled over the Abbey above Wharcombe Bay and Ivy found herself grateful for warmth of the peacoat. How anyone could possibly be cured sitting outside in weather like this boggled her mind but she had to admit that even the fog was a welcome change from the rust and gloom of the Infirmary.

There were five people outside that she could see. Agnes Tidy was pushing a man in one of the wheeled chairs. He was perhaps forty years old, quite thin and she could hear his breathing from where she stood.

"Mr. Home," said Frankow though he pronounced it *Hume*. "He has the Tuberculosis. Many of our patients come here for the cure."

She nodded. Consumption was a terrible disease killing most who contracted it. The toxic Pea Soup fogs of London, Manchester and

Birmingham were notorious culprits. Those who could afford to would retreat to sanitaria such as Lonsdale where large doses of fresh air, moderate exercise and good food could often stave off the symptoms for years. She was surprised the Abbey wasn't full on account of it.

Her eyes wandered to a table where another nurse sat with a wild looking young man. His hair was very dark, uncombed and longer than hers. His moustache and beard were tangled and his eyes darted about as if watching a swarm of bees. Suddenly, he spied her and rose to his feet, making the sign of the cross and shouting in a strange tongue. To Ivy, he looked the very definition of the word insane.

"Grigori is new here," said Frankow.

"Grigori?"

The man snatched a stick from the dining table, began to lash it backwards across his neck and shoulders.

"Yes. Grigori Rasmussen, Rastafarian…Raspberry…something like that. At any rate, Grigori comes to us from *Pokroyskoye,* Siberia. That is in Russia, Miss Savage."

"What is he saying?"

"Oh, that. He is calling you the Virgin Mary."

"How odd." She turned to Frankow. "Why is Grigori here at Lonsdale? Does he have the consumption as well?"

"No. He stole a loaf of bread from a church so they sent him here as penance."

"I'm afraid I don't believe you, sir."

His spectacles whirred and clicked. "He is calling you the Virgin Mary."

She smiled now.

"Aha. We are finally getting somewhere. He is here, Miss Savage, because of two reasons. One, he is believed to be a clairvoyant mystic and his government is afraid of him. They wish me to confirm or disprove his claims and two, because he cannot die."

"He cannot die?"

"That is what I said."

She took a deep breath, thought a moment.

"I do not see with the eyes of a cat," she said finally.

As they continued their tour of the grounds, she heard the sound of flapping wings and Ivy looked up to the roof of the Abbey. Almost a silhouette, she could see a young woman with pigeons on her head and shoulders. She waved down at them and Ivy recognized her as the young woman from Frankow's office.

"I'm afraid Sebastien was quite right," Frankow sighed. "Not even the cowboys of America are prepared to handle our Lizzie. Oh look, over there. A breakthrough…"

Agnes Tidy was talking to Mr. Home as he rose to his feet and took a few steps. Smiling, he raised his arms up to the sky.

"How wonderful," said Ivy. "It certainly must feel—"

And began to rise from the ground.

Ivy blinked. The man was rising from the ground. He was smiling and rising from the ground. One foot, two feet, a yard now, and higher. She couldn't believe her eyes. The man was at least ten feet above the ground and far below him, Tidy was clapping her hands.

"…good." Ivy finished.

Now the levitating man began to spin, slowly making circles with his body in mid air. Once, twice, three times he circled before slowly, ever so slowly, he began to descend. Tidy fussed over him and tucked him back into his chair.

Together, man and nurse turned and wheeled out of sight.

"Mr. Home is doing much better now," said Frankow.

It was remarkable the things she was simply taking in stride.

There was the rattle of another chair and Ivy's breath caught in her throat. Her mother was being wheeled across the lawn and Frankow waved them over. Ivy waited, her hands wringing like damp dishcloths until the chair came to a complete stop.

"Hello, Mum. It's me, Ivy."

There was no response. She bent down and hugged her, fighting back the rush of tears. She kissed her cheek and took her hands.

"She's looking well," she said softly. "Her colour is good. And she looks to have put on some weight."

"Three pounds, miss," said the nurse. "She's eating well, sleeping well. She sits outside most days, even the rainy ones."

She nodded, squeezed her mother's hands.

"Have you…tried…anything on her, Doctor? Any of your scientific techniques, I mean?"

"Do you mean to ask if I am experimenting on her, Miss Savage?"

"No! Yes... Maybe. I don't know, sir."

"Not to worry. I understand completely." He inclined his head. "We have tried two things since she has been here. The first is the Baths."

"The Baths?"

"It is essentially a soundproof tank of salt water. There is no light, there is no scent, there is no sound. The water is warmed up to exactly the temperature of the human body and the salt content makes it dense enough to float without exertion. It is most relaxing."

"And what do you do in the Baths?"

"Well, there is nothing to do in the Baths, but 'Be.' The mind is freed from all external stimuli and therefore opened to explore its own mental acuity and spiritual pathways."

She swallowed, remembering Franny Helmsly-Wimpoll and her *Hypersensory Mental Acuity, Spiritualism and Communion with the Realm of Departed Souls.*

"And the other?"

"Just like Sebastien. Small electrical charges into her cerebellum."

She should have been outraged. She should have been shocked.

"I see," was all she could say.

Yes, quite remarkable the things she was taking in stride.

"As I said earlier, there is little I may be able to do."

She sighed, nodded, squeezed her mother's hands again. "Thank you for doing this. For trying."

"Not at all, child."

And they continued their walk along the grounds of Lonsdale Abbey, Ivy pushing her mother in the wheeled chair, fighting back the tears and being both the happiest and the saddest she'd ever been in her life.

***

There were at least thirty bodies in the morgue of the Royal Hospital, all wrapped in tarp. The mortician had gone home for the night and the room was cold and dark and smelled of formaldehyde. Christien didn't care. He was certain his heart was colder, his mood darker and he felt as dead as those on the slabs.

He moved over to a table where a body lay shrouded in black. He didn't need to check her tag. He himself had wrapped her.

"I'm sorry, Annie," he said quietly and he looked down at the ring. It was turning his finger a sickly purple, the skin around the ring puckering and tight. "I know it's yours but it's stuck. I've tried everything. It won't come off."

He could make out the outline of her face, the bump of her nose, the hollow of her eyes.

"Marie Kelly has one too, just so you know, and Albert Victor. What a strange trio to have your rings." He sighed, turned to lean against the table. "Did you love him? I doubt it. Eddy's not terribly lovable, is he? I do hope you loved someone, and that someone loved you. This is a lonely place to end up."

It was raining outside and he could hear dripping from the ceiling pipes onto the floor. Water was not good for cadavers, he thought. The hospital needed to invest in a better room, but then again, he doubted anyone complained overmuch.

"Do No Harm, says the oath," he sighed. "But that's not the same as doing good. I don't know where to draw the line anymore. I have to talk to Williams. I know he's trying to help you girls, but all this has gone terribly wrong. It seemed clear at the time. All about the research, he said, but it's grown far too complicated and I think he's covering for someone. If I talk to Trevis or Bondie, they'll investigate and we'll all get the sack. All my schooling gone, because of you, Annie. You and your three damned rings."

A rat slipped through the shadows. Terrible, the state of things.

"But if I don't say anything, then I know this ring is going to get tighter and tighter and I'll lose my finger and my career will be damned anyway. Then how will I take care of Ivy or anybody else?"

There was only the sound of the dripping from the pipes, the hissing of the gaslight. It was almost peaceful down here in the morgue and he looked at her again.

"Is your spirit alive somewhere? Up North maybe? Is that what Bastien sees? Can he really? I can't believe it. I just can't. It's impossible. And yet…"

He sighed.

"And yet, here I am, sitting in a bloody tomb, talking to a dead woman and a rat. I'd never thought I'd do such a thing. Wouldn't the Ghost Club be pleased?"

And he sat like that for some time, with only the rat and the body of Dark Annie Chapman for company.

***

Someone had been singing.

Strange tunes, sure enough and in another language, but it was singing nonetheless. He didn't think it was his mother. His mother used to sing all the time, in the nursery, in the hallways, in the gardens. He didn't remember much of her but he did remember singing.

He opened his eyes to the ghoulish green lights of the infirmary and the sight of Otto hovering over him with his tarnished faceplate. He could see a series of lights flash, knew that outside the door Karl was being notified of his waking, knew that very soon Frankow would be down to see him and that all would be well.

His mouth was sharp and he realized that there was a respirator covering the lower half of his face. He reached up, removed it and inhaled deeply the damp, rusty smell of the infirmary. A sudden stabbing pain at the simple act of breathing and he remembered the fact that sometime, at some point last night, he had been shot.

She had done it. She had got him here and he had lived. That was a bit of a surprise. He hadn't expected to live. Truth be told, he hadn't expected to be shot either. Life had a way of throwing things at him. There was always something different around the corner. He would miss her, though, for she would have disappeared the moment she'd dropped him off at the gates of the Abbey. She had looked sweet in her breeches and bowler.

Otto spun along the track and stopped at his left side. Calipers extended from the metallic body, and a set of hoses lowered from the ceiling. The calipers caught the hoses, attached them to suction pads already placed over his heart, at his throat, on his forehead and wrist. He sighed, waiting for Otto to do his work and let his eyes wander around the recovery room, as familiar to him as the stables of Lasingstoke.

He spied the metallic brace holding his right arm in place, the bandages brown with dried blood. He flexed his fingers, relieved to find everything in working order. Bertie would love a friend with a prosthetic arm. If he ever took up smoking, the flint could come in handy.

And at the foot of the bed, Mumford.

He smiled.

A yellow light flashed over the doors, and they began to swing inward. He could hear the whirring of Frankow's wheels and he waited for the bearded face to appear. It did, the great spectacles causing his eyes to warp and bend with the lenses. He was worried, Sebastien could tell, but he masked it well with an arched brow and a patronizing smile.

"Ah. You have finally decided to see what it is like being dead."

"I keep trying." His voice was hoarse. "It never takes."

The doctor grunted and moved to the side, checking the numbers that were now scrolling from the slit in Otto's mouth like a very long tongue.

"Hmm. It appears you are quite fine."

Sebastien raised the brace slightly. "Bertie will be disappointed if I don't keep this."

"I can arrange to surgically remove your arm whenever you feel the need."

"Thank you. I shall think on that." He moved to sit up, groaned, sank back into the pillows. "Too soon, yes?"

"Your brilliance is a constant amazement," muttered Frankow as he read the papers and for the first time since his awakening, Sebastien realized there was someone else in the room.

"Miss Savage…"

She slipped out of the shadows toward the bed, the locket radiating softly as it nestled between her breasts.

"How are you feeling?" she asked.

He shot a glance up at Frankow, who was ignoring them both.

"I don't like the infirmary."

She smiled.

Frankow's large eyes flicked up from the scroll.

"Well," he said. "Since you are invariably recovering from this disastrous injury, I shall leave you now. I have other patients to attend. Ones that have not inflicted grievous bodily harm upon themselves." He nodded. "Sebastien, Miss Savage…"

And with that, Arvin Frankow rolled out of the infirmary, leaving the pair with Otto, Mumford and the green gaslight.

The locket was calling him, but he could barely look. He felt his breathing quicken as she moved over to the bed.

She reached down, picked Mumford up in both hands. "Your mother made this?"

He swallowed. "Before I was born. She wasn't much of a knitter."

"He's charming." She looked at him, and he realized immediately that he had never felt so exposed. She moved over to lean against the bed and he saw that not only was she wearing the locket, but the breeches, blouse and oddly enough, a red leather corset. Her hair was loose, rare for women, and he thought he had never seen one look so very good.

"Frankow says he speaks Latin."

"Yes. But he won't speak when you're here. Only to me."

"I see. He's a shy woolen."

He reached out with his good hand and snatched Mumford out of hers, tucking him under his arm.

She smiled at him.

"Why are you still here?" he asked, trying desperately not to look at her.

"I was concerned. I wanted to make sure you were going to be fine." She shrugged, pushed her hip up onto the bedframe. "Also, I saw my mother and then found this amazing corset in the Wardrobe room upstairs. I've never worn a corset like this—look. It cinches at the waist by these little tiny gears. Isn't it scandalous? Hmm, what else? Oh yes, I saw a man levitating on the lawns, got called the Virgin Mary by an undying Russian. You know, usual fare for a sanitarium, I suppose."

"Well, I am indeed fine, as is your mother. So you can leave now, your conscience clear."

"But I don't wish to leave, Sebastien. After all, you promised to see what you could do for my mother if you lived and apparently, you did."

Finally, she noticed his attentions to the pendant around her neck. It was spinning only slightly. She smiled, reaching for it with her fingers.

"Christien said it had been in your family for years."

"Periculosa est," he said aloud and nodded at Mumford. "I know."

"What is he saying?"

"He is saying you should leave."

Suddenly, she was touching his face.

"Gray," she said with a smile. "Today, at least, your eyes are gray."

He did not know what to say to that.

"And these... They're almost healed," she said now, running her fingers along the scratches from last week. "Thank you for doing this, whatever it was that you did. You saved his life."

"And you saved mine last night. I believe that makes us even. So leave."

She smiled again. Curse her and that damned smile.

"I have no pressing engagements, and you are fascinating company. I've never followed in the footsteps of a murderer before."

And to his complete and utter surprise, she leaned down and kissed him on the cheek.

She rose from the bed and moved away, turning back only once.

"Get up soon, will you? I wish to explore the lands around Wharcombe Bay and can think of no better way than on horseback."

And she left the room, its double doors swinging outward to let her through.

As for the Mad Lord, he pulled a pillow over his head and waited for the heartbeat of her to leave the room.

***

"Alexander Dunn," said Penny. *"He is an international jewel thief and rogue. He has stolen the Clockwork Heart, but I suspect he has already left the country."*

"Damnation, Penny," groaned her father, Charles Dreadful. *"This is a disastrous end to the affair. Regina Imperiatrix will not be amused."*

"And what about the key?" asked Claryss, her dearest friend. *"How did Alexander steal the key?"*

Penny hesitated. "Perhaps, this is a mystery that will never be solved."

And for the first time in all her years as a Girl Criminologist, Penny Dreadful and her boys in blue did not have an arrest on their hands.

Later, days after they had returned to London, Penny slipped into her room to retire for the night. She had just attended a swank soiree for the Belgian Ambassador and was happy on the finest champagnes imaginable. A man stepped out of the shadows.

"Thank you," said Alexander Dunn/Alexandre Gavriel St. Jacques Lord Durand. "For not revealing my identity."

Penny raised an eyebrow. "Do not think, sir, that my good will extends beyond the Affair of the Clockwork Heart. It was, after all, yours."

"Indeed." He stepped closer. "It is difficult to steal a heart."

She stepped closer. "So I've been told."

"And thank you also, for not incriminating Dr. von Freud."

Closer.

"He is like a father to you, I suspect," she said, stepping even closer herself.

"He gave me the key." Now almost upon her. "I simply returned it when I was done."

"And that was your mistake." She could feel the warmth from his body, looked up into his eyes. "It seems perhaps you do have a heart, after all…"

He leaned in closer, his lips only a kiss away. "Perhaps I do…"

Penny held her breath. Her own heart was pounding like a fist on a door.

"Penny! Penny, are you in there?"

It was Julian Terrence Hull, Penny's fiancé, a-knocking on her door.

And suddenly, Alexander Dunn/Alexandre Gavriel St. Jacques Lord Durand was gone, along with most of her breath.

And apparently, her pearl necklace as well.

The End of "Penny Dreadful and the Ghost of Lancashire."

Chapter 25

Of Red Ink, Killing of Two Birds and a Letter from Jack

The steamcab pulled up in front of the long white row of houses. Christien paid his fare and trudged up the steps to Hollbrook, exhausted, cold and, after a night spent talking to dead women in the morgue, damnably sad.

"Hallo Remy," called the voice from next door. "You're looking tired, my boy! That Ripper fellow giving you more headaches?"

Christien sighed. It was Jekyll and like before, he was standing in his dressing gown, holding the paper in one hand, a pipe in the other. Christien could barely manage a smile. Civility was, he told himself, a very English mask.

"We haven't heard from him for a while, sir," he called. "I'm certain he's left the city."

"Right, right. I'm sure you're right." And the man put the pipe to his teeth. "Probably gone back to France. That's what the papers are saying. That he's a French anarchist, wot?"

The London Steam News sat folded on his step and in a deliberate move Christien turned his back to the doctor to pick it up. From under the paper, a square brown envelope fell out onto the step.

"Not that there's anything wrong with being French, dear boy. Don't get me wrong on that account. Nothing wrong at all..."

The address was written in red ink.

"Post come early today, did it?" called Jekyll. "I really must talk to the post master. I rarely get letters anymore. Most of them are for some fellow named Hyde…"

Slowly, Christien straightened, cursing the fact that the letter was trembling in his hands. He was a surgeon. His hand should never shake. He breathed and breathed again, willing himself to remain calm, to remain detached. Above it all. In control. It had been the only way to stay sane in this mad, mad world.

"Remy?" called Jekyll. "Remy, are you quite all right?"

Carefully, he peeled back the seal, read the letter in its entirety and closed it up again, neat and precise.

"Remy?"

Slowly, he turned to look at his neighbour next door.

"Dr. Jekyll," he said. "Could you kindly flag me another cab? I'm afraid I must go to Whitechapel."

And without waiting for a response, he looked back down at the letter and the rather unusual terms of address.

'Dear Boss', it began.

***

Dear Christien,

How are you? I am fine. The weather has been nice if a little blustery…

"No."

Dear Christien,

I am at Lonsdale because your brother got shot whilst murdering someone in Milnethorpe. And by the way, I want you to quit the Ghost Club.

"No, no."

Dear Christien,

How are you? I am fine. I kissed your brother last night.

Ivy growled, crumpled the paper into a little ball and dropped her head into her hands.

What had she done?

She sat now, knees up, with her back against a Gothic brick corner of Lonsdale Abbey. It was cold and windy and she could see a bank of dark clouds looming over the Bay. But still, the nurses sat with their patients out on the lawn, blankets drawn, umbrellas at the ready. Her mother sat, staring with unseeing eyes at the grass. Grigori was on the roof high above them, shouting in Russian and threatening to leap to his death but no one seemed to pay him any mind. Lizzie Borden was apparently chopping wood for fires but the automaton assigned to help her was now in pieces across the lawn. Agnes Tidy had tucked Mr. Home into his chair after finishing his levitations for the day. He had completed an entire circuit of the Abbey this morning and he was tired.

Madness, thought Ivy. It was all an exercise in madness and she was certain it was catching.

She wrapped her arms around her knees and shuddered. She had kissed the Mad Lord of Lasingstoke last night and the taste of him lingered on her lips. She had rarely even kissed her fiancé. Kissing was not proper behavior for respectable folk in London and Christien, of all things, was a gentleman. She knew the feel of his hand in hers – soft and supple and skilled. She knew the smell of his skin, his clothes, the slightly sharp odor of carbolic soap and astringent. She knew the lean, graceful strength of his body – she would make a point of leaning into him when on a walk or in a crowd of people. And he had kissed her on the cheek, on the forehead and always with utmost respect. She had never been a romantic girl but last night, she had stolen a kiss, become the romancer and she found her mind racing with the implications.

She had finished her story last night as well. *Penny Dreadful and the Ghost of Lancashire* had almost ended with a kiss but she'd stopped short, afraid of what that might mean for Penny and Julian. Julian would certainly never approve of the rogue Alexander Dunn, would never understand how a girl's heart could be stolen as easily as a necklace or a locket or a ring. No, most certainly, Julian would never understand.

Would Christien? Did she?

There was a rumble of distant thunder but the nurses made no move to take the patients indoors. Ivy shook her head. Lonsdale was a strange place indeed.

The locket around her necked began to hum and she looked up to see Sebastien walking from the Abbey to the lawn. He had been shot less than two days ago and she was surprised he was up and moving. He was checking a pocket watch, hair and greatcoat whipping in the wind.

Behind him, Frankow wheeled on the little contraptions strapped to his feet, the mallard's-head cane doubling as an umbrella, and she wondered if his legs would rust in the rain.

"No, Sebastien," she could hear the doctor say over the wind. "This is not a good idea."

"It doesn't matter," the Mad Lord answered. "The *Chevalier* will be here shortly and I made a deal with Victoria."

"You are still losing blood."

"Your wire stitches have me put together most ably."

"You do not need to do this. I will speak to Bertie."

"They are using Christien to get to me," growled Sebastien. "I won't have that. Not Christien. Not while I live."

"Christien is a grown man," said Frankow. "And he does not believe. He will be hard pressed to do what they ask of him."

"Bertie said they'd already met with success."

"Bertie would say anything to get you into the Club."

Suddenly, the locket around her neck leapt with colour and Sebastien turned his head in her direction. She was certain her heart stopped beating.

"Periculosa est," he said. *"Periculosa et pulchra."*

Ivy swallowed and pushed herself to her feet. His eyes were changing colour again, of that she was certain, cycling from brown to the lightest blue and it seemed the locket was matching shades. She could not tear her own eyes away and her heart thudded like airships over Lasingstoke.

She was not a romantic girl, she told herself. She was not a romantic girl.

"Dangerous and beautiful," he muttered. "Everything has changed."

And once again, all time seemed to slow save the beating of her heart.

Frankow glanced from Mad Lord to Girl Criminologist and back again. The skies were growing darker, her heartbeat growing louder.

"Shall we continue this inside, Sebastien? Miss Savage? It seems we are all expecting storms tonight…"

Thudding, racing, roaring, causing umbrellas to pop and nursing caps to fly and Ivy threw a hand over her bowler to keep in on her head. A black shadow fell across the Abbey and they all looked up as, once again, the underbelly of airship came into view.

***

Through the high-paned window of Frankow's office, Ivy watched the *Chevalier* drop cables to the grassy grounds, trying to steady herself in the buffeting winds over the Bay.

It was a beautiful airship, she thought, and the canvas a work of art, with horses and hounds and red-coated riders chasing a fox around the balloon. Depending on the light, the fox appeared then disappeared at different points in the design. The gondola was polished oak and the bowsprit a rearing golden horse. A name was carved into her stern – *Chevalier*. French for horseman.

"It seems our Christien has got himself into some small trouble," said Frankow, sitting behind his desk, sipping his tea. "Is this why he gave you that bauble, Miss Savage? You do not seem the type for fine jewelry."

"He said the Ghost Club was interested in it," she said, turning back from the window. "He said they wanted to take it apart."

Frankow sipped his tea but said nothing.

"Why, sirs? What does it do?"

"She," Sebastien said, his first words since entering the office. He had not touched the tea that had been poured for him. "Her name is Ghostlight."

Frankow turned his bespectacled gaze on the Mad Lord.

"Ghostlight, yes. It belonged to your father, a very long time ago. It's a very powerful device but it seems to have no effect on Miss Savage. I wonder what effect it may have had on Christien for him to give her away. Or, for that matter..." He smiled his patronizing smile. "What effect it may be having on you?"

"She is having no effect on me," Sebastien said.

"My mistake."

"But what does it do?" asked Ivy again. "Why would the Ghost Club want it so?"

"I can only imagine," said Frankow. "Renaud was a secretive man, not given to sharing his discoveries with others. But obviously, the locket has some strong connection to the de Lacey men. It has not stopped dancing."

It was true. The locket was continuing to spin and flash, and Ivy was thankful there were no snowflakes like the night in Milnethorpe.

"Do you want it, Sebastien?" she asked.

"Yes. No. Yes." He shook his head. "No. I think she would not be best with me. She is far too loud and seductive. I could destroy the world with her power."

Ivy swallowed, wondering then if he had even noticed her kiss.

"Now, now, Sebastien," said Frankow, rising to his feet at the whoosh and thump of the pneumatic pipes. "Be content with your pistol and bullets, please."

The doctor slid the capsule open, his lenses spinning and clicking as he read the note inside. He looked up.

"You will excuse me," he said. "Grigori has jumped from the roof yet again and has broken all his bones. This is the third time this week. It is most annoying."

And with that, he hissed and clanked out of his office, leaving Sebastien and Ivy and the uncomfortable silence.

"Why do you do that?" asked Ivy, tucking the locket into her corset to mute its flashing. "Shoot people, that is."

"To quiet the dead," he sighed. "They are persistent."

"So, you see them, then? With your eyes, the way you would see me or Christien or Rupert?"

"The same way," he said. "Although I feel them first. They invariably bring the frost with them."

"I see." When, in fact, she did not. "Would things have gone differently in Milnethorpe if I hadn't been there?"

"Quite likely. I'm certain that's why I slipped up. She is so very loud."

"Slipped up? You mean—"

"Got myself shot. Yes. That."

"Oh." She swallowed, feeling her throat grow tight. "I'm very sorry, then."

So they sat for a few minutes more, the only sound being the thwupping of the airship's engines and the shouting of the men as they sought to moor her against the powerful winds.

"No, Miss Savage, I'm sorry." Sebastien sighed. "I'm sorry you had to witness it."

"You killed a man, sir. You shot him in the head."

"I am a crackerjack shot."

"It was a horrible thing to do."

"He was a murderer."

"And so are you."

"No, Miss Savage. It is entirely different."

"Please tell me how, Sebastien. Because I'm not seeing it."

"You weren't meant to see it, Miss Savage. I distinctly remember asking you to look away."

She folded her arms across her chest, like armour.

"Do they...*tell* you...whom to shoot?"

"They?"

"The voices. The ghosts. The women of Seventh. Do they tell you somehow and you do it? You may as well answer me, sir. I am quite persistent, if you hadn't noticed."

"Indeed. You are a bloody badger."

He looked down at the tea cup next to him. There was a thin film of cream spreading across its surface, consequences of letting it sit too long. He sighed and raised his head, but oddly enough, did not look at her.

"The dead show themselves to me and I must deduce who they are, how they died and hopefully, who killed them. If I do make these connections, then I am at liberty to dispense justice as dictated by the victims and permitted by the Crown."

"So you work for the Crown?"

"I am loyal to Lonsdale and Lonsdale is funded by the War Office. For some reason, they have a stake in my welfare. Don't ask me why. I certainly don't shew for the sittings of the House of Lords. I hate London. I would rather die than set foot on its accursed streets."

She studied him as he sat, wondered at the trauma that had created someone like him, wondered if such things could possibly be true and lastly, wondered at the strange tightening in her chest. She was not the sort of girl be carried away by starry-eyed notions of love or fairytales or princes on white horses. She was a mystery writer, cerebral and detached, preferring a good murder to a love-story any day.

And besides, she told herself, Sebastien's horse was grey.

The office door opened and Frankow entered, hissing and clanking toward his desk.

"Grigori has indeed broken all his bones, but he is healing well," said the doctor. "He should be up and about by tea time."

Behind him, Agnes Tidy wheeled the unseeing, unmoving form of Catherine Savage in her wheeled chair.

"Oh," gasped Ivy. "Mum..."

"I thought, Sebastien, that you might wish to meet Catherine Savage."

"Why?" asked the Mad Lord.

"Life is funny, yes?"

"You did promise," said Ivy.

Sebastien sighed and rose to his feet.

"How long has she been like this?"

"Seven years," said Ivy, moving from the window to take her mother's pale hand in hers.

"No," Sebastien snapped. "Let her go. Move away. Move away."

Ivy did as he asked.

"Curious," he said and then nothing more for some time.

Very patiently, Ivy waited, watching for him to do something miraculous. Frankow pushed back his spectacles, waiting as well. Sebastien stood for several minutes studying the woman, arms folded across his chest, forefinger tapping his lips as if deep in thought.

Ivy glanced at Frankow, who shrugged.

Finally, the Mad Lord knelt down, took Catherine's hands in his, pressed his thumbs into her palms. Turned her palms over, slid his hands up to her wrists. Ivy remembered that he had done the same thing to her in his study, wondered what it meant. He moved them up to her forehead now, first with his palms, then with all fingers pressed into her hair.

Finally, he rose to his feet and moved over to the window, began to scan the lawns and grounds of the Abbey.

"Sebastien?" asked Frankow.

"She's not here," he answered quietly. "I can't make her out anywhere. How long has she been like this again?"

"Seven years, sir," said Ivy.

"And where did she die?"

"She...she's not dead, Sebastien."

"Right. Where did *he* die? Your brother, I mean. The little one. Where did he die?"

"In the Thames. St. Katharine's Docks."

"Right, then. Miss Savage, you will accompany me."

"I don't understand," said Ivy. "We're going back to Lasingstoke?"

"No, Miss Savage. We're going to London."

"But...but why?"

He sighed but smiled, and for the first time in days, Ivy saw the man she thought she knew.

"Your mother is not here. Her 'soul' is not here. There is a dichotomy in her mind and body. You said once that she died when Tobias died, therefore we must go to 'where' Tobias died."

"This is a bad idea, Sebastien," said Frankow.

"Yes, quite probably," he said. "But we can kill two birds with one stone, so to speak. Miss Savage, if we wish to find your mother, we must go to St. Katharine's Docks. We will find her and I will send her home, here, to her body. Then, I will hunt down this London Ripper for the Ghost Club and I will kill him with my father's pistol. I will then contact dead Prince Albert at Sandringham for Old Vic and be back by All Hallow's Eve. Unless, of course, Arvin is right and it all goes to hell in a hand basket. Then, I'm in very big trouble and might never return. Have you ever been in an airship?"

And this time, his smile was as bright as the regal French sun.

Her heart skipped a beat as she realized one very strange but sure thing. The Mad Lord of Lasingstoke was the greatest mystery she had ever encountered, greater by far than anything she could have ever written in one of her Penny Dreadfuls. She could never settle now for a 'normal' home somewhere in Kensington or Stepney, could never abandon her writing in favour of elegant parties or games of whist. Not when there were stories like him in the world and places like Lonsdale filled to brimming with the fantastical. It wasn't the fantastical she was searching for anyway, she had begun to realize, but simply life. Proof that she was young and alive and that the world was truly an amazing, tumultuous, breath-taking place. As much as she loved her parents, as much as she admired Christien, she knew needed to write her own story, not simply be a character in someone else's.

She had no clue what that might mean for her mother, for her fiancé or for her doomed, blossoming career but of one thing she was certain— wherever the Mad Lord would go, like one of his dogs, she would follow.

***

September 27, 1888
Dear Boss,
I keep on hearing the police have caught me but they won't fix me just yet. I have laughed when they look so clever and talk about being on the _right_ track. That joke about Leather Apron gave me real fits. I am down on whores, and I shan't quit ripping them till I do get buckled. Grand work the last job was. I gave the lady no time to squeal. I love my work and want to start again. You will soon hear of me with my funny little games. I saved some of the proper _red_ stuff in a ginger beer bottle over the last job to write with but it went thick like glue and I cant use it. Red ink is fit enough I hope. ha.ha. The next job I do I shall clip the lady's ears off and send to the police officers just for jolly wouldn't you. Keep this letter back till I do a bit more work, then give it out straight. My knife's so nice and sharp I want to get to work right away if I get a chance. Good luck.
Yours truly,
Jack the Ripper
Don't mind me giving the trade name
P.S. Wasn't good enough to post this before I got all the red ink off my hands curse it No luck yet. They say I'm a doctor now. Ha.ha.

End of Part I

Part II: London

Chapter 26

Of Butchers, Mortuaries and Meat Pies in the Clarence

September 28, 1888
Lambeth Road, Southwark, London

It looked like a butcher's packet, tied in brown paper and lying on the side of the road.

The boys had been out early that morning, shoveling coal at the Blind School on Lambeth. It was a hard job, but it was a job and at the ripe old age of nine, all three of them could boast a regular pay of a shilling a month, split between them. For nine-year old boys, it was enough to keep them in taffy and Penny Dreadfuls for weeks at a time.

Sharpie spied the package first in a puddle under the wrought-iron railing of the fence.

"What's that, then?" he cried as the others moved round to see.

"Looks like bacon," cooed Martin Alcorn.

Sharpie's eyes gleamed. "Y' think some butcher dropped it, then?"

Martin shrugged. "Or Mrs. Tumblemorrey. She's always losing her markets."

"We could sell it," whispered Ronnie Shipley. "Me mum's always selling old meat in the rooks."

"Can ye get it, then?" asked Martin. "Try and get it."

The package was wedged beneath the railing and Sharpie dropped to his knees, pushed his arm through the grass and slid the package through the puddle towards them. He tugged at the string when white powder spilled through onto the stones.

"Salt?" offered Ronnie.

The three of them began to tug on the strings now until the paper unfolded on its own. Cyril Sharpie screamed and dropped the package, bolting down the road as fast as he could. Martin Alcorn began to back away, tripped over his feet before turning and scrambling after him. Ronnie Shipley watched them for a moment but peeled the paper back to reveal the contents.

"That's not bacon," he whispered to himself and he peered closer.

It was an arm, tied off with a piece of string and laying in a puddle on Lambeth Road.

***

She had never dreamed she'd be arriving at the Westminster Port Tower in an airship. The tower was a common sight for all Londoners, better known as the Clock Tower of Big Ben and there were always airships tethered to the top. But she had never been up, never set foot in the adjoining palace of Westminster either. No one in her family had but now, as the wind buffeted and the thunder threatened, she was about to experience it all firsthand as the *Chevalier* moved in to dock.

It had taken the entire afternoon to make the trip from Lonsdale to London, and she had spent the duration sitting with an iron pot in her lap. She was not a good air traveller, she reckoned, not with the way the airship rocked and bucked like a frigate on the high sea. The skies had been dark and occasionally split by lightning and they had outrun the storm by mere hours. It was dinnertime now as Castlewaite piloted the great ship through the gusting winds to the dock.

Three other airships were moored and the narrow gangplank was open to the skies, flanked only by a thin copper railing. It allowed her a terrifying bird's eye view of the city and given the wind, she wasn't surprised that there were always hats, gloves and umbrellas littering the streets below. It was a haven for quick-handed thieves. A fine hat could bring a pretty penny in the secondhand shops of Piccadilly.

The gangplank made landing high in the tower at the *Clock and Bell Club*, a lounge that served tea and spirits to the politicians who made airship travel a routine part of their schedules. She couldn't fathom it.

The trip had been far too bumpy for her to carry on any sort of conversation, let alone a political one, and for his part, the Mad Lord had polished off an entire decanter of port before starting on the Scotch.

As they trotted down the steep steps of the tower, she could feel the glances of men in black overcoats and top hats. The Mad Lord did not look fit for a day in London, being plucked from the wilds of Lancashire as he had, and she herself was still in her breeches, red corset and riding boots. She wondered what Christien would think if he saw her.

Finally, out onto Whitehall Road and the late afternoon crowds flowed around them like a river. Down the street, she could see the buildings of Greater Scotland Yard that served as home for the Metropolitan Police Service. Her father used to have a desk in A-Division, before transferring over to Stepney's H and she had fond memories of riding his shoulders through the halls of the building. Her father would often remind her of the time when she was six, and had announced to his entire unit that one day, she would be a crimes investigator like her tad.

She didn't need to wonder what *he* would think if he saw her like this. She knew well enough.

"We have some time before Castlewaite fetches the coach," said the Mad Lord. "Perhaps we might have time for tea? The Clarence is just down the road and it makes a dandy steak pie."

The mention of steak pies made Ivy wish she was still holding the cast iron pot.

"Tea would be lovely," she said. "But I would like to go home soon, if I may? Leave a note for tad, let him know I'm in London. Would that be alright, Sebastien?"

But her breath fell like ice to the walk and she looked up to see the Mad Lord, hands in his pockets, staring across the road at the Yard. His eyes were changing colour and around her neck, the locket began to flash. Her heart sank, dreading now what that meant.

"Sebastien? The Clarence," she said. "How about we g—"

Without warning, he turned and stormed across the street, unmindful of the squealing of horses and shouting of cabbies as he went. She scrambled to catch up as the crowds parted for him but closed in on her, and she fought her way through wave after wave of black wool and scowls. Finally he slowed at one of the many backstreets rabbiting the Yard. She reached his side just as a door swung open and a man was pushed out into the lane.

"But you need to listen!" moaned the man, a slim, middle-aged fellow in a charcoal suit and spectacles. "He's a medical man, I tell you. I've seen it! Please listen!"

"We already listened, Lees," said one officer. "You're a lunatic, you are!"

"You need to take this up with the City Force," said the other. "Or the Hs, not us."

"But I've already talked to H-Division! They said the Ripper was your jurisdiction!"

"But dreams, visions and other such 'communications' *ain't*. Now, beat it or we'll ship ya to Bedlam."

"Here," said the man called Lees. "Take my calling card. Call me if—"

They smacked the cards out of his hands, causing them to fly up like leaves before falling into the mud.

"Mark my words, sirs," he grumbled as he bent to collect them. "He will strike again soon."

"If he does, we'll throw *you* in the claps."

"Bloody lunatic…"

And they disappeared back into the door of the Yard.

She glanced up at Sebastien. He wasn't moving and she was certain that, right now, his eyes were greener than hers. She stepped forward into the lane, the locket sending colours all across the shadowed brick.

"Mr. Lees?" she called.

"Leave me alone, miss."

"Sir, we overheard your conversation—"

"Then you heard what they said." He rose to his feet, began to straighten the cards in his hands. "They think I'm a lunatic. They'd ship me off to Bedlam if they could."

His tired eyes flicked over Sebastien. "Him too, by the looks of things."

"We can help."

"Can you shoot me?" He strolled over towards them, slipped a card into her hand. "Your friend's got a pistol, I can tell. Shoot me in the head and put me out of my misery. Will you do me that kindness, pistol man?"

She swallowed, wondering if Sebastien would consider doing that very thing.

"You said 'he' is a medical man, sir. What did you mean?"

"Nothing." Lees smiled now, but it wasn't a pleasant sight. "Nothing at all. What do you see, pistol man?"

The Mad Lord was staring at him, cocking his head like a dog hearing a faraway sound. At her waistcoat button, the locket was humming like an engine.

"A Highlander," said Sebastien. His voice was hollow, his eyes as green as emeralds. "There is a Highlander behind you."

"Been there ever since I was a boy. He protects me. I have no clue as to why."

"He was killed by a sword to the belly. He died in agony."

Lees laughed.

"By God, you've got it worse than me." He stepped forward, slipped the rest of his calling cards into Sebastien's waistcoat pocket. "Do yourself and your young lady a favour. Take that pistol of yours and shoot *yourself* in the head with it. Let her find someone normal and get on with it."

And with a pat on the chest, Lees pushed around them and departed the alley.

Ivy didn't know what to think, even less what to do. The crowds were moving to and fro in their suits of black and gray. Coaches and steamcabs rolled along the streets and the shadows of airships fell across the skies but as they stood toe to toe, hearing the distant rumble of thunder and waiting for the rain to fall, there was no one else in the entire city and the locket called Ghostlight had fallen silent once again.

***

It was dark in the Mortuary of the Royal. It was always dark in the Mortuary of the Royal. Shapes were distorted by the flickering gaslight on the walls and the leaded glass of the door and Christien rapped once before rolling it aside. Bond, Henry and Rosie looked up from the dissecting table.

On the table, lay a pair of arms.

"Christien," said Bond. "I told you not to come, boy. We've got this handled."

"All we got is arms," grunted Bender. "You got another letter from the Ripper."

"The Police have the letter now," said Christien. "And Inspector Savage told me about the arm. I want to help."

"You can go *home*, boy."

"Home is where I find the letters, sir," said Christien. "I feel much safer here."

Bond studied him for a moment before stepping back.

"Very well. Second arm found on Lambeth Road by the Blind School wrapped in lime. The hypothesis is that they are from the same woman. Henry, refute."

"Aw, Dr. Bond, why do I always have to refute?" Bender ambled over to the table. "Right limb slimmer than left, less subcutaneous hemorrhaging, seems to have been removed from the trunk at a radically different angle than the other..."

"Removed, not dissected?"

"I see no evidence of medical skill, sir. Any competent butcher could have done this. Joints of cows and joints of people are all the same, really. All you need is a good strong blade."

"Continue."

"Nails of the right hand shaped differently, perhaps indicating a different line of work. *If* she worked. Ah, let's see...this one found in the River tied with string and black tape and this one..." He rolled the other arm. "This one found wrapped in paper and cased in lime. Radically different methods of disposal. And weeks later to boot. Not likely the same perpetrator so therefore, not likely the same victim."

"Brief and to the point. Verdict?"

"Found dead, sir."

"Christien, are you sure you're up to it?"

"Yes, sir."

"Very well. Defend."

Christien moved in, lifted the limbs one by one. "They are the same length of bone. I'd put her height at five seven, or five eight. She's well fed but not gluttonous and her hands are long and fine. She's used to a comfortable life."

"Maybe she lived in a lunatic asylum," grinned Rosie but Henry smacked him.

"Shut it, you git."

"It were a joke, is all…"

Christien glared at him before turning back to the cadaver. "Probably young, given the state of the hands. No wedding ring found or indicated."

"Speaking of rings," said Bond. "That one of yours seems to be cutting off the circulation."

Christien studied his hand. "I can't get it off, sir. I've tried everything."

"You 'aven't tried the bone saw," grinned Rosie and Bender hit him again.

"Try some of the carbolic soap," said Bond. "You'll want to get that off before it damages a nerve. With your skill, that would be a loss."

The boys rolled their eyes. Christien was Bond's favourite and they all knew it.

"So then, getting back to our girl. What do *you* make of the difference in the nails, Christien?"

"I would warrant that everyone has a slight difference in the length and style of their nails, sir, depending on their handedness."

"So then. Professional anatomist, butcher or murderer?"

"I cannot express an opinion, sir. There is conflicting evidence."

"Indeed?"

"Well," said Christien. "To me, it looks to be different perpetrators but the same victim."

Rosie snorted out loud but ducked before Henry could hit him.

"Gruesome theory," said Bond. "Right then, boys, let's hope we find the torso to whom these belong. Bonus marks to whichever of you is correct."

"Aw, now Dr. Bond…" groaned Bender. "That ain't fair, is it?"

The Police Surgeon turned to leave. "Put our girl away. And I want you all to scrub up good. Lister's rules, remember?"

"But the ladies love a bloody frock," said Rosie. "They practically swoon for it!"

"Off you go, boys. See you tomorrow. And Remy, if you need anything…"

"Yes, sir. Thank you, sir."

As Dr. Bond left the mortuary, Bender swung around on his companion.

"Rosie, you git! You're going to see us all sacked."

"It won't 'appen," moaned Rosie. "Williams won't let it 'appen."

"He will, mark my words," said Christien as he wrapped the first arm back in canvas. "He will retire if anything goes wrong. He's protected by the Club."

"And so are you, Remy," said Bender. "You Clubbers stick together something fierce."

"I'm not sure I'm in, boys. This has become entirely too complicated. Bond is bound to put it together sometime and the Hs are all over the hospital."

"What's wit' yer finger anyways, Remy?"

"Yeah, it's disgusting!"

Christien shook his head. The little finger was purple and twisted, looking more a slip of dried tendon than live flesh.

"I can't get it off," he repeated.

"'ere," said Rosie. "Take this, then. It 'urts me eyes just lookin' at it."

And he held up a glove made of fine black leather.

"One?" asked Christien. "Why do have only one glove?"

"You find all sorts of flash gear on the streets under Big Ben," Rosie grinned. "It's cause o' the gangplanks. I got myself a new topper last week, traded it for a pint at the Bells."

Christien slid the glove over his hand, hiding the decaying digit from view as the boys turned to clean up the arms, one from the River and one from the Road.

***

The Clarence was both pub and restaurant and it was a favourite of royals, lawyers and Parliamentarians alike. It was crowded and full of smoke and she thought them lucky to find a table on their own. So they sat tucked into a corner by a street window, drinking tea and saying nothing at all to each other.

Their meals were delivered by a stout automaton whose chestplate slid open to rolls of billowing steam. A tray cranked out, two plates of golden meat pies slid off and onto the table. A hose snaked out, refreshing both cups of tea before it turned and wheeled back in through the crush of patrons at the bar.

She didn't want to look at him. She had prided herself on her expanding sensibilities but she had to admit, all this talk of the Ghost Club and secrets and now Lees, had left her wondering if she really knew what she was doing at all. Life had seemed so simple back in Stepney. Flat and safe and two-dimensional, like the pages of a book. In a book, you started at the beginning and went on to the end. Life, she was beginning to realize, was not like that.

She turned the card over in her hand—*Robert James Lees. Psychic. Spiritualist. Clairvoyant.* She wondered if he too saw with the eyes of a cat.

She looked at Sebastien. He had picked up his knife, but was only prodding at his food. He glanced up at her, eyes brown once more.

"Why did you kiss me, Ivy?"

Her heart thudded once in her chest. So he *had* noticed.

"In the infirmary," he went on. "You kissed me. Why did you do that?"

"I don't know," she said. "I suppose I was happy you'd lived and it was my fault that you got shot in the first place, really. I'm terribly sorry. It was too bold."

"It was entirely pleasant. I never get kisses like that. Sometimes..." He sighed and pushed his plate away. "All the time actually—I find myself wishing I were normal. I wish I could have friends that didn't have four legs, a pretty fiancée, perhaps marry. Have children and a regular occupation. Like Christien, you know. I think it would be wonderful to be normal."

"But why can't you marry, Sebastien? I can't see why you couldn't."

"Christien has told you, surely…"

"About?"

"About my parents."

She lowered her eyes. "He hasn't told me but I have heard."

"My father killed my mother, because *his* father killed *his* mother, for how many generations I honestly can't say. Madness runs in the family and it needs to stop, you see. And so it does. It ends. With me."

Her throat was growing tight.

"Christien says the lithium would help, but honestly, Miss Savage, I can feel nothing at all on the lithium. I'd rather be on laudanum if that were the case. I do prefer laudanum to the lithium. My mind is free and the darkness is beautiful. Really, it is."

He reached for his tea and she noticed his hand shaking. *A ghost hunter,* Fanny had said. *Drove him mad.*

"It's been good for me at Lasingstoke lately. I have my dogs, I have my horses. And while he may be prickly, Rupert is very fine company. I do what I can, and if I'm not forced to be around people for too terribly long, I manage well enough. For you see, the spirits are getting louder, more insistent, certainly more gruesome and it is to the point where the dead and the living look alike to me now. It is very difficult to tell them apart."

He paused, the cup hovering over the table in his hand.

"What does that mean, Miss Savage, when I can't tell a living person from a dead one?"

She bit her lip. "I don't know."

"I don't know, either." He looked out the window. "And so I stay up north and do what I can to keep out of trouble. Dash the broadsheets for hounding me. Poor Christien. I know why he is driven as he is."

"I don't know why the papers hound you, Sebastien. I think you're a brilliant, gifted, fascinating man. But I don't think you should be shooting people, no matter what the reason. There must be a better way."

"Can you think of anything? You heard the officers. You know what they think."

"What about Edward, or Albert Victor, or even Victoria? Surely, there is someone who can assist you."

"A Royal?" He arched a brow and smiled. "No, I fear I am very much alone in this pursuit."

"You are not entirely alone, sir."

"No?"

She saw something odd and hopeful in eyes that were brown now like chocolate.

"You have Rupert," she said quickly. "And, and Frankow and Castlewaite and, and the dogs…"

She cursed her inadequate, foolish tongue and her fear.

"Yes," he said quietly. "I do have them."

She leaned forward, keeping her voice deliberately low.

"In Milnethorpe, you said, 'You are forgiven and the Crown has been served.' So *do* you work for the Crown, sir? Do you murder murderers for the Crown?"

"No, I murder murderers for me," he said. "It is the only way I can have peace."

"That's criminal."

"It is no different than a hanging at the Old Bailey, Miss Savage. The Empire rigorously pursues stability and order. I serve at the pleasure of Her Majesty."

"It's not the same at all, Sebastien. A hanging at the Old Bailey is the result of an investigation and trial by judge and jury."

"In Wharcombe, a drunk kills his son with a poker to the head. Tell me, in a town with one overworked police constable, who is going to investigate the death of an eleven-year old fishmonger's boy?"

"That is why we have a police service, sir. To do that very thing."

"But a dead boy doesn't go to the police, Miss Savage. He goes to me."

"And what if you make a mistake or what if you don't find the killer? What happens then?"

He sighed.

"Seventh is very full."

"But why Seventh? Why do these ghosts go to the Seventh House of Lasingstoke?"

"Because bad things go to Seventh," he said. "That's what my father always said. When I first started seeing them, I was younger than your

Davis and my first inclination was that they belonged at Seventh. What sense does a young boy have?"

Thunder rumbled once again and the old beams in the ceiling shook cobwebs onto the floor.

"Nature is a powerful force, Miss Savage. If there is a hole in a barrel, a crack or a flaw in the wood, the water will find it. I am that hole, Miss Savage, that flaw in the integrity of the world. Spirits come to me and I send them to Seventh."

"You're not a flaw, sir." She looked out the windows. The sky was very dark. "But what I saw in Milnethorpe, the cold, the frost, the wind—it defies rational explanation, it defies reason and it makes me afraid. What if the dead asked you to shoot me?"

"But they wouldn't, Miss Savage. You're not a murderer."

"You are putting peoples' lives into the hands of angry dead spirits. Your women almost killed my brother and yet Davis is no more a murderer than I."

"They are not my women."

"I can't see how the dead are more trustworthy than the living. You put more faith, more value in a departed soul than in a living one. It's not only dangerous, sir, but I believe it morally wrong."

He looked away and she sighed.

"I'm sorry, Sebastien. I am speaking out of turn as usual. I just wish you could involve an officer of the law in your investigations."

"Your idealism is charming, Miss Savage, but unrealistic. It is only the increasing frequency and brutality of the murders in Whitechapel that are attracting attention. I guarantee you that if there had been only one woman—even one woman a month, there would be nowhere near the clamor for justice."

She sighed, knowing this to be true.

"What I do is a laborious and subjective process, dependent entirely upon my ability to interpret supernatural communications. You saw how Lees was treated by the police. They would never take me seriously."

He was right. People regularly reported their dreams and visions to the police and London's Whitechapel killer was no different. In fact, people were crawling out of the woodwork claiming supernatural knowledge of the villain and she could hear her father's voice deriding them as lunatics, fantasists and crackpots.

Even he would not take the Mad Lord seriously.

She took a deep breath.

"I would."

"You would what, Miss Savage?"

"Take you seriously. We made a crackerjack team in Milnethorpe. I could be that moral compass in your quest for justice. I have a good mind for a mystery and I do know the law. My father's unit made sure of that. I sat and listened at their feet for hours. You asked me what I want for my life, back in Lasingstoke. Well, this is what I want. Please say that you'll consider it?"

He smiled sadly.

"Now you are reaching a little too high, Miss Savage. Crumb's bullet could have struck you. Christien would never forgive me if something were to happen, nor would I be able to forgive myself." He shook his head. "No, we'll head straightaway to the Docks but once I have found your mother, I will insist you fly back to Lasingstoke while I stay in London alone. I will find this London Ripper, I will kill him and the Crown will be satisfied. I will turn myself in to the Ghost Club and Christien will be freed to marry you. You see? It is much better for everyone all around."

"Turn yourself in…?"

"Don't worry, Miss Savage. They won't find me as tractable as my father. In fact, Christien says that St. Mary's Bethlem has crackerjack surgeries for people like me."

"Bethlem? You mean, *Bedlam?*"

"The very one," he said, looking down at the golden crust of the meat pie in front of him. "In his last letter, Christien mentions a procedure in which the surgeon drills three tiny holes in the forehead like so…"

He picked up his knife and poked the crust gingerly once, twice, three times. Gravy oozed out onto the plate.

"Sebastien…"

"And then a long aluminium probe is inserted—"

"Sebastien, no."

"Christien says it is quite effective."

"Sebastien, *stop!*"

She threw her napkin onto her plate. "You don't need surgeries, Sebastien. And you most certainly do not need Bedlam! You simply need to exercise a little restraint, obey the law and stop shooting people!"

The pub had suddenly grown silent and she glanced around to see all eyes on her.

He lifted the tea to his lips.

"Oh I do believe they heard you in Over Milling *that* time, Miss Savage."

And a roll of thunder announced the commencement of rain.

Chapter 27

Of Wet Streets, Dry Cabs and a Head in the Thames

The rain was pelting down as the coach pulled up in front of a little rowhouse house in Stepney. The street was dark, the brick of the buildings streaked with coal and the odor of fish hung heavy in the air. There was a factory at the end of the street, the large stained sign reading *Fermier's Fish and Crab*. Sebastien thought the entire neighbourhood looked weary and sad.

"Yes," Ivy said. "I live in a neat little rowhouse by a factory."

"Funny how life is," he muttered.

"I'm just going to leave a note for my tad," she said. "He doesn't know I'm in town."

He continued to stare out the window.

"You won't leave without me, right?"

"I won't."

"Promise?"

"I promise."

"Castlewaite?" Ivy called and the trap swung open, revealing the gap-toothed smile of the coachman. "You promise not to leave without me?"

"Aye, miss. Ah promise."

"Right." She reached for her umbrella. "We'll do this tonight, and have a better day tomorrow. Agreed, Sebastien?"

"Yes, Miss Savage," he said, trying to smile. "We will have a better day."

"Because every day spent living is a good day, isn't that right?"

"Yes, Miss Savage."

She stepped out of the cab, popping her umbrella and trotting up the steps. He dropped his chin onto his palm, watched her let herself in with a very old key. Immediately, figures began to rise out of the floor.

"Castlewaite?" he called.

"Aye, sir?"

"Did you see anyone else in there?"

"Other than Miss Ivy, sir? Naw sir."

"You didn't see a bearded woman, a clown and a sword-swallowing acrobat?"

He could hear the old man grin.

"Naw sir, Ah din't see any o'tha."

He sighed.

"Castlewaite?"

"Aye, sir?"

"If a man kills a killer, is that wrong?"

"Sir?"

"What I mean to ask is…ah…" He leaned his forehead against the glass. "Is it wrong to kill someone that you know is a killer? If you know beyond a shadow of a doubt that the person has killed not just once, but several times. That he is a murderer and a villain and will kill again unless stopped. Then is it wrong to stop him…or her… by means of a bullet to the brain?"

"Without a trial, sir?"

"Yes, Castlewaite, without a trial."

The coachman thought a moment and Sebastien could see rainwater drip from his top hat onto the roof of the coach.

"'And if he strike him with an instrument of iron, so that he die, he is a murderer: the murderer shall surely be put to death. And if he smite him with a throwing stone, wherewith he may die, and he die, he is a murderer: the murderer shall surely be put to death. And if he smite him with an hand weapon of wood, wherewith he may die, and he die, he is a murderer: the murderer shall surely be put to death. The Avenger of Blood shall slay the murderer: when he meeteth him, he shall slay him.'"

Castlewaite looked down at him, his copper eyepiece whirred and clicked.

"Th' Avenger of Blood shall slay the murderer, sir. Tha's wha' Ah think, sir."

"Thank you, Castlewaite."

"Tha's from the Bible, sir."

"You're a good friend, Castlewaite."

"Aye, sir. Thank ye, sir."

He leaned his forehead back on the window, waiting for Ivy and a break in the rain.

***

"Dr. Williams!"

Christien pushed through the crowd toward the streamcab. He could see the Royal Physician's face through the rain-streaked window, looking very fine in his top hat and cloak.

The cab door swung open.

"Get in, boy," shouted the doctor. "You'll catch your death in a torrent like this!"

Christien climbed in and dropped himself onto the red velvet seat. Rain dripped down his forehead and cheeks but he did not move to wipe it.

"I'm headed to Buckingham, Remy," said Williams. "But I can give you a lift as far as the Park."

Christien nodded but said nothing.

The coach lurched forward with a sputter and pop, and forward again as it pushed into the crowd. The smell of coal filled the cab.

"What is it, my boy?" said Williams, leaning back in his seat. "You have the look of a lost soul about you."

Christien held his breath for only a moment before pulling the black glove from his left hand.

"What the deuce?" said Williams and he leaned forward.

The little finger looked like a slip of drying jerky. Tendons were stark against the purpling flesh and the skin had peeled and blistered around the circumference of the ring. Bone and nail looked as one.

"It's a miracle," Williams breathed.

"A miracle?" said Christien. "A miracle? It's a nightmare, that's what it is!"

Williams looked up at him now, eyes shining.

"It is proof, son. Success."

"It's a cursed ring from Annie Chapman, isn't it?" He snatched his hand away, slipped it back inside the safety of the glove. "Why did you give it to me and why is it behaving so?"

"Oh Remy," sighed Williams and Christien was certain he saw tears shining in the grey eyes. "You have no idea what this means."

"I most certainly do not."

"She's trying to contact you, boy. Through the ring."

"That's nonsense, sir. You know how I feel about that sort of thing."

"It doesn't matter how you feel, Remy. What other explanation can there be?"

"That it is too tight and is now cutting off circulation to my finger."

"Really, boy? That is what you believe?" Williams leaned back in the cab. "Or is that what you are telling yourself?"

Christien set his jaw but said nothing.

"You see?" said the surgeon with a grim smile. "If you believed that, why wouldn't you have simply asked one of the boys to remove it with a hack saw? Easy enough done, I should think. And why else would you have been going through my medical journals in the Doctor's Rooms at Bethlem? Oh yes, I do know that's what you were doing. I'm not a simpleton and you'd do well to remember that. Why were you looking for Dark Annie Chapman in my journals if you thought a brass ring simply too tight? And finally…"

He inclined his head, smile widening.

"Finally, why would you be sitting here in a cab with me, telling me that such things cannot happen if you knew, beyond a shadow of a doubt, that they could not?"

Christien was shaking with fury, a sensation altogether new for him, and it took all of his nerve to keep his face passive and his breathing controlled. The coach bumped and rattled as its wheels exchanged mud for cobbles and he knew that they had left the East End for a better part of town.

Williams patted his knee.

"You see, Remy? This is why the Club wanted you. You are your father's son and your brother's superior in every way. I will call an emergency meeting for tonight, ten o'clock. We will share this amazing discovery and all will be explained. How does that sound, Remy my boy? You will have all the scientific, metaphysical and parapsychical answers you seek."

Christien eyed him for a long moment before turning his face to the window. Fleet street now, tall limestone and brick buildings, arched windows, gothic spires and squared roofs. Men and carriages, women and horses crowding the streets with the noise of their lives. It was deafening and suddenly he understood his brother far too well.

"Tonight," he said through tight lips. "At the Ghost Club."

***

On the street, umbrellas bobbed as their owners trudged along beneath them. It was very late, nearing midnight now and the wet streets were lit with gaslight.

"Are ye sure ye want to be doin' this, now?" Castlewaite called down from the dickey. "We can come back in the mornin', we can."

They had pulled up on Tower Hill Road, waiting for the downpour to ease, neither wanting to admit defeat and retire to the places they both called home.

Ivy looked at him, her eyes heavy. "We can come back, Sebastien. I don't mind."

"No, Castlewaite," he called up but he was looking at her. "This won't take long."

"Aye, sir. Ah'll wait right 'ere for ye, then sir."

"Certainly, but do wait inside," said Sebastien. "The cab is good and dry."

The old man grinned, his eyepiece whirring as he left the dickey to climb down.

"It's bad enough the horse has to be out in this," the Mad Lord grumbled and he held the door open. Ivy popped her umbrella and stepped out into the rain.

The formidable dark shape of the Tower rose above them as they made their way onto the road. She was still wearing Davis' peacoat. It was several sizes too large but served to keep the water off. The bowler did the same, and together they strode past the Tower down St. Katharine's Way toward the docks.

She could smell fish and oil as they neared the river. There were some longshoremen working, some shipsmen, and she could hear shouts and laughter but for the most part, the docks were quiet. Still, she hoped Sebastien had his strange three-barreled pistol at the ready, just in case, and she led him away from the cloistered docks toward the pier.

Finally, in the rain and the darkness, she stopped.

"Here," she said. "A ship from the East India Company was reported to have brought elephants as cargo and mum had taken Tobias to see. The elephants were being unloaded and mum was watching them when Tobias chased a kitten toward the pier…"

Her voice trailed off. She had not been there. She had not seen.

"Here?" asked Sebastien. "Not inside the locks but this pier, right here?"

"Yes. Down there…"

He moved slowly to the edge of the water, the umbrella hiding head and shoulders but she saw his hand move, turning upwards as if to catch raindrops in his palm. He had called it "asking," back in Milnethorpe.

She glanced around the dark waterfront. Smokestacks billowed above the engine-works house, its massive steam engines running constantly to keep the water in the locks and basins level. The Tower of London rose darkly on one side, the arched windows of the Ivory House on the other and in the distance, cranes—idle now, but in daylight, busy with the construction of the new bridge across from the Tower. It was an elaborate project that had already taken two years. It was rumored not to open until well into the next decade.

Suddenly, the locket began to hum and glow and she looked back at the Mad Lord. He was standing as he had been, palm upraised, and she felt her heart breaking at the sight of him. He moved her more than a thousand stories.

Suddenly, he dropped the umbrella and strode toward the far end of the pier. She thought he would walk straight off the edge but he turned and began to climb down the ladder that accessed the framework beneath the dock. He disappeared and she stood, clutching her umbrella and peering over the side.

"Miss Savage!" she heard him call. "Miss Savage, come here!"

She climbed down after him, once again grateful for the practicality of breeches. The framework was dark but the locket threw light across the beams. The water lapped at the posts and timbers and the smell of the river was strong here. Fish and sewage, silt and oil. Wharcombe Bay had smelled so much better than this.

He was suspended like a monkey in the framework of the pier, arms and legs braced against angled beams but when he heard her, he turned his face and smiled like the sun. It was a pleasant change after the last few hours. Slowly and carefully, she climbed toward him, not trusting her handholds on the water-slick timbers. He reached down and wrapped an arm around her waist, hoisting her up so she could see where he was looking.

It was a strangely intimate grip, entirely flattening her chest into his body, but she pushed it out of her mind.

"Look there," he said and he pointed with his free hand. "In the far corner, under the truss."

"I don't see anything."

"No?"

"Honestly. No."

"Tobias. He looked like you, yes? Dark hair, green eyes?"

"Yes…"

"Did he have freckles?"

Her throat began to tighten. "Yes…"

"Missing one front tooth. He was very young."

"…oh God…"

"Your mother is here, with him. Over there, under the truss." He narrowed his eyes to study them. "I thinking they're playing cat's cradle. She is singing to him."

The tears came and she leaned her forehead on his chest.

"No, no. It's good, Ivy. She's happy. Her body is just a shell. Here, with Tobias, she's happy."

"Tobias is dead, Sebastien. And my mother is still living. It what way can that possibly be good?"

"Ah, you're quite right. I'm sorry."

"Is she choosing this?"

"No...maybe...probably...yes..."

"Death is not an acceptable choice," Ivy whispered. "Not when you *have* the choice. It's cowardly and defeated and it's just not fair."

He focused his attention on the truss and the damp air grew cold very quickly. Ice began to form all along the beams in direct lines from the corner and there was a rush of cold wind. Abruptly, Sebastien turned away, eyes tightly shut.

"She's angry with me. Made quite a terrifying face actually." He peered back at the corner. "They've gone now. But they'll likely be back tomorrow. Perhaps we should try again in the morning?"

"Yes," she said. She was still pressed tightly against him and she looked up into his eyes. She had given up trying to track their colour. They changed like a London sky. "In the morning."

"Yes, in..." he swallowed. "In the morning."

She could feel his heart beating against hers and she held her breath. She very much wanted to kiss him again. Just a little. It wouldn't take much for this choice to be made. Just a simple push with her toe and Christien would be little more than a porcelain memory.

"So..." His voice no more than a whisper. "You think I should stop...shooting people?"

"Yes, Sebastien," she whispered back. "I really think you should."

"Well...I'll, I'll give that a try..."

His eyes had found her lips, as if seeing them for the very first time.

"Sound good?"

"Sounds very good."

Yes, she very much wanted to kiss him.

"So," she began. "If I were to reach a little higher..."

"Just a little."

And she pushed with the tip of one very fine boot...

The thudding of her heart was growing louder, although this time it was more a thump, thump, thump. With a sinking feeling, she knew that this was not her heart.

Someone was walking on the pier above their heads. They could hear voices, whispering, sniggering, and Ivy bit her lip. Sebastien grinned and pulled her closer.

"Shhh…" he hushed as if it was a great game and she supposed it was. The Mad Lord and the policeman's daughter, looking for ghosts under St. Katharine's Pier. "It's the Beak!"

"The Blue Bottle!" she whispered.

"Coppers."

"Peelers."

An entire host of slang terms for her father's profession were on her tongue, when there was a splash into the water just beyond their feet. Ivy let out a little whimper as water sprayed onto her legs and she knew she would be miserable if she caught cold because of it.

Something white and brown bobbed in the water by their feet. Sebastien grew very cold and she craned her neck to see.

A cry died in her throat as a woman's head rolled in the water once, twice before being swept under the dock toward Whitechapel.

Chapter 28

Of Purl, Strauss Waltzes and a Chance Meeting in Dutfield's Yard

The head bobbed, rolled once, twice then disappeared into the blackness of the water.

The air under the pier crackled with ice and slowly, Sebastien de Lacey reached behind his back. Ivy could barely breathe, her pulse was roaring in her ears, but she most definitely heard the sound of a hammer being cocked and quite reflexively, she pushed away from the man holding her. For with slow and painstaking control, he aimed the tri-barreled pistol up, corrected the angle and fired into the underside of the pier.

"Shite!" bellowed a voice from above and suddenly, the dock thundered with boots. Sebastien swung like a monkey through the beams and within seconds, had disappeared up the ladder, over the edge in pursuit.

It took Ivy several moments longer and when she finally pulled herself up and onto the pier, there was no one but a small group of dockhands gathering nearby. She snatched up her umbrella, for the rain was pelting hard.

"Oy!" shouted one man. "You all right, lad?"

"Yes!" she called back.

"Lad?" said another voice. "That ain't no lad."

"A bird? In breeks?"

"I never seen no bird in breeks…"

"Did you see anyone just now, sirs?" she called. "Anyone at all?"

"Aye," came another. "We heard a shot and two blokes tore outta here like they was on fire!"

"And an'over un chasin' em, dat's wot I saw!"

"Which way, sirs?"

They all turned and pointed and Ivy sighed. Back down St. Katharine's Way.

"Thank you, sirs. Could someone please fetch a bobbie?" She moved across the pier, scanning the black water for a sight of the head. "I fear there's been a dreadful murder."

She could hear the men as they murmured amongst themselves but she could see no sign of the head. It was too dark. However, she did find a sizable hole made by Sebastien's bullet and knelt down to study a puddle of rainwater. There was a scrap of fabric floating that looked like trouser material. It was gray wool with a thin blue pinstripe, and there appeared to be blood on one edge. She marveled, thinking that Sebastien may have scored yet again. The man was a crackerjack shot. She rose to her feet, slipped the fabric in the pocket of her breeches and looked around to wait for a police officer.

Naturally, of Sebastien de Lacey, there was no sign.

***

The dead stared at him as he raced down the black alleys of Smithfield. The pair had a decent lead but they were careless. Knocking things over in attempt to slow him only left a bang-up trail for him to follow. He was soaked to the bone with the greatcoat growing heavier by the minute, so he slipped out of it as he ran, dropping it on a box of cornhusks by the side of the road.

The streetlamps were bright as he raced onto Butcher Row and he could make them out darting right toward Mansell. He was tempted to pull his pistol and take one down, but there were pedestrians even now in this downpour and he knew it would be a risky shot at best. And Ivy Savage's words were still ringing in his ears. He continued in pursuit.

He could feel eyes on him and it was impossible to ignore them all. The Tower was a terrible place. People had died by the hundreds over the centuries and he could see them now—men, women, children. The plagues had taken their toll as well and he could feel their deaths, frozen in time, as he raced past.

One of the men was limping now and he secretly prided himself on his accuracy. They were not making a straight go of it and he knew they were hoping to lose him in the chaos of the streets. Up Smithfield to Glasshouse and east again on Cable and it occurred to him that if they hit Commercial, they might be able to hail a cab. If they did that, he realized his chances of finding them then would be slim.

He bumped into a woman, or rather, when he reflected upon it later, *she* bumped into him. She was very small, dressed in green and black velvet, and he tried to swing out of her way but she had hold of his arm and he could not shake her off.

"Hallo, han'sum," she purred and the smell of liquor hit him like a wall. "What's yer hurry?"

"Go home," he snapped. "You should not be out tonight."

He tried to bolt but she had his arm, was reaching for his trousers. He slapped at her hand and suddenly the cold threatened to crack his skull.

Blade slash throat ear kidney liver slice

She laughed and pulled him to her, but he clapped a hand over her mouth and pushed her backwards into the wall.

"Go home," he growled. "You're not safe! *Go home!"*

"Oy missus, need some 'elp?"

Two longshoremen standing there and Sebastien released the woman, staggered back into the street. There was no sign of the fleeing men.

To Commercial, he told himself. Just beat them to *Commercial.*

He set off again in the rain heading west.

***

Ivy tugged the umbrella lower over her head.

"Yes, sir. I'm quite certain it was a head, sir."

"A woman's head, you say."

"Yes, sir. A woman's head."

"And you saw it where, miss?"

"Under the pier, sir. We heard feet, we heard voices, then there was the splash." She watched him writing. "Of a head. In the River."

His name was Constable Pleasant Poole and his moustache twitched as he regarded his notes. His dark helmet kept the rain from his head but his notebook was a soggy mess.

"And what, pray tell, were you and your friend doing under the pier, miss?"

Damnation. She heard Sebastien's words ringing in her ears. They would never believe her. She almost didn't believe it herself.

She raised her chin. "Investigations, Constable Poole. And when you do find the head, or the unfortunate torso to whom it belongs, do remember to contact Ivy Savage, daughter of Inspector Trevis Savage, Metropolitan Police, H-Division. Do write that down, sir."

His dark eyes flicked up at her, before heading back down to his notes.

"Yes, miss. Thank you, miss. Do you need a cab 'ome, miss?"

"No, thank you, sir. I have a very fine one waiting. French Warmbloods, you know. All the rage in Lancashire."

She stepped away from the officer and marched off the pier, through the gawking crowd of dockworkers who had gathered to watch. She prayed Castlewaite was still parked by the Tower and hadn't accompanied de Lacey on his pursuit. It was very late now, and she had no money. Sebastien had carried a sum in his pocket for expenses but she had no idea where he would have gone or if he would even remember to come back for her. He was like a bloody hound on a scent.

There was a coat thrown over a pile of cornhusks and she paused to nudge it with her boot. Yes, it looked like his, so she picked it up, shook it off and threw it over her shoulder like a sack.

With a deep breath, she tucked her hair up under the bowler, straightened her brolly and headed off to find the coach.

***

"Damnation!" he hissed under his breath.

He had reached Commercial Street and true enough, there was no sign of them. Cabs and hansoms jammed the streets, crowded even for this gusty Saturday night and he realized there was no way he could find them to follow.

There was an automabob on the corner of Commercial and Backchurch and he was sorely tempted to approach it and register. Dressed in tin-plated officer's uniforms and helmets, automabobs were stationary automatons in the service of the Met, rather like short, automated police boxes. People could ask for directions or register a complaint and the automabob would do its best to provide assistance. They routinely took photochromes of the street life as well, which had proved to be a deterrent to all manner of petty crime.

They also played audiochromes of Strauss waltzes, which Sebastien believed was a greater deterrent. It was a well-known fact that most criminal types abhorred fine music.

He shivered and rubbed his hands together to warm them. He wished now that he had not ditched his greatcoat and debated going back for it. He leaned under the canopy of a shop front, cursing his ineptitude. The torsos were angry and of all the dead at Seventh, it was the torsos that disturbed him most. He had been presented with a perfect opportunity to rid himself of them only to let it slip away because of a drunk.

Blade slash throat ear kidney liver slice

He rubbed his eyes, wishing he didn't see the things he saw and not for the first time he wished that Frankow had just let him die.

There was a single chime from the clock tower at the end of the street. He glanced up. 1:00 a.m. It was late. Very late in fact and he marveled at the number of people still out and about at this hour, most especially the number of women. He shook his head. They simply didn't understand the dangers of walking the streets as they did, how some men hunted them like deer, how like little lambs they were, amongst a forest of wolves.

Ivy Savage! He let out a groan, clapped a hand over his forehead. He had completely forgotten her under the pier. Hopefully, she hadn't slipped. Hopefully, she hadn't drowned. He'd never forgive himself if she died like that.

However, he might be able then to send her to Seventh and visit her from time to time.

He rather liked the idea so he pushed himself off from the wall and headed back toward Batty Row and the Docks.

***

"Hello, Castlewaite."

"'ello, miss." The old man held the door open for her as she climbed in. "Did you and 'is Lordship find what ye was lookin' for?"

"Yes, thank you. And a fair bit more."

Castlewaite grinned his gap-toothed grin. "So tha' was 'im I seed chasin' them boffers, eh?"

"It was indeed." She dropped the greatcoat to the floor of the cab. "I have no idea where he's gone, or how long he'll be."

"Aye. That's 'is Lordship, miss. Always on the town." He had a small clockwork light pinned to the ceiling of the cab. With a few twists, it would set the gearworks in motion, creating a contained spark that, once magnified, provided a beam of golden light. Her father had mentioned the Met was outfitting their patrol officers with them for better visibility on the streets.

Pocket torches, he had called them.

She noticed his hand, sliding something behind his back against the seat cushion. She breathed in the air.

"Castlewaite? Something smells very good in here right now…"

"Aw now, miss. Don't be angry…" He produced a copper container. "Just a bit of purl, miss. Ah gets chilled on a night like this."

"Purl?" She flashed him a great smile. "My grandfather used to make purl all the time. May I?"

He averted his eye. "Aw, miss. It's a might stronger than wha' yer grandpa used to make, Ah'll wager…"

"Castlewaite, I grew up in Swansea," she said as she removed her bowler and shook out her hair. "I'll wager it's exactly like what my gran'tad used to make."

He handed her the container and she twisted the lid, breathed the rich bitter odor.

With a smile, she lifted it to her lips.

***

It was a mistake taking the cut down Helen Street. He didn't know this part of town. Knew very little of London actually and he hoped he could figure out how to make it back to the river. There was no gaslight here, for in truth it was little more than an alley behind a walled yard. A horse and cart would have great difficulty making it past the rubbish piled against the walls. The footing was soddy earth and puddles.

Suddenly, the cry of a thousand banshees threatened to split his head from the inside. He clapped his hands over his ears and staggered against the yard's wall, the cold cutting through him like a knife. The air in the lane fogged and warped and slowly, a ghostly woman rippled into existence. She tried to speak but the blood at her throat bubbled like a brook. He had never seen anything like it. The air sizzled with frost.

Cursing then footsteps and silence once again. The cold was blistering, causing his teeth to chatter as the dead woman gestured and gaped. He placed a hand on the brick to steady himself.

Suddenly, a bag was tossed over the wall followed by the dark figure of a man. He was wearing a Coburn—a greatcoat with shoulder cloaking, and a very fine a felt hat. He dropped quietly to his feet, looked first left then right then froze when he saw the Mad Lord staring at him from the shadows.

Sebastien knew, without a shadow of a doubt, that he had just stumbled across the infamous London Ripper.

Even though there was no lamplight and the sky was blackened with rain, Sebastien could see the man's face as clear as day. He needed no light, for it was a face of the dead.

"Father?"

The man snatched the bag and bolted down the lane, disappearing around the corner in a heartbeat.

And it was less than a heartbeat before Sebastien was hot on his heels after him.

Chapter 29

Of Metal Spades, Left-Handed Villains and Dead Women in the Hall

The rain poured down like Noah's flood, but inside the cab, they were warm and dry.

"Aw yes, miss. That Davis is a right smart lad, 'e is! 'ave ye seen 'is plans for the boilers?"

Ivy stretched across the seat of the cab, toes tapping together happily, the flask of purl clutched contentedly in her hand.

"I have not, sir. I have been busy chasing Sebastien de Lacey all over Lancashire, Lonsdale *and* London. That's what *I've* been doing."

"Well, Ah think 'e's the best, Ah do. A right smart lad."

"I'm so glad. Did I mention I saw a head tonight?"

"Yes, miss. Many times, miss."

"But it was a *head,* Castlewaite. A single, bobbing head."

"That's terrible, miss."

"It was, Castlewaite. Truly terrible. I've never seen a head before, just bobbing like that. And the eyes! It still had eyes! Did you know I received a heart in the post? A human heart! That's why they sent me up north, they did. What is it about me that attracts all manner of misplaced body parts?"

"Ah don't know, miss."

"Ooh look!" she exclaimed and glanced down at the locket. It was spinning once more.

"Honestly, Castlewaite, I have never owned a single piece of jewelry in my life, but now, Christien has given me two. A ring that belonged to his dead mother and this infernal thing."

"It's right pretty, miss."

"It talks to ghosts, Castlewaite. In *Latin.*"

"Does it, miss?"

"Yes, Castlewaite. Believe me, I know how it sounds, but I have seen far too much in these last weeks to think anything but."

"Well then, Ah believe it, miss."

"It snows, Castlewaite. You just wait. We'll be shoveling before the morning."

He grinned, toothlessly.

"I should have given it to Frankow. I don't know why I didn't. Stubborn, I suppose. It was a stubborn thing growing up Savage." She swirled the flask in the air. "Castlewaite?"

"Yes, miss?"

"What is your Christian name, Castlewaite?"

"Jerry, miss."

"Jerry Castlewaite, may I ask you a personal question?"

He grinned again. "Aye, miss. Ye may ask."

"How did you lose your eye, Jerry Castlewaite?" And she passed him the purl.

He took a swig, wiped his mouth with his sleeve.

"Well, miss, it was one of the Master's 'orses. It was wearing iron shoes and it kicked me in the 'ead, right 'ere..." He tapped his copper-plated brow with the flask. "Broke the bone and squished me eyeball like a grape."

"Oh, Jerry. That's terrible. One of Sebastien's horses?"

"No, no, miss. The Master. That's wha' we called 'is dad. Renaud Jacobe, miss. A right nasty piece, 'e was. An 'ard man, sure enowt."

He drank again, passed her the flask. "But Rupert, now. There's a good 'un. Felt bad fer the way 'is brother treated me, so 'e paid for me new eye. Took me down to Manchester himself, to the Manchester Royal Eye there."

She took the flask. "Can you see out of it?"

"Aye."

"Yes, I mean your eye. Can you see out of your eye?" She took a swig. It was wondrous strange how everything was blurred. Even the motions of her hands were slow and echoing. Her lips felt like rubber.

"Yes, miss. Ah can see. Rupert says it's got a mina'chure AE program in it tha' lets me brain decode the light. 'e says the brain is a right remarkable piece of machinery, which, Ah suppose it is."

"Well, I think it is too. And I'm so very glad you can see. Now… why don't you have any teeth?" She raised the flask, frowned, shook it. "It's empty, Castlewaite? What are we to do?"

He grinned and reached under the seat, slid a tarnished silver flask out now.

"Ah'm quite sure yer granddad didn't make nowt like this, Miss Ivy…"

She grinned back and reached across the cab.

"A toast," she said, lifting it to her lips. "To the head."

***

For a dead man, his father was very fast but Sebastien would not give up, not after losing the other two earlier on. So he dogged him through every deserted lane and dark alley in Whitechapel. There was not even the opportunity for a shot, as the villain dodged and wove like a hare. In the pouring rain, the ground slopped and slid and he was hard-pressed to keep his feet under him. His father obviously knew the vicinity well for he kept his trail to the back streets where no one could lend a hand.

Renaud flailed his arms and suddenly, the Coburn was released, catching Sebastien like a sail and causing him to stumble before he tossed it to the side. The villain darted toward an alley yard with a four-foot stone wall surrounding it and with cat-like grace, he leapt into the air, pushing off the copes with his right arm and swinging both legs over. He was gone in a heartbeat.

Easy enough, thought Sebastien and he increased his speed and sprang, reaching out with his right arm. Something in his shoulder gave way however and the arm buckled beneath his weight. His body continued over the wall but his legs did not catch him and he fell to his knees on the other side. Stars popped behind his eyes and he cursed the fact yet again that, only days ago, he had been shot.

He struggled to his feet when he spied a dark shape moving toward him. He ducked but not quickly enough and the broad side of a spade struck him flat on the cheek, sending him thudding into the wall. He rolled as the thin edge struck the stone with a force that would have split him in two. He staggered backwards, reached for the pistol. His right arm was useless, but he was proficient with both and pulled with his left, cocking the hammer as it came.

"That is *mine...*" growled his father and the spade came down again, this time across his wrist and the pistol was sent sailing out of his grip.

Ice crackled up the stone even as the blood ran down his arm and he knew he had little fight left in him. The yard spun and the spade circled in for another go. He couldn't move fast enough and it connected with the side of his head, sending him to his knees once again. One last time it came, metal clanging against the metal plates in his skull and sending him the rest of the way to the ground. He could taste dirt and grass and his own blood.

The cold was blistering now as a hand twisted into his hair, raising his chin, and he felt a blade at his throat. A left-hander, he thought in a detached sort of way. He'd never known his father was left-handed. It made a certain sense. Handedness, like madness, ran in the family. He hoped the cut would be quick.

"That pistol is too good for you," growled the voice.

"The people I shoot with it stay dead," Sebastien grunted, spitting out bits of dirt on his tongue. "Pity you can't say the same."

A heartbeat of hesitation and suddenly, both the blade and the man were gone. Sebastien lay there for a long moment, trying to catch his breath before he managed to crawl over to the wall and sit against it. He wondered now if it really had been his father who had just beaten him down and if so, why in the world he had stopped his blade. Didn't matter. He cast his eyes across the yard in hopes of seeing the pistol, but somehow he knew his father had nicked it. Failed again. He had lost the head, the head's men, his father and his pistol, all in one night.

To top it all off, a dead man was the London Ripper. Not even Ivy was likely to believe him now.

Bad luck all around.

He pushed himself to his feet, hauled his bruised body over the fence and headed in what he hoped was the direction of the cab.

**

"And how many grandchildren, sir?"

"Eight, as of last month."

"Oh well done. Eight grandbaby Castlewaites. Do they have all their eyes and teeth, sir?"

"Aye, all 'cept the little 'un. But she'll get her teeth soon enough."

She waved the flask around. "That's grand, Jerry! Absolutely grand! I would love to have *wyrion* someday, oy? That's Welsh for grandchildren, in case you didn't know. But first I'll need some *plant* and even before that, I'll need a *dyn*. Ah, the *dynion*. Damn 'em all to hell…"

"Aw, now miss," he said, reaching for the flask. "Ah think Ah should be takin' that about now…"

"Oy? Who's the greedy girl, now, eh? Not me, sir. No sir." And she clutched it tightly to her chest.

The cab door rattled and swung open, and the Mad Lord stumbled up the high step. Ivy raised her brows.

"And where have you been, then?"

He flopped himself onto the seat next to Castlewaite, bloody and bruised. His breathing sounded as if he had tried to outrun a steamtrain and failed.

"You look like shite, sir."

"Ah'll get up in the dick, now," said Castlewaite and he slipped out of the cab to climb upwards.

"I found your coat in the rubbish."

"Are you drunk," Sebastien panted. "Or are you Welsh?"

She raised the flask. "I'm both, sir. And proud of it."

The trap swung open. "To Holbrook 'ouse, sir?"

"Please."

"And Miss Ivy? Where shall Ah be takin' her?"

"I'm sure she's not particular, Castlewaite. Not at the moment."

Ivy rolled her head and pouted. The bowler was tipped at an odd angle, so that it almost covered one eye.

"I am *so* particular. Just ask Christien. I am very, very particular. But *you*, sir, *you* are *peculiar.*"

"Are you Welsh?" He frowned. "Truly?"

She swung herself over to sit beside him and perched her chin on his shoulder.

"I am indeed. Did you really not notice?"

"Honestly, no."

She smiled a ridiculously wide smile. "You, sir, are adorable. With your eye blackened like that, you look like a regular rogue. Alexander Dunn is a jewel thief, you know. Did I mention I saw a head tonight?"

The coach jerked and started to move. He swallowed, not knowing what to say.

She raised the flask. "Would you like some purl?"

He was bleeding out of many wounds, his one wrist useless due to the spade, the other useless because of the wall. The side of his head was red and purple and he was soaked to the very bottom of his toes. His dead father was the London Ripper and his brother's fiancée was rather pretty and very, very close.

He snatched it out of her hand and downed it to the last as the carriage rattled its way to Holbrook House in Kensington.

***

The servants were discreet, he had to give them that. Even Pomfrey—prim, wigged Pomfrey—had not said a word as the master of the house showed up at the door looking as if he'd just lost a round with a pugilist, hoisting his brother's fiancée like a bag of fermented apples.

He carried her up the stair of Holbrook House before deciding on the Blue Room, the one with the wallpaper. He nudged the door with his foot, carried her in and dropped her onto the spread. He placed her hat on the night table, began to unlace her boots. They were very fine boots, he thought. Perfect for riding. She couldn't possibly have purchased them in Over Milling. No very fine shoe shops in Over Milling. He'd closed the last one down years ago.

He pulled the spread over her and she didn't move at all. The locket lay in the cove of her breasts and he stared at it for a moment. It was pulsing like a heartbeat, calling him like a siren the way mermaids called sailors to their deaths.

He raised his hand over it, willing it to move.

It did. First spinning, then flashing—a lighthouse on a darkened shore. It moved from its nest in her corset, rising to hover just beneath his palm.

Aperi me, it sang in Latin. *Open me.*

The voice of angels.

He wanted it more than anything he had ever wanted.

He reluctantly moved his hand, not watching as it dropped back down to her chest. He tucked her in, smoothed her wild hair across the pillow and for the first time he noticed the freckles, just a few across the bridge of her nose.

Amazing all the things he wanted now.

"You're too perfect, Christien," she purred and rolled over, a wide happy smile on her face. He straightened, feeling an unexpected sense of loss.

He rose quietly, closing the door and leaving the room in total darkness.

There was a woman waiting for him in the hall.

She was hideous. Her mouth and nose were gone. Ears too, from the looks of it. Her bodice was opened and her skirts torn so that her organs were exposed and hanging. A shawl of intestines draped across her right shoulder and her entire torso was splattered with blood. What was left of her clothes were shabby, all green and black velvet and it struck him instantly who she was.

Blade slash throat ear kidney liver slice

He sagged against the wall, ran a hand down his face.

"I'm sorry," he moaned and suddenly, there were eight others in the hall—seven whom had previously been in Seventh and an eighth—the one who had died in the lane before his encounter with his father. Nine women, standing in the fine Georgian hallway of Hollbrook House. The cold began to descend as he slid down the wall to sitting, and he cradled his head in his hands. He closed his eyes, but that did not remove the image of them from his mind, nor the feel of them in his bones.

The wailing began soon after and his teeth chattered in time. He wished he could be very small, wished he could escape. Wished he still had his father's pistol. He would follow Lees' advice and shoot his own head off with it tonight.

And so he sat like that for hours, shivering and wanting and numb until his brother pulled him to his feet and into his room.

Chapter 30

Of Bond's Boys, Criminal Behaviour and Another Letter from Jack

"Good Lord, Bastien," groaned Christien as he peeled the shirt from his brother's chest. "Have you been shot?"

Sebastien nodded and closed his eyes, teeth chattering, head sinking into the soft pillow.

"Two days ago, in Milnethorpe."

Christien pulled the old bandages away, tossed them to the floor. Began to examine the stitches that were pulling loose from the flesh.

"Damn Frankow and his wire stitches…" He shook his head. "They can hold a bull together but not you…"

"Is there any Scotch downstairs?"

"I'll fetch some as soon as I've cleaned you up." Christien rose from the bed, moving to the doorway where he had dropped his bag. He spied the chalk symbols across the doorframe, along the walls. The *ligaturae spiritus,* his brother called them. Prayers of binding and protection. They were old, but apparently still worked. A psychological crutch, he knew and was thankful for the power of the mind. It was the only way the two of them could be in the same room. Sebastien would normally be clawing his eyes out by now.

With a sigh, he resumed his seat on the bed. "Why do you do this, Bastien? Why can't you stay up north? You know what London does to you."

"Bertie…"

The wound was oozing from where the stitches had pulled away. He dabbed at them with alcohol and cotton.

"Gads, Remy, you should have seen her face. She had no mouth, no nose. It was dreadful."

"Who was, Bastien?"

"The little woman from Whitechapel."

"God, no wonder the Club wants you," he muttered under his breath. He reached for his brother's wrists, made sure they were not broken. They were however purple and swelling. "Is Bertie asking you to search for this Ripper now?"

"Of course. But I would be obligated anyway. I have a houseful at Seventh and they're beginning to follow me around. It's Father, by the way."

"What's that?"

"Father is your Ripper."

"Father's been dead for years, Bastien. Do you hear what you're saying? How you sound?"

"I sound mad. I know. You tell me every time."

Christien continued flexing the bruised wrist, twisting it to test the integrity of the bones. Sebastien winced

"Sorry. Did you ride or take the airship?"

"The airship." Sebastien grinned, eyes still closed. "She gets airsick, you know. Sat with a pot in her lap the entire time."

"She…?"

"Ivy."

Christien blinked slowly. "You brought Ivy to London with you?"

"We were going to try to find her mother at the docks. She's fixed there with the little boy, the dead one. Tobias I think his name was. I'm not sure if she's willing to come back. I couldn't ask, for someone tossed a head in the river and I was rather preoccupied after that."

"By God, Bastien…" He sat up stiffly. "Where is she now?"

"Hm… The Blue Room. The one with the paper. She likes paper, I think."

"She's here? In Hollbrook?"

"Yes. She's drunk and her father's a policeman." His words were growing slurred. "I don't get on well with policemen so I brought her here."

"You got drunk with my fiancée?"

"Castlewaite…He keeps a little flask for nights…like this…"

Christien sat for a long while on the edge of his brother's bed, his mind spinning in many different directions. The locket. Surely, she'd have brought the locket with her. No wonder he'd lost two hours tonight.

He sat that way until a pounding on the door roused him from his thoughts and he went down to tend it.

***

"By *God*, boys," he groaned at the sight in the doorway. Pomfrey was holding it open, eyes sleepy, wig miraculously in place. It was well past three in the morning, but a well-paid houseman was never off the clock.

Henry Bender was at the door, supporting Ambrose Pickett under one arm.

"Remy!" cried Bender, pushing into the foyer "Rosie needs tending!"

"I been shot!" wailed Pickett. "By some bloke under the pier!"

"Quiet," hissed Christien. "Into the study. *Now.* Pomfrey, my bag is upstairs in Bastien's room."

"I'll fetch it at once sir," said the man and he disappeared like a wraith into the darkness. He would ask no questions. He was good that way.

Christien slipped his arm under his friend and the trio hobbled to the study, dropping Rosie into a chair.

"Start up the fire, will you Henry?" Christien closed the French doors and moved to the side table to pour three glasses of port. He passed one to Pickett before kneeling by the chair.

"Drink," he ordered. Rosie did, all in one go.

As Bender stoked the fire, Christien pulled up an ottoman for the injured leg. "What the hell happened?"

"We thought we were clear so we tossed it," said Bender. "And some bugger shoots up from under the bloody dock!"

"Shot my leg, he did!" moaned Rosie. "Shot my bloody leg!"

Bender snorted. "Took out a perfect hole in his trousers, too…

Bloody hilarious, if you ask me..."

"It was *not* funny, you git! *You* get shot next time."

"Enough," growled Christien. He tore open the trousers to reveal a long, white leg with two perfect holes at a steep angle. He turned the leg, twisting it and eliciting a whimper from his friend.

"Damn him," he smiled coolly. "He *is* a crackerjack shot."

"Who?" said Bender. "Who's a crackerjack shot?"

"My brother, that's whom. Bullet went clean between the bones."

Bender swung around from the fire. "Are you saying—?"

Christien cleared his throat as Pomfrey entered the study to lay the medical bag at Christien's side.

"Would you be wanting some cheese and biscuits to go with that port, sir?"

"No but warm up a bit of that soup from supper, Pomfrey, if you would be so kind."

He disappeared as quietly as he had come.

"Are you saying that your *brother* shot Rosie?" Henry hissed. "The Mad Lord of Lasingstoke? What the hell was he doing under the pier?"

"I didn't think he was in town," groaned Rosie.

"Arrived tonight." Christien was cleaning the wound now, dabbing it with alcohol from a dark bottle. "Not in town eight hours and he nails one of you. Williams is right. You're bloody useless, the pair of you."

"Shut it, Remy. We had the arms *and* the head. You just had to do the legs."

"Which they have not found, by the way..." He continued his work. "Is Lewie joining us here afterwards?"

"Yeah." Bender straightened, downed his port in several anxious gulps and shook his ginger head. "He thinks he's got a bang-up place for the rest of her."

"It's not meant to be bang-up, you ass. It's meant to be disposed of. Williams will not stand by us if this goes poorly. He could get fired for giving us those cadavers."

Bender snorted again. "He could get fired for doing what he did to those girls, Remy. Or to the Royals. It's still illegal, even for him. In for one, in for all. That's the way of it."

There were voices from outside and the French doors swung open once again, admitting Lewis Powell-Smith. Marie was under one arm, looking very pretty in jewel-toned velvets and golden curls. Powell-Smith frowned as he took in the scene.

"What the hell, Remy?"

"Keep it down, Lewie."

Powell-Smith closed the door behind them. Bender straightened. "Marie."

"Henry." She smiled lazily and flopped her backside on the arm of Pickett's chair. It was clear she was drunk. "What's happened to poor Rosie?"

"He got shot."

"Poor baby..." She ran her fingers up his cheek. Rosie pouted at her but Henry flushed red.

"Remy's brother shot him."

"Oh God," groaned Lewis. "Not him, again. I thought he was up north."

"War Office." Christien began wrapping the leg with gauze.

"Does he know you're a Clubber, Remy?"

"You won't mention it to him, will you Lewis, or I'll ask him shoot you next." He straightened, reached for his bag. "There, Rosie. All done. All you'll need is a shot of morphine and a new pair of trousers."

"It hurts, Remy..."

"Did you just toss it off the pier, then?" Lewis rolled his eyes. "You git."

"Well, we didn't see no-one," moaned Pickett and he laid his head on the back of the chair. "It were dark as pitch, it were."

"Poor baby." Marie leaned over and kissed him.

"And we ain't been caught yet, have we?" growled Henry.

"Well, you 'ain't' been caught,' but you *have* been shot..." Christien glanced at Lewis. "And the rest of her? What did you do with that?"

Powell-Smith tossed his head.

"I ditched 'er," he sniffed. "The Bottle's gonna blow when they find her. It was brilliant. I'll go down in history most likely."

And he smiled.

From his seat on the ottoman, Christien removed a small bottle of liquid, began to assemble a very long brass hypodermic syringe. "You will see us all disbarred, Lewie. Williams will sell us out and Bondie won't be able to do a bloody thing."

"Ah come on," groaned the blond man. "They were dead anyway? Who's going to miss a few dead lunatics?"

"They die all the time at Bedlam," said Bender. "This way, it saves room in the infirmary for the next. It makes sense, Remy. You know it does."

And he washed it down with the last of his port.

"I been to Bedlam," cooed Marie. "Once, with John. He took me there for me surgery. Said it were more clean there than a clinic. He takes lots o' the girls there."

She looked up at Christien. "He's a very clean man, John."

"Still, I will make a point of telling Williams that we're not on for any more extracurricular business. It's too dangerous now," said Christien and he lifted the hypodermic syringe to the light. A drop of morphine dripped from the needle's tip. "Rosie, I need your arm…"

"Dangerous is right," groaned Pickett, raising his arm. "I'm not dying for a few bonus marks – what the bloody hell?"

His breath was creating frost in front of his face.

"Shite!" Bender turned his glass upside down, and a chunk of golden ice dropped to the floor.

"Damnation," hissed Christien and he bolted to his feet. "Shut up, all of you. Shut up and don't move!"

"What the hell is going on?" Lewis' breath was frosting now and Marie shrank back to cling to his arm.

"It's freezing in 'ere," she moaned. "Take me 'ome, Lewie…"

Christien reached for the handles of the French doors but snatched them back for they were slick with ice. He took a deep breath and swung the doors open onto the sight of his brother, waistcoat and shirt hanging like bloody rags. There was an unnatural wind plucking at his hair and he looked like a dead man.

"Bastien, get back to bed."

"Who's in there, Christien?"

"Just the boys, Bastien. We've talked about this before."

"There is wickedness in there, Christien, I can feel it. They must be stopped."

He tried to push past his brother but Christien stepped in front of him, barring the way and pulling the doors closed behind him.

"The boys haven't murdered anyone, Bastien. I'm telling you the truth. Why can't you believe me?"

"The torsos are angry. I need them out of my head."

"I'll get you your Scotch, Bastien. Or the laudanum, if that's what you want. Just leave my friends alone."

The ice was crackling up the walls, up the doors, along the floors. Even their breath hung like a wall between them.

"You see them even now, don't you?" said Christien. "They want you to kill me."

Sebastien swallowed.

"Do you think this is good for you? Are you happy with how your life is rolling along?" Christien stepped forward. "Because you can change it, you know. You only need to say the word and I will do everything I can to help you."

Sebastien stared at him, eyes changing colour as quickly as a London sky. Not for the first time, Christien wished Frankow had just let him die.

"You could have everything, Bastien. A wife, children, a normal life. Everything I know you want, deep down. But not with this affliction. Not if there is the hint of possibility that when your demons tell you to kill, you listen. That, Bastien, is simply not acceptable."

"I know. I do—I know it, Christien. I would shoot myself if I had the pistol. I would."

"Would you consider the lithium? Please, Bastien."

He watched as his brother glanced at the door. There were shapes visible through the curtain over the glass, shapes of Henry, Lewis, Rosie and Marie, watching, gawking and whispering. Christien hated all of them at this moment.

He took a deep breath.

"They haven't murdered anyone."

"I will consider it," Sebastien said quietly.

Christien took his arm, sighed when his brother flinched. Not from flesh, he knew, but spirit. It had always been this way.

"I'm sorry, Christien."

"Come on, get back to bed and I'll bring you a Scotch immediately. How does that sound?"

"Good," Sebastien nodded. "Yes, good."

"Right. Off you go, then."

And the Mad Lord of Lasingstoke turned and slowly made his way back up the stair, taking the cold and the ice with him.

Christien turned to find Pomfrey standing behind him, eyes sleepy still. But the wig was straightened and he was holding a slip of cardstock in his hands.

"I found this at the door, sir, when the boys came in," he said. "I fear your dreadful night is not yet over."

It was a post card, smeared with blood.

***

I was not codding dear old Boss when I gave you the tip, you'll hear about Saucy Jacky's work tomorrow. double event this time number one squealed a bit couldn't finish straight off. ha not the time to get ears for police. thanks for keeping last letter back till I got to work again

Jack the Ripper

Chapter 31

Of Circus Monkeys, Vitamins and a Conversation Under a Blanket

Evening Steam
1 October 1888

The East-end of London was yesterday again much excited by the discovery of two more revolting murders. About one o'clock in the morning, the body of a woman, with her throat cut, was found in a yard belonging to a work-men's club, in Berner-street, and an hour later another woman was found murdered in a corner of Mitre-square, Aldgate. In the latter case, the body was also mutilated, and as this was not the case with the woman found in Berner-street, it is supposed that the murderer was disturbed before completing his dreadful intentions, and that then he proceeded towards the City and committed the second crime. The body of the woman found in Berner-street has been identified as that of ELIZABETH STRIDE and the body of the woman found in Mitre Square as that of CATHERINE EDDOWES.

Police are continuing to investigate.

***

Ivy awoke to the pounding of her head.

She sat up slowly and thankfully, the room stayed put. As she let her eyes adjust to the morning, she did realize that she was once again in an unfamiliar bedroom and her heart did a somersault. She had heard tales from friends of her father—respected officers of the law—of the consequences of too much drink. Usually they involved strange bedrooms, tattoos and circus monkeys. She glanced down, praying that she would find neither tattoo nor monkey. Of the two, she wasn't certain which would be worse.

It was the Blue Room, she realized, in Christien's home at Kensington-Knightsbridge. She vaguely remembered Castlewaite's eight grandchildren, a potent silver flask and Sebastien carrying her up the stair.

Her boots were neatly placed beside the bed but she was still dressed in her breeches, corset and blouse and she was grateful that while the Mad Lord was indeed mad, he wasn't a cad. A murderer, yes and a screwsman, but not a cad.

She slipped out from under the brocade and held still while the room did a little spin. On the vanity was a pitcher and bowl of water, and a folded tweed skirt on the chair by the door. She remembered the last time she'd awakened in a room not her own, so she set her mind to clean up before heading down for tea.

***

The staircase and foyer was flooded in light. In Stepney, almost every day was gray but here in Kensington-Knightsbridge, the sun seemed stronger, golder and she knew it had to do with the money. Fancy houses simply attracted the light.

Pomfrey watched as she moved very carefully down the stair.

"Mr. Christien is in the dining room," he said and Ivy smiled, grateful that she had taken the time to wash her face, repin her hair and slip on the skirt. Rupert had been right so many weeks ago—Christien had never seen her look anything other than her best and even then, that was a struggle. She wasn't sure how he would react to the thought of her escapades last night.

He sat at the head of the long table, dressed in a suit of charcoal gray. He was reading the paper and at this moment he reminded her very much of Rupert. In fact, as he looked up at the sound of her footfall, his face was stern.

"Good morning, Christien," she said, forcing cheer into her voice.

"Good morning, Ivy." He did not do the same.

"Is there tea?"

He waved a hand toward the hutch, where a French breakfast of croissants and berries was set. Normally, she would have dug in, but suddenly, she found her appetite gone. She did, however, decide to fix herself a cup. Tea worked wonders for frayed nerves and sticky situations.

He folded the paper and she noticed he was wearing a glove on his left hand. It looked out of place.

"There were two more murders in Whitechapel last night," he said.

"The same man?"

"Apparently so. What were you doing out with my brother?"

His face, so perfect, lips drawn in a very tight line.

"Christien—"

"And what, for that matter, are you two doing in London?"

She tried to stop the trembling of her hand as she poured the tea.

"We came to Whitechapel," she said. "To find my mother."

"To find the *ghost* of your mother, Ivy." His face still showed no emotion. Blank, neutral, porcelain. "How can you find a ghost of someone who's still among the living?"

"Sebastien said we'd find her and we did."

"Ivy," he began, smoothing the newspaper. "My brother is mad."

"Christien—"

"He's mad, Ivy, and yet you brought him along with you for a little romp through the East End on a whim. On a farce. Did he shoot anyone last night?"

She opened her mouth but no words came.

"You don't know, do you? Because you weren't with him the entire night. You were drunk in the cab with Castlewaite."

For some reason, when her eyes should have been filling with tears, she felt her chin rise inexplicably.

"Do you know how many people he's shot because the 'ghosts' tell him to? I don't. I don't have a clue how many murders he is responsible for. I cleaned him up last night when I put him to bed. Imagine my surprise when I see wire stitches holding his arm in its socket, and what looks like a fresh bullet hole, no more than a few days old. Were you with him, Ivy, when my brother was shot?"

"Yes," she whispered defiantly.

"I see." He nodded. "And so, you decided it would be jolly good fun to bring him to Whitechapel, see if he could find that devil who's ripping whores. Maybe he could even shoot him for you. Wouldn't your father be proud?"

"He's worried about you, Christien!" she snapped. "You're a member of the Ghost Club and he's worried."

He blinked slowly as he processed her words. He was too clever. She couldn't allow him the chance.

"There are strange things going on, Christien, otherwise you wouldn't have given me the locket. I know you're trying to find out what happened to your father but dismissing your brother is no way to do that."

"Ivy, you don't understand…"

"And you've made certain I never will. But that's wrong, Christien. Hiding things is no way to discover truth."

He rose to his feet and she stepped back. He cocked his head.

"Are you afraid of me?"

"No—"

"You run around the countryside shooting people with my brother, yet you're afraid of *me?*"

"I'm not."

"How do you know he's not the Ripper, Ivy? There hasn't been a murder for weeks, and now, the very night he arrives, two."

"He's not the Ripper."

"And how would you know? You were drunk in a coach. And Bastien *is* a killer, you know he is." He moved over beside her, picked a fresh cup, began to pour. "Two whores this time, Ivy. Two in one night, a Double Event, the papers are calling it. Took a kidney and a womb this time and I believe, an ear…"

"Christien, please."

He arched a brow by way of asking. She shook her head.

"It's not true."

"But I say again, you don't know that. He's black and blue, Ivy. How did that happen if he was with you on the Pier? What happened afterwards that you don't know about?"

"Why do you hate him so?"

"Because it's his fault our father is dead! If he hadn't...If he had just..."

She saw the tears in his eyes as he struggled for control, took a deep breath, and then another and for the first time, she wondered what he remembered. He had been in the room when his father had killed himself. Two little boys living with the same horror. Her heart broke for them both.

"I love him, Ivy, and I hate him. He's my brother and he's mad and dangerous and yet, to see him with his dogs and his horses and he's so very happy, I wish life could be that way for him always. I wish he would just stay north. I just... I wish..."

He released a long deep breath, doing it again – placing the mask tightly over his face. The fine black glove and the methodical stirring of the spoon in the china cup. It was a very English ritual, tea.

"He doesn't need to be encouraged." The splash of milk, the level spoon of sugar. "He needs to be medicated, hospitalized and treated." The slow, hypnotic circles caused by the stirring. "He is an innocent, Ivy. A wild, brutal child. He needs to be protected from people and people need to be protected from him."

She swallowed, watched him drop two tablets into the tea.

"Vitamin supplements," he said. "He doesn't eat when he's manic."

She remembered the pasty, three knife holes bleeding gravy.

"And what if he decides that I'm next? You know his women want him to shoot me."

"He won't," she said. "He's promised."

"What about you then? What if he decides to shoot you? Or stick a knife into you just to make sure you're real?"

"He won't hurt me," she said.

"Until the ghosts tell him to." He smiled sadly and held her the cup and saucer. "I'm sending him back north. Take this to him, say your good byes and never see him again."

Her eyes flashed now and he could tell but it was he who raised his chin.

"The last door on the right before the second-floor terrace," he said, and he raised the cup once more. "Go on. Be a good girl."

Be a good girl.

She *was* a good girl. She had *always* been a good girl.

Reach a little higher, then...

For some reason, the tears began to sting.

She took the cup and fled back up the stairs.

***

The tears were flowing down her cheeks as she knocked on the door, the last door on the right before the second-floor terrace. There was no answer, so she tried the handle, relieved to find it unlocked. She nudged it open and peered inside. A great expanse of draperies were drawn shut and the fireplace had dwindled down to a few glowing coals. She glanced at the bed but it was empty.

There wasn't even a spread on it.

She stepped in and closed the door behind her.

"Sebastien?" she called softly into the room. "Sebastien, it's me, Ivy. I, I have tea..."

In the far corner, she saw a strange shape and she moved closer. Someone was sitting on the floor underneath a blanket, like a little child hiding from its parents. She crossed the room to kneel beside it.

"Sebastien? Would you like some tea?"

The spread moved and a hand to slipped out. It was then that she saw his wrist, swollen and blue from his late-night adventures. Christien had been right—she had been drunk in the cab. She barely remembered him after the pier.

She passed him the saucer and it disappeared under the blanket.

"May I join you?" she begged, wishing just for one moment that she were a little girl. She and Davis would make tents under their blankets, pretend they were adventurers in Africa and India, fighting lions and tigers on the frontier of the Empire. She had been eleven. She'd had to grow up very quickly after that.

He said nothing so she lifted an edge and peered under.

The side of his face was purple and he was cradling his right arm as though it were still in its brace. The spread draped from his head and he was staring into the teacup, although, like her mother, she doubted he was seeing anything. She could imagine him very much like this at Lonsdale. The only thing missing was Mumford.

It broke her heart all over again.

She slipped underneath the blanket, wrapped her arms around her knees as tears spilled fresh from her lashes. And so she sat, weeping silently until he raised his eyes to look at her.

"Why are you crying, Miss Savage?"

She smiled through her tears. "I'm a good girl, aren't I?"

"Yes. A very good girl."

"I hate it," she sniffed. "I hate being a 'good girl.' I hate having to follow orders. I always have. I am so stubborn but I hate being told what to do, when to do it, how to do it, why I should do it, what I should think, how I should think. I wish, I wish…"

Her breath shuddered in her chest. "I wish life was very different…"

"Me too."

"And I try to reach higher, really I do. But I think I only succeed in making a mess of things. Do you ever feel that way?"

"Always," he said. "I am a madman and a failure."

"No, Sebastien. At least, no more than me." She smiled and this time it didn't feel forced. "Quite a pair, we make, yes?"

"Hm."

"Are you going to drink your tea?"

"Oh, yes," he said, and raised the cup to his lips. "Thank you."

"How are you feeling this morning?"

"Not so good."

"I'm terribly sorry. Can I help?"

He shook his head. The blanket moved when he did so.

"I think you shot one of the men on the pier," she said. "I found blood and fabric next to a hole in the plank."

"Hm."

"Did you find them, then? The 'head' men?"

He shook his head again.

"Oh. Well, how did you get so clobbered up?"

"The Ripper is as good with a spade as he is with a blade. He is also left handed, by the way."

She felt the blood drain from her face. "Sebastien…"

"He was going to kill me, but he didn't."

"You need to tell the police."

"I saw him."

"What? You saw him?"

"The Ripper. I saw him. It's my father."

She stared at him.

"My father, who's been dead for years, is killing women in Whitechapel."

"But…but he's dead…How can he?"

"It's a challenging question. I think I'll stay in here for a while. The dead don't come under blankets."

She didn't know what to say to that.

He sipped his tea and once again, she noticed a tremor in his hands. She had never seen that before London.

They sat in silence for a moment and finally, he laid the empty cup on the floor. Between his feet was a small golden tin, which he picked up and began to fold over in his hand. Inside, it rattled like crushed stones.

"Lithium," he said. "Christien wants me back on it."

"I know. What do you think?"

Finally, he looked up at her.

"I felt a woman die last night. I've never felt that before but I was no more than fifty feet away so it stands to reason. It was like nails in my skull. My dead father almost beat me to death with a spade and when I came home, there were nine women in the hall. One of them had barely a face. They don't want to be dead and they're very angry about it. There are four torsos, Ivy. Four dismembered women everywhere I go. I'm not doing enough but honestly, I can't do anymore and I want it to stop." He looked down at the tin in his hand. "I want it all to stop."

"Oh my dear Sebastien…" She frowned, hugged her knees. It never occurred to her that it was odd, conducting such a personal conversation under a blanket in the corner of a room. "So, with the lithium, you don't see the dead?"

He frowned now, blinked as if trying to focus.

"No," he said slowly. "I don't see the dead. But the problem is that I don't see much of the living either...Hm..." He frowned again, rolled his head on his shoulders. It caused the blanket to bunch and pull. He said nothing more for some time, and so they sat, toe to toe, saying nothing.

"Would you talk to my father, Sebastien? If you fought off the Ripper, you should tell him what happened."

"No."

"Maybe it was someone who looked like your father. You could describe his height, his frame, his clothing—"

"No, Ivy."

"Sebastien, you are a witness to a terrible crime."

He said nothing, didn't even seem to have heard. In fact, he was blinking very slowly.

"Sebastien?"

"Hm," he said again, and reached for his cup, fumbled with it, then stared into it as if it were a puzzle. "Lithium in the tea. Quite clever. I never expected it..."

Ivy looked up. "What?"

"It dissolves quickly in hot water. Well done. Rupert was right." His voice was sluggish and slow. "You'd make a tidy spy. Christien has you trained."

"What? Sebastien, *no*. He said they were vitamins..."

"Please leave."

"I—"

"Now. Please. You are filled with shadow." He pulled away so that the blanket slid off of her head and suddenly, she was sitting on the floor in a corner of a bedroom of a man she barely knew.

He won't hurt me, she had said.

Shaking, she rose to her feet.

Not until the ghosts tell him to.

She fled the room and ran down the stairs, seeing neither Christien nor Pomfrey when she left the house, a fact for which she was grateful.

Chapter 32

Of Alexander Dunn, Henry Babbage and an Engine named ERICA

If the sun was sweet in Kensington-Knightsbridge, then it was positively sugar along the ivory streets of Pall Mall, where all the clubs of the civilized world set up shop. She kept her head down as she walked past each and every one of them. It would take many hours to get to her home in Stepney, for she didn't have the money for a cab and her mind raced faster, more furiously, with each step.

Christien had deceived her.

She had trusted him and he had deceived her.

She twisted the ring on her finger as she walked, wondering if this was really what she wanted for herself, this marriage to a very fine man from Kensington-Knightsbridge. It had made sense, once upon a time. It still did. Her father liked Christien, liked the stability and security he brought to her life, and the fact that he could help the family with Catherine's care. And she liked him too, liked the fact that he was interested in Forensics and crime and mysteries. He was better than she could have hoped for, better than she deserved, as stubborn and willful as she was. But still, she couldn't shake the image of the Mad Lord from her mind, sitting like a child under a blanket, standing under an umbrella on a rainy pier, laying on a hospital slab with a knitted dog under his arm. He had managed to strike a chord deep inside. She barely knew him, and yet he resonated like a very familiar song.

Alexander Dunn had stolen Penny's heart.

She shuddered to think of it, it had happened so quick. Penny had been happy until she'd met Dunn but now, how could she ever look at Julian the same way after that? Not when there was always the possibility of Dunn lurking around the corner with his thievery, his tricks, his devilish smile. What did that mean for her stories? What did that mean for her?

No, she told herself, it was better for Sebastien in the north. London was hard on him; she'd seen clear evidence of that this morning. He was stranger than he'd ever been and she found herself wondering what to believe. She *had* seen the head in the water but had he really fought off the Ripper? How in the world could she believe that same Ripper was his dead father? How could she possibly believe any of it?

Perhaps Christien was right to question his brother's sanity. Could Sebastien be not only a killer of killers, but of women as well?

A pair of gentlemen laughed as they passed her and rang the bell onto one of the black-painted doors of Pall Mall. She watched them, eyes drawn to the plaque on the wall by the door. Memories ran through her mind of an evening goodbye, a newly-purchased steamcar and a locket, given as a gift. *It's probably nothing,,* Christien had said, *simply a Pall Mall club for gentlemen with scads of money and far too much imagination.*

She paused, looked around the street. Plaques beside every door announcing all manner of Gentleman's clubs and it didn't take her long to find it between the Reform Club and the Athenaeum. *The Ghost Club – London, est. 1862.* She took a deep breath, raised her chin and pushed open the door.

It was entirely what she would have expected. Wood paneled walls and golden portraits, elegant furnishings and books. It smelled of pipe smoke and brandy and old, old money and she felt a rush of nerves as she closed the door behind her. At the foot of a long, spiral stair, an elegant automaton raised its golden head.

"Welcome to the Ghost Club," it droned in a clipped Sussex accent. "My name is CHARLES. *Chippendale's Handy Automated Representative for Licensing, Etiquette and Service.*"

"Hello CHARLES," she said. "I was wondering—"

"This is a Gentleman's Club, I'm afraid. No women allowed."

She could hear raised voices echoing down the stair.

"I, I'm here to see Dr. John Williams."

"Do you have an appointment?"

"He told me to meet him here," she lied.

The lights on its faceplate flashed several times.

"Williams, Dr. John. Logged in at 8:20 Greenwich Mean."

She swallowed. Jolly good luck, that.

"Where is he, please?"

"You may await Williams, Dr. John, in the Red Room. Do follow me."

And his shiny head turned on his shiny neck, followed by shoulders, then torso and all the parts of him turned one after the other like a slowly spinning top, until finally the contraptions that served as his feet turned and he clanked away to the right, toward a room decorated entirely in red.

Ivy waited for him to disappear before trotting up the stair. The voices led her down a long hallway filled with the sharp odor of cigarettes, cigars and pipes. She slowed as she neared a set of doors.

"Dashitall, Bookie," said one voice. "This is bad! Very bad indeed!"

"Two women, last night! It's impossible!"

"Now, Westie," said another. "The truth is almost upon us. It's not our fault there's a madman loose in the city. If anyone, it's Jackie—"

"Here, here," said a voice that she immediately recognized as Williams'. "I resent that implication!"

"Tosh," said the voice called Bookie. "Bertie will see us all cleared if events do surface. He stands to lose the most."

"Damn that Eddy and his infernal whoring…"

The voices dropped down low and she leaned in to listen when there was a sound on the stair. It was the automaton clanking up the steps with slow, methodical movements, its head spinning on its neck, a thin beam of red light searching out ahead of it.

With heart in her throat, she pushed open the doors. Through the smoky haze, a dozen men looked up.

"A woman?"

"A woman, indeed! Where is CHARLES?"

"CHARLES! CHARLES!"

"Ivy?" snapped Williams. "What the deuce are you doing here?"

"Dr. Williams...I...I..." She froze, suddenly realizing that she had just stepped over her head and out of her league. "I need to speak with you, sir."

"Not now, Ivy," he growled. "We have a situation."

"Is *that* the locket?" asked one man and a charge ran through the room. Suddenly, all eyes fell upon the pendant, hanging sweet and coy around her neck.

She looked across the sea of the gentlemen. Not one of them was younger than her father and they all had the look of academia. These were learned men, scholars and politicians of the *Empire of Steam* and she had just turned their world upside down, simply by stepping a very fine boot inside their doors.

These were very strange, modern times indeed.

She raised her chin.

"Ghostlight sends her regards."

"Come with me, Ivy dear," said Williams. "We can talk in another room."

A fellow with a white-beard and bushy brows laid a hand on the surgeon's arm.

"Can she leave the locket, Jackie?"

"Not now, Bookie."

"But look at it..."

The men surrounded her, pressing in on every side until Williams took her elbow and escorted her out the doors.

"Ivy," he said, keeping his voice low. "What are you doing in London? Does your father know you're home?"

"No sir. I only arrived last night."

"Don't tell me you're here with Sebastien de Lacey?"

"Yes, sir," she said. "We have some questions for you regarding these Whitechapel killings."

"*We?* Is he putting you up to this? Damn the man. Damn him to hell."

"No, sir. These are my questions and mine alone."

At the end of the hall, there was an open iron-grilled door and above it, a clockwork eyeball studied them as they approached. Williams pulled a card from his pocket, held it up. It blinked and the grille door rattled open with the groan of interlocking gears. An hydraulic lift, she realized. All the rage in London. She stepped onto the cage floor, could see black and gold cables in the shaft beneath her boots. As Williams closed the grille, the entire platform shuddered and massive hydraulic gears began lowering them down.

"Now Ivy," he said, over the rattle of the cables. "You're not writing *that* story, are you? You know what your father thinks about that."

"I know, sir, but—"

"You are not an investigator, Ivy."

"Is there a chance that Annie Chapman may have been pregnant?"

He hesitated. Gaslight on the walls cast moving shadows across their faces as they descended and for the first time, she realized that he had a very grim mouth.

"Now why would you ask something like that, Ivy?"

"It's a thought I had regarding the removal of her womb. I just can't fathom a killer taking something like that. Why remove the womb?"

"This Ripper is an ill man, Ivy. Nothing more."

"But would there be a way of telling, sir? Please, just answer me that."

He smiled in a fashion that reminded her of Arvin Frankow. Patronizing. That was it. Patronizing.

"Yes, Ivy. There would be a great many ways of telling."

"So," she said. "What if she were pregnant but couldn't keep a baby?"

"Well, she certainly wouldn't carve herself up like that, now would she?"

"No sir, that's not what I meant."

"I'm an obstetrician, Ivy. Many women have need of my services. My 'extracurricular business.' Not every pregnancy brings happiness."

The hum of machinery grew louder, louder even than the grinding of the hydraulic gears. Steam billowed up from below, hissing in bursts from behind their backs.

"So you *are* helping them, sir? In the clinics?"

"I'm one of the few legitimate physicians who care to try, Ivy. You know that."

"But isn't it...?"

"Illegal? Yes, Ivy dear. Quite."

She nodded. "And there are others, less legitimate than you."

"They call it *Restellism*, on the street."

"I see." She thought for a moment. "No, perhaps I don't. But that's quite expected, given the last few weeks..."

"Are you certain Sebastien de Lacey didn't put you up to this?"

"Quite certain, sir. It is my own belligerence."

"So you know Remy is a member, then?"

"Yes, sir. It's one of the reasons I'm here. I want him to quit."

The lift shuddered to a halt and he stared at her for a long moment.

"Come this way, Ivy," he said. "There is someone I want you to meet."

He pulled the iron grille door onto a room deep underground and she wondered at that. The Infirmary of Lonsdale was underground. The Mortuary of the Royal was underground. It seemed all manner of unnerving operations took place underground. Perhaps it was the seclusion, away from windows and prying eyes. Perhaps it was the air or the darkness or the magnetism of the earth. She had no clue but there had to be something that drew dark pursuits underground.

The room was dim and gleaming with old gold. As her eyes adjusted, she could see sparks arcing through tarnished pipes and glass tubes along the ceiling high above her head. The walls themselves were lined with machines – flashing lights and spinning shafts and shuttling levers that reminded her of automated weaver's looms. They ran nonstop, these pipes, drums and plates, moving with clockwork precision. In fact, it looked like a factory and workers manned various stations along the wall, inputting cards and punching keys and pulling levers at amazing speeds.

It was an Analytical Engine, she knew, had heard the boys of Leman Street Station talk about the hopes of getting one working for the Met. Hundreds of numbers spun on brass plates and she wondered how information could be communicated to and from such a device. Difference Engines were helpful but Analytical Engines could almost think.

A man with gray hair and grizzled chops marched up to meet them, his shoes echoing on the tarnished floor.

"What the devil is a woman doing here, Jackie?" he growled, thumbs hooked in his waistcoat pockets. "It's against Club rules."

"Henry, this is Ivy Savage," said Williams. "Remy's fiancée."

"Henry Babbage." He did not offer her his hand. "Can't say I'm pleased to meet you. Inviting women into the Club is worse than inviting Anarchists. Or the French."

"Manners, Henry," said Williams.

"Remy's fiancée, you say?" His eyes flicked down. "Is that the locket?"

"It is indeed. She's brought it to London, along with Sebastien de Lacey."

"Good Lord!" said the man named Babbage. "Explains a few things, wot? Very well. How can I help?"

"I want her to meet Erica."

Babbage held wide his arms. "And so she has."

"I don't understand," said Ivy.

"ERICA," said Babbage. *"Engine for Rational Input, Computation and Analysis."*

"But why would the Ghost Club have an Analytical Engine?"

"Despite our name, we are a scientific organization, my dear," said Williams. "And Analytical Engines are the cutting edge of science."

"Science *and* socialism," said Babbage. "This way, girl, keep moving. Don't stop to gawk."

Up a set of steps that clanked underfoot and a small man in shirtsleeves turned at their approach. He was a diminutive fellow with kind eyes and a timid air.

"Ninian," said Babbage. "This is Ivy Savage, Remy's woman. Shake, boy. Shake."

Reluctantly, Ninian held out his hand. It was blackened with grease.

"Mathematicians are notorious rude," grumbled Babbage. "Good thing Lovelace had a hand in *my* raising. *Ahem.* Ninian is a northerner. Comes from Newcastle, don't you boy?"

"Yes, sir. I do indeed, sir," he said shyly. "Ninian Liddell, from Newcastle 'pon Tyne."

"Ninian Liddell." Ivy cocked her head. "Do you know a woman by the name of Fanny Helmsly-Wimpoll?""

"She was the light of my sorry life."

"She still speaks of you, sir."

The young man dropped his eyes to the floor. "And I still dream of her…"

"Does she know of your current occupation, Ninian?"

"Alas, she does not approve of datamancery."

"Even in Pall Mall?"

His mouth opened and closed. Apparently, he had no answer for her.

"I will be sure to tell her of your improved station when I see her next."

He smiled shyly. "I would appreciate that very much, Miss Savage."

"Miss Savage wants to know if we have anything regarding the Whitechapel villain," said Williams.

"The papers are calling him 'The Ripper' as of last night," said Ninian. "Apparently, there was another letter."

"And why would a girl want to know about this Ripper?" asked Babbage. "It's not a romantic topic."

"I am not a romantic girl," said Ivy.

"She is Remy's fiancée. Poor boy works with Bondie. He's up to his eyeballs in body parts."

"Two more last night, wot?" grunted Babbage. "One in the back of some foreigners' club and one in Mitre Square. Does that scare you, girl?"

"The mortuary is my second home, sir."

"Indeed," he said. "Remember the arm off Grovesnor Bridge? They found another yesterday morning on Lambeth. Bond is checking them out as we speak."

"As he should," said Ivy.

"I say," said Babbage. "This girl's got pluck."

He turned to face her and she steeled her will, determined to bear up.

"Right then, girl. The Met is looking for someone who has knowledge of anatomy, has access to a six inch blade and can work quickly in the dark."

"Mr. Robert James Lees believes he's a medical man," said Ivy. "A surgeon would have access to a blade like that."

"Robert James Lees is a fraud," said Williams. "Crookes debunked his claims not last year."

"ERICA has suggested a list of professions, miss," said Ninian. "At the top of which is butcher, closely followed by leather craftsman. Surgeon is well down."

"The police are questioning every butcher and leatherman in Whitechapel," said Babbage. "They're not about to start questioning surgeons, are they, Jackie?"

"Not bloody likely."

"And what if he's not from Whitechapel?" asked Ivy. "There was an article in the Lancaster Guardian recently. A woman named Clara Clements was murdered and her heart and womb removed from the scene, just like the women in Whitechapel. There was also, I believe, a young woman in Pelling—"

"Honestly, Ivy," warned Williams. "This is not the subject for a young lady."

"Seriously, sir? Considering the high percentage of crimes against women that occur in the Empire, wouldn't it be sensible to have women in the field?"

"Suffrage is the path to anarchy," said Babbage, arching a brow. "Has she been sent by Frankow?"

"She's a mystery writer," said Williams.

"Tutored by Trevis Savage and the boys of H-Division." Ivy arched a brow. "Let's talk this through. All of these London women were prostitutes, as was Clara Clements of Maudgate. They have all experienced some mutilation of their hearts and their womanly organs. And I understand that Miss Barton had her heart removed from the scene. I propose that there may be an emotional connection that we are simply not considering."

"Oh gads," groaned Babbage. "Trust a woman to bring emotions into the mix."

"And trust a man to ignore them."

The mathematician laughed.

"She's a bold one, Jackie," he said. "How much has Remy told you, then?"

"Nothing, sir. He aims to protect me."

The mathematician grunted, turned to Williams.

"Show her, Jack," said Babbage. "I have real work to do."

And he left them, his shoes echoing on the metal steps as he went.

Ivy looked back at the Surgeon. "What does he mean, sir?"

Williams sighed. "Come along, Ivy."

They followed the walls toward a filing station, where punch cards sat in neat rectangular piles, wrapped with leather straps and buckles. Williams took one pile, slid a card out and studied it under the golden gaslight of the room.

"ERICA has been a busy girl," he said quietly. "The mathematicians have input every known variable into her algorithms for weeks now, with the same result."

"A name?" she asked. "You have a name?"

"We do."

"Why haven't you brought this to the attention of the Met? That should be your first duty!"

"Because they wouldn't believe us, Ivy."

And he handed her the card. She read it, then read it again. There was indeed only one name on the card.

Renaud Jacobe St. John Lord de Lacey.

Chapter 33

Of Conflicting Storylines, Coraline Candymore and the Sentinels of Leman Street

This just proved it. The light *anywhere* was much sweeter than the light in Stepney.

Her key let her in and as her eyes adjusted to the dimness, it seemed as though there were a film over everything. Perhaps it was dust. Her father wasn't much of a housekeeper, and while everything was neat, she doubted that anything was particularly clean. He was a crimes investigator. For him, there were more important things to do with his time.

Renaud de Lacey, the print-out had said. *Renaud Jacobe St. John Lord de Lacey.*

A dead man was the Whitechapel Ripper.

She headed into the tiny kitchen, found the kettle in the same place as always. Filled it with water and set it on the gas stove. Sat at the small table under the window, waiting for the kettle to boil.

Penny Dreadful and the Terror of Whitechapel. She had started it before she was sent north. She needed to write. Writing helped organize, clarify, simplify. Penny Dreadful would help her. Penny was so very much better at that than she. Penny was engaged to handsome Julian, but then again, Penny had let the rogue Alexander disappear with the stolen heart and her pearls. Strange. That was not at all like Penny.

They saw their mother in a bloody bed, her heart in their father's hand, Fanny Helmsly-Wimpoll had said. It had broken her heart, had made her sick to her stomach.

The kettle whistled now, but Ivy didn't hear. She tried to recall Fanny's voice, her manner of speaking, her words in the Lancaster Mews, while Franny ate crumble and went on about Czechs.

Something about their mother…

She twisted the ring on her finger.

Something about their mother…

It was rumoured she was having a scandalous love affair with another man and in fact, that she was pregnant with his child.

But there was more.

So Renaud Jacobe St. John de Lacey killed her with a hunting knife and cut out her womb and her heart.

He cut out her womb and her heart. Just like the Ripper.

Could Renaud de Lacey possibly be alive? Or was it something worse?

She looked out through the window at the small gray yard beyond.

Clara Clements of Lancaster had her heart and womb cut out. Sebastien had cheerfully admitted to being in Lancaster the night of her murder. It was the night he had bought her the breeches.

And then there was Miss Barton from Pelling, whose heart was still missing. Pelling was a three-hour ride from Lasingstoke.

Sebastien was a killer, this she knew, but a murderer of women? She couldn't believe that. But he was mad, wasn't he? He would have happily shot Celia Crumb back in Milnethorpe. Why was this so very different?

She had a story now, but it was one she didn't want to write. Alexander Dunn was not the Terror of Whitechapel.

And yet…

And yet…

Fortunately, she did remember to turn off the flame as she left the little rowhouse by the factory.

***

The Sentinels of Leman Street had always frightened her, just a little. Unlike the Great Steam Expostion Sentinels, no effort had been put into covering up the mechanisms that made them work. While other automatons had hats, bowties, moustaches, or other human metalwork, these Sentinels had no such attempts made. They were pure clockwork mechamen, and they guarded the doors of the stationhouse, reminding everyone not only of the laws of the Royal British Empire, but of the very ability to see those laws carried out.

She slipped in under their inhuman gaze to the registration desk and Mrs. Coraline Candymore, the registrar.

The woman was easily in her late fifties, and her blueblack hair was piled high on top of her head under a little hat with a single black feather. She was sporting a leather waistcoat and had a brass pistol tucked in the pocket of one breast. With thin lips over protruding teeth, she reminded Ivy of a crane or a stork or some other spindly wading bird. She had worked this desk for longer than most detectives could remember.

"Yes and what are you wanting?" Candymore did not look up, merely continued punching her type-writing machine.

"Mrs. Candymore, I need to see my tad. Is he at his desk?"

"Your *'tad.'* And what is your *'tad's'* name, girl?"

Ivy sighed. They went through this every time. "Trevis Savage, Inspector, H-Division."

"And your name?"

"Ivy Savage, daughter of Trevis Savage, Inspector, H-Division."

"One moment." Candymore spun and wheeled on her chair towards a second desk where the officers clocked in. She flipped the cards, located one, studied it, looked at Ivy, studied her, before putting the card back and wheeling to her desk once again.

"Yes, he's at his desk. Be brief. The H's have work to do."

"I understand, Mrs. Candymore. Thank you."

As she left the foyer, Ivy wondered if the Empire needn't simply hire Coraline Candymore to guard the doors of stationhouses across the nation. She was as fearsome as a sentinel, and almost as inhuman.

Down a short hall, up a flight of stairs and Ivy breathed in the scent of old coffee, cigarettes and pistol-grease. More familiar than baking bread, she thought as she opened the door onto the bustling center that was H-Division.

As usual, the floor was packed with officers, most of whom she knew by name. Leach and White, Lamb and Brown. Through the glass on one of the doors, she could see Thompson and Thicke poring over some papers with Chief Arnold. She'd served them all tea at some time or other. They'd told stories by the fire, brought presents on her birthday. They had been her family growing up.

There were no women on the floor however and she'd always wondered why. With half the Empire's population female, it made no sense. Victoria was down on any woman having a profession but Ivy knew a woman's perspective could come in handy in many an investigation.

"Hallo Ivy!" called a voice and she turned to see Carter Beals, one of her tad's partners. He was a tall man with brown hair and a rather long, pleasant face. "What are you doing home?"

Home. The Leman Street Station House was home.

"I'm here to see my tad, Mr. Beals. Where is he, please?"

"In with North and Bond. I'll fetch him toot-de-sweet." He grinned and disappeared into one of the offices down the hall.

She looked over at her father's desk. There were three photochromes, two of his children and one of Catherine, back when she'd been alive. She looked robust and cheerful. Not a stitch of black lace to be found.

"Ivy?"

It was her father. He moved quickly toward her, catching her up in his arms for a squeeze. He didn't seem to want to let go.

"Ivy," he breathed into her hair.

"Tad?"

"There were two more last night. I found your note and when you didn't come home..."

"Oh, oh tad, I'm so sorry, I didn't think..."

"Where were you?"

"I was out late and...and..." She bit her lip. "Tad, can we talk somewhere?"

He released his hold but continued to stare for a long moment. "Of course, my girl."

"Somewhere private? I have a question..."

He glanced at Beals, who shrugged. "Wheaton's office?"

"Right. This way, my girl."

And he led her down to the end of the floor to a small windowless room that looked more a broom closet than office. Wheaton was a clerk, and was responsible for much of the press releases and reports filed from H-Division to the newspapers and the Yard. There was a set of pneumatic pipes on one wall and a steam-powered type-writing machine on the desk. Type-writing machines were all the rage in London now. They made her fountain pens seem like antiques.

Savage closed the door behind him, turned up the gaslight on the wall. "What's wrong with you, my girl? Why are you back in London?"

"It's a long story, tad and I'll tell you everything but I need to ask you a question first. Please?"

He raised his brows and she took a deep breath.

"The Ripper. Is he left-handed?"

Savage stared at her.

"Well? Is he?"

"Ivy, what are you doing?"

"Please, tad…"

"You're not writing your novel again, are you? We've talked about that—"

"Tell me if he's left-handed and I'll tell you everything."

"You are stubborn as your brother, you know that?" He folded his arms across his chest. "Llewellyn thinks so, but Bondie disagrees and Phillips is on the fence. It's a bloody bugger having all these specialists working the case. They all have their opinions and they contradict each other like politicians. Why do you ask?"

She frowned as she thought.

"Please don't tell me you are conducting your own 'investigations,' my girl. This villain has been taunting Remy and once he knows you're back in town, he'll set his sights on you. I couldn't bear losing my last girl. I couldn't."

She glanced up.

"Taunting Remy? What do you mean?"

"Been sending him cards and letters. We have no idea as to why."

"Oh dear God," she moaned. "Poor Christien. Oh it makes sense now, why he wanted me safe."

"Your turn, my girl."

She sighed.

"We were at the Docks last night, Sebastien and I, and he says he saw the Ripper and fought him off with a spade."

"Sebastien? Sebastien *de Lacey?*"

"Yes, Sebastien. I suppose I should call him Your Lordship, but honestly—"

"Good Lord, he's in town."

"Tad?"

"Stay here!" And suddenly, her tad bolted from the room, leaving the door wide open. Beals glanced in and she shrugged.

He returned a few moments later, closed the door behind him. He held out a photochrome. It was of a London street at night.

"An automabob took this last night on Cable." He moved in closer under the gaslight so she could see.

"Look at this. Look at these two here…" He pointed to a grainy image along the shopfronts and she could make out a man holding a woman against a wall. She swallowed, recognizing him immediately.

"This woman is Catherine Eddowes. She was one of the victims of the Ripper last night. This man…" He looked at her now. "Is this man Sebastien de Lacey? Lamb said he recognized him from one of the tabloids but I said he was up north."

Her heart was racing and she could feel her knees trembling. She was actually grateful for the sweeping fabric of the skirt. It hid many things.

"Ivy? Is this man Sebastien de Lacey?"

She took a deep breath.

"No," she said firmly. "It is not."

His green eyes tried her like fire. "Ivy, you've always been a good girl. You tell me the truth."

"No." She swallowed again. "That is not Sebastien de Lacey."

Suddenly, he grabbed her wrist and dragged her out of the tiny room, down the hall towards the first office. All the officers, including Beals watched them and even the automatons swiveled their heads to follow. Savage paused only to rap on the door before pushing it open and dragging his daughter in. She recognized the gray moustache of Dr. Bond and he frowned as they entered.

"Trevis? Ivy?"

The walls were covered in photochromes of mutilated bodies and Ivy looked away.

"No, Ivy," growled her father. "You look. Look at these women. Study them hard, my girl. This is what our Ripper is doing in the back streets of Whitechapel. This here…"

He pulled her over to a set of fresh chromes and Ivy felt the bile rise in her throat.

"This is Catherine Eddowes, the woman in this chrome."

The tears stung her eyes once again and he raised the automabob image up to her face, gave it a shake.

"Now, you look one more time and tell me that this is not Sebastien de Lacey in this chrome. Tell me that and if you're lying, let every one of these murders be on your head."

"Sebastien de Lacey?" Bond frowned again. "Remy's brother? I didn't think he was in town."

Tears spilled down her cheeks and her chest pressed in on itself so that she could barely breathe.

"No," she whispered. "It is not Sebastien de Lacey. He was with me last night."

"*All* night?" She saw the flash in his eye. Lowered hers. But she did find her chin rise and that, of all things, surprised her.

"Yes," she said. "All night. I spent the night at Hollbrook House."

The silence in the office was crushing. He had not closed the door and several officers drained away, not wanting to see, not wanting to hear of the fall from grace of Trevis Savage's "good" girl. To his credit, Dr. Bond said nothing.

"I see…" Her father straightened. "Does Remy know?"

She nodded.

"How could you?"

"Tad—"

"Go. Leave, my girl. I have work to do."

She did, feeling the eyes of the entire department on her as she fled the floors of H-Division, out under the inhuman gaze of Coraline Candymore and the Sentinels of Leman Street.

Chapter 34

Of Obfuscation, Fabrication and a Room in Scotland Yard

She hailed a cab for the ride back to Hollbrook House, rushed up the steps to bang on the door. Within moments, Pomfrey answered, looking prim in his wig and satin coattails. He did not move to let her in.

"Pomfrey, is Christien in?"

"I'm afraid Mr. Christien has been called to work, miss."

For some reason, she felt a wave of relief. "And Sebastien? Is he here?"

"Is His Lordship expecting you?"

"No. But he'll see me. He must."

He seemed to consider this and stepped aside.

"Please wait in the foyer, miss."

Her heart was still racing and she dreaded the feeling sinking into her bones. What had she done? She had lied to her father both *as* her father and as an officer of the court. It *had* been Sebastien in the photochrome and if he was the Ripper, she was playing a very dangerous game. It likely would have gone better for him had she told the truth. Now, she was wrapping him in lies. That would not sit well with any court of law.

Within minutes, Pomfrey returned.

"This way, miss."

She followed him to the sitting room of Hollbrook House. It was large and very ornate with cream papered walls and a marble fireplace in the centre. A bank of high windows at the west end invited the struggling October sun and under the windows was a piano, much like the one back at Lasingstoke. Sebastien was sitting at that piano now, staring at the keys.

She turned to Pomfrey. "Please have Castlewaite ready the coach. Sebastien is needed back at Lasingstoke."

The houseman raised a wiry brow.

"Please, Pomfrey," she said. "If you care at all for your masters, do as I ask."

He nodded primly and left the room.

"Hallo, Sebastien..."

He said nothing, merely stared at the keys. He was dressed now, which was a good thing, but whether he had done it himself or if Christien had taken care of him, she couldn't tell. His clothing was fine and his hair was swept off his forehead like a regular gentleman, so she suspected the latter.

She wondered if Christien felt the same way about his brother as she felt for her mother. It was a common thread, ties that bound them together as caregivers and prisoners both. It broke her heart all over again.

She sat on the piano bench.

"Sebastien?"

Still nothing. She touched his hand and he breathed in as if suddenly awakened. Slowly, he raised his head. Slowly, he blinked at her. Slowly, a smile spread across his face.

"Oh. Hallo Ivy."

His words were slow as well and she knew it was the lithium. He was still drugged. This could be problematic.

"Sebastien, I'm having Castlewaite take you to the airship. You need to get back to Lasingstoke."

"I can't play," he said slowly. "My hands... they won't work."

"I know. That's the lithium. Its effects should wear off soon. You need to leave. Do you understand?"

"Why did you do that, Ivy? I would never hurt you."

Damn those tears. They were calling again.

"I'm so sorry, Sebastien. I know you won't hurt me. Will you go back to Lasingstoke?"

"My dogs are at Lasingstoke."

"Yes. They're missing you. Here, I want you to take this with you…"

She reached under her collar to the clockwork locket, slipped it off and over his head. It began to hum and glow.

He looked down at it as it sat just over the first button of his waistcoat.

"Mumford says it's dangerous."

"Take it to Frankow. He'll know what to do."

"Frankow has good laudanum…"

"Will you go?"

He nodded, slowly looked back at the keys.

"Miss?"

It was Castlewaite in the doorway of the sitting room. He looked surprisingly fresh and well rested after a night of cold rain and hard purl.

"We're headin' to the airship, Ah take it?"

"Please, Jerry. We need to hurry. I'm afraid I've made a calamity of things and Sebastien is in a bit of trouble."

"We'll get him home, miss. Not to worry."

She turned on the bench seat. "Sebastien, the coach is ready."

"I can't play," he said quietly. "My hands won't work…"

She looked back at the coachman. "Perhaps Lonsdale instead…"

"Aye. Lonsdale it is."

Castlewaite crossed the floor, and together, they slipped arms under Sebastien's to help him to his feet when there were voices in the hall.

"Quickly," she hissed but it was too late. Flanked by several constables, her father stood in the doorway of Hollbrook House.

***

Once, when he had been very little, he had been angry at Cookie so he had set out to break some windows at Fourth. Passing the pond, the swans had chased him, but being the ruffian that he was, he chased them right back. Straight into the water and then some but he was only seven and half English, and he didn't know how to swim. The sensation of going under, of trying to move heavy arms and legs, of looking up through the water and seeing sunlight and trees through walls of liquid glass. He remembered very little of his life before Lonsdale, but that particular memory had stayed with him forever.

He felt that way know.

"I'm sorry," Sebastien said, holding his head in his hands. "Can you repeat the question?"

He was in a room in what he assumed was the Metropolitan Police on Great Scotland Yard. The gaslight was very bright and there were men in the room with him. Most of them were older, mustachioed and hard as tack and one of them was Ivy's father, Trevis Savage. Another, with a great handlebar and chops, loomed over him and had been introduced as Chief Inspector Henry Moore.

"I said what were you doing in Whitechapel last night, de Lacey? Answer it this time or I'll throw you in the claps for a night. You'll be happy to talk tomorrow."

There was an apparition flickering around the man and Sebastien felt a chill. The lithium was wearing off.

"Answer me, damn it."

"Aaah…We were looking for a woman…"

"A woman? Well, you went to the right part of town, sir. More whores in Whitechapel than pigeons."

"No, not that kind of woman."

"A particular woman, then. Who is this woman? Does she have a name?"

"Aaah…" He racked his brain. The name was there, on the tip of his tongue, but neither tongue nor brain was operating on all gears at the moment. Just like being underwater. "Savage, her name is Savage."

Moore glanced at Trevis. "Ivy Savage? Are you referring to the girl, Ivy Savage? Was that her name?"

"No," he shook his head, but the motion made him dizzy. "No. We were looking for Catherine Savage, her mother."

***

"Your mother?" Carter Beals scratched his head. "But Ivy, your mother is alive."

"I know, but Sebastien sees things that we don't. He thought that since Tobias died in the water at St. Katharine's Docks, we might find

317

her there. Her soul, that is. Sebastien says that her soul is disjointed from her body and that is why she lives like she is dead."

"And this made sense to you, Ivy?"

She looked up now. She was very fond of Beals. He had a young wife and four happy sons and for a detective, he was a very kind man.

"No, not at first. But I've seen things that defy explanation. Talk to Dr. Williams. Talk to Henry Babbage or Ninian Liddell or Arvin Frankow. Honestly, sir, talk to Prince Edward or Albert Victor. They are in this thick."

"I would never talk to a Royal about issues of sense and nonsense."

She smiled now, grateful for his friendship.

"So you were lying earlier, weren't you Ivy? About spending that sort of night with de Lacey? A woman's reputation is a hard one to gain back once lost."

"He's not the Ripper, sir. I know he's not."

"Well, we shall have to prove it then, shan't we?" He straightened, took a long deep breath. "But that's going to be difficult. The public believes the Ripper is a madman, and the way I'm seeing it, they don't come much madder than the Mad Lord of Lasingstoke."

***

"Are you a ghost hunter, sir? Is that what you are saying?"

The apparition was flickering over the man's shoulder. It was a boy of perhaps thirteen with a very white face and sunken eyes. He looked as if he had drowned but there was a hole in the side of his head, likely from a bullet.

A hand slammed down on the table in front of him and Sebastien flinched.

"Answer the question, man!" Moore leaned in again. "And how did looking for a ghost under a pier lead you to be assaulting a woman on Cable, sir?"

"Someone dropped a head in the River so I gave chase. And I did not assault her. *She* assaulted *me.*"

"That is quite unlikely, sir. We have a photochrome." He placed it on the table, turned it with his fingertips and slid it across. "Hard evidence of you with a woman who turns up violently murdered less than an hour afterwards."

"Yes. That is she. I saw what he did to her. It is unspeakable what a man can do to a woman." He looked up. "Do you have any other chromes?"

Moore snarled but another man cleared his throat.

"Yes we do, sir. The 'bobs snap every minute like clockwork."

"I was chasing two men. One was limping from a shot to the leg. Is there a chrome of their flight?"

"A shot to the leg?"

"Yes I'm quite certain I hit him and most likely in the leg."

"You shot a man last night?"

"It was a crackerjack shot, if I do say so myself. I could have taken them down whilst in pursuit but I did promise Ivy not to shoot anymore people if I could help it."

The room grew strangely still.

"You shoot people, sir?" said Moore.

"From time to time. As I presume, do you."

"I am an officer of the law."

"I am a sorry wastrel of the Crown."

"That is obfuscation, sir."

"Victoria asked me to come to London to shoot hoodlums. I'd prefer not to but it is very difficult to say no to Victoria. She has her ways."

"Balderdash. It is a fabrication, sir."

"I do not fabricate, nor do I obfuscate. Would you please check on those chromes? If we have an image of them, we might be able to locate the torso killers. That would be a blessed relief."

"Torso killers?" Moore frowned, glanced at his men. "What do you mean by torso killers?"

de Lacey sighed, dropped his head into his hands again.

"This game does not play far with me, sir," growled Moore. "I believe as much in your madness as I do in your ghosts."

"According to the reports, there was a woman's arm found September 11 off Pimlico Bridge in the Thames. Two evenings ago, another arm on Lambeth. Last night, I myself saw the head. It does stand to reason that there would be a corresponding torso and possibly legs, yes? Not many heads around without torsos and legs."

"You are bordering on contempt, sir."

"And you shot a boy."

"What?"

"You shot a boy in the head so yes I do hold you in contempt."

"What the devil are you talking about?"

"A boy, thirteen, perhaps fourteen at most. You shot him in the head then dumped him in the river. Why? Was he a thief? A pickpocket? Yes, I think a pickpocket. He looks the type. Could you not be bothered bringing him to trial? I see what Ivy means now. Honestly, I do."

"Sounds like Billy Clarence," asked Savage. "We haven't seen him 'round the docks of late..."

"Does he have brown hair and brown eyes?" asked de Lacey.

"Why, yes, I think—"

"That's enough!" snapped Moore. "Clap him and take him downstairs. A night in the brig will chase the bloody insolence out of him."

"But he's a Baron, Henry," another man grumbled. "He sits in the House."

"The peerage is not above the law, Donald. They more than all of us should behave in a conduct becoming an Englishman." He narrowed his eyes in scorn. "But then again, I believe de Lacey is French..."

Sebastien sighed.

Moore turned to Savage. "Take him down, Trev. For your daughter's sake."

"Aye, sir." He moved around the desk, helped the Mad Lord to his feet.

"There will be a torso, sirs," said Sebastien. "I can attest to that. Where it will turn up I haven't a clue, but she will turn up sometime. And please, have someone check on those chromes."

"Have a good night, sir," growled Moore, and he turned his back to them both as Savage led the Mad Lord down.

***

"There will be a report of a head in the Thames that I filed last night with a Constable Poole. The times will coincide and our story will be vindicated. You'll see, sir. I am telling the truth."

"Ah." Carter Beals smiled at her. "You're telling the truth *now.*"

"There's a time for every purpose under heaven, sir."

There was a rattle at the door and Christien slipped into the room.

Beals glanced up. "I'll, ah, I'll go see if your Poole filed that report in the archives, shall I? Back in a jiff."

And he was gone, leaving Ivy by the window while Christien sagged against the door. He looked very pale, and perhaps sadder than she had ever seen him. He was usually so controlled, so calm, so perfect.

It was a mask, she realized, a fine, perfect, porcelain mask, cracking now and revealing someone very fragile underneath. She remembered a time when she had wanted to be his partner but now things had changed. He was a stranger to her. Or perhaps she was the stranger.

She felt the ring tight on her finger.

"I'm sorry, Christien," she said. Her throat was closing but her hands had curled into fists of their own accord. "I'm sorry I've made a calamity of things."

"What were you thinking, Ivy?" His voice was very thin. "How could you do this to him?"

"You drugged him, Christien! You slipped the lithium into his tea and used *me* to do it. How could you do *that?*"

"Please stop." He held up his gloved hand, drew a long shuddering breath. Fighting for his calm, she knew that. Smoothing the porcelain. He was so very different from his brother.

"Your father wants you to go home. I've arranged a cab—"

"No, I can't leave hi—" She caught herself. "Now. I can't leave now."

But he had caught it too and he took a long deep breath.

"Well, you don't have much choice, Ivy. They've taken him downstairs to the pen."

"Oh…"

"Eloquent response for a writer."

"I'll…I'll talk to my father…"

"It was your father who ushered him."

Ivy bit back any further eloquence. In truth, she didn't know what to say.

"I do care for you, Ivy. Do you not believe that?"

"I know you do, Christien."

"What more, then, do you need? What does he give you that I cannot?"

A word that popped into her head and she tried to chase it out as quickly as it came to her. But there was no denying it, she knew it full well. It was the very key to her heart, her mind, her soul, the key to Penny Dreadful and her winning ways. Just as quickly, she realized that it was very unlikely that Christien could ever give it to her. He was as much a prisoner as she.

She looked up at him.

"Freedom," she said.

***

His name was WILLS. *Westinghouse Institutional Legal-Lockdown Sentinel.* He was the sergeant-at-arms of the holding cell and he was easily twice the size of a man and much more formidable.

At the end of one of his arms was a skeleton key that spun as he unlocked the large iron door to cell. Inside, the room was small with gray walls, plain linoleum and a a single window very high up. There were currently five men incarcerated and the odor of them struck like a fist, as unwashed men have a way of doing. A covered bucket and a low bench were the only items, other than the men, in the room.

Other than the men and the dead, that is.

Sebastien hesitated as one by one, like wolves in a forest, they appeared, until there were at least twelve along with the living. He suspected there would have been more, but it was these twelve alone who were the most insistent and were aware enough to sense him. Not for the first time he regretted the loss of his pistol.

He turned back to Savage.

"And why am I being locked up, sir?"

"Having second thoughts, are you?"

"Not at all. I am just recovering from a rather large dose of lithium and am a titch addled. I would just like to know. For the sake of clarity."

Savage raised a thick brow. "You pissed off the Chief Inspector, that's why."

"Ah. And that is a crime, now, is it?"

"In."

Sebastien stepped through the door as Savage leaned in.

"Stay *away* from my daughter."

The door closed in his face.

Sebastien stood quietly for a moment, before slipping his hands in his pockets.

"Apparently, I pissed *him* off as well."

He turned to the other occupants of the room. By the looks of them, this was not their first night in a cell. One by one, they stood and moved toward him as if to jail him with their very bodies alone. One was short, stout and smelled of cooking oil and beer. Another was very hairy and reminded him of a warthog. Even one sharp tooth protruded from his lip like a tusk. The third was bleeding from a wound to the head that was obviously not his first. The fourth was very tall with a beaked nose and tattered clothes, but oddly enough, very fine riding boots. And the fifth was the largest man Sebastien had ever seen, a great tattooed bull of a man with a shaved head and burnsides that swung up and formed a moustache.

This man alone brought six of the dead.

He towered over the Mad Lord, and his breathing was the only sound in the room.

Sebastien looked up at him and smiled.

"Your tattoos are quite remarkable, sir. Do you know by any chance when they bring the tea?"

A massive fist turned out the lights, which was as good a start as he could have hoped.

Chapter 35

Of Repentance, Remembrance and a Trio of Unexpected Visitors

Pall Mall Steam Gazette

TORSO FOUND AT WESTMINSTER.

At twenty minutes past three this morning, workmen on the construction site of the New Scotland Yard made a grisly discovery. It was of the torso of a young woman, missing the head, arms, legs and several internal organs. She was wrapped in a dark skirting and was assumed to be a bag of lime until a workman tried to move her. How or when the torso was brought to the site is unknown, but it is believed to be the original owner of the arms of Pimlico and Lambeth Road. Dr. Thomas Bond is on the scene and the Offices of the Metropolitan Police have declined to comment.

Whether this is a prank on the part of medical students or yet another victim of the Whitechapel Ripper is still unknown. Police are continuing to investigate.

***

"He was in there all night?" asked Carter Beals as he trotted alongside his partner, Trevis Savage. "With Rusty and the Millhouse gang?"

"Aye," muttered Savage. "Half hour with Rusty is enough to make most men cry like a baby. That'll teach him to mess about with my daughter after midnight."

"Trev," groaned Beals. "I've told you. Nothing happened. Ivy was lying."

"I don't care, Bealer. She was a good girl 'til she went up north."

"He was right about those chromes, you know. Two fellas in the chrome before his, one limping like a lame nag."

"That says he's either observant or he's good with a pistol. Nothing more."

"Did he have a pistol on him?"

"Probably in the house."

"Did we search the house?"

Savage rolled his eyes.

"Well then, maybe we should," said Beals.

"Well then. Maybe we should."

They came to a halt at a registry desk outside the row of the cells. Savage presented his badge, as did Beals.

"Block D, Prisoner 777," said Savage.

The registrar peered up at them through thick reticulating lenses.

"We 'ad a bi' of a problem… wif d' 'eat," he said. "Cold as 'ell, in 'ere. But ovver'n 'at, no incident."

Beals glanced at his partner and the pair of them entered the cellblock row.

The ceilings were at least twelve feet high and their footsteps echoed on the linoleum. There was a peculiar odor to the cellblock as well. The pots were cleaned daily but that was a part of the "charm" of a cell. No amenities. Intended to make a villain think twice about committing another crime.

They pulled up in front of the Sentinel. It patrolled the row like a soldier.

"Identification code," it said and Beals punched a series of numbers into the panel on its chest. A green light flashed on the sentinel's faceplate.

"Alright, WILLS," said Savage. "Open 'er up."

The sentinel rolled forward, raising his key arm in the air and attaching itself to the heavy iron door. The key spun three times and the door groaned as it began to wheel back on its hinges. A wall of cold hit them like a fist and both detectives peered in on a most unusual sight.

Four men—the oily one, the warthog, the bleeder and the tattered fellow—knelt in four corners of the room, hands clasped under their chins, praying. The fifth—large, tattooed, mustachioed Rusty, sat on the bench weeping, his meaty hands grasped within de Lacey's. He was also wearing de Lacey's cravat around his thick neck.

Savage and Beals exchanged glances.

Sebastien de Lacey looked up. "Please give us a moment. We're almost done here."

He turned his attention back to the big man. "So Rusty, what do you say to Ponce?"

"I'm sorry, Ponce!" the big man wailed, and his breath frosted in front of his face. "I shouldn'nae poonched yer head in! I shouldn'nae rammed ye into the bricks or cut yer forks off like kippers and I shouldn'ae hung ye up by yer sausages till ye was blue! I' was in me cups but it was wrong! Can ye ever fergive me?"

Savage looked around as a wind picked up and blew at their clothing and hair. It died as quickly as it had come.

"James Russell, you are forgiven and the Crown has been served."

Sebastien sighed, dropping his hand on the top of Rusty's bald head, patting it like he would a dog. It made a slapping sound.

"So, can you promise me that you will try to control your temper from now on? I really don't want to have to come back down to London and shoot you, because I will, Rusty. Next time, I will. Honestly, it is so much easier."

"I will, Laury! I will control my temper!"

"And watch the drinking."

"Aye. No more gin fer me! I'll be dry as a nun."

"There's a lad." Sebastien rose to his feet. He was wearing riding boots. Savage was certain he hadn't been yesterday. "And remember to call the Heath Row Fields. They can always use a big lad like you to help with the ships. Ask for Neville Scully and tell him Laury sent you. Can you remember that?"

"Neville Scully. Aye."

Sebastien glanced around at the others. "Promise me, lads. All of you. Remember, bullets are expensive."

The four others nodded, and the tattered man looked up from his knees, smiling like the sun. "Dese are de most flush docks I ever owned."

And he looked down at his feet, shod now in fine spats with brass buttons.

"And they suit you, Percy. Like a glove."

"Bless you, Laury."

"Yes, bless you, Laury," moaned the warthog. He wore a fine gray waistcoat.

"Bless yew, Laury," moaned the greasy one. He made the sign of the cross. "Amen."

Sebastien turned to face the detectives. "May I leave now?"

Beals glanced at his partner.

"Aaaah, no," said Savage. "The Chief wants to talk with you awhile."

"Oh good Lord." The Mad Lord's shoulders sagged. "I'm desperately tired and need a cup of tea. Ivy would be proud but honestly, sirs, a bullet is so much easier."

Savage grumbled and shoved Sebatien de Lacey from the room, leaving WILLS to close up the iron door on a now reformed James Russell and the repentant Millhouse gang.

***

She sat on the edge of her bed, staring at the floor.

She hadn't slept at all after the cab had dropped her off, merely climbed the stair to her room and sat the way she was sitting now. Christien had not come with her and her father had not come home. She felt entirely alone.

What had she done?

And so she sat for a very long time more, thinking very little, feeling even less. At some point, sometime, she realized that someone was rapping on the door downstairs. Finally, like an automaton herself, she rose to attend it.

"Open up, you petulant thing, you! Open up I say!" came a familiar voice and Ivy's heart leapt within her. She flew down the stair and threw

327

open the door on a tall slim horsey brunette in an aubergine jacket and tiny top hat, and a short round blonde in red cloak, massive touring hat, goggles and long paisley scarf. With a cry, Ivy threw herself at the sisters, pulling them both into a great teary-eyed embrace, to which the sisters wailed, shrieked and exclaimed their surprise. Finally, Ivy pulled them both into the house.

"Dearest!" exclaimed Fanny. "That was a most unusual welcome. Splendid and hearty, yes of course. We Helmsly-Wimpoll women are used to splendid and hearty welcomes..."

"Most splendid and hearty," agreed Franny.

"But from you, dearest and darling, it is most unusual."

"Most unusual."

"Oh," said Ivy, wiping the tears from her eyes. "I've just missed you both terribly. Please come in."

Fanny studied her with a now-familiar scrutiny. "I suspect there is more that you are not telling us, surely, dearest..."

"Surely more," said Franny.

"But you will tell all over tea, won't you? I know you will." She laid a hand on Ivy's shoulder. "You can keep no secrets from us, dearest."

"Are there biscuits?" said Franny.

Ivy beamed at them. "I am so glad you are here!"

And she led them into the kitchen, where she set the kettle to boil for tea.

***

Sebastien de Lacey glanced around the new holding cell, hoping to spy a tea service but there was nothing of the kind. It was as gray as the former room but smaller and on the third floor. However, it had a desk and two chairs, and he had to admit that, as of this morning, his station was much improved.

Trevis Savage was the only other occupant of the room, and he leaned against a wall, arms folded across his chest. Very little in the living world frightened Sebastien de Lacey but for some reason, this man did. He wondered if it had something to do with the fact that he was a father. All in all, fathers were very frightening creatures.

He looked up, put on his best smile. It was difficult for he was very tired and he couldn't remember the last time he had eaten. His stomach had been rumbling all night.

"And how is Ivy, sir?"

Savage glared at him but no answer was forthcoming.

There were no apparitions. It was a strange thing. Such animosity from an obviously good man. Yes, it had to be fatherhood and for the first time, Sebastien felt thankful that he was not in that camp. His mind and instincts still functioned without compromise.

"She's a persistent thing, isn't she? Quite a little badger. And I must say, she has a good nose for a mystery. She would make a wonderful detective. In fact, I think she'd—"

"Don't you dare speak to me of my daughter, sir," Savage growled, pushing off from the wall. "Not one more word. *Ever.* Do you understand?"

Sebastien nodded, although he didn't understand in the least.

"You have effectively ruined everything for her. She could have had a life with your brother. She could have had a nice, sensible life with a fine house and a fine husband so she could stop writing those dreadful stories of hers. Don't you understand? Christien de Lacey was her way out, man. Her way out of the East End."

"But he—"

"Not. One. Word!" There were tears in his eyes as he continued. "All I wanted was for her to be safe. All I wanted was for her to have a better life than she could have with me in Stepney. She would care for her mother until she died, my Ivy would. She is that sort of girl, but *you!* You step right off the pages of one of her Dreadfuls. How could she possibly be safe with you?"

He loomed over the table, bringing his face down until they were almost nose to nose.

"There is scandal in your every footprint, sir. No one will have her now but she's far too young to realize it. Your madness has only fueled her imagination and I'm certain she will have nothing to do with a quiet sensible life now. You have been her ruin, sir. You have been her ruin."

Sebastien swallowed again but to his credit, said nothing.

"I don't think you're the Ripper, but if you are, you will hang. If you are responsible for the arms of Lambeth and Pimlico, you may still hang. But for this, this *ruination* of a good young girl, I wish I could see you hang for this crime alone."

The door rattled and Savage stepped back as Moore and Beals entered the room. Beals had in his possession a folder of papers and he glanced at his partner, who wiped his eyes and stepped back to the wall. For his part, Sebastien quickly stared at the floor.

"Are these your men, sir?" asked Beals. "The ones you were chasing last night?"

He slid a chrome under de Lacey's nose.

The Mad Lord did not even look at it.

"And Constable Pleasant Poole does have a record of a Miss Ivy Savage reporting a woman's head dropped into the River Thames at St. Katharine's Pier at 12:52 yesterday morning. Is this correct, sir? Is this your remembrance of things?"

"There was no head," said Sebastien softly.

"Sir?"

"There was no head. In the river. There was a splash. Nothing more."

Beals glanced between his partner and his superior. Moore leaned in over Sebastien's shoulder.

"There was no head, you say?"

"No," said Sebastien. "There was no head."

"That's interesting. Are you certain there was no head?"

"Yes."

"Because we have a torso, now, de Lacey."

Slowly, Sebastien looked up.

"You did say we'd find one," said Moore. "And we did. Do you know where we found her, sir? Any idea at all?"

Sebastien shook his head.

"The Embankment. In the foundation cellar for the New Scotland Yard."

There was silence in the room.

"Clever, don't you think?" asked Moore. "I think that was damned clever. Brazen, in fact. Anything you can tell me about that, sir? Anything else we need to know?"

"The torso," began Sebastien. He cleared his throat but his voice was thin. "No head, no arms, legs taken off at the hip joints, part of her abdomen missing?"

"Exactly, sir. Looks like a butcher or a surgeon."

He nodded, let his eyes drop once more. Moore straightened.

"Do you have anything to say for yourself, de Lacey?"

He did not look up. "This other woman, the small woman on the street who was murdered…"

"Catherine Eddowes?"

"She was alive. She was alive when I met her. I saw what he would do. I saw it all. I should have taken her home, made sure she was safe but I chased after the men instead. I did not value her life."

It was like a Tesla charge in the room, and the three officers moved in as his talk turned to the foremost of crimes.

Moore placed his hands on the table's edge. "Is this a confession, sir?"

"Ivy was right all along. I place more value on the dead than the living. The dead plague me and the living are of no consequence. It is morally wrong." He lifted his eyes to Savage. "You are correct, sir. She would not be safe with me. No one is safe with me."

"Fetch Abberline," said Moore.

Savage nodded and slipped from the room. Beals frowned.

"Are you saying you killed Catherine Eddowes, Lord de Lacey?"

"I am responsible."

"But did you *kill* her, sir?"

Sebastien looked up at the tall man. "I would like to speak with my brother, please."

Moore loomed in between.

"I thought you might. He's right outside the door." He leaned in close one last time. "You'll hang for this, de Lacey. You will hang from the neck until dead."

And quietly the two men left the room as Christien entered, closing the door behind him.

They said nothing for some time before Christien took a chair to sit at the table, laced his fingers across it. Sebastien couldn't bring himself to look at him. Too many damned cadavers.

"Bastien…" Christien began.

"I'm sorry, Christien," said Sebastien. "I'm so very sorry."

"I know. But you didn't do these things. I know you didn't. They have nothing. They're simply trying to bully you, that's all."

"Will you still have Ivy, Christien? She's a good girl. Very industrious and clever. She needs a good stable fellow, someone to keep her safe. Someone to give her a fine house and fine children and..." He took a deep breath. "And you are the finest man I've ever known."

"I do care for her, Bastien," Christien smiled sadly. "But not the way she needs. And I know she does not love me the way I need."

"But she does, Remy. I know she does."

The young doctor cocked his head. "How?"

"Well, she is still wearing mother's ring, yes?"

"I don't believe she has taken it off. But I also gave her a locket and look who is wearing it now."

He glanced down. He had not even noticed. It pulsed like a heartbeat, beautiful and coy.

He sighed.

"Christien, that surgery..."

"Surgery? Which surgery?"

"The one with the holes in... in the forehead..."

"The prefrontal leucotomy?"

"That will cure me, yes?"

"Oh that," Christien swallowed. "It has met with some success in the treatment of violent schizophrenia, yes."

"Could you arrange it, please?"

"Bastien..."

"Please?"

It was Christien's turn to take a deep breath. "I'll talk to Williams. We'll have you transferred out of here. They'll want to send you to Broadmoor but I'll make sure it's Bethlem. We can discuss it then."

"Thank you."

Christien rose to his feet and stepped to the door. He paused and turned.

"How many women do you see, Bastien? Here in this room, right now with me?"

Sebastien cleared his throat again but did not look up. "There are nine women and three torsos, although the torsos are not as clear."

"Torsos? What do you mean?"

"Three dismembered women. They are gruesome to behold."

"By God," said Christien and he looked at the ceiling. "They discovered the torso of a woman today. At the construction site for the new Scotland Yard."

"I have seen her for a month or more. Why have they only found her now?"

"Perhaps she wasn't murdered, Bastien. Perhaps she simply died and people needed to dispose of the body."

"That is no way to do it."

"Is that why they are angry?"

Sebastien shrugged. "I don't know, Christien. They don't speak."

"Right. You've said that before." He studied his brother for a few moments more. "Dr. Williams is a member of the Ghost Club."

"And so are you, it seems."

"Yes, well, that is a matter of debate. Would you consent to speak with some of his fellows?"

"Why?"

"You would present evidence of the validity of their pursuits. They are honest scientists, Bastien. They believe in life after death."

"But you don't," he said quietly.

"I don't want to believe it, Bastien. I'm terrified by the fact that they still want to talk to our dead father."

"They don't know what they are seeking. It's not illumination, it's damnation."

"Will you consent to speak with them?"

Sebastien nodded once again.

Christien sighed. "Remember, Bastien, these officers are only trying to bully you."

Sebastien said nothing.

"I'll talk to Williams and see what we can do. Right?"

"Thank you."

With one last look, Christien left the room but no one entered in his stead. The women folded up on themselves and blew away and for a short while, Sebastien was alone. However, he could hear voices from outside the door, heard words like "lunatic," "illness," "surgery," and "Bedlam." He wished for his father's pistol. In fact, he wished for any pistol. He had sincerely tried his best last night with the Millhouse gang but some problems could not be solved without the pull of a trigger.

He wondered if it were possible for a surgeon's drill to accomplish the same result. He had his doubts.

No, he was convinced he would never leave Bedlam a normal man. In fact, he was convinced that, once there, he would never leave Bedlam at all.

***

"Ninian?" exclaimed Fanny. "*My* Liddell Ninny? In the Ghost Club?"

"That's so exciting!" squealed Franny.

"Indeed," said Ivy and she smiled. It was amazing how the sisters raised her spirits so. They were natural forces for hope and she adored them for it.

"Well, then," Fanny sniffed and raised her cup. "Perhaps I shall drop him a post when I return home. To congratulate him, of course. Nothing more."

"I love datamancery," said Franny.

"Ah, that is London, is it not?" asked Fanny. "All this mystery, romance, intrigue and fine, fine men?"

"Very fine," said Franny, although she looked happily preoccupied with the plate of biscuits on the table.

They were on their second pot of the morning. Ivy had found the biscuits in the larder along with toast, and so she had made a cheap and easy breakfast. Truth be told, nothing could quell the sense of unease in the pit of her stomach.

"But you, dearest and darling," said Fanny, placing a hand on Ivy's sleeve. "You have certainly had a rough time of it."

"A rough time, certainly."

"No, Sebastien has had a rough time of it. I've simply made everything worse." Ivy sighed. "I am a meddlesome, impulsive calamity of a girl and a very good man will pay the price for it."

"Oh dearest," exclaimed Fanny. "That is a most terrible tale of woe."

"Most terrible," said Franny.

"But he will be cleared, surely."

"Most surely."

"Yes," said Ivy, although with considerably less conviction. "Most surely he will."

Fanny sat back, raised her cup. "They have found the torso, you know. The torso belonging to that dreadful head of yours."

"Oh, that's terrible," sighed Ivy. "It was a terrible sight. Poor, poor girl."

They sat for a moment, each one, sipping tea and thinking of the unfortunate woman now in pieces all throughout the city, when once again, there was a rap on the doorknocker.

Ivy looked up.

"Oh, that would be Marie," said Fanny. "Our mother's sister's husband's sister's cousin's daughter. We told you about her once. She's a friend of your Christien Jeremie. Remember?"

"Of your Christien," said Franny.

"We told her to meet us here so we girls could go out for a spot of lunch. I hope that wasn't too forward of us?"

"Was it forward?"

"Not at all," said Ivy. She bustled to the door and opened it upon a vivacious woman of perhaps twenty-five, with strawberry curls and a rosy complexion.

"'allo, Miss," said the woman, and when she smiled, there were dimples in her cheeks. "You Ivy Savage?"

"I am indeed."

"Helo fy chwaer!" said the young woman. *"Cyfarchion o Aberystwyth!"*

"Dear cousin," said Fanny hovering over her shoulder now. "This is our friend Ivy Savage. Ivy, meet our **mother's sister's husband's sister's cousin's daughter** Mary Jane Kelly. We call her Marie. She's Welsh, you know. Just like you."

And Mary Jane Kelly called Marie smiled as Ivy invited her in.

Chapter 36

Of Women Restelled, Women Released and Women in the Morgue

The Snooty Fox was a well-frequented pub between the neighbourhoods of Stepney and Whitechapel, and even at the early hour of eleven, men of all ages sat, smoking, drinking and chatting amongst themselves. Not so different than women, thought Ivy, with the exception of the smoking. And the tea in the Fox was almost as strong as the tobacco or the ale.

Mary Jane was a talkative girl and Ivy learned more about her in half an hour than she knew about any other living soul. She had been born in Ireland but raised in Wales. She had been married at a very young age and three times no less, firstly to a coal miner, secondly to an Ironclad longshoreman and thirdly to member of the Submersibles Navy. She had been widowed in each circumstance. She had worked as an artist, singer, actress, governess and seamstress. She traveled on the stage to Paris but returned to London to find work in Knightsbridge, very near Hollbrook House. Her parents had been well off and friends with Dr. John Williams back in Swansea. In fact, it had been Dr. Williams who had introduced her to Christien and the boys years ago. They were "thick as thieves," as she put it. "Thick as bloody thieves."

Ivy did not know what to make of her stories. They were grand for such a young woman, but she was obviously a girl of intelligence and pluck. With a well-connected family, it was possible to have done all these things and yet she was living in a common lodging house off Dorset. Ivy suspected that while she dreamed of many grand adventures, she made do with what she had.

Ivy understood it quite well.

As Mary Jane lifted her tea, Ivy noticed a brass ring on her finger.

"Mary Jane?"

"Call me Marie. It's French. French is so much more 'phisticated than English, don't you think? Just like your Remy. 'e's very 'phisticated, ain't 'e?"

Ivy smiled. "Marie, your ring? Where did you get it?"

Mary Jane held out her hand to admire it. "Oh, funny you should mention it. John gave it to me. 'e's a regular gentleman, my John is."

"John Williams gave you this ring?"

"Aye. *Annwyl fy meddg,* John."

"You must know him well, then."

The young woman blushed but said nothing, merely twirled the finger around a lock of strawberry hair.

Three matching rings, thought Ivy. One for Christien, one for Prince Albert Victor, one for Mary Jane Kelly. She shook her head, entirely boggled.

"Dear friends, I think I must get back to the Yard. They're bound to have released Sebastien by now and I feel the need to make things right between us before he returns to Lasingstoke."

"Alone," sniffed Fanny. "All great romances end in misery, I fear. Misery, death and then of course, ghosts."

"I love ghosts," said Franny.

"I thought you was Remy's moll." Mary Jane leaned forward. "'oo's this 'Bastien, then?"

"Have you not heard, cousin?" scoffed Fanny, waving a hand in the air. "Sebastien Laurent St. John Lord de Lacey, the Mad Lord of Lasingstoke himself?"

"Christien's brother," said Ivy. "He's being wrongly held at the Yard."

"The Mad Lord!" Mary Jane sat upright. "Why, 'e shot poor Rosie, 'e did. Shot 'im right up from under a pier."

There was silence at the little table. Both Fanny and Franny turned to look at Ivy for she had told them the tale that very morning. Ivy blinked slowly.

"What did you say, Marie?"

The girl glanced between them. "I was there at Hollbrook House with Lewie the other night. Christien was fixing up Rosie's leg. Henry said some git shot him right up from under the pier, just like that! Your Christien said it was his brother who shot him and he would get him to shoot Lewie next."

Ivy felt the world lurch underneath her.

"I saw him through the glass. He looked like a lunatic, sure enough, but the room grew right cold, then. There were frost all over everything. Old houses are poor for it, ain't they? But I thought Hollbrook House were finer 'n that…"

Ivy took a deep breath but it did not help steady her racing heart. "Did Henry say what they were doing on the pier?"

"Naw," she answered. "Something about Bedlam. They die all the time in Bedlam, he said. John's been helping them with some schoolwork and it has to do with Bedlam, but for the life of me, I didn't listen. I was in me cups that night, I was! Lewie's right generous with the gin!" And she laughed at the memory.

Ivy looked at the sisters. "What would Ambrose Pickett be doing dropping a head into the Thames in the middle of the night?"

"Disposing of it, I should think," said Franny and Ivy turned to her. She was eating a steak and kidney pie and did not bother to look up. "It is an ideal way to rid oneself of an unwanted body. The Met pays well for human remains fished out of the river, so it's a win-win situation all round. Ah ha, me me. Medical students and their pranks…"

She laughed to herself as she sopped up gravy with a bit of bread.

Ivy stared at her. Franny Helmsly-Wimpoll was not a woman given to many words.

"Franny? What are you saying?"

Franny raised her head, licked the gravy from her lips. "Nothing…?"

"No, no, continue. Please."

"Well," she said tentatively. "It's in all the papers, isn't it? The arms of Pimlico and Lambeth? And now the torso on the Embankment. I read all of them. The papers, I mean. I do love to read the papers. They have so many wonderful stories in them, almost as good as yours, Ivy. And the papers have always maintained it was students and their pranks.

They have access to cadavers for their studies and are usually high-spirited young men. Your Christien Jeremie is a medical student, is he not?"

"Is he not?" echoed Fanny in an odd reversal of role.

"Yes," said Ivy quietly. "He is. But I can't imagine Christien being involved in such hijinks. He is simply too... too..."

She had no words. She wanted to say, too perfect, but he had deceived her into bringing his brother drugged tea. *He still can't bear to be in the same room as me*, he had told her back at the house called Seventh. Says *the cadavers are too much for him.*

She sat back in her chair, puzzling.

"Oh, they're pranksters, the lot of them," said Mary Jane. "Remy stays out of most of it, though. He's too good for them, says Lewie. He's right in thick with Bondie and my John. He only had to do the legs."

"The legs?" barked Fanny.

"They get 'em from Bedlam," whispered Mary Jane. "Patient girls who die from the bleeding. He's not s'posed to do it, you know. Lewie says its illegal an'all."

"What, Marie?" asked Ivy. "What is illegal?"

"The Restellism." The woman glanced around and leaned in close. "The 'bortions, girlie. John's good that way. He helps us at the clinics when we need him. They need him at Bedlam too. There's men and ladies together at Bedlam. Of course it's going to happen."

Ivy frowned. She knew Williams performed abortions. He had admitted as much in the lift at the Ghost Club.

"But why would they die at Bedlam, Marie?"

"It's not an easy job, no miss. Not easy at all. Sometimes it works with just them pills, or the tonic, but if it don't, then that's when they need our John. He has these instruments to do the job right quick. But there's a lot of blood, miss. And sometimes, the girls get sick. They run fevers and sometimes they die."

"Abortions are illegal, dearest," said Fanny, raising her teacup. "Even in Bedlam."

"That's why it's bad if one dies."

Her blue eyes were earnest and Ivy believed her.

"He gives it to lots of the girls. He gave me one last year at Bedlam.

He's a saint, our John is. A true saint." She sat back. "'Cept for the ones that die. Not a saint for them, then is he?"

And she raised her teacup to her lips. "No, not a saint if they die."

***

Carter Beals entered the little room, carefully balancing two cups of tea in his hands. He bumped the door closed behind him and laid the cups on the table.

The Mad Lord looked up at him, eyes baleful and asking.

"Yes," Beals grinned. "They're both for you. You did something right peculiar with that Millhouse gang. I'm not quite certain I understand it but I figured you deserve a cup or two."

"Oh thank you so much," said Sebastien and he grabbed one of the cups in a most ungentlemanly fashion. "One never knows how utterly dependant one is until one is deprived for a spell."

And he gulped it down like a greedy little boy.

Beals sat across from him, studied him for a long moment. "You didn't kill those women, did you?"

Sebastien hesitated a moment before draining the first cup to its dregs. Slowly, he pushed it aside in favour of the other. He seemed prepared to take his time with this one, savour the taste on his tongue.

"Would you be kind enough to answer me, de Lacey? Did you kill those women?" He sat back in his chair. "Because I don't think you did. I think you're a strange one, sure enough, but I've met stranger. And Ivy Savage speaks very highly of you."

de Lacey said nothing.

"In fact, she says you didn't kill those women..." He leaned forward now. "Because you were spending the night with her..."

"What?" The Mad Lord looked up sharply. "No. Absolutely not. I would not. She is engaged to marry my brother. I would never—"

"I believe you, sir, I believe you."

"She said that?"

"She did."

"Well, that explains her father, surely," he said. "He must love her very much."

"He does, sir. Don't think to badly of him. Trev's a good man. Losing his wife bit by bit like that broke his heart, made him very protective of his last girl." He smiled sadly. "And Ivy's a handful, believe me. She gets herself in a world of trouble. But she's a good girl, too. Cared for her mother better than most nurses. Raised her brother, wrote her little stories. Yes, she's a very good, sensible, clever girl. So, tell me ..."

He looked up.

"Why would she lie?"

Sebastien sighed, ran a hand along his face. There was considerable scruff now. His chin had not seen a razor in days.

"de Lacey?"

"I cannot say."

"She doesn't believe you're the Ripper, sir. She will gladly ruin her reputation to see you cleared. And yet you don't seem to care about that. You don't seem to be a callous man, but then again, I don't know you from Adam, do I?"

"I do care, Inspector. But, it's for the best. It's honestly for the best."

"What is, sir?"

"Bedlam." He leaned forward, crossed his arms on the table and began to tap with one finger. "You see, I need to know if I am truly mad or not, for I saw the Ripper the other night. I spoke with him after he beat me senseless with a spade. I know who he is and who he is—for him to be doing the things we all know him to be doing—is impossible. And so, I am either bound to comb London for a man who cannot exist, or I am utterly mad. I would sincerely like to know before I begin to exert incredible amounts of energy and willpower in what could very well be a futile search. I would quite happily spend the rest of my madness at home in Lancashire with my dogs."

He lifted the second cup to his lips and sipped while Beals blinked very, very slowly.

"Did you just say you know who the Ripper is?"

"I did say that, yes."

"You know who the London Ripper is."

"Yes. Yes, I do."

"You spoke with him."

"Yes. I did."

"After he beat you senseless with a spade?"

"It was most humiliating."

"And who is he, sir?"

"Renaud Jacobe St. John de Lacey, Sixth Baron of Lasingstoke." He set down the cup. "My father."

"Your father."

"Yes."

Beals blinked again. "Isn't he dead, sir?

"Yes. He shot his head off with a pistol fifteen years ago. You see my dilemma."

After a moment, Beals rose to his feet, turned and moved away to the door.

"Say," said Sebastien. "Do you know if anyone from the circus owned the Savage house before they did?"

"Why would you ask that?"

"Because I distinctly saw a bearded woman at the door, along with a clown and a sword-swallowing acrobat."

The detective stared at him and the Mad Lord sighed, looked down at his hands, knowing he had done it again. There was silence for a long moment.

"This man whom you saw," said Beals. "Your father…"

"Yes."

"Was he your father in flesh or in spirit?"

Sebastien looked up.

"Well? In flesh or in spirit, sir?"

"I…I cannot say." He sat back in the chair, frowned. "That is a very good question, sir. Damnation. That complicates things entirely."

"Right," said Beals, not knowing what to say to that.

"But thank you, Inspector. The tea was delightful." He rose to his feet, extending his hand. "Actually, it tasted like cabbage but I'm not picky. Honestly, not. It was delightful, nonetheless."

Beals took the man's hand, frowned when he did not let go.

"Hm…" said the Mad Lord and turned the hand over in his grip, running his fingers along the man's palm and up his wrist. He gave it a final shake, released and smiled.

"Five children. You must be very happy."

"Four," said Beals, cheeks flushing red. "Four strapping sons."

"No daughter?"

"No, sir. God has not blessed us with a girl."

"No little girl with big brown eyes and red curls? I see her quite clearly. Her name is Claire."

Beals stared at him. "Only sons."

"My mistake."

"Well, good day to you," said Carter Beals and he slipped quietly out the door.

***

He only had to do the legs.

He only had to do the legs.

The cadavers are too much for him.

He's mad, Ivy.

He only had to do the legs.

It took them less than half an hour to drive to *London Royal* in the steamcar. Franny seemed to have an endless supply of goggles and steam, and Mary Jane joined them as they puffed and chugged down the narrow streets. Ivy couldn't think, needed to keep quiet and stay still and perhaps she might just manage to keep her heart from bursting through her chest.

He only had to do the legs.

At some point, the steamcar bumped and lurched to a halt, parked almost on the front step of the hospital and Fanny slipped her goggles up on her forehead.

"Are you quite all right, dearest?" she asked.

Ivy nodded woodenly.

"Yes. No. I'm not sure. I will be." She took a deep breath. "Yes, I will be."

"Spoken like Penny Dreadful, dearest. Take heart."

Even though she had known these women less than a month, Ivy was certain they were the best friends a girl could ever have.

Together, the four of them headed up the steps and into the green corridors of the hospital. She led them down several flights of stairs to a small surgical theatre, dark save the few gaslights on the wall, and they could see a thin shape moving through the leaded glass of the door.

She rolled the door wide, seeing first the saws, drills, masks, coils and other macabre devices hanging from the ceiling over their heads. Beneath it all, a cadaver lay naked on a steel table in the centre of the room and beside it Pickett wearing goggles and leather apron, holding a long sharp-edged knife.

"Oh my!" cried Fanny.

"Oy!" Rosie snapped. "Marie? Ivy? What the 'ell?"

The cadaver was a woman, her colour the sickly gray of the dead. Her abdomen was opened from her naval down and the room smelled of ammonium and blood. For her part, Franny patted her sister's hand but could not tear her eyes away from the sight.

"Rosie!" said Ivy. "What are you doing?"

"Schoolwork, Ivy!" He glanced quickly between the women. "What d'you think?"

"I don't know *what* to think, Rosie. Is this schoolwork for Bondie or schoolwork for Williams?"

He glared at Mary Jane now, his eyes made all the larger by the goggles he wore. "What 'ave you told 'er, Marie?"

"Answer me, Ambrose Pickett," said Ivy. "Or I will go to my father straightaway. Is this schoolwork for Bondie or for Williams?"

He studied her now, as if there were no other person in the room.

"You can't tell yer dad, Ivy. You promise you won't tell yer dad?"

"I can't promise, Rosie. You know that."

His eyes flicked down to the body on the table, to the blade in his hand. His shoulders sagged and he pulled the goggles down under his chin.

"For Williams," he said in a quiet voice. "He's teaching us the obstetrics and the gynaecologies. I'm failing the class."

"You are practicing abortions on cadavers?" Ivy felt her chin rise. It just seemed to do so on it's own now.

"I'm practicing all kinds o' things. It's better than learning on a live girl, ain't it? We get 'em from Bedlam. They die all the time at Bedlam."

"And what do you do with these unfortunates once you are finished your practicing, Rosie?"

"Ivy…"

"Tell me, Rosie. I need all of my friends to hear it so they will know that I'm not mad. And that Christien's brother is not mad, either."

"But he is! He shot—" He stopped himself, glanced quickly at a cane leaning against the table.

"Tell me what you do with them!"

"Ivy…" he moaned. "We'll get the boot, we will! We're six months out. Six months! And these is dead already! They don't feel nothin'!"

"Say it, Rosie. What do you do with the cadavers when you're finished with them?"

"You promise you're not going to tell yer dad, are you, Ivy? I promise we won't do this no more. Christien said it weren't worth it and I agreed. I got shot for all me troubles. That crank brother of Remy's…"

"I will ask one last time." She stepped forward again. "What do you do once you are done?"

"We…"

"Go on."

"We cut 'em into pieces and chuck 'em in the River."

"And how did the arm get on Lambeth Road?"

"It dropped out of the bag when we was leaving. It were a mistake, it were! Henry wouldn't do that by purpose! It's not right."

"No, Rosie. It's not right. None of this is right, is it? These poor girls deserve a burial just like everyone else."

"It's got honour, Ivy, just like a sailor! But we take out the wombs and such, just in case."

"In case?"

"In case someone finds 'em and brings 'em to Bondie and he sees she's been Restelled. He'd get suspicious. He's a smart one, is Bondie."

"So how did one get in the construction site of the New Scotland Yard?"

"That was Lewie being an ass!" He flung his hands in the air. "You know it, Marie! You was with him that night! He's an ass, that man is!"

"'e said 'e were dropping off some lime," said Marie. "Fer the workers. I didn't know it were a… it were a… you know…"

Ivy nodded, sighed. "I'm sorry, Rosie. I'm sorry for all of you."

"You can't tell anyone, Ivy."

"Come with us, Rosie," she said. "It'll be easier if you do."

He swallowed and Ivy was glad it wasn't Bender or Lewis. Rosie had no fight in him. She couldn't say the same for the other two.

Of Christien, she had no clue.

Finally, Rosie sighed. "I gots to put 'er away. Wait for me outside, will you?"

They did, waiting outside the ghoulish surgical theatre for almost ten minutes before Ivy rolled the door open once again.

Ambrose Pickett and the cadaver from Bedlam were gone, a fact that did not surprise her.

***

Sebastien de Lacey suddenly stopped as Savage held the door open to the laneway behind Great Scotland Yard.

"Bastien?" asked Christien but he did not touch him.

The Mad Lord blinked and blinked again, looked around the dark hall, past the constables, detectives and his brother, all surrounding him like Queen Victoria in a May Day Parade. The locket was spinning and flashing, creating a kaleidoscope of colour across the brick.

"They're gone," he said. And he looked around again.

Savage glared at Christien, shaking his head.

"Who's gone?" asked Christien.

"Just a moment…"

Sebastien closed his eyes, turned his palms upwards, but they were manacled together and the chains made it difficult. The temperature in the hallway dropped immediately and they could see their breath in front of their faces.

"What the hell is he doing?" grumbled Savage

"Two gone," said Sebastien, and he smiled at the inspector, as bright as the regal French sun. "Two of the torsos gone. Released. I don't know how. Life is wondrous strange, isn't it? New surprises every day."

"Get him out the door."

And they pushed the Mad Lord out of A-Division and into the lane that led to the Central Offices of Scotland Yard.

Chapter 37

Of Parking, Policemen and the Unfortunate Punch Card

Ivy had begun to realize that "parking" for Franny Helmsly-Wimpoll simply meant stopping the forward motion of the steamcar. As they piled out at the Met's A-Division Station on Whitehall Road, most of the tires were on the paved walk and the car was almost blocking the doors. In fact, it was directly under the cold gaze of the A-Division Sentinels, and Ivy thought it was a very safe, albeit illegal, place to be.

It had begun to rain on the drive over from the Royal and A-Division was crowded with seas of people rushing to lodge protests, file complaints and get out of the rain. She began to despair of getting anywhere, when suddenly a woman with great brown eyes and red curls swept through the crowd on her way out the door. It was Ginny Beals, Carter's happy wife and as she swept past, she caught Ivy's hands and clung for dear life.

"Ivy, my girl!"

"Ginny! It's wonderful to see you!"

Ivy held on but the crowds were like a current, straining to pull the woman out of her arms.

"I just brought Carter his tea but Ivy, I have news! I'm pregnant!" she exclaimed over the roar of voices. "Can you imagine? Pregnant again! Number five on the way!"

"I'm so happy for you, Ginny! Maybe it will be a girl this time!"

"That's what I'm hoping! Oh dear, this crowd!"

"Best of luck, Ginny!"

"God bless, dear girl!"

And just like that, Ginny Beals was swept out of her arms and out the door of A-Division.

People were pressing in on them now, and she began to fear that the four of them might be sent in different directions, but they grasped hands and plowed through the crowd. They were stopped before they made the stair.

"Only staff, miss," growled a large ironclad of a man. His nameplate read Constable Twist and he looked utterly formidable.

"Hallo sir. I'm the daughter of Inspector Savage, H-Division," she said. "He's upstairs with Inspector Beals, Chief Inspector Moore and the de Lacey brothers. I was here with them all only last night."

"Sorry, miss. They've all gone to Central Office across the way."

"To Central?" She blinked. "But why?"

"Don't know, miss. They're with Bondie and Abberline now."

Ivy felt all the air leave her body. "Abberline…"

"Now, darling," hushed Fanny, catching her arm. "Dr. Bond and Inspector Abberline are upright, virtuous men. This can only be good for your Sebastien Laurent, surely."

"Surely," said Franny.

"I seen Abberline once," added Mary Jane. "'e looks like a banker."

"But he is the most familiar with the Ripper cases. They must be thinking…" Her voice trailed off. "Oh dear Lord, what have I done?"

"None of this is your fault, dearest," said Fanny. "The police are simply investigating every lead. Isn't that right, officer?"

"They do, miss," said the constable. His eyes were darting under his helm at the women. Altogether, they made a very unusual puzzle.

"There, you see?" said Fanny. "Not to worry. Besides, I'm quite certain your Christien Jeremie is with him, isn't he?"

"Isn't he?" echoed Franny.

"Yes," said Ivy. "I'm sure he is. But he believes Sebastien to be mad."

"But dearest," said Fanny. "He is, isn't he?"

"Isn't he?" echoed Franny.

"Well, yes…" Ivy frowned. "But not *terribly* mad."

"Is he handsome?" asked Mary Jane. "Like yer Remy? Is that the problem, then? You've got it fer both fellas?"

Ivy found herself at a loss for words, while the sisters merely sniffed and looked off in opposite directions.

"Coo," said Mary Jane, and she smiled wickedly. "And here, I thought you was a *good* girl..."

Ivy looked up at Constable Twist.

"Sir, she said. "I must insist we be taken to Inspector Savage at once. We have knowledge of a most heinous crime."

That was when Mary Jane smiled at him, dimples dazzling. Ivy could have sworn the man's cheeks reddened and his moustache twitched just once.

"This way."

And the ironclad of a man turned and carved a path through the crowd that parted like the Red Sea. The four women followed in his wake.

***

The room at Central Office was much the same as the room in A-Division, only minus the bed and covered pot. The two buildings were virtually identical, with only a narrow lane separating them. In fact, there were so many of these red-bricked addresses now that made up the Yard that police services were much impeded, hence the need for a comprehensive new building on the Embankment. It would have been a wonderful, progressive thing, had there not been a torso in the cellar.

Damn those torsos. But there were two less to plague him and it was all he could do to keep from smiling. That, Sebastien concluded, would simply not go down well at the present time.

"Well," said the man sitting across the table from him, closing up his medical bag. "These injuries do seem consistent with the blows from a spade. Had you not the metal plates in your skull, sir, you could easily have been killed."

It had been a pleasure to finally meet Dr. Thomas Bond, the man who had been so instrumental in his brother's life and he desperately wished it could have been in happier circumstances. There was little shadow in him and no malice, only pride, a quick, inquisitive mind and strong sense of justice. However Sebastien could not shake the feeling that life would not end well for Dr. Bond. Some people just dragged sorrow like a chain.

"In fact," Bond went on. "I have never seen anything quite like them. A Dr. Arvin Frankow, you say? Neurosurgeon?"

"Psychiatrist."

Bond raised a gray brow. "A talented man."

"I am alive and sensate so I will give him that."

"Now, de Lacey," said the other man. "You are maintaining that it was the Ripper who took this round out of you?"

He looked like a banker, with thinning dark hair, large deep-set eyes and a fine up-turned moustache. He had been introduced as Inspector Frederick Abberline, and while the other officers had paid him great respect, Sebastien had yet to see why. He seemed much like the others, pedantic, authoritarian and sharp. They all threatened like bullies.

He was tired. Every bone in his body ached. He hadn't eaten for days and was desperately beginning to long for either the wide fields of Lasingstoke or the solitary comfort of Lonsdale.

"de Lacey?" the banker reminded.

"In my mind, the man I encountered and pursued through the entirety of Whitechapel could only have been London's Ripper, so yes, I maintain that he is one and the same. But it is my private opinion. A man cannot be held for having an opinion, surely."

"And you maintain that this man was left handed?"

"He swung the spade with his left. He pressed the blade into my throat with his left, so yes, I do maintain that."

"So why did he stop?"

"I have asked myself the very question. I have yet to discover the answer."

"The arms fit, sir," said Bond now. "To the torso they found at the construction site."

"I would expect that they should."

"So did you, or did you not, see a head in the Thames?"

Sebastien was silent.

"de Lacey?"

"May I tell you the truth, sir?"

Abberline snorted but Bond nodded earnestly. "Please do."

"I did, in fact, see a head in the Thames. But I have also seen the entire torso for over two months and sent her to a little house we call Seventh at Lasingstoke. But she's free now, for whatever reason I cannot imagine. She and the other from last summer are gone, although there are two more, very old. I doubt your boys had anything to do with them."

"My boys?"

"Your boys, sir. The medical students."

"You suspect my boys because they are medical students?" asked Bond. "You read far too many papers, sir."

"I do read many papers but I suspect your boys because the dead despise them."

There was silence once again in the little room for several moments before Dr. Bond leaned forward. "Your brother is very concerned for you, de Lacey."

Sebastien leaned forward. "And your boys are very wicked, Dr. Bond. If I had my pistol that night, I would have shot the lot of them. Without hesitation."

"Your brother included?"

Sebastien set his jaw. "I would never shoot my brother."

"Ah," said Abberline. "Only those who have little or no value to you."

"The dead are self-absorbed, sir," he said. "I am preoccupied with their business and leave the living to themselves."

"The dead speak to you, then?"

"The dead rarely speak."

There was a rap at the door and a uniformed constable peered in.

"Dr. Bond? You're wanted on the floor."

With a deep breath, Bond rose to his feet but paused at the door, throwing a glance at the Mad Lord.

"Have you ever considered lithium, sir? It might help with the delusions."

Sebastien stared at him a moment.

"Thank you," he said finally. "I will consider it."

And Bond left the room.

"So, de Lacey, you're a clairvoyant?" Abberline asked. "A psychic channel of the other side? A spiritualist?"

"If I say yes, will you boot me out the door like you did Mr. Robert James Lees? For I would very much like to be booted out this door."

Abberline grinned. "I like you, de Lacey. And in fact, I don't believe you are the Ripper. Can you give me any hard evidence at all that can corroborate your testimony? I have a public that very much wants a hanging."

Sebastien sighed and sat back in his chair, the chains making a scraping sound across the table.

"When the first woman died, a man in a dark Coburn dropped over the fence. He had a black bag that is similar to a medical bag. When I gave chase, he loosed his Coburn, so perhaps it is also on the street, although it was a very fine coat and I think someone would have nabbed it. There is a yard with a four-foot wall and a spade that might still have my blood on it but it was raining so any blood will likely have been washed away. Other than those things, sir, there is little I can give you."

"And your pistol, sir," said Abberline. "You told Moore that you shot one of the men you were chasing with a pistol. What has become of that?"

"I lost it in the scuffle. The Ripper has it in his collection, surely."

"Was there a serial number?"

"No serial number, but it was a musket-bore three-chambered piece commissioned by my father and signed by William Westley Richards. Walnut and steel, with ivory grip. If you find it, I would very much like it back."

"So you can shoot more villains?"

"Indeed."

"Moore wants to send you to Broadmoor, you know."

"Not Bethlem?"

"Bedlam doesn't take the criminally insane." He pushed off the wall. "Are you, de Lacey, criminally insane?"

Can't tell a living person from a dead one. The Avenger of Blood. I believe it to be morally wrong. How could she possibly be safe?

Sebastien looked down at the cuffs on his wrists. "Maybe so."

And with that, the man who looked like a banker shook his head and left the Mad Lord of Lasingstoke alone in the room.

***

Each woman had been taken to a separate room and it was a strange, unnerving feeling to be separated from these women who had grown so close, so quickly. But now, she sat across from both Dr. Bond and her father, looking at her hands and trying desperately to keep her chin from rising.

"You know these are serious allegations, Ivy," Bond was saying. "Williams could be disbarred for this."

"Are you telling the truth, Ivy?"

She glanced up at her father, who was staring at her, arms crossed over his chest. He looked weary.

"Yes, tad. I am. I'm sorry for lying earlier. I've always been too quick with my tongue though, haven't I?"

He said nothing, telling her everything.

"Just a moment," she said and slipped a hand down, past the fabric of her skirts to the breeches she was wearing underneath. She ignored the strange looks of the men as she found the tight pocket, fished around and produced a scrap of fabric in her fingers. She held it out to Bond.

"I found this on the pier that night, very near the bullet hole."

Bond took it from her, turned it over in his hand.

"I believe if you check all of Rosie's trousers, you will find a pair with a corresponding hole. Unless of course, he's disposed of them, which he may have done entirely."

"Evidence…" Bond looked up at her, a faint tug of approval on his lips. "Trevis, why haven't you trained this girl? She has a good mind for forensics."

"You know how many of us die in the line, Bondie. I'll not have my daughter in danger. I'll not. Not for my last girl."

"She's an asset, Trev," muttered the surgeon and he leaned forward now, lacing his hands across the table. "And you say that Williams admitted performing these abortions at Bethlem?"

"Yes, sir. Mary Jane and Rosie confirmed it."

"The physicians of Bethlem are bound to deny these allegations."

"Of course they would," she said. "If Williams was being called in to do these because of inadequate supervision in a public lunatic asylum, do you think the staff are going to admit it? Even worse if a patient dies because of it. It would look very bad if this came out."

"The boys will be suspended," said Bond quietly. "They always were pranksters, but what they've done to the bodies... As medical men, this is unconscionable."

"Remy too," added her father. "Is that what you want, Ivy? Do you want to see Remy's career ended before it has even begun? He's a fine man, Ivy. He's been very, very good to us."

"I know he has, tad." She felt her throat tightening once again. "So don't pursue it. Leave it. Ignore it. Sweep it all under the rug. But don't make Sebastien de Lacey spend another night in irons because of it. He is innocent of these crimes and you know it. Even if you don't want to believe it, you know it."

Savage sighed, looked at the ceiling.

"No, the boys are guilty," said Bond sadly. "I should have seen it earlier, I should have known..."

He leaned back in his chair. ran a finger along his gray moustache. "Williams has been running clinics for years, now. We've all known it, but he kept it quiet, kept it discreet. God knows, the street girls need the help and he was the perfect one to do it for them, with his connections and his research. But if a girl died because of it, it's unlikely that even Victoria could intervene if a family chose to prosecute."

"We've had these torsos for years, Bondie," said Savage. "Are you suggesting Williams has been using students all along?"

"I am out of my depth, Trev. He would have suggested it surely as an easy way to dispose of the evidence. And from a purely pedantic point of view, it is no different than using our John Does, vagrants and paupers for teaching purposes. The boys would not think twice if asked by an instructor. Lewis has no morals. Bender and Pickett only slightly more so but Remy..." He shook his head. "I had such high hopes for Remy. He usually stays above it all."

"Please don't think too harshly of him, sir," said Ivy. "He thinks of you as a father. And Dr. Williams too. He would do anything to please either of you."

"That's very astute of you, Ivy. The gate to hell is flanked by approval and rejection."

There was a buzz at the door and Savage opened it to reveal an automaton the size of a child. It held a letter in its pincer-like grip, telescoped it up so the investigator could take it. He peeled it open, read it quickly, raised his brows and gave the communiqué back to the little robot. It wheeled on its axis and disappeared down the hall.

"Bondie, the boys are in room two thirty. Williams is on his way."

"Ah, me. What a night…"

As the Police Surgeon left the room, Ivy looked up at her father, tried to stop the quiver of her chin.

"Tad, will you have Sebastien released? Please?"

"I'll do what I can, my girl, but it's not my call. Moore's the Chief and he doesn't like your Mad Lord one bit. He'd be happy to see him swing for anything."

She swallowed, feeling quite undone.

"You really care about him, don't you?"

Damn those tears. She could not stop them this time.

"Oh, tad," she moaned. "I thought I was helping. I thought I was being clever but I've made such a mess of things…"

And he crossed the floor and wrapped his arms around her as she wept into his chest.

"You *are* clever, my girl," he hushed, stroking her hair and rocking her like he did when she was little. "Too damned clever for me."

He held her face in his hands, brushed the tears away with his thumbs. "I've never given you enough credit. I was afraid of losing you and I thought Remy would keep you safe. Maybe I'm the one who's made a mess of things."

"Growing up Savage," she took a deep shuddering breath and tried to smile. "Please help Sebastien, tad."

"I'll do what I can, my girl."

He kissed the top of her head, lingering a moment before following the surgeon out of the room, leaving Ivy alone for the first time in hours.

After a long moment, she pulled out the punch card from the pocket of her skirt and set her mind to figure out exactly how a dead man could kill.

Chapter 38

Of Flying Corpses, Sitting Pigeons and a Dead Man Walking

No one had come back and at some point, he had fallen asleep, head down on the wooden table, cheek resting on the cold links of iron that were his claps. The dead had come and gone, leaving him once they realized he would not help and his sleep had been restless, with dreams distorting in a brew of memory and fear.

Suddenly, the room grew cold and he lifted his head from the table. The locket was spinning madly, causing light to flash across the room.

His father was standing at the door.

Sebastien studied him for a long moment, blinking the cobwebs from his mind and trying to harness his thoughts. They were rushing like wild horses.

"Damnation," growled his father, eyes glued to the locket. "I knew it was back."

"Are you flesh," Sebastien began quietly for his voice was merely a croak. "Or are you spirit?"

His father's lip curled and he turned the key to lock the door before gliding into the room.

"I had you for ten years, boy. You know the drill. When the spirit is willing…"

"The flesh is weak…" Sebastien finished, staring up now as his father circled the little desk. The room was very cold, with long slicks of ice growing up the walls. His own breath frosted the air, but truth be told, his father's was as well, answering his question. "Why are you here?"

"To kill you. Your flesh is weak."

Sebastien nodded. He knew it was true.

"Frankow should have let you die all those years ago. He did no one a kindness, least of all you."

His father stood beside him now, hands clasped behind his back. A dozen dead women began to rise from the floor.

"Your brother is the strong one," Renaud growled. "He should be running Lasingstoke, not you. And certainly not my damned brother."

The iron around his wrists burnt his skin and his teeth had begun to chatter on their own. There were sparks arcing from the locket and he could feel heat and cold radiating from it in waves. The door was locked from the inside. No one would be coming to help. No one would be coming at all.

"Remy is a bright, clever, obedient boy. Not you. You are a bastard. Your mother doted on you, but I should have drowned you then when I had the chance." He looked down his nose, blue eyes narrowed and cold. "I did not try hard enough."

Sebastien swallowed.

"And so, somehow, you ended up with my estate, my pistol, and my Ghostlight."

He reached a hand for the locket, but was repulsed by an arc of blue light. Renaud hissed and pulled back.

"So this is how you're going to end it, boy. Listen up and pay attention."

The man leaned down and Sebastien could see the bullet hole in his temple. The skin was puckered and proud and he was grateful the other side was turned away from him.

"They're going to take you to Broadmoor. Not Bedlam. Bedlam refuses to accept the criminally insane now. Far too upscale for murdering lunatics like yourself. There will be no little surgery for you, not even a chance of a normal life. They do not do that for criminals and bastards. So very soon, they will come to take you to Broadmoor, but you will escape them en route—I don't care how you do it, just do it and make your way back to Hollbrook House. There, you will find my pistol in Remy's bag. It's a fine pistol and you don't deserve it. You never have. You will leave the locket in the bag, take the pistol up to your room and you will blow your own damned head off with it. Do you hear me, boy? For if you do not..."

The stench of death from his mouth, the smell of blood, the writhing and wailing of the women.

"If you do not, the Ripper will strike again, and this time, he will take your little novelist, Miss Ivy Savage. He will remove the skin from her face, cut off her breasts and the flesh from her thighs, move her organs around like chess pieces. He will cut out her heart the way she has cut out my Remy's, the way your mother cut out mine. He will make her the worst of all of them and will cut her into one hundred pieces and turn her into your mother, lying on a bloody sheet. And that will be only the beginning...

Sebastien closed his eyes.

"Next, he will head up north for her brother. He will feed him to the furnace and watch him burn to a cinder. Then he will flay the skin from his little Lottie until she curls up like ash and dies. He will take Cookie and Castlewaite and all your miserable dogs—I might spare the horses, mind—before I set my hand to my dear brother Rupert. Oh my, what a time I shall have with him... He the adulterer, the spoiler of women, the ruin of my perfect home..."

His breath had grown raspy and hoarse, and it seemed to take a moment before he had composed himself once again. But when he did, it was complete.

"That is what will happen if you don't do as I say. Do you understand, boy?"

There was a sound at the window and when he looked, he saw a face. A familiar face but he could not place it. It was likely dead, for the window was three stories up and there was no ledge. Dead inside, dead out. All spectators watching the grim show.

"Do you understand?"

He nodded, felt everything slipping away in a swirl of ice and madness. Lees had been right. It was for the best, he understood that now.

"Good. You have no idea how much I look forward to reading your obituary."

And his father patted his shoulder once, twice, three times, sending the ice like blades into his flesh.

With that, the sixth Baron of Lasingstoke moved like water, flowing across the floor towards the door. Slowly, with deliberation, he turned the key and left the room, not bothering to look back before closing the door behind him.

They came for him at midnight.

***

Ivy stared at the card in her hands.

Renaud Jacobe St. John Lord de Lacey.

Williams had given it to her. It was there, in grease and ink.

Slowly, she slipped it back into her pocket, wondering what her father or Dr. Bond would say if they saw it.

She wished she had a pen or pencil with her. It always helped her to write her thoughts down, follow them like rabbits as they led down trails to mystery and adventure. She was alone in a room in Scotland Yard with a terrible mystery to solve and no tools with which to solve it.

No, that was not right. She had all the tools she needed – her imagination and her mind. This was a perfect opportunity, she wagered, so she folded her hands under her chin and began to think.

According to Sebastien, similar crimes had been occurring not only in London, but in Lancashire for several years, Tillie Barton and Clara Clements to name a few. Obviously, there had to be a connection. It seemed to have had its start fifteen years ago, when Renaud Jacobe St. John de Lacey took a hunting knife to his wife.

As they sat, toe to toe under the blanket in his room, Sebastien insisted he had seen his father in a Whitechapel yard.

But his father was dead, shot his head off with that damned three-chambered pistol. Sebastien had to be mistaken. He was either mistaken or mad.

She sat back in the chair now, wished her mother were here to listen. While she would never answer, it had always been helpful to talk her mysteries through. Perhaps that was the reason she had taken so quickly to the sisters Helmsley-Wimpoll. They were natural foils.

She looked over at the window, where a pigeon sat on the outside ledge. Ivy turned her chair to face it.

"Right, let's talk this through, shall we? Fifteen years ago, Renaud de Lacey killed his wife in her bed, cut out her womb and her heart, and then shot himself with his pistol. That is the story, isn't it?"

The pigeon blinked.

"Well?" she said. "What if he didn't?"

The pigeon cocked its head.

"Do we know for a fact that Renaud Jacobe St. John de Lacey is dead? We have only gossip and rumour. Is there a death report? An autopsy? Who found the body? Who identified it? After all, the only witness is Christien and he was six at the time."

A second pigeon landed.

"Was there in fact ever a full investigation into her murder or was it simply closed and forgotten? Believe me, that's often the case when the police have an open and shut case."

And then a third.

"And there was a lover, yes?" Ivy added. "Who was this lover, this secret lover of Jane Penteny of Eccleston? Surely, he would have had some involvement in the affair, something to say about how the investigation was handled. I understand she was a beautiful woman. He had to have felt some remorse over her death…"

Her words trailed off as a memory came to call, a memory of a stormy morning by a fire at Second, drinking bitter coffee with a man who had lost his heart fifteen years ago.

The sweetest, fairest flower in a wild flower meadow.

"Oh no…" she whispered. Another pigeon landed and they all cocked their heads as she rose to her feet. "Oh, no no no…"

"Ivy?"

The pigeons took off from the ledge and she spun around.

Carter Beals was standing quietly at the door.

"I'm sorry Ivy," he said. "They've taken him to Broadmoor."

"To Broadmoor?" she repeated as all the air left her body. "But I thought it would be Bedlam…"

"Moore's orders. He's being committed to a facility for the criminally insane. A company of four warders just packed him into a carriage not twenty minutes ago. He's gone, Ivy and I doubt you'll be seein' him for quite some time."

She couldn't move. She couldn't think.

Beals sagged against the door frame.

"Ivy, just this morning he told me I was going to have a little girl. A little girl with red curls and brown eyes and her name would be Claire. That's me mum's name, Ivy. How in hell did he know that? I didn't know Ginny was pregnant until a few hours ago."

She felt emptied, numb.

"I need to speak with my tad."

"He's in with Williams and the boys upstairs. It's a bloody mess."

With a terrible sinking feeling, Ivy threw a glance at the window ledge where there were no pigeons.

***

The rain was hard as the carriage rattled its way down Finborough Road, causing the windows to steam and frost inside the cab. The chains at his wrists were white with ice and the locket sang a sweet, strange song inside his head.

The voice of angels.

His chest was tight, his nerves tense and he began to wonder if it was fear. He had never experienced anything quite like it in his life. It was most unsettling and he realized most people lived their lives to avoid this at all costs.

No wonder he preferred the company of dogs.

There were two warders in the cab with him, stealing glances and trying not to stare as his breath fell like icicles to the floor. They hadn't spoken a word since ushering him into the coach, but he was grateful for it. They had been on the road for half an hour and he needed to think, but the damned locket was so loud, drowning out all thought. He wished he could take it off, but he knew now that he would never have the power to do so. She was terrible and beautiful and better than the laudanum by far.

In flesh or in spirit. That was the question. He had simply assumed it was flesh when he'd seen him in the lane. Definitely flesh to have killed a woman, swung a spade, pressed a blade into his throat. Never in his experience could the dead do anything like this. It was a mystery far greater than anything he had ever come across, certainly greater than anything he or Frankow had ever prepared for.

But if it were in spirit? His father was a ghost hunter and a founding member of the Ghost Club. If it was a matter of spirit, then that might explain a great many—

Suddenly, the screech of tires on metal as the coach jerked violently across the road. The flashing of bright lights, the scream of horses and Sebastien was thrown against the roof of the coach as the world turned upside down.

Chapter 39

Of Allegations, Recriminations and Things One Can Buy for a Penny

Beals took her first to the sisters who were waiting for her outside the women's docket. They knew very little of the affair, only what they had heard from Ambrose Pickett in the mortuary of the Royal. Their cousin Mary Jane knew far more, having accompanied Lewis in placing the torso in the cellar of the Embankment Building the very night Pickett was shot. She was a key witness, in fact but according to the police, something about her profession made her an unreliable one. It made Ivy very angry, realizing that "freedom" was a word that few women truly knew.

It was after midnight and the Central Office was quieter than usual. The sisters shuffled nervously as Ivy rushed down the hall toward them, catching them in her arms.

"Dearest," said Fanny.

"It's very late," said Ivy. "You should go home. Where are you staying, by the way?"

"Our mother's sister's friend's chemist's cousin's residence. In Highbury."

"Highbury," said Franny.

"Are you free to go?" asked Fanny.

"Are you free?"

"I want to stay. Christien is in with the detectives now and I think they'll be keeping Mary Jane for a while longer as well. She has history with the boys. She's a prime witness."

"Of course she is," said Fanny.

"I'll see to it that she gets home. Actually, I might ask her to stay with me. It's going to be very cold and lonely in my house tonight...."

"Are you not going to Hollbrook?" asked Fanny.

"No," she said quietly. "Sebastien..."

Fanny reached out, laid a hand on her sleeve. "We've heard, darling. This entire station is abuzz with the scandal. The Mad Lord being committed and to Broadmoor, no less."

"Nasty Broadmoor," said Franny.

"He shouldn't have to go. He's done nothing wrong. But I see now how difficult it can be in dealing with the police. I've never known that before. I mean, I've known, but I've never *truly* known..." She stared at the doors leading off the hallway. "I wonder if Prince Edward could help... Or Albert Victor...?"

"Ooh, Albert Victor," sighed Franny. "He's sweet."

"Of course he is, dearest," said Fanny, patting her hand. "I'm sure he would return your letters if ever he got them."

Ivy smiled sadly at the thought of dear, odd Franny Helmsly-Wimpoll with a little corner of her heart reserved for the scandalous Duke of Clarence. Women were deep and complicated creatures, she realized. They all had secret places.

"Right," said Fanny. "We'd best be off then, dearest. If you are certain you can manage on your own..."

"If you are certain," repeated Franny.

"Yes, of course. I'll just wait for Mary Jane and Christien. We'll be fine. And thank you both, for everything."

They gathered their brollies, buttoned up their buttonables, straightened their hats and pulled themselves together. Fanny sniffed, took Franny's arm, and the sisters set off down the hall, the syncopated rhythms of their footsteps echoing as they went.

She rejoined Carter Beals and together they headed down the quiet halls of the Central Office. It was very late and she wondered what the next few hours would hold. She would wait for Mary Jane and Christien. Of the two, Mary Jane would be by far the better companion tonight. She wondered if Christien would even look at her, if he would demand the ring back, if he would ignore her presence like a beggar on the street. She had effectively ruined his life tonight. He would never consider marriage now and she wondered what that might mean for her mother.

She missed her terribly and she missed her father too. He had surprised her with his belligerence but she had to admit that she was a chip of the old block. Belligerence and tenacity, two things that the Savage household had by the trunkload. Growing up Savage had been a difficult thing.

She could hear shouting in a room down the hall when suddenly, the door swung open and a blonde blur stormed out. Mary Jane Kelly whirled and lashed her finger out at the men in the room.

"I am *not* lying!" she snarled. "And I am not cheap! You take that back, John! You take that back!"

Seated inside, John Williams flashed a grim smile. Bond, Moore, her tad and the boys all sat around a large table. Papers were scattered everywhere, giving the impression they had been at it for a while.

"You are indeed a cheap whore, my dear," said Williams coolly. "Your body is bought at the price of a brass ring worth less than a penny. How can your testimony possibly be worth any more?"

"Lewie?" Mary Jane wailed. "Say something!"

"I think I paid less than a penny," Powell-Smith sniffed and tossed his head. "In fact, I could have sworn she paid me…"

The boys sniggered at that.

"Rosie? Henry? Remy?"

"Cheap," said Rosie.

"Dirt cheap," said Henry. He was looking at her, pale eyes glittering.

For his part, Christien said nothing.

"That's enough then," came the voice of Inspector Moore. "Miss Kelly, we'll need you to sign—"

"I ain't signing nothin'!" she snapped. "No wonder you ain't caught this Ripper, the way you jacks think of us working girls! We may be of low profession, but we ain't low of character like the papers says, or low of value! We have value, we do! We have worth!"

"About the price of a penny," muttered Lewis and the boys sniggered again.

"Enough," growled her father.

The young woman spied Ivy standing beside the door and they locked eyes for several moments before Marie spun on her heel and stormed out of the doorway. Her boots echoed on the linoleum until there was only silence in the hall.

An officer approached and handed Beals a note. As he read, she peered into the room. Williams had said something, causing the boys to snigger anew. It boiled her blood and she wondered how Christien could call these friends.

She leaned against the wall, wishing life had gone differently, but then again, in which direction? Could she say she would prefer to have remained blissfully ignorant of Christien's part in the torsos of London? He surely must have known how it affected his brother and yet, insisted on the madness, the "schizophrenia," as the culprit rather than admitting to any guilt. Not for the first time, she wondered if she really knew him at all.

Beals folded the note and looked at her before leaning into the room.

"Trev," he called in. "I need a word."

There was the scraping of a chair and Beals led her father to the other side of the hall. Trevis read the note and together, the detectives began to speak quietly. She sighed and looked away. The room beside her smelled of coffee and smoke and she wondered if this night would ever end.

She noticed her father shake his head and glance her way. All this conspiracy. All this secret talk. The world of men was filled with bitter secrets. It made her very angry, and she realized that this world was for men alone. Women like Mary Jane, even like herself, skirted the edges but never really got in. She had always thought that she belonged here, in this world of detectives and mysteries, but now she wasn't sure if she wanted to, even if she were allowed.

The detectives returned and her father put a hand on her arm as he leaned in.

"Remy, a word if I may?"

The sound of another chair and she held her breath. Christien appeared in the doorway, face set in his fine porcelain mask. He did not look at her and Trevis touched his arm as well. Ivy frowned again. Her father was not a touchy man.

"Both of you come this way. I need to talk to, ah… to talk to the pair of you."

"Two-twelve?" suggested Beals.

"Aye. Two-twelve. Just here, ah… down the hall…"

And her father turned and led them down the quiet hall, Beals following like a shepherd.

Savage opened another door, held it wide for the young physician.

"Wait outside, will you, my girl?"

He looked grim as he closed the door and disappeared inside with her fiancé.

She glanced up at Beals. "What's going on, sir?"

He smiled but without his eyes and her heart lurched within her chest. Surely, they couldn't deal with any more blows tonight. This night had already shipwrecked their futures. Truth was a pitiless thing.

Behind her, Chief Inspector Henry Moore walked out into the hall, accompanied by Drs. Bond and Williams and what was left of Bondie's boys. They were laughing and chatting but Ivy thought their voices sounded strained, their joviality forced. Once they spied her, all conversation ceased and they left the hallway in silence.

Suddenly, she felt very sad and wondered if there wasn't anyone who didn't hate her tonight.

The door opened and her father peered out. She could see Christien, sitting at a far table, head in his hands. Her heart thudded once again.

"Come in, Ivy," said her tad, his voice unexpectedly gentle. "I need to tell you something."

With a deep breath, she stepped into the room and he closed the door behind her.

Chapter 40

Of Blood, Rain and an Obituary in the Times

It was raining hard as the coach clattered down the cobbled streets of Kensington-Knightsbridge. The line of fine white houses was a blur, the blanket on her lap as heavy as a stone. There was no sound. There was no heat, no light, no taste, no feel. Not even an ache to indicate life. Just the deep hollow pull of emptiness, a hole that had no sides, no roof and no end in sight.

It was amazing how quickly the emptiness had come. Frightening, almost, and that too she realized was a kindness. She wondered if this was her mother's world, this place of quiet apathy, where the only sound was the rushing of blood through the veins and the steady pulse of the heart. Hands on her, moving her, directing her, up into the coach, sit here, look there. Yes, this was her mother's world. She understood now it all too well.

An automaton sat next to her, a perfect machine-man with dark hair, clear blue eyes and skin like porcelain. He did not move, did not flinch as the coach rattled and bumped over the stones. He was in his own world, she knew. Of all of them now, he was the most alone.

Her father sat across from her, his eyes darting from his hands to her face and back again. She wondered in a detached way what he was thinking but didn't care overmuch. Carter Beals next to him, his day starting with the announcement of new life and ending like this. Together the four of them rode through the narrow dark streets toward Hollbrook House and the dead Lord of Lasingstoke.

"It was a steamcar," she could hear her father saying, although his voice sounded hollow and very far away. "A bloody four-wheeled steamcar flipped in the rain and hit the cab on the way to Broadmoor. That's how he made his escape. He would be safe at Broadmoor if it hadn't been for that steamcar. Damn those bloody four-wheeled death traps..."

At some point, the coach halted and the automaton was gone from her side. A hand was held out for her and obediently, she took it but did not feel it in the least. The water splashed her boots, the hem of her skirts and she remembered vaguely that she was still wearing the breeches he had bought her underneath. She couldn't feel them either, but that did not surprise her.

There was a black coach parked on the street in front of Hollbrook House. It was a distinctive carriage, one she had seen too often lately in Whitechapel. It was drawn by black horses, heads low, tails dripping in the rain.

They moved up the steps and into the large foyer, where policemen stood with a rumpled-looking man with thinning light brown hair, neatly-trimmed chops and a rather common face. The sleeves of his smoking jacket rolled up to his elbows, he was wiping his hands on toweling provided by the servants. It was stained with red.

"Ah, Remy," said the man and he strode over. He extended an almost-cleaned hand. "Terrible business, this."

Christien shook stiffly like an automaton. The porcelain was set tight.

"Ivy, this is Dr. Henry Jekyll, my neighbour."

She nodded, shook his hand, but could think of nothing to say.

"I heard the shot," Jekyll said. "Came by to see if I could be of help."

"Is he...?"

"Quite," said the doctor, shoving his hands in the pockets of his smoking jacket and looking at the floor. "The undertakers are upstairs now, bagging him up. Metal skull, wot? Fascinating."

Christien stared at him.

"Ah. Sorry, Remy. Well, damn peelers want my statement, so..."

Christien reached for his hand again, shook long and hard. "Thank you, Henry."

"Not at all, Remy. Miss Ivy. Good night, then." And he left their side for the company of the constables. Savage motioned from the stairs.

Down the hall, last door on the right before the terrace. The door was ajar and the room was dim, lit only by a single gaslight over the fire. Castlewaite was standing by the window, watching as two men were intently wrapping a body in black cloth. There was a long wooden box, a dark pool on the floor and blood splattered across the paper on the wall.

"Oh," she gasped, her first utterance in almost an hour, and she felt the urge to turn away. Christien stepped in front of her.

"Ivy," he said. "You don't need—"

"No," she said. "No, please, may I stay?"

He said nothing but stepped into the room. On hands and knees, Pomfrey was scrubbing at the stains, producing a pink foam with his brush. His wig was in place but it looked hastily put.

Castlewaite approached, wringing his hands.

"Ah'm so dreadfully sorry," he moaned. "Ah tried to stop 'im but 'e was set on it, 'e was. Said it were the only way."

Christien nodded, watched with dull eyes as the undertakers finished the last of their wrapping. Together, they lifted the body and deposited it inside the box with a thump.

"'e made me promise you'd take 'im to Lasingstoke. 'Lasingstoke, not London', 'e said. 'Tell Christien. Just not London.'"

She swept her eyes across the floor again, noticed a fresh dent in the floorboards, and several links of chain nearby.

"What's that?" she whispered.

"Ah 'ad to take 'is claps off, Ah did. Used me axe from the stables."

"And where is the axe now?"

He glanced up quickly, his copper eyepiece whirring and clicking. "In the stables, miss. 'is Lordship asked me to ready the coach, said we was 'eadin' back to the 'all, so Ah put it back afore Ah got the 'orses."

"But weren't you with him when he... when...?"

He nodded quickly. "Aye, miss. Ah felt sommat weren't right, so Ah came back up. 'e had the pistol in 'is 'and, 'e did."

"Please, Ivy," whispered Christien. "Not now."

She swallowed and shut her mouth, not for the first time wishing she could restrain her tongue. That trait had cost her, and the de Lacey brothers, everything.

Christien took a deep breath. "I'll contact Rupert..."

"Already done, sir. Ah telegraphed 'im at once."

"Thank you, Castlewaite."

"'e were a good man," he said and for some reason, he looked at Ivy. "At the 'eart of it all, 'e were a good fine man."

With that, the coachman turned to help the undertakers with the nailing of the lid.

Her father approached, holding the clockwork pistol in cloth, its three chambers polished and gleaming in the gaslight.

"I thought he'd lost it," she said softly.

"That's what he told me too," said Savage. "He said the Ripper had it."

They all flinched as the first nail was hammered into the wood. It sounded like a gunshot, again and again and again, and Ivy found herself shaking quite uncontrollably. Finally, after several minutes, it ceased.

With the help of two constables, the undertakers lifted it up, across the floor and out of the room. Now there was only Pomfrey, the scraping and the terrible pink foam.

"Pomfrey," said Christien. "You don't need to do that now."

The prim man looked up. His eyes were red and puffy. "Oh no, sir. Blood stains so. I shall never get it out if I don't do it now."

"We can replace the flooring, Pomfrey. And change the paper. I don't care. It doesn't matter."

"But sir, I do feel the need—"

"I said stop!"

Everyone glanced at him, the man who rarely raised his voice in laughter let alone anger, and silently the houseman rose to his feet and left the room. Castlewaite did the same, along with Ivy's father, leaving the pair of them in the dark gaslight of the room.

The tiny muscles in his jaw were twitching and she longed to stroke his face, to hold him, comfort him. But it was simply an inclination, for inside, she was as dead as the body in the box. She looked down at the ring, the single pearl with two diamonds, and slowly, deliberately, slid it off her finger. She held it a moment before slipping it into the pocket of his waistcoat. He made no move to stop her.

"It ends. With me," he had said over tea and pasty at the Clarence. She should have known what he was thinking.

She should have known.

She stood on tiptoe to kiss him on the cheek and turned to look one last time at the room, at the blood of the man who had changed everything. The corner where they had sat toe to toe under a blanket, the scrawls of chalk and Latin on the walls.

And she turned and left Christien in the room, alone.

***

"Ivy, wait."

She paused at the front door but did not turn as a gust of wind buffeted at her face, rain pelting in from the darkness outside. She had no umbrella but she doubted she would feel either cold or wet or darkness. She watched the undertakers load the box into the back of the carriage and slap the door shut. There was a man at the dickey, a small man in overcoat, reticulating goggles and a beard that looked silver in the gaslight of the street. He pulled his cap down low and with a flap of the reins, the black horses headed off into the night.

"Ivy." Her father stepped in at her side. "I'll have Bealer take you home."

"No, tad," she said. "I'm going to walk."

"Aw, my girl, you can't walk in this. It's a long way, a bad night and in this weather—"

"Tad, I think it's time you stopped telling me what I can and cannot do."

"I know, my girl." He reached out to stroke her hair. "And I'm sorry. I just, I don't want to lose you. I can't lose you. Please, please understand."

She turned her face, saw tears brimming in his eyes, forgave him of everything, although the numbness did not sway.

"It's alright, tad. I understand. I'm sorry too." She leaned forward to kiss him on the cheek. As she did, she spied a small amount of debris on the floor, lifting and swirling in the wind from the doorway.

Odd, she thought. Feathers.

"I'll see you at home, tad."

And she tugged her bowler down on her head and stepped out into the night.

***

The Steam Times: Obituaries
October 6, 1888

Sebastien Laurent St. John Lord de Lacey
Baron Lord of Lasingstoke, Lancashire

It is with sorrow that we announce the sudden and shocking death of Sebastien Laurent St. John Lord de Lacey, Seventh Baron of Lasingstoke, Lancashire. He was found two nights past at his family home of Hollbrook House in Kensington-Knightsbridge, a victim of a bullet to the head in what police are calling an apparent suicide. Long troubled by mental instability and given to lengthy stays at Lonsdale Abbey, a sanitarium on the shores of Wharcombe Bay, Lord de Lacey held a seat in the House of Lords and will be missed by the French Warmblood Society of Europe for his contributions in the field of equine husbandry.

Son of Renaud Jacobe St. John de Lacey, Sixth Baron of Lasingstoke and Jane Penteny of Eccleston, he did not marry nor are there heirs to the de Lacey estate. He is survived by his uncle Rupert Therrien St. John of Lasingstoke Hall; and his younger brother Christien Jeremie St. John de Lacey, a physician studying under Thomas Bond. Christien Jeremie is expected to be conferred the title as Eighth Lord of Lasingstoke on January 1, 1889, by Prince Edward in a special ceremony at Buckingham.

He was last seen in the company of a young brunette whom our Society columnist believes to be Ivy Savage, daughter of Metropolitan Police Inspector Trevis Savage and fiancé to the aforementioned Christien Jeremie. This correspondent wonders if perhaps some scandal involving the young woman played a part in de Lacey's unfortunate decision to take his life. Neither Miss Savage nor Dr. de Lacey was available for comment.

According to one Times source at the Met, Lord de Lacey was en route to Broadmoor Criminal Lunatic Asylum in Berkshire for random attacks on citizens in Whitechapel and Smithfield when he escaped due to a steamcar accident on Long Wood near Heston Park. This is the fifth such incident involving four-wheeled steamcars this week and the group Six-Wheeled SteamCar Alliance (SWSCA) is petitioning parliament for the banning of four wheels on steamcars. (See article, Four Wheeled Death Traps, Sunday Lifestyles D3)

Bethlem Royal Hospital's resident physician George Henry Savage, MCRP, (no relation to the aforementioned Ivy or Trevis) has called the suicide tragic, and is calling for greater education on psychiatric conditions for all police officers, and most especially Met and City forces.

The private funeral will be held at All Souls Christchapel, Lasingstoke, on October 10.

Chapter 41

Of Morning, Mourning and the Helmsly-Wimpolls of Over Milling

From hell.

Mr de Lacey, Sor, I send you half the Kidne I took from one woman and prasarved it for you tother piece I fried and ate it was very nise. I may send you the bloody knif that took it out if you only wate a whil longer

Signed, Catch me when you can Mishter de Lacey

***

November 2, 1888

It was late, it was raining and she had been walking for hours, thinking nothing, feeling even less. In fact, the rain was a comfort, the constant tapping on her hat, her face, her shoulders. It was like music, she thought. Like sweet, sad music and was a perfect accompaniment to the symphony of misery playing in her heart.

It was nearing dawn as she stood on the pier at St. Katharine's Docks, a weathered carpetbag at her side. The river rippled like a living thing, the rain dancing on its oily surface. Her mother lived under this dock where her brother had died. Sebastien had held her here, warm against his body. She had tempted him to kiss her and he had almost given in. She had lost everything here, on this bloody dock.

It had been almost a month since that terrible night, a month spent either in her room, or here, on this pier waiting for ghosts. Despite her father's protests, she had started *Penny Dreadful and the Terror of Whitechapel* and it had all but consumed her. She had reached an impasse however, for she needed an ending. A pine box and a black carriage seemed far too bleak for such a tale. She felt her throat constrict every time at the thought. But the tears wouldn't come anymore. She had cried them all out over the last month and now she stood on this dock like an empty canvas, waiting for paint.

Soon, the first glimmers of purple stole across the water and she gazed eastward to where the sun was rising. There were ships and dorrys, trawlers and barges. Factory stacks were black spires in the distance, silhouettes of airships floated quietly over the city, and around them birds swooped and dove for fish. Slowly, ever so slowly, there was colour, painting water and sky first purple then pink, red then orange as the sun rose over the city of London.

For the very first time in her life, she thought it beautiful.

She picked up the carpetbag and left the docks, heading for the *Whitechapel-Mile End Station.* There she boarded a steamtrain heading north. She did not take a sleeping car but was content to sit and watch the gray-green countryside roll past her window. She was content to watch the stars and the moon and the night and the trees with their skeleton hands. When she stepped onto the platform at Over Milling the next morning, she breathed in the sweet, damp country air. Even in dull, dark, dreary November, Lancashire was green and she marveled at the change in her. It was a new thing.

She had been to the Helmsly-Wimpoll family home once on the morning of their Lancaster visit, a whistle stop for a thermos of tea and a biscuit. But it was half past ten in the morning and she was resourceful, so she hailed the first (and only) cab waiting at the station and made her way to the colourful limestone house known simply as *Wimpolldon.*

She trotted up the steps to rap on the front door. After several moments, it creaked open and a very old woman peered out. She was wearing a traditional servant's smock, white apron and mob hat.

"Yes," croaked the woman.

"My name is Ivy Savage," said Ivy. "I was wondering if Fanny or

Franny would happen to be in?"

The woman muttered something and closed the door in her face.

It wasn't long however before she heard the stomping of feet and the shrill squeal of girlish laughter and the door flung open, unleashing the collective whirlwind that was the sisters Helmsly-Wimpoll. Still in nightgowns and bedcaps, they caught Ivy up in a great embrace and dragged her into the house.

"Dearest, you came!" exclaimed Fanny, holding her out at arm's length. "We knew you would. It was only a matter of when."

"Only when," cried Franny.

"Granny, this is our dear friend Ivy Savage," said Fanny to the housekeeper. "Can you please put on some tea and ready up some biscuits?"

"Ooh, yes," said Franny. "Biscuits."

The very old woman turned and shuffled off to the kitchen, muttering the entire time. Ivy smiled.

"Granny? That's an odd name for a housekeeper."

"But she is, dearest."

"Oh, she is."

"She is what?"

Fanny blinked slowly. "Our granny, dearest."

"Not your housekeeper?"

"Oh, tosh! You are an imp. Come, let us dress and prepare for a most wondrous, most amazing…"

"Most adventuresome!"

"Most adventuresome day!"

And with a Helmsly-Wimpoll on each arm, Ivy was hauled up the stair to the bedrooms.

***

Penny Dreadful and the Terror of Whitechapel.
A Novel
by Ivy Savage.

Chapter 1: of Floating Arms, Blobs of Ink and a Murder in

Manchester

September 11, 1888
Grosvenor Railway Bridge, London
It looked like a dead dog floating on the River… "

As she read, they dined on tarts, biscuits, preserves, hard-cooked eggs and sandwiches. The family sat around the table, spellbound and eager, drinking tea and shouting comments with every twist and turn of the plot. Ivy felt happier than she had in a very long while.

Mr. Helmsly-Wimpoll was a short round ball of a man, with a mop of fair curls on his head and enormous chops. Mrs. Helmsly-Wimpoll however was a beanpole of a woman. She was less equine than Fanny but perhaps more mulish, and her clothes had been the height of fashion a decade past. Ivy couldn't tell whose mother 'Granny' was, and she served them all, shuffling around the tables and muttering to herself all the while.

Finally, Ivy laid down her papers.

"Is that it?" asked Fanny, tea cup frozen in mid air.

"The end?" said Franny.

"No more, my peony?" Mr. Helmsly-Wimpoll now, blue eyes bright in his pink face. "My pet?"

"You must end it, dearest," said Mrs. Helmsly-Wimpoll. "That is why you're here, surely."

"Yes, surely," said Fanny.

"Surely, surely," said Franny.

"Oh end it, surely!" said Mr. Helmsly-Wimpoll.

Ivy smiled, wondering if she'd ever get used to quadraphonic Wimpolls.

"That is, in fact, why I'm here. I was hoping to enlist the aid of my fellow sleuths. Franny, would you kindly drive me in your wonderful steamcar to the little church by Lasingstoke? I think my story needs to begin its end there."

"Spoken like a true novelist," sniffed Mrs. Helmsly-Wimpoll and she sat back in her chair. "You are Emily Bronte reborn!"

"Emily Bronte indeed!"

"Oh yes. Emily loves her ghosts!"

"Wonderful ghosts with all Brontes, my poppets," said Mr. Helmsly-Wimpoll and his blue eyes gleamed. "Perhaps you shall find a ghost or two of your own at Lasingstoke, wot?"

Mrs. Helmsly-Wimpoll laid a long, bony but gentle hand across hers.

"Not to worry, dearest and darling. Your heart will mend. It always does. Even the most tragically broken beaters manage to carry on." And she smiled the way a mule might bare its teeth. "Life is like that, you know."

"Life is like that," echoed Franny.

"Poor pigeon," said Mr. Helmsly-Wimpoll.

"So you think it's the Scourge, don't you, dearest?" said Fanny.

"Nasty Scourge," said Franny.

"A brute of a man," said Mrs. Helmsly-Wimpoll.

"Now, now, my partridges, Rupert St. John is a pillar of the township and keen businessman. Kept the Hall running in the black for years now, so don't be too quick to point your pretty pinkies. Your plucky Penny would wait to glean all the facts, first, wot?"

"And I respect him, sir. I really do," Ivy sighed, sat back. "But it is the only explanation."

Mr. Helmsly-Wimpoll raised a bushy blond brow. "*Only*, my poinsettia?"

"Only, darling?" said Mrs. Helmsly-Wimpoll, a phrase echoed by both sisters.

Ivy gazed into her tea, suddenly unsure.

"Well, off to work, my petals, my pearls," sang Mr. Helmsly-Wimpoll. "I have a limestone fact'ry to run. Someone needs to pay for the wedding event of the season! Ah ha! Ah ha!"

Ivy could not help but smile. Fanny had been busy this past month, renewing her correspondence with one, Mr. Ninian Liddell of the *Ghost Club,* London, and after several letters, an offer of marriage was once again presented. This time, however, it was accepted.

"Oh, the wedding!" sang Mrs. Helmsly-Wimpoll. "Our princess and her peculiar mathematician! It is indeed a marriage made in Pall Mall!"

"And Over Milling!"

"Oh, Mr. Helmsly-Wimpoll! You are too clever!"

"My pickel! My pansy!"

And for the first time in hours, Mr. and Mrs. Helmsly-Wimpoll pushed away from the table and with a kiss on the cheek for each of their girls, headed off hand in hand. Granny continued shuffling around the table, grumbling and wiping and picking up crumbs.

"My dear Liddell Ninny," Fanny beamed quietly. "He has become entirely respectable, even with such a superfluous profession."

"I've invited Albert Victor," said Franny.

"And I'm certain he will respond," said Fanny. "It is simply too prestigious an invitation to deny. You will help us find a dress, darling?"

"In Chester," said Franny.

"Oh yes, in Chester. Only the best dresses to be found in Chester."

"I would be delighted," said Ivy.

"Even with all this joyous talk, I can tell you are troubled, dearest." Fanny sat back. "You are committed to confronting the Scourge, aren't you? Is that wise?"

"Is that wise?"

"I need to speak with him at the very least. I need to ask him some questions, find out why…"

"Are you going to the grave?" asked Fanny and Ivy started.

"I… I hadn't considered it…"

"Oh, you should, dearest."

"You most certainly should."

She honestly hadn't thought of it. Of course, Sebastien had been buried there, at the little graveyard by the chapel. She would have seen it had she been invited to the funeral. Life was so very strange. Flat, now and strange.

She took a deep breath.

"Right. Let's go."

"Let's go!" exclaimed Fanny.

"Off to Lasingstoke!" cried Franny.

And so the sisters jostled and bumped and pulled and dragged their friend to the steamcar, where Franny spent over an hour preparing goggles, bricks of coal and of course, scarves and finally, as the November sun was beginning to wane, they packed up the steamcar and set out on the road for Lasingstoke.

***

It was quite dark by the time they chugged up to the small church. There were no lights inside and Ivy felt her heart sink. It was Sebastien's church after all. There would be no one to light candles or scrawl Latin on the walls in chalk and blood.

She stepped out of the wild little steamcar and turned immediately to the sisters. Fanny followed her out, Franny beginning to climb down from the dick so she stopped them in their tracks.

"No, my dear, dear friends," she began. "This is something I must do alone."

The sisters stared at her.

"Alone?" asked Fanny. "Are you sure that's wise?"

"Is it wise?"

"With the graves, the night…"

"The ghosts…"

"And how will you get to Lasingstoke, dear heart? Will you walk?"

"Will you run?"

"I know these roads. I know these trails. Besides, I stole this from my father."

And she reached into her small bag, pulling out a foot-long aluminium device. She twisted the gears and immediately a beam of light burst forth.

"What the devil is that?" shrieked Fanny, shrinking back from the light.

"A pocket torch!" Franny clapped her hands. "I've heard of them!"

"Yes, indeed," said Ivy. "It's a wondrous new invention. All the bobbies have them."

"Hmph," sniffed Fanny. "It may be wondrous for a bobbie in Whitechapel or a foolhardy girl criminologist in Lancashire, but for good normal folk, I can't say there'd be much of a use."

"No use?" asked Franny.

"None whatsoever. I can see simply no future in pocket torches, I'm afraid. And a Helmsly-Wimpoll woman is never wrong about such things."

Ivy smiled. "It doesn't matter. After the last few months, I can honestly say there is very little I fear here at Lasingstoke."

"Save the Scourge."

"He's a Scourge."

"Yes, well, there is that." She took a deep breath, gazed off to the distant lights of the Hall. "My brother is still there so I think Rupert will be civil. But if not…"

She turned back to them. "If not, you both are witness to the fact that I was going to confront Rupert St. John of most terrible crimes. The police will be certain to believe you both."

As expected, Fanny arched one brow. "Indeed. I fear our experience has proven otherwise."

"Nasty Peelers," grumbled Franny.

"And poor Mary Jane! She has received such terrible treatment that her husband has left her, yet again!"

"Wait? What is that?" asked Ivy. "Mary Jane is married?"

"Well… *you* know…"

"You know…"

Ivy frowned, for in fact, she didn't know. It didn't matter. She had a single purpose tonight, a single reason for being here in Lancashire in the first place, that being the dreaded conversation with Rupert St. John. She looked over her shoulder. That, and the grave.

"Very well," sniffed Fanny. "If you are most certain…"

"Most certain…"

"I am most certain. I still have my things at the Hall. And I believe Castlewaite will be kind enough to bring me back to Milling when I am ready." She could see the sisters' concern, their knit brows, their setting jaws. "Besides, we have a dress to find in Chester, don't we?"

That did it.

"Oh my, the dress!" Fanny brightened. "We shall have *such* a time finding that dress!"

"Such a time!"

Fanny sniffed. "Very well, dearest. We shall take our leave. But if you do not return by tomorrow, we shall be forced to consider more desperate measures."

"Much more desperate."

"I would hope for no less."

And with that, the sisters packed up into the four-wheeled steamcar and barreled off down the road to Over Milling.

Ivy stood for a long while watching them go, before turning back to the little church, a freshly dug grave, and the forbidden house called Seventh.

Chapter 42

Of the Women of Seventh, the Men of Second and a Killer Revealed

As she made her way through the grass, the beam from the torch swept over the graves in the dark. Some had frail wooden crosses, others smooth stones set into the earth. There were a few headstones as well with names carved into the plinth but for the most part, all were simple and very plain. There was none of the pomp and pageantry that was common in London cemeteries now. The 'Culture of Mourning' was currently all the rage in London. There, death was a hobby, a philosophy, a way of life, and it was not uncommon to see widows dress in black for the rest of their lives. Victoria was a trendsetter at twenty-seven years and counting.

Her breath caught in her throat when she spied the newest stone. It was unadorned save for a name and a horseshoe engraved in the plinth. No dates of birth nor death and it conspired to make her feel very sad. The grass was wet, the earth damp, but she knelt anyway, touched the soil with her fingers, breathed in the sweet scent of twilight and November pines and old, cold stone.

She would miss him terribly when she began to feel again. She wondered at that, wondered if the stirring of taste and touch, sight and sound would bring with it raw and painful sensations, or rather a clean slate and altered perspectives. She had no clue. She had always been the sort of girl to get on with it, chin up, bully through. Unlike her mother, she had never truly experienced loss. No wonder her father feared it so.

She frowned and glanced around the little graveyard. Everything was neat, everything normal. The church, the trees, the cold night sky. But something was wrong; she could feel it in her bones. Something amiss, undone, simply "off" in this little cemetery by the church. She set her mind to look for what was missing rather than what was there. She closed her eyes and rose to her feet, took a deep breath and looked back again.

She couldn't see it. Or perhaps it wasn't there.

At some point, she would need to admit she was not a Girl Criminologist, no matter how hard she tried.

With a sigh, she turned back, feeling an odd warmth at the distant lights of Lasingstoke. She remembered fondly Cookie and Castlewaite and dear sweet Lottie. She remembered the library and the piano, the warm fireplaces and the cold stone, the photochromes and paintings of fine men, finer horses and the great many happy laughing dogs.

Suddenly, she knew.

She lifted her chin and turned back to the grave, seeing as clear as day the missing element that would have completed the charade. It was an easy oversight and she felt a rush of pride that she had caught it. She set off, making her way through the headstones and wooden crosses and crunching under the dark canopy of trees still dripping with rain. Her torch cut swaths in the darkness, allowing her to find the path. Finally it bounced off stone and she knew she had found the Seventh House of Lasingstoke.

The windows were boarded up and a chain roped across the door, but she strode up to the door darker even than the night sky. She pounded on it with her fist, once, twice, three times.

"Sebastien! Sebastien, open this door! I know you are not dead, and I know you are in there! Open this door now!"

A cold wind picked up, plucking leaves and debris from the forest floor and whipping her skirt against the door. She pounded again, undeterred.

"I'm not going away, Sebastien, so I suggest you open up!"

The winds moaned now and for the first time, she felt fear rise in her chest. This was Seventh, after all. All manner of terrible things might be inside. She glanced around at the trees, bending and creaking like skeleton hands, the crosses in the distant graveyard rattling free of the earth and suddenly there was a thump from within the house. She whirled, casting the torch upward. The wall thumped again and one of the boards burst free from its nails, swinging a moment against the stone before sailing towards her like a spear. She ducked as it shattered on the path where she had been standing. The winds threatened and groaned.

"You will hear me, Sebastien. Whether you are inside here or at Lasingstoke Hall, you will hear me and you will come! I know it! Your women will wake you and call you here! So just come now, dammit! Just come for me!"

The winds threatened to push her off her feet and now, the boards covering the picture windows began to rattle as they fought against the nails holding them in place. She yelped as one by one, they flew from their moorings, whipping through the air like cannonballs from an ironclad.

The winds deafened her now, and her bowler flew from her head up into the branches of the trees.

"I'll not leave!" she shouted. "I don't believe it for a second, Sebastien! You are not as dead as you would like me to think! I know you are not. Your women don't scare—"

There was a clink of metal and she glanced down sharply as the chain that locked the door somehow wrapped itself around her wrist. It burned her skin with the cold.

She tried to pry it free with her fingers. She tugged at it, pulled with all her might, but it would not be moved. Finally she struck the chains with the pocket torch but the torch snapped in two. Instantly, she was plunged into the shadows cast by the trees and the house and the pale moon. The chain drew tight, the iron links digging into her flesh and suddenly, the wind died like the drawing of a deep breath.

The door thumped once, as did her heart.

"…Sebastien…?"

The door thumped again, this time on its hinges and made a terrible, grating sound, like nails on slate. The paint peeled long jagged ribbons into the wood like the claws of a giant cat. In fact, she could see slices tearing both paint and wood from the hinges now. The entire door thumped yet again, trying to shake itself loose from its moorings and suddenly it occurred to her that if the women of Seventh could almost kill her brother, a simple doorframe would not likely stand in their way.

And now, she had to admit that she didn't know which was more frightening—falling into the clutches of the women of Seventh, or the thought that the Mad Lord might not in fact be alive to stop them.

The wind picked up again and she strained to free her wrist from the chains when something brushed against her ankle. She looked down to see the figure of a hand pressing out of the door. It was long and misshapen, pushing through the door like an oaken glove. It was the most unnatural thing she had ever seen—more unnatural than a levitating man, a clockwork doctor or a face rent by ghostly claws and she found a scream building in her throat.

She stretched her feet far from the door but was constrained by the chains at her wrist and now a second hand, pushing from the surface of the door towards her face, reaching like a demon for her throat. The first hand caught her ankle and she screamed but it was deafened by the winds and the whipping trees and the howling house. Kicking and thrashing, she fell to the step as the horrible fingers wrapped around her boot. They began to drag her toward the door as if they meant to drag her through the wood and into the house. She knew she would surely never leave if they did that.

She grabbed the wooden wrist but could not stop it, turned her face away as the fingers reached the curve of her cheek, scratching her jaw, splintered nails reaching for her flesh, reaching...

She closed her eyes and whispered a prayer.

Movement all around her, the rush of fur and fang and heavy breathing and the squeal of a horse over the roar of the winds.

"Sedate vestras iras," barked a voice from above. *"Dimittite hanc mulierem. Ea non est inimica tuarum."*

Immediately, the rushing of winds and chains and fingers and doors quieted and she opened her eyes. Leaves dropped all around her to the dark floor of the forest.

And with the thud of boots on hard ground, a figure swung off the horse and loomed over her, leaning forward and placing palms against the door. Strange light flashed across the wood and up into the night sky.

"Habete pacem, mulieres spiritales."

It was as if the house called Seventh released a deep breath. The chains at her wrist fell away, the reaching hands sank back into the wood and the door laid flat against the walls, leaving her trembling on the step. Dogs whimpered all around her, nuzzling her with their noses and she slipped her fingers into their wet fur.

"Conabo durior," he said, sighing and he turned to lean back against the door. *"Habete pacem."*

And all was quiet in the forest, save for the whimpering of the dogs.

She looked up at the face silhouetted in the pale moonlight, the locket swinging around his neck.

"Hello Sebastien," she said in a small voice. "I knew you would come."

***

"'ere, girl," said Cookie. "Yer weak as a drowned cat. Some tea'll be good for yer bones."

And the housekeeper pressed the cup and saucer into her hand. Ivy took it, noticed the tremor as she did but lifted it to her lips nonetheless. Cookie tugged the blanket higher up on her shoulders, fussing over her like a mother hen.

"Enough of that," growled Rupert. "The skirt needs a Scotch, not tea."

They were in the Library of Second and a hearty fire was roaring in the hearth. Rupert St. John leaned against his wing chair, arms folded across his chest, staring at her with eyes as hard as flint. Sebastien stood facing the fire, a silent silhouette, and while Cookie fussed and coddled, the tension in the room was thick. Not one of the dogs on the floor was wagging.

"Ah'll go fetch some toast and honey. That'll set ye to rights."

"Thank you, Cookie," said Ivy and she managed a smile for the fearsome woman but Cookie merely shook her head before bustling out of the dark room. She was alone with the fine but frightening men of Lasingstoke.

"So?" said Rupert. "You want that Scotch then, skirt?"

"Yes, sir. A double, if you please."

He moved to a table, lifted a crystal decanter and set about pouring three glasses. The crystal clinked, the liquid lapped, the fire crackled. For the first time since Hollbrook House, her senses worked, every sound magnified, every scent amplified. Wet dog and leather, wood smoke and whiskey. She was trembling from head to toe, but her jaw was set and she would not back down. She would end this story if it killed her.

The Scourge of Lasingstoke stepped over to his nephew, pressed a glass into his hand, which was accepted and downed in one go. Rupert moved over to her, passed her a glass and this time he took his seat, swirling the Scotch around in the glass and watching it as it splashed within.

She sipped it now, feeling the burn as it slid down her throat. She was intent on emptying the entire contents when the Mad Lord of Lasingstoke spoke for the first time.

"You are a foolish girl," he growled, still looking at the fire. "A foolish, foolish little girl."

She said nothing, quietly sipped the Scotch.

"You could have been killed. You know that, don't you? I think you know that very well."

She had never seen him angry. Had even wondered if he was capable. Still, she concentrated on her Scotch. Like it, the whole world was a golden, intoxicating, mind-numbing blur.

"What if I weren't here at Lasingstoke? What if I were away, or in Lonsdale or Manchester or Wharcombe? What if I was—"

"Dead?"

He smashed the snifter into the fire and Rupert sighed.

"Expensive Kosta Boda, Laury," grumbled Rupert. "We'll have none left if you keep breaking them this way."

The Mad Lord turned now and the locket swung on its pendant, happy to be home. She could see the patch of hair shorn from his skull where the bullet had grazed. He looked older somehow, almost gaunt, and for the first time since meeting him, she was afraid.

"What were you thinking, Miss Savage? Please tell me. I truly wish to know."

Ivy tossed the rest of the Scotch back the way a man would, gagging as it lit a fire in her throat. But to her credit, she kept it down. Rupert smirked and she felt a flash of pride that she had caused it.

"Actually," she said. "I was thinking that if I rode up to Lasingstoke Hall, knocked on one of these many doors and asked to speak to the dead Lord de Lacey, you simply would not be available. Dead people generally aren't, I'm told."

"It was the only way. He said..." He stopped himself. "Damnation, woman. You are a bloody badger."

"*Who* said, sir? And what did this mysterious 'he' say? It must have been pretty terrible to make you want to pretend to kill yourself like that."

Suddenly she felt the heat rush to her cheeks and she rose to her feet.

"In fact, I hope it was a terrible thing, because what you *did* was a terrible thing. Poor Christien. He looked as though he had been hit by a four-wheeled steamcar. You tore the heart right out of him, you did. That was a terrible, terrible thing to do. To both of us."

Sebastien stepped toward her. "You should not be here."

She stepped toward him, her hands curling into fists at her sides. "Neither should you. You're dead."

"I should have let them have you, if only for a little while. It might have taught you some sense."

"But then you would have felt the urge to take my wounds on yourself like you did with Davis. I know you, sir. Chivalrous to the core."

"Rupert?" For some reason, Sebastien looked at his uncle. "What do I do with her?"

"Not *my* skirt..." Rupert rolled his eyes, swirled the Scotch and grinned his lazy cat grin. "How did you know he wasn't dead?"

She struggled to control her breathing, for she had never downed an entire Scotch so quickly. Or ever, for that matter.

"No pawprints on the grave."

Rupert looked down at the six dogs laying across the floor. Clancy raised his head, wagged.

"I know how these dogs adore him. Had there really been a body in that grave, I would have seen pawprints, digging, impressions of laying dogs, something. It was as unmourned as a parliamentarian's."

"Not bad," said Rupert.

"But that was not my first clue. No, that simply served to reinforce what I was already beginning to suspect."

"Your first clue?"

"Feathers." She looked at Sebastien now. "In the foyer of Hollbrook House. Feathers and an axe blow to the floor in the bedroom. That had Miss Lizzie Borden written all over it. And the undertaker's carriage. It was Frankow at the rein. Even with his silly cap and overcoat, I could tell it was he. I knew something had to be up, but still, it did take a while to come together in my head."

Her fists began to relax. "But there was so much blood…on the floor. On the walls. Poor, poor Pomfrey. And the doctor next door. How could you fool him?"

"She's caught it all, Laury. May as well tell her."

"You are both utterly impossible," growled the Mad Lord and he strode over to the small table for the Scotch, looked around for a glass. Rupert shrugged. Sebastien snatched up the decanter, took a long deep swig, set it down with a bang.

"Sit," said Sebastien.

"I think I'll stand."

He turned and raised a finger. *"Sit."*

She sat.

Rupert snorted. "Good dog."

"Jekyll," began Sebastien. "Is one of Frankow's men."

"Dr. Jekyll? Christien's neighbour?"

"The very one. Twenty years ago, when the Lovecrafts of Kent lost their fortune in petrol stocks, the house came up for sale. The War Office took it, leased it out from time to time. They figured it would come in handy to have an ear to the wall of a de Lacey residence."

"But why?"

"Because of my father, that's why." He sighed, pulled up an ottoman, dropped himself on it this time, the decanter still in his grip. The locket pulsed like a heartbeat, glittered like a star. "It was something your Mr. Beals said that got me started thinking, about whether my father was flesh or spirit? When he was a member of the Ghost Club, he and Frankow had been experimenting on soul transference—what the spiritualists might call 'possession.' It's a terrifying process and was quite likely the thing that drove him mad. It was, in fact, the last thing he had been working on before he killed himself, so naturally the Club was suspicious. Had he learned these techniques himself? Could a spirit truly ever be gone? And if he was not, in fact, gone, where was he these last fifteen years? Not heaven surely, and not likely hell, not if he could come back so easily. So where had his spirit been for fifteen years?"

She swallowed. The thought of such an horrible man moving through the body, the soul, of another was perhaps even more terrifying than all the women of Seventh.

He took another swig, wiped his mouth with his wrist and she wondered how he handled it so well. He drank rather heavily, she reckoned.

"In the holding cell of the Yard, my father entered the room. Told me if I did not do exactly as he said, then you, my dear Miss Savage, would be his next victim. First you, then your brother, then all the rest of this household, Rupert included."

"He could have tried," muttered the Scourge. "I'm quite certain I would have prevailed."

"While he was in the room, I noticed a face at the window. At first, I thought it was simply another of the dead—there were so many in the room at that time—so paid it no mind. On the way to Broadmoor, the carriage was struck by a steamcar. Spooked the horses something terrible but it was Carl at the stick—"

"Carl? Carl Feigenbaum? From Lonsdale?"

"The very one. He helped me escape, and it was then I realized the face at the window belonged to Mr. Home. Arvin had sent him to locate me in the building, keep an eye on me in order to best secure my release. Three stories up. He's got his skills back right smartly, he has."

Ivy sat forward, frowning. "Did Frankow bring them all to London? Lizzie, Carl, Home? All of them?"

"And Grigori as well."

"The undying Russian?" she said. "Grigori Raspberry?"

"Rasputin. His name is Rasputin. The boy can surely bleed. I'll attest to that."

She looked at his head, the shorn patch and red welt. "But you did shoot yourself, didn't you?"

"A mere graze across a metal skull. I am after all, a crackerjack shot. But I kept the locket with me. I could not bear what he might do with my Ghostlight…"

And he reached up, brushed it with the tips of his fingers. It pulsed and purred, a clockwork cat arching its back to the stroke.

Ivy glanced at Rupert, who did not look back.

"And so you planned to 'kill yourself' and slip out of the city… But why? Not to live somewhere else under an assumed identity. You would not have returned to Lasingstoke if that were the case, surely."

"Surely."

"So? Why return here?"

He now glanced at Rupert, who did not look back.

"Tell me, sir. Or I will simply continue my sleuthing. I can be quite persistent, as I'm sure you have noticed."

"To continue our investigations. My father is still at large in London, and while there hasn't been a Ripper murder for over a month, I'm positive it will not be in his constitution to stay down for much longer."

She cocked her head, puzzled. "I thought you said you'd lost the pistol?"

He said nothing, lifted the decanter, took another swig.

"So did your father give you the pistol that night? In the room at the Yard? Surely not, for they would never have let you onto the Broadmoor coach armed like that."

"No. He did not give it to me. It was waiting for me at Hollbrook."

"How odd." She puzzled for a long moment, saw the men exchange glances. There was something they did not want her to know, something she was very close to uncovering. She furrowed her brow, finding the thread, following it. "You said that Home saw you through the window…"

"Yes," he said. "I did say that."

"That Mr. Home saw you 'while your father was in the room with you.' You did say that, did you not?"

He rose to his feet, turned back to the fireplace.

"Well?" asked Ivy, glancing now between Mad Lord and Scourge. "Whom did he see? Did he see your father, Sebastien? Did he see

Renaud Jacobe St. John de Lacey?"

"No," said Rupert quietly and he stared at the fireplace. "He didn't see Renaud at all."

"But did he see someone, then? Anyone? I mean, if the spirit of Renaud was inhabiting the physical body of another man, surely Mr. Home would have seen this other man's face, yes?"

Neither Rupert nor Sebastien answered her. There was only the crackling of the fire now, the occasional sigh of a dog on the floor.

"Well?" She was not above begging. "Please, sirs. Out with it. I've been through far too much to see this affair ended so. Who did Mr. Home see in the room?"

Rupert smiled, but it was strained and sad.

"Christien," he said quietly. "Home saw Christien."

Ivy stared at him. He cleared his throat, tossed back the last of his Scotch.

"Yes. It appears that our Christien is the man all of London is calling Jack the Ripper."

Chapter 43

Of Brothers, Father's Sons and a Violet from Mother's Grave

November 8, 1888

The Good Samaritan was thick with smoke and the sharp tang of beer and unwashed bodies, but he didn't care overmuch. He had just cleaned out his locker from the students' row at the Royal, and everything had fit neatly into his medical bag. On his way out, he had shared a sad but civil conversation with Bond in the halls. The police surgeon was a decent man. He did not mention the torsos, nor the scandal, nor the suspension. Christien was grateful for that.

He had not seen the boys in weeks. Theirs had been a respectable profession with a promising future but now, with a disgraceful blot on their records, no hospital in London was willing to offer them internship. Lewis Powell-Smith had moved back to the family home in Cambridge, where it was said he was registered in the Law School there. Bender, also from a well-heeled family, was reported heading into the army to serve as a medic in Afghanistan. Williams had retired to private practice, citing a decline in his health and Rosie had simply disappeared. The boys had lost everything while in less than two months time he would have Sebastien's seat in the House of Lords. Life was funny that way.

He wondered if Ivy would have him then.

Girls had come tonight and girls had gone, each one trying to catch his eye. He was flash, he knew that full well and he stared at his reflection in the glass. He wondered if that was all they saw when they looked at him, wondered if that was how a woman might feel as she walked past a group of men. Did she turn the eye, melt the heart? Is that what was needed to catch and keep a man? If so, what was needed to catch and keep a woman?

He took a long swig from his beer and not for the first time, wondered what she was doing now.

"Oy, Remy de Lacey. If it ain't you, I'll skin me gran."

He raised his eyes to see a young woman in black velvet with fair curls and dazzling dimples. She was arm in arm with a mousey-haired woman of similar age. They were eying him up like a pearl necklace in a shop window.

He looked back into his drink and sighed. "Mary Jane."

She was smiling from ear to ear but her eyes were daggers.

"Marie Jeanette and mind the French."

He rubbed his temple, feeling his stomach lurch with the vertigo. *Damn these headaches.* He hadn't had one in weeks.

"Jules, this here's Christien Jeremie St. John de Lacey. Remy, say hallo to me mate, Jules. She's…" Mary Jane grinned slyly and nudged her companion. "She's Italian!"

"Italian," the woman giggled back. "I'ma froma Italia. Calla mia Julia." And she giggled again. Christien rolled his eyes. Julia was as Italian as Mary Jane was French. It was clear they were in their cups.

Mary Jane swished forward, pushed his shoulder so that he was forced to look at her.

"You owe me, Remy. All you gits do. Me man left on account o' yer lies and I got no money for me kife, let alone kippers." She moved closer, brought her face almost nose to nose and he could smell the gin. "You owe me Remy, an' I mean to collect."

"I have ten pounds," he said finally. "That is all I am willing to pay."

The woman called Julia squealed, but Mary Jane moved even closer still. She was a beautiful woman and she knew it.

"Ten pound, eh? Well, that's a start…"

He ran his eyes down past her face to her bodice, her tiny waist, the old bustle increasing the size of her hips. This was not Ivy's body. No, Ivy was small and slim, almost boyish. Mary Jane was all woman, and his head throbbed again, causing him to grimace with the pain of it.

She noticed, and stroked his cheek with her finger. It occurred to him that she would have made a tremendous nurse if life had been kinder.

"Oh, 'e's a poor lad, my Remy is. So 'ow's about a trade, then?" And she pushed him back in his chair and sat on his lap, straddling him with her skirts. "You pay me what you owe me, and I'll keep you company tonight." She kissed his forehead tenderly and he closed his eyes. "Me an' Julia both. We'll both keep you warm tonight. How's about that, me Remy boy, me pretty lad?"

He opened his eyes to see her face full of mischief, her coy mouth, those marvelous dimples. He was very sad tonight and had just received a fine offer.

She kissed him again and this time, he did not think of Ivy.

***

She held on to the pot for dear life as the *Chevalier* shook in the violent winds. They were approaching the Airships Docking Port at Whitehall and once again, there was lightning flashing across the skies. *Honestly,* she thought to herself, *how could people employ these contraptions?* It was worse than riding a drunken horse through a minefield in a snowstorm.

They had brought all six dogs with them but they were locked in the galley. Apparently, she was not the only one who disliked air travel.

"See here," Rupert was saying, and he passed her a bill. It was for a steamcar, purchased from Lancaster Motors on September 17. "He did in fact fly up on an airship, mostly likely coming to visit and in full control of his faculties. At some point, Renaud took over, killed Clara Clements of Maudgate, purchased the steamcar and drove back to London the next morning. We have receipts from all the steamstations along his route."

She took a deep breath. It was too difficult to believe. Christien, her Christien, the Ripper. Even now, as Rupert sat, smoking and shuffling through papers, she found it far more palatable to think Rupert the villain, Dr. John Williams or even dear, strange Sebastien. Anyone but Christien.

"He was up in June during the Solstice festival. Here's his receipt from the Tumblestone in Pelling the same date Tilly Barton was done. I believe her heart is still missing..."

"I think I know where he sent it."

Rupert glanced up at her. "You still don't believe it, do you?"

She clutched the pot tightly as ballast. Storms were rough everywhere tonight.

"I don't want to," she said.

"Well, that's honest. Sebastien found the pistol in his medical bag. Just like Renaud said."

Easier even to believe a dead man killing in the streets of Whitechapel.

"Remy saw him do it," Rupert went on. "He told me once when he was little. Renaud had just thrown Sebastien out the window and he turned, saw Remy staring at him with those great blue eyes of his..."

He sighed, flicked ash onto the floor of the airship.

"He put a hand on Remy's head, pulled the pistol and fired. It must have happened then. I can only guess how much our Remy has suffered."

"He never let on," Ivy said softly. "He is always in control of everything, what he says, what he does..."

"A mask. A bloody English mask on a very French face."

Rupert flicked his cigarette again and bent back to his papers.

She looked over at Sebastien, sitting cross-legged on the floor under the window. His eyes were closed, hands cupping the locket that was hanging from his neck and she could see snowflakes spinning in circles around his palms.

"That thing is killing him," said Rupert without looking up.

It was obvious. His eyes and cheeks were sunken, lips blue as they moved to unspoken words—prayers most likely, in Latin.

"Remy had it all along. I don't know how he managed to lay his hands on it—he was never allowed in their room."

"Is that why Renaud was able to wear Christien's body like his own, to be able to kill? Because of the locket?"

"Most likely, but I don't know, to be honest. This is not my world."

She nodded. "And the murders stopped when he gave it to me, but started again when I returned with it to London."

"Which is why we'll need to move quickly once it's back in the city."

"Yes." She looked over at the Mad Lord. "What is he doing?"

"Practicing."

"Practicing what?"

"Tracking. Something that Frankow was supposed to teach him, but didn't. Something about following a trail. Cold trail. Spirit trail. Something like that."

"Oh."

She could feel Rupert's eyes on her now and she looked away, heat growing in her cheeks.

"You've made your choice, then?"

"Sorry?"

"Of my boys. I assumed that with the 'death' of one and the ruin of the other, you'd see clear to leave well enough alone but yet, here you are back with a vengeance." He blew smoke out through tightened lips. "What are you thinking, little skirt?"

She looked down at her left hand. "I am wearing no man's ring, sir. I am a writer pursuing a story. No more than that."

"No more? Really?"

"Yes, sir." She swallowed, looking back at the Mad Lord sitting under the window. "No more than that."

But she was wearing tan breeches, riding boots and a red corset laced over her blouse so she imagined she had made a choice after all.

She clutched the pot a little tighter in her grasp and waited for the ship to dock.

***

Only a violet I plucked when but a boy,
And oft' times when I'm sad at heart, this flow'r has given me joy,
But while life does remain, in memoriam I'll retain
This small violet I plucked from mother's grave.

It was strange—wonderful strange and sad how a scrap of a tune forgotten since childhood comes back to mind so easily once begun. As they wandered the streets from Commercial around to Dorset and all the way to Osburn and Brick, then back around on Buxton towards the

Bells, they sang *'A Violet From Mother's Grave'*, again and again and again. He had a woman tucked under each arm and while it may have looked like they were supporting him, it was clearly the other way round. Both Mary Jane and Julia were quite drunk and he wondered how they could not afford food nor rent, but seemed to find enough for gin and beer. Gentlemen, he knew, hoping to buy their company with a drink or two. These girls had likely not paid for their own drinks in years.

For his part, Christien was not near as drunk as he would have liked tonight.

It was dark now and the streets were filled on this Friday night. The rain had held off but the fog had rolled in, keeping everything damp and chill. It wasn't toxic yet but he had masks in his bag, just in case. The Ripper had not struck in over a month and it seemed good times were returning to the worst street in London. For one night it was a wonderful and desperate delusion.

Scenes of my childhood arise before my gaze,
Bringing recollections of bygone happy days,
When down in the meadow in childhood I would roam;
No one's left to cheer me now within that good old home.
Father and mother they have passed away.
Sister and brother now lay beneath the clay;
But while life does remain, to cheer me I'll retain
This small violet I plucked from mother's grave

"My mum's dead, you know," said Christien and both girls turned their faces to look at him. He nodded seriously. "My dad killed her. Cut her into a hundred pieces in her bed."

"Like the Ripper," cooed Julia.

"Just like the Ripper."

"Did your dad swing for it?"

"He did not." Christien made a face, pulled his gloved left hand to his temple, made a pistol with his fingers. "Popped himself, he did. Right in front of me too. *Bam.* Have you ever seen a man shoot his own head off? It's a terrible thing."

"Just like yer brother," said Mary Jane.

He looked down at her. She was so very beautiful. "Just like my brother."

And he kissed her as they walked, bumping into a streetlamp and laughing it off.

"So you see, it's just like the song... *But now all is silent around the good old home, They all have left me in sorrow here to roam; While life does remain, in memoriam I'll retain This small violet I plucked from mother's grave.*"

And they all joined in on the chorus and sang as loud as they could as they walked drunkenly back towards 13 Miller's Court on Dorset.

***

It was clear that poor old Pomfrey had not been let in on the ruse as they pushed open the door into the foyer of Hollbrook House. As he took their coats and gloves, he looked as though he had just seen a ghost. Which, thought Ivy, was perfectly reasonable.

The dogs had stayed in the carriage with Castlewaite, to be taken to the mews to be fed. She couldn't imagine poor Pomfrey tending six happy, wet dogs the way Cookie did.

The three of them stomped up the steps to the long hall that led to the sleeping rooms. They stopped at one of the doors.

"This one?" asked Rupert, and Sebastien nodded sharply. He had not spoken at all since boarding the *Chevalier* and Rupert had warned her on more than one occasion not to touch him. The air around him was brutally cold, frosting up the windows in the carriage on the way in from the Big Ben Tower and she had found her teeth chattering on account of it. Even now, it was fogging the breaths in front of their faces as the door swung open onto Christien's room.

Rupert moved in to start a fire and she let her eyes sweep around the room. It was green. *Odd,* she thought. She had never seen Christien's bedroom, could not have imagined it. The colour was exquisite however, rich and velvety and elegant and she had to admit that it did suit him so. There were books everywhere, and strange mechanical devices with lenses and gears and wire. There was a birdcage in the window but no bird and by the bedside, a vial of pills. For his headaches, she knew. The neighbouring physician, Jekyll, had written him a script. Everything was neat, orderly, meticulous. Everything had its place.

She swallowed, fighting back the rush of emotion but she felt Rupert's eyes on her and was determined to hold up under them.

As St. John spoke to Pomfrey, Sebastien moved slowly into the center of the room and dropped to sitting, cross-legged on the floor. He took a long, deep breath, his exhale sounding like tinkling crystal and Ivy thought she had never seen a man so otherworldly as he looked now. His skin was pale, his pupils wide, almost fully black like a cat's in the night and she wondered what he was seeing.

"I need..." His voice hollow, echoing.

Rupert turned to him.

"Yes, Laury? What do you need?"

"I need something of his..." He turned his strange gaze to Pomfrey. "He sleeps here? In this room?"

"Why, yes sir. He does, sir. Most nights, sir. That is, when he is not working. Which he is not, these days..."

"Personal effects?" asked Rupert and Pomfrey shrugged.

"He had a bird, a pretty little songbird, but it died. It looked as if someone had wrung its neck, but who would do such a thing to a pretty little bird?"

Sebastien exhaled again and Ivy could have sworn she saw his breath fall to the floor like ice.

"His pillow. Give me his pillow."

Ivy glanced at Rupert, who nodded, so she moved quietly to the bed, lifted one of the pillows. It was heavy with the softest down, its case pure silk and she carried it as though it were the Crown Jewels as she crossed the floor.

"Carefully," said Rupert. "Don't touch him."

She nodded and passed the pillow into the Mad Lord's waiting hand.

He closed his eyes, ran his palms over the fabric, crushed the feathers in his grip. The locket began to spin once again and tiny sparks flashed in the darkness.

"A hospital... The Royal... He has gone to the Royal...why?"

"Ah, to collect his things, sir." Pomfrey answered. "His studies have been suspended."

Rupert crouched down close beside him. "It's closing on eleven, Laury. He's not at the Royal now. Where is he?"

"I don't know."

"You need to ask."

"I don't want to."

"You need to."

Rupert leaned closer and she could swear she saw the scruff of his chin begin to freeze.

"We need to find him and take him to Lonsdale. He will be safe at Lonsdale, Laury. Frankow will help him."

"Yes," said Sebastien. "Frankow will help."

"So, you need to ask."

Sebastien nodded and slowly Ivy watched as he dropped the pillow and turned his palms upward. A wind picked up in the bedroom.

Pomfrey stepped back, eyes wide and Ivy took his arm in hers. Truth be told, she wasn't any less afraid.

The wind lifted their hair and clothing, the drapes along the window, the papers on the dressers. Everything was moving and moaning and whirling in circles in the center of the room. She thought she could see faces in the swirling of the wind and she shuddered at the thought.

Ghostlight was spinning madly now and sending sparks into the wind. It began to rise off his chest as if being pulled heavenward by a powerful magnet.

Or angels.

There was a strange sound and the light of the fireplace began to reflect on the floor. She narrowed her eyes to see. It was ice growing in a slick across the floor. Like a shot, the ice flashed out the door and down the hall. Sebastien leapt to his feet and out the door after it. Rupert grabbed her shoulders, hauling her out of his way.

"You see?" said the Scourge. "Tracking. *Castlewaite!* Fetch the dogs!"

And together, the pair of them followed the Mad Lord out onto the streets of Kensington-Knightsbridge.

***

She fastened the last button of her bodice, slipped her feet into the boots and propped her foot onto the desk to draw the laces. There was a healthy fire in the hearth and she threw a look over to the bed. Julia was asleep, her mousey hair spilled across the pillow, one arm across de Lacey's chest. He was watching her with sleepy eyes.

She smiled.

"Yer a bonnie boy, my Remy," she said. "You were always better than the rest."

He blinked slowly but said nothing.

"The ten pounds? Where is it, then?"

"Why?"

She snatched her shawl from the chair, wrapped it around her shoulders. "I have bills, Remy and I likes to pay 'em."

He nodded at the pile of clothes on the floor. "Trousers, back pocket."

She snatched it up, pulled the bill from the pocket, slipped it into her bodice before folding the trousers neatly and laying them on the desk. She turned and swished over to the bed.

"But I'll be back, not to worry…" And she sat one hip on the edge, leaned over to stroke his fine face. "Ten pounds is too much for a mop like me…"

He gazed up at her. "You're beautiful."

"I could be," she said, running a finger along his cheek. "For a man like you, I could be anything. I could be yer moll, Remy. I'd like that. And I wouldn't have eyes for no other man, I wouldn't. I would be yers, all yers. Miss Ivy had it fer yer brother, but I'd only have eyes fer you."

She bent over, kissing him, felt his hands begin to move across her body once again. She caught them, brought them to her lips.

"I'll be back soon. And I'll be all yers."

She rose to her feet and left the room, closing the door quietly behind her.

***

It was very dark on the street and Sebastien tried to get his bearings. Late at night, from the looks of the sky and London judging from the skyline and the people. Only in London would people be out after dark, masked now because of the fog. It was difficult to remember how he had arrived back in London. He hated London. He would rather be dead than be here.

He was in a park, a city park and he ran through the list in his mind. Hyde Park, Green Park, St. James' Park, Regent's Park, Kensington Gardens, Battersea...

He smelled water, heard it lapping quietly on a shore. A bridge mirrored in a lake, a silver blue bridge over water.

Blue Bridge, St. James' Park. He was on the Mall at St. James, by Buckingham.

He had been following the ice. *Damnation.* He had been tracking.

He took a long deep breath, turned both palms upward to the sky.

"Adiuvate me," he whispered. *"Ostendite mihi viam."*

He could feel the chill start from his ribs, up his back to his throat and his teeth began chattering.

"Adiuvate me. Ostendite mihi viam. Adiuvate me. Ostendite mihi viam. Adiuvate me. Ostendite mihi viam."

He repeated the plea over and over until he was shaking with cold. He scanned the street, caught a flash of lamplight in the gutter. He stepped over toward it, eyes straining in the darkness.

There was ice in the gutter.

It crackled and stretched like a living thing, pointing like a finger, leading him eastward.

He went east.

***

The fire was dwindling as he slipped from the bed. It was late and she had not returned. He cared nothing for this Julia in this bed. She was a warm body, nothing more. But he did try not to disturb her as he raised the thin sheet and left her alone to begin the process of dressing.

He rolled up his stockings, pinned them to the garters before stepping into his trousers. He slipped into his shoes, pulled the spats overtop, watched with fascination the tendons in his hands as he worked the buttons. The cold air and warm fire made his skin prickle and he noticed the gooseflesh raise the hairs across his arms. Bodies, he thought. Bloody marvels.

Their clothes were strewn everywhere in the tiny room and he noticed a broken window, stuffed with paper and cloth. He shook his head, wondering how people lived this way. Hollbrook House must have seemed a palace to her. He bent to pick up a skirt, folded it neatly, placed it on the desk. A blouse, stockings, a chemise, a shawl, all he carefully handled, placing them in a meticulous stack. His shirt he plucked from the floor, shook out the ashes and bits of straw and gasped as his head suddenly split with the pain that had plagued him for years.

He dropped the shirt and lowered to a stool, rubbing his forehead until the ache subsided. He had not had one of these for weeks and he released a long breath, looked for and spied his medical bag by the door. Not a good place for it, he reckoned. In this lodging house, anyone could slip a hand in and nick it.

He swung it on the desk next to the clothes. There was a whisper in his ear, and he turned. No one was there, only the girl and she sleeping soundly as the grave. He frowned, turned back to the bag. His pills were in there and he reached in for them, somewhere between the hypodermic syringes and the stethoscope. There were his surgical instruments as well – his haemostats, gauzes, forceps and blades. The Lister, one of his favourites. A beautiful knife, producing a smooth cut. And Williams' surgical blade, a fine black-handled piece, razor sharp and easily gripped.

Pick it up, whispered a voice. *Feel it in your hand. It is a good blade. That's my boy. My saucy boy.*

His head throbbed and he closed the bag quickly, let his eyes slide over to the figure of the sleeping woman.

"I could be yer moll, Remy," she had said. *"I'd like that. And I wouldn't have eyes for no other man, I wouldn't. I would be yers. All yers. Miss Ivy had it fer yer brother, but I'd only have eyes fer you."*

Marie had been right. From the moment she had set foot in Lasingstoke, Ivy had had eyes for Sebastien. She had tried to deny it, but he had seen it, plain as day. She had strayed and lost her heart. She had given it away, a heart she had once promised to him.

But now all is silent around the good old home,

They all have left me in sorrow here to roam;
While life does remain, in memoriam I'll retain
This small violet I plucked from mother's grave.

His mother had given her heart away, and so his father had taken it back.

There had been so much blood.

He shook his head, trying to clear it. The whispers were growing louder.

Bloody marvels. Bloody, bloody marvels.

He looked back at his bag. It was opening all on its own, something grey reaching out.

The voice of angels.

And that was the last thing he remembered for the rest of the night.

Chapter 44

Of Six Dogs, Ten Bells and a Cry of Murder on Dorset Street

She pressed her nose against the window glass, trying to catch a glimpse of fur among the carriages clogging the streets at this hour. Apparently, Sebastien was tracking his brother and the dogs were tracking him. She wondered how Castlewaite in the dickey could keep them in his sights as they wove between the wheels and horses legs but the dogs were well-trained and did not bolt off after cats, steamcars or other distractions.

It was very late and she threw a weary glance at Rupert. He had a cigarette in his teeth, chewing rather than smoking it. He noticed her look.

"What?" he asked flatly.

"How is he doing this?"

"You think I understand, skirt? From what Frankow has said, the women are using the locket to track their killer."

"The dead women?"

"It would be rather difficult for a living woman to track her killer, since she is living."

She scowled at him. "But if he can do this, why doesn't he do it all the time?"

The man shrugged, pulled the stub from between his teeth, tossed it to the floor of the cab. "Because he doesn't know how. Because he isn't trained. Because he never had the locket. Because it's what led to the madness of his father. Take your pick, skirt. This is not my world, remember?"

"Why can't we touch him?"

"By God, you're a badger," he grunted, began lighting a second cigarette. "He used to have seven dogs. Once before, when he gave it a try, one got worried like Tag, got too close, nudged him with her nose. Sucked all the heat out of her in a heartbeat. Shattered into a thousand pieces all over the Persian carpet." He blew out a long stream of smoke, stared out the window. "Cookie was not amused."

"Oh…" was all Ivy could think to say as she tried not to imagine a shattered dog or Cookie.

They continued their journey through the bleak streets in silence.

***

He had followed the ice for hours. He was cold, wet and exhausted, and now the ice was gone and he stood under the gothic limestone pillars of Christ Church Spitalfields.

A church. Trust dead women to lead him to a church.

He knew it. He should have sent the very first one to the little chapel the moment he'd laid eyes on her. He had been too young. He hadn't known what to do.

Damn these cursed spirits. He would if he knew how.

His legs were shaking so he sank down onto the curved steps beneath the pediment. There were two gaslights by the doorway and one across the street above a pub that looked to be very busy. He squinted as he tried to read it. *Bells,* the sign said. *Ten Bells.* For the church bells, most likely. He wondered if they indeed rang ten.

At least the church was quiet. He would check and see if it were open in a moment, once he caught his wind. He had been on the move for most of the night and while Hollbrook House seemed worlds away from this terrible corner of the city, he knew it couldn't have been more than twelve miles. Didn't matter. He had failed.

He felt his muscles tremble in the aftermath of the tracking. It was brutally cold in their clutches, cold and black and empty like a grave. He had given himself over, they had led him here and left him, and now he was alone, sitting on the cold wet step of a church and no closer to finding his brother. *Pointless,* he thought miserably. *Useless. A Failure.* Even Ghostlight hung darkly against his chest.

He hoped the automabobs got good shots of him tonight. The Mad Lord de Lacey back from the grave. That would be poetic justice, he figured. The Peelers would chew on it for weeks.

He closed his eyes and leaned against the pillar, wishing for sleep. Instead, he got a wet nose.

He opened one eye. "Tagger…"

And then many wet noses and kisses as finally, a carriage rattled to a halt at the foot of the steps. Rupert stepped out with Ivy Savage at his heels. He shook his head. The woman was worse than one of his dogs. It was a wonder her nose wasn't wet.

"Laury?" asked Rupert, towering over him in the darkness.

"All done," he sighed. "All gone. Nothing. Nowhere. Pointless. Useless. Failed again."

"Oh stop grousing," said the man and reached under his arm to haul him to his feet. "Come on, little skirt. It's three a.m. and the pubs never close in Whitechapel. Let's get my boy a drink."

And Miss Savage too now, slipping her arm under his and together they lifted him to stand.

"Wait," he said. "Dogs. In the coach. Go. Go now."

One by one, the six dogs slunk off to hop into the coach, with tails— those that had them—tucked between their legs. Ivy wrinkled her nose.

"That is going to smell dreadful when we are finished."

Rupert grinned. "Then the point shall be to drink enough not to notice."

And they set off across Fournier Street to the pub.

***

It was nearing three a.m. when they pulled chairs at the *Bells.* An automaton furnished crudely as a woman, with large colanders for breasts, twisted copper wire for hair and tin petticoats, had taken their order and they sat now, Rupert drinking bourbon and Sebastien a second large dark ale. Ivy nursed an absinthe, not certain if she enjoyed the strong taste but also fearful of repeating her 'purl' experience of the month before. She was, she had convinced herself, a teetotaler.

Sebastien looked terrible. His eyes were completely different colours, his clothes muddy, his hair a wet, disheveled mess. He had in fact, just ran through a good half of London, and through a toxic fog to boot, but there was more than physical exertion playing a role. She was beginning to appreciate how taxing his abilities must be and wondered if he regretted not making that last shot count.

"Well, maybe the locket led you here," said Rupert, one hand on his bourbon as his eyes swept the crowds. "This place is close to the hospital and we know he was there tonight."

She watched as Sebastien finished his second ale and laid his head in his arms across the table. There was a peel of laughter and she looked to a doorway off the bar where a woman hung onto the arm of a man. Ivy recognized the dimples in a heartbeat.

Across the floor, their eyes locked for the briefest of moments before Mary Jane looked away, quickly ducking into the crowd with her companion. Ivy felt a pang of regret that friendship was not in the cards. She had liked the woman immensely.

Sebastien raised his head. The locket about his neck had begun spinning once again, but in the opposite direction.

"Rupert…"

"Mm-yes, Laury?"

"Oh God, Rupert…" he moaned.

St. John moved his bourbon aside. "Laury?"

And suddenly, Sebastien bolted to his feet, knocking his chair backwards in haste. He staggered towards the door, pushing patrons and knocking over their drinks as he passed. People grumbled at him but then again this was a public house in Whitechapel. A night was not a night without a brawl or a good drunk.

The fog hovered like a blanket and the air smelled of sulfur as Sebastien staggered onto the street. Many coaches parked along the roadside, making the narrow street narrower still and Ivy spied him leaning against one of them, retching into the gutter. Steam rose from storm drains and from the horses' breaths and from the gutter where his beer had landed.

They waited for him to finish before approaching.

"Laury?" said Rupert once again.

"There's another one…" he moaned, wiping his chin with his sleeve. "Oh Rupert, she's… I've never seen… Oh dear God…"

"It's alright, Laury," said Rupert. "We can still find him."

"Make her go away…"

"I can't, Laury. You know I can't."

"Where?" he moaned to the empty side walk. "Where are you? Lead me! *Ducite me!"*

And he gestured wildly, pleading with an invisible someone and to Ivy's eyes, she had never seen a man look so utterly insane as he did now.

Suddenly, he froze, turned his head back as the pub door swung open spilling light out into the dark street. Two patrons stepped out—Mary Jane Kelly and a man—laughing. The man pressed something into her palm and she kissed him on the cheek before wrapping her shawl and rushing off between the parked coaches on Fournier.

Sebastien's eyes had not left her for a moment and without a word, he set off to follow.

Rupert turned to look at Ivy. "I'm not certain—"

"Let's go," she said, darting off after the Mad Lord. Rupert shook his head and did the same.

***

Mary Jane moved swiftly, glancing behind her from time to time, as they followed in her footsteps. In fact, Sebastien was like a hound on a scent, Rupert only paces behind and Ivy was forced to run to keep up with them both in the darkness. Castlewaite followed with the coach but the streets had grown narrow and he was forced to wait for them on Shepherd. The fog was a Pea Souper, and she wished they had thought to bring their masks. Prolonged exposure to the Soup was toxic, and there was a thriving black market in stolen gas masks. Now, it was creating a strange illumination, catching the light from the streetlamps, bouncing it all around as if it were a strange silver dawn. In reality, it was very likely near four in the morning and for once, the streets of

Whitechapel were as silent as the grave.

Suddenly, the young woman swung around.

"Leave me!" she snapped, marching back toward them. "I know 'oo you are! You leave me and Remy be!"

Sebastien did not stop but caught her by the arms, forced her backwards into a wall.

"Where is he? Where?!"

"Murder! You let me be! *Murder!*"

"Where!?"

Rupert caught him, hauled him off the young woman as Ivy slipped in between, pushing the Mad Lord back and reaching for Mary Jane.

"Don't you touch me!" shouted the woman. She swatted Ivy's hands now and backed up down the street. "I'm not givin' the money back, I'm not! He owed me, fair and square so's I took it!"

"We don't want your money, Mary Jane—"

"*Marie*, you little mop! I told you! So you take yer Mad Lord and shove off! Remy's mine now, not yers!"

"Marie, I don't—"

"You left 'im, you did! Broke 'is poor 'eart! Picked *'im* instead." She stabbed a finger at the Mad Lord, still bound in Rupert's grip. "You made a bad choice of it, my girl. Remy's worth ten of him."

"Marie, Remy's not well—"

"He did right well tonight, I'd say. Kept up with two of us, he did. Aye, he did right well." The young woman tossed her blond curls. "Not like *you'd* know."

"Marie, we just need to see him. He has a condition." She reached into her pocket. "He has pills, see?"

Mary Jane eyed the bottle with suspicion.

"Fer his headaches?"

"Yes, Marie. For his headaches. Please, we just want to help him. Please."

She eyed Ivy now with equal suspicion.

"Your word, now. I know where you live. I could make big trouble fer yer dad."

"You have my word, Marie. We just want to help him."

"I'm not givin' up the money."

"I'm not asking—"

"I have one hundred pounds," said Rupert, stepping into the conversation. "Take us to him, and it's yours."

Mary Jane waivered. "You can't buy me."

"In point of fact, I can."

And he pulled a one hundred pound note from his pocket, held it out to her as one might a bone for a hungry dog. She snatched it from his grip, tucking it into her bodice.

"If you hurt 'im…"

Rupert sighed. "We're not going to hurt him, skirt."

"Marie." She fairly spat the name at him. "Marie Jeanette."

"Marie Jeanette." He grinned his lazy cat grin. *"Très jolie."*

She eyed him now and Ivy marveled at how quickly she shifted. She needed to, undoubtedly. She had lived on these streets a long time.

"And what about him?" She nodded her chin at Sebastien. "If he so much as lays a finger on me…"

"Then he'll wait in the coach with the rest of the dogs."

Sebastien glowered but said nothing.

"I'm not a cheap whore," she growled under her breath.

"I've just paid one hundred pounds, *chéri.* And I'm quite certain you're worth every penny."

She stared at him a long moment before nodding swiftly once.

"This way," she grumbled, turning and hiking off down Shepherd St.

***

Miller's Court was a crowded tenement building on an alley off Dorset. The arched entrance to the yard was long and narrow, and the odor of rotting garbage very strong. Ivy was sincerely wishing for gas mask now. The rubbish smelled worse than the Soup.

Mary Jane led them down the yard, stepping over a milk canister, a water bucket and several broken carriage wheels lying on the ground. Grass attempted to grow between the stones and heaving had made the footing treacherously uneven. They could see the light of a flickering fire but little else as the glass was blackened with soot. Mary Jane pulled a skeleton key from her skirts and fumbled with the lock.

415

"No," said Sebastien and Ivy turned. He was hanging back in the yard now, shaking his head. Around his neck, the locket was spinning and steady. "No, no, don't go in…"

Mary Jane snorted, twisted the key and stepped inside the room.

As if struck in the belly, she doubled up, a strangled cry escaping her throat. Rupert moved swiftly, covering her mouth with his hand and her dragged her out of the room into the shadows of the yard. Ivy watched as the woman thrashed in his grip until finally, she grew still. The Scourge of Lasingstoke turned her and held her while she wept.

He looked at Sebastien.

"He's not there."

The Mad Lord nodded, stepped past him into the tiny room and Ivy moved to follow. Rupert shook his head.

"No, skirt. It's best you not."

And for once, her chin did not rise.

"Take her to the coach. Castlewaite has a flask that will help with her nerves."

Ivy nodded, reached for the mother's sister's husband's sister's cousin of her best friends. The young woman was trembling, her breathing coming in ragged gasps, but she allowed herself to be passed into Ivy's care, did not struggle as Ivy slipped an arm around her waist and began to usher her from the yard.

"Murdered…" she moaned. "Julia…murdered…"

"Ssshh," hushed Ivy and together, they left Miller's Court. She did throw one look back over her shoulder to see Sebastien emerge from the lodging. He leaned against the doorframe, ran a hand across his face.

"…murder…"

She took Mary Jane's arm and led her toward the coach. She didn't know what to say, even less knew what to think. It was all true. Christien, her Christien. The man to whom she had pledged her heart, a murderer. Even as she walked, she began to shake as the horror of that thought sank deep into her bones.

Suddenly, a masked figure loomed out of the fog and into their path. The bulbous eyes glowed green and slowly, the man slid the mask up onto his fine forehead.

"Hello Ivy," said Christien and he held up a pearl ring in the gaslight.

"I believe you've lost something."

Chapter 45

Of Life, Death and Those in Between

"Christien!" she gasped.

"You..." growled Mary Jane. "You killed her! You cut her into pieces like a bloody sow on market day! How could you?"

"Easy," said Christien, slipping the ring back into his waistcoat pocket. "With a sharp enough blade, even tough meat like an East End whore carves like Sunday roast."

The sound that came from Mary Jane's throat was not a sound Ivy would ever forget and she lunged at the man she knew as Christien de Lacey. But before she could get close, he swung the clockwork pistol in a smooth arc from behind his back, cocking the hammer and aiming it between her pretty eyes. She pulled up short, fists clenched, seething.

"Ivy," he purred. "Come here."

She swallowed.

"Come here or I will put a bullet in her head."

"Run, girl," growled Mary Jane. "I don't care what he does t'me. But you run and tell yer dad who this bastard is. I want him to swing for what he did to Julia. In my bed."

Through the fog, Ivy could see his gloved finger move on the trigger.

"In my bed!" she screamed at him.

"Wait," said Ivy and her heart thudded in her chest. "I'll come, Renaud. I'll do whatever you say."

His blue, blue eyes brightened a moment and he cocked his head at her. "You know, girl?"

"I do, sir. I understand." And she took a step toward him.

"I doubt it very much." His perfect lips quirked but he grabbed her wrist and yanked her to his side, the remarkable pistol still aimed squarely at Mary Jane's head.

"You will do two things for me, whore. Firstly, you will greet my brother in my name. Tell him Renaud Jacobe St. John Lord de Lacey sends his regards. Tell him everything I have done has been for him, a gift from brother to brother. You like the French, don't you? Tell him, *une centaine de putes pour son seul.* A hundred whores for his one. Tell him that for me, will you? And secondly, for my bastard son—tell him..."

He yanked Ivy very close now, tucked her under his arm.

"Tell him to look for her head under St. Katharine's Dock."

For a brief moment, the two women locked eyes and while there was no friendship offered, there was one thing that was deeper, more intimate even than that.

Survival.

"I'll tell 'em," growled Mary Jane, moving side to side like a snake. "I'll tell them and they'll hang you from your neck 'til yer dead, they will."

"Au revoir, petite putain."

And he backed out of the alley, dragging Ivy with him. They were instantly swallowed by fog.

Mary Jane released a long, shuddering breath, wiped her face with her sleeve. She looked over her shoulder, fought off the tears and the helpless fury, looked back now in the direction the killer had gone, dragging the young writer with him.

She was alone in the lane. It would be easy to slip away into the crowds of London, seek lodging elsewhere in they city. She could even find haven back with her relations in Ireland or Wales or disappear entirely across the channel in the teeming streets of Paris. It would be so easy.

She raised her chin, just a little.

She turned and bolted back in the direction she had come.

***

Rupert closed the door quietly behind him, turned the skeleton key that had been left in the lock and slipped it into his pocket. He had found Remy's medical bag squared beside the neatly folded clothes, decided it would be best not to leave it for the police. He did not look inside, however. The unfortunate girl looked like she was missing some parts and he didn't want to see more than he had tonight. And so he stood just outside in the gaslight and released a long breath, waiting for his nerve to return.

He had witnessed a scene like that only once before in his life. It was remarkably similar in fact—the bed, the blood, the organs moved with great care around her body. Yes, remarkably similar, with the exception of the boys. He would never forget the boys. One lying as dead on the grass three stories down, the other fragile as a porcelain doll in the middle of it all. He would have died had it not been for the boys. They had needed him to live, and so he did. He would have killed himself that night had it not been for the boys.

Life, it seemed, was a mutual thing.

He turned and strode from the lodging, laying a hand on his nephew's arm.

"Let's go."

Together, they headed out under the long narrow archway that led to and from the yard. The fog was still thick as the smoke from the countless chimneys sank to hover over the ground. It smelled of rotting eggs and made him glad they were not out for long tonight. Once in your lungs, the Pea Soup was a bugger to dislodge.

They made their way back down Dorset, past the many lanes, alleys and narrow streets that rabbited this old part of the city. Finally they spied Castlewaite and the coach parked nearby on Shepherd. There were a few carts as well, no steamcars at all, and the street was quiet as a tomb.

Which, of course, it was.

With his own mask hiding his face, Castlewaite was huddled in a blanket on the dickey seat and he stirred at the sound of the dogs whimpering from within. He pushed the mask up onto his forehead.

"Aw, there y'are, sirs," he said, climbing down to the cobbled street. "And Miss Ivy? Where's she at, then?"

They slowed as the realization sunk in. Sebastien stopped but Rupert continued to the coach. He took a quick glance inside, through windows fogged by dog breath. He straightened.

"Damnation."

He passed the medical bag into the coachman's hands and turned, looking over at his nephew who was watching from the curb. Saw the gaunt cheeks and sunken eyes, the locket that beat a strong steady rhythm like a heartbeat. He felt his own heart break for both his boys. Damned the fascination with the arcane that had plagued his family for generations. It killed them all every time, just as it was killing them now.

Sebastien would do it. He only had to ask. He would call on that accursed clockwork locket, lose himself in the blackness of the spirits and die just a little bit more. He would do if asked. He would do it in a heartbeat.

"Laury," he began. "I think you need…"

But Sebastien had turned his head away, cocking it like a dog hearing a faraway sound. Presently, Rupert heard it too, footsteps running hard down wet cobblestones and soon, a figure in dark velvet and woolens appeared in the fog, blonde curls damp and weighed down by the night.

"He's got her," Mary Jane panted and she grabbed Rupert by the hand. "Come on, quick now. To the River!"

And she pulled him off his feet and together the three of them headed back into the fog.

***

It was a terrifying thought that in such a modern age that a man could still drag a woman around the dark streets of London undisturbed. Then again, this was the East End. There was more crime on one street in Whitechapel than in the rest of the city combined. Union Jack. Saucy Jack. It was all the same in Whitechapel.

He was taking her through the back lanes and alleys toward the river and the Docks, where he had told Mary Jane Kelly that he would take off her head. He was an expert in the streets, knowing when to pull her in close like lovers on a late night stroll, knowing just when to pause to avoid the click of an automabob or the sweep of a copper's pocket torch. He had slipped the mask down over his face, so he would be unrecognizable in either event, and the sight of him with huge green goggled eyes was terrifying.

St. Katharine's Way now and she could smell the water as he dragged her, could hear it as waves lapped against the hulls. The cables of huge cranes creaked in the breeze and bells from moored ships carried across the water. The fog was lifting over the River and she had a clearer view of the sheds, shanties and warehouses that littered the piers. She wondered if he was searching for a secluded spot. The quays, she reckoned, were a good place for a murder, but honestly, not for dismemberment.

"I would like to speak to Christien," she gasped. "Please, sir. May I speak to Christien?"

"Shut up, girl," he growled, voice hollow through the mask. "Or I will take out your tongue right here, right now."

"You are about to do far worse to me, sir. Why shouldn't I ask?"

He swung her around and brought the pistol up very close to her eyes.

"Because you hope, girl. Because if I cut you now, then you know for a fact how it ends and you don't want to believe that. And so, you hope."

She swallowed, knowing it to be quite true.

He turned and yanked her off her feet once again.

The sound of their boots had changed, so she knew at some point they had exchanged the cobbles of the Way for wood. Wood meant the pier, the shantytown that was the dock. So very near the place where her brother had died and her mother had stayed. She could smell tar and coal and the sharp tang of iron, and she wondered if there were shipsmen still working at this hour. And there it was, the faint flicker of hope that someone might be around to come to her aid. But she needed more than a willing longshoreman or dockworker.

She needed a miracle.

He dragged her between the cranes that unloaded the ships from Spain, Portugal, the West Indies and the Caribbean. To her left, the basins and the docks, the Ivory House, full to brimming with tea, feathers, shells, sugar and rugs. As they neared the door to the engineworks house, she noticed an iron bollard with an inscription—St. Katharine by the Tower. She had seen these bollards before, had once told Davis the story of St. Katharine of the Wheel, a young martyr who was forced to choose death by beheading or death under a massive iron wheel. While Renaud's blade was most certainly sharp, she sincerely doubted it would take her head off in one go.

Their boots clanged as they crossed the gangwalk toward the engineworks house, where massive steam engines pumped thousands of gallons of water for the locks and the basins. There were oars leaned up against the walls, captain's wheels and buckets on the ground. Her mind spun as she thought about using something, anything against him.

Suddenly, he froze and she could hear footsteps echoing on the pier. She spied the shapes of three people in the darkness, picking their way over the ropes and cables as they moved across the quay.

Renaud pulled her in close, slipped the mask up onto his forehead once again.

"Which one shall I kill first?" he whispered. "My brother, the bastard, or *la petite putain?"*

She swallowed. In the distance, she could see the lights of the locket flashing across the faces, across the water, across the pier. It was like a beacon, calling a ship to shore.

"Yes, you're right. The bastard, I think. He's the dangerous one." He looked down at her, smiled. "He is a crackerjack shot, don't you agree? Does he have an iron with him?"

"Christien, hear my voice. Stop this. Please."

Renaud lifted the pistol in his gloved hand, cocked the hammer, took aim.

"My... bastard... boy..."

Her eyes flicked once again to the oars.

His finger moved across the trigger.

***

The locket was spinning madly, flashing lights across their faces, across the water, across the pier. Sebastien paused as one after another, figures had begun to appear from the damp night air. Silver figures of mist and shadow taking shape before him. Women and men, some familiar, some not, all dead and very angry.

"Sixteen, seventeen, eighteen…Good lord, Rupert," he moaned. "How many has he killed?"

"I don't know, Laury," said his uncle. "Ren wasn't in his right mind for years."

The Mad Lord narrowed his eyes past the shantytown of wooden planks and sheet metal to the dark silhouette of the engine house. "He's there. Right in there. I can feel him."

And he raised his palms to the dark sky. Snowflakes began to circle and bend.

"No, Laury," said Rupert and he reached for his nephew. "Not here. It's too exposed. I don't like—"

Suddenly, there was a cry from the shanties and the sound of wood hitting bone.

Rupert lunged into Sebastien as a pistol shot broke the quiet of the night, and both men staggered.

One went down.

***

"You little whore!"

The pistol swung in a savage backhand, sending her into the side of the engine house with a thud. Lights popped behind her eyes as he hit her again with the pistol, and again until she dropped to her hands and knees onto the wood of the pier. She heard the pistol fire a second time, and then a third, before it clattered to the planks. She fumbled for the oar, caught it again but his heel stomped her wrist. Fire as he kicked her ribs and belly and chest until it was difficult to draw breath. There was no light at all now and she tried to scramble away but he caught her easily, felt him twist his fingers into her hair. He yanked her head up, bending her neck so far back that she felt as if it would surely crack.

She tasted blood on her tongue when a blade pressed onto her throat.

***

Mary Jane screamed as the second shot bored in through the fabric of her skirts, slicing open the flesh of her thigh. Sebastien grabbed handfuls of fabric, hauling them both out of the range of the final shot and to the cover of a nearby longshoreman's shed. The planks immediately grew dark underneath.

The young woman pulled herself to Rupert's side, fumbled with his bloody shirtfront but he stopped her, taking her wrist in his hand. He looked up at his nephew.

"Go, Laury… Stop him…"

"Rupert?"

"I'm fine. See? Just a scratch. *Jolie Marie* will tend me. I could not be in better hands. Now go. He's done his three shots. Save them if you can, but stop him."

The Mad Lord rose to his feet, the locket whirring and sending sparks now up into the sky. He stepped around the dock, palms upward and winds picked up as the frost began to descend.

"Homines et mulieres qui laesi sunt, nunc est ultio vestrum," he murmured. *"Accipite spiritum huius hominis et dimittite innocentem intra."*

As he walked forward, ice crackled along the planks, up the bollards and down the chains of the dock. Boats in the nearby water groaned and rose, hulls buckling as the mighty Thames itself began to freeze.

"Homines et mulieres qui laesi sunt, nunc est ultio vestrum. Accipite spiritum huius hominis et dimittite innocentem intra."

Ropes and cables snapped in the winds now and even the rooftops of the sheds began to peel and sway. Figures which, only moments before had been but shapes of mist and fog, began to solidify, forming arms, legs, torsos and finally faces out of the frost, until there was an mob of ghostly white marching with him along the quay. It was an army now, of flesh and bone, skin and ragged cloth.

"Homines et mulieres qui laesi sunt, nunc est ultio vestrum. Accipite spiritum huius hominis et dimittite innocentem intra."

An army of the dead.

***

"Damn him to hell!"

Suddenly, she was on her feet. The cold had rolled over them like a wave and she could not stop her teeth from chattering. Renaud's breath frosted the hair at her ear. The edge of the knife burnt with cold, creating blisters in her skin and he hauled her to the door of the enginehouse, swinging it open and shoving her inside. He bolted the door behind him.

At their feet was a spiral staircase gleaming black in the dim gaslight and she could hear the hiss and hum of the steam engines that operated the locks. He dragged her down after him, her boots clanking as they scuffed against the metal. Soon, they were in the basement, and he dragged her toward the golden glow of the engine room.

Underground once again.

Two massive steam engines flanked the room, their drums, cylinders and pistons chugging like trains on a track. Two great geared flywheels—each as large as an ox—drove the engines and she was certain that a grown man could stand up straight within the cylinders had they been still. Steam collected in long copper tubes to be reused in the pumping process that raised and lowered the canal to the level of the river. Still with the heat from the roaring twin boilers, water dripped from the ceiling and formed rivers of its own across the concrete floor.

To her dismay, the only dockman manning the boilers was an automaton. It swiveled as they entered.

"Security code?" it droned, its eyepieces whirring with its attempts to identify them. Renaud released his grip on her, strode up to the robot and efficiently twisted its head from its shoulders. The head bounced on a few wires, which he cut with the blade. It dropped to the floor with a clang. He turned to her and smiled.

"Your turn."

She bolted, diving between the engines, searching for something, anything that might prevent what was rapidly becoming her fate. Out of the corner of her eye, she could see him lunge in after her but she was small and quick and far less elegant than he. The flywheel rattled and hummed alongside her, creating friction of its own and she was grateful that she was not wearing skirts. One slip—of a lock of hair, a lace, a sleeve—any small misstep could cause her to be pulled into the machinery and crushed in a heartbeat. Like St. Katharine of the Wheel.

Like St. Katharine of the Wheel, she began to pray for a miracle.

She could see him dogging her behind the great iron gears, moving through the machine-works like a stalking cat but in his pursuit, he left the way to the stairwell open. She steeled her nerve, slipped out from under the drum and rushed for the stair. She made it up the first three steps before he caught her ankle and dragged her back down. Still, she kicked at him, striking his chin, his shoulder, his chest before he wrenched her foot and she heard something snap. She lunged forward now, clawing at his eyes, ignoring the pain as his blade opened red slices in her arms. He slammed her head into the metal rail and light flashed behind her eyes. It was all the opportunity he needed.

Dragging her from the stair, he spun her around and tugged her in tight against his body. His right hand clapped over her mouth. Through a haze, she saw the knife flash in the gaslight and closed her eyes.

***

He paused at the door to the engine house, at least two dozen dead pressing in on him from the air. He was not surprised to find it bolted, so he reached out the tip of a finger to draw a circle on the metal, leaving a slick of ice as it went. A star within it now, and placed fingers onto each point.

"In nomine Patris et Filii et Spiritus Sancti…"

He raised his other hand to cup the locket.

"Amen."

***

There was a moment when everything changed and the hand dropped away from her mouth.

"Ivy?" said Christien.

Chapter 46

Of Physics, Metaphysics and the Opening of the Clockwork Locket

She drew in a breath and then another and another, grateful for the sweet sensation of air filling her lungs. She breathed until, from the damp concrete floor, she looked up at the man who only moments ago had been trying to kill her.

It was Christien.

Amazing, she thought to herself. Exactly the same and yet so different. He was shrinking back, eyes wide, staring at the blood on his hands. The blade clattered to the floor at his feet.

He looked at her now, an expression of horror on his face.

"What is happening to me?" he wailed and she could see him shaking in the dim gaslight. Her eyes flicked to the blade, to the puddles on the floor that were slowing beginning to crackle and frost. She looked back up at him again.

"You're ill, Christien," she said, carefully pulling first one then the other knee underneath her. "The locket—"

"Yes, the locket," he moaned. "The locket makes me ill. It makes me lose myself…"

There was a stab of pain from her ankle and she could see her breath as she gasped. She glanced up as a droplet of condensation froze in a perfect icicle, hanging like the sword of Damacles over their heads. Slowly, ever so slowly, she reached for the blade.

"But we can help you. It's not your fault…"

"What's not?" He reached for her but she shrunk back now. He blinked in bewilderment and she could see tears brimming behind his lashes. "What's not my fault? Ivy, please?"

It was very cold behind her and she turned to see the black staircase growing white.

Suddenly there was a boom as the door above them shattered open. She ducked her head as a thousand frozen pieces rained down on them from above.

Illuminated by the locket's flashing lights, the Mad Lord stood at the top of the stair.

"Renaud Jacobe St. John de Lacey," he began, his voice hollow and echoing down like an automaton. *"Iudicium est in anima tua,".".*

"Bastien?"

"Iudicium est in anima tua," he repeated as he began down the stair, the locket throbbing like a heartbeat. "There is judgment on your soul."

"Bastien, please?" Christien moaned, pulling the gas mask from his brow as if it had grown too tight. He threw it to the ground.

Sebastien continued down the stair. In the flashes of Ghostlight, she could see the bones through his skin, his face empty like a skull, hands searing as they touched the cold metal of the railing.

Christien pulled the glove from his hand next and Ivy gasped at the sight. The finger that held the little brass ring was withered and black, tendons and bones visible beneath the rotting flesh. It was beginning to crackle with ice.

"Ego te ligo. Ei te ligant. Tu ligaris es."

Christien was shaking now and it broke her heart into a thousand shattered pieces. Like the door. Like the dog.

"Renaud Jacobe St. John de Lacey, *tu remittitur es et corona servita est.* You are forgiven and the Crown has been served."

Christien's eyes snapped open and he froze in place as the locket began to rise from his brother's chest.

"May God have mercy on your soul."

Christien stared at the locket and she let her eyes fix on it as well. Not only was it hovering in the air, suspended at the end of its chain, she was certain it was slowing. It had been spinning madly up to this point but now it was slowing, its rotations almost ticking like the hands of a clock. Like a countdown. Like a breath.

The Mad Lord merely closed the paper-thin layer of skin that covered his eyes and suddenly, all sound ceased.

Faces white and long dead surrounded them. Rising up from the floor, floating down from the doorway, peeling from the walls. Ivy could see them all now, real as her own flesh. A faceless woman hovered at Sebastien's side, gesturing with her hand and in her hand, was her heart.

Finally and for a brief fleeting moment, Ivy could see with the eyes of a cat.

She did not feel revulsion. She did not feel wonder. She felt very little at all, and she wondered if in fact, she was also dead but simply unaware of it yet.

It was Ghostlight. Somehow, the strange, beautiful artifact possessed a power she had never imagined. In fact, it was as if she had stepped out of time as everything around her now seemed to slow. The fire did not burn in the boilers. The belts and the pistons and the wheels slowed without so much as a squeak. The gears in the machine-works ground to a halt. All sound had ceased, all thought, all sensation, all life, all death for even the dead were silent now, empty eyes drawn to the pendant about de Lacey's neck. Everything was focused on that one thing, a simple clockwork creation of undiscovered elements, glass and angels.

The locket was holding its breath and everything in the world held with it.

And with a click that sounded like the roaring of a waterfall, it opened.

***

A small crowd was gathering on the quay. Dock workers, shipsmen and drunks, all claiming to have heard pistol shots and come to see. A bobbie had been sent for along with a surgeon and Mary Jane sat, stroking Rupert's forehead with her fingers as he bled all over the planks. She seemed numb to the world, a fragment of a woman pushed too far, but she refused help when the few men offered, preferring to sit and wait for the surgeons herself.

His breathing was raspy and she knew what that meant. She had seen her share of dead and dying. There was little a surgeon could do.

"It were right brave," she said softly. "Pushin' 'im outta the way, like that. I never seen no-one do nothin' like that before."

"My boys," he said. "I'd die for them."

"Still, it were right brave, all the same."

Suddenly, the crowd around her gasped and she looked up.

The engine-house of St. Katharine's Docks was shining.

***

Once, when she was little, she and her tad had driven out to the ring of great stones on Salisbury plain. It wasn't a solstice, it wasn't a festival, it was simply a night and they lay on their backs in the middle of the stones to watch the stars. Being a city girl, she had never seen a sky so big, so black and yet so amazingly bright at the same time and star after star shot across the night like fireworks.

Her tad had told her they were angels.

Inside the locket—so small and delicate—spun a universe of stars. Shooting stars, twinkling stars and collapsing stars; clouds of rainbow colours in hues she had never before seen. It was hypnotic, drawing all light into itself and she could not help but look. The spirits were equally drawn, abandoning their fleshly forms for heavenly ones, lifting into the air and circling the Mad Lord and the entire universe cupped in the palm of his hands.

And, just like that night on the Salisbury plain, she could have sworn she saw angels.

They came from within the Ghostlight as if it had no glass, no metal, only the unlimited expanse of sky. They were creatures of light, bending and folding like colours from a kaleidoscope and they swooped out from the rings like the shooting stars of Salisbury Plain. She watched, amazed as they swept around the engine-house, each one reaching for and catching one of the dead in their arms and she heard music like the rushing of great waters and a choir of a thousand voices lifted in song.

She could have sworn they were singing in Welsh.

She glanced at Sebastien. He was smiling like the sun but his eyes

431

were space. It was if they were windows open to the vast expanse of night sky and she could see stars and coloured clouds and suns spinning within him and she realized that at this moment, he was not a creature of this earth.

Perhaps he never was.

Behind him, the stairway, once black iron now gleamed gold and her eyes swept the engine room, marveling as gear after gear changed colour as well. They were turning into the colours of the locket – gold, brass, silver, copper and bronze and they had resumed their working, trading their hiss and hum for an increasing roar. The room was radiating with an iridescence that was at once beautiful and terrifying and the throb of otherworldly power pulsed like a drum.

Angels and spirits swept back in a rush, spinning in on the locket that swelled with their company. The light throbbed larger and larger, like a heartbeat and she found it difficult to keep watch, wondered if her eyes would burn out of their very sockets with the intensity. There was a great heaving of breath and a final burst of light and then silence.

A woman appeared before them all.

***

"Can you see, *jolie* Marie?" croaked Rupert.

"Aye," she said. "It's flash."

"Flash?"

She looked down at him. "Beautiful."

"Let me see."

She pulled him to sitting, wrapped her arms around him for support. The blood rushed up with the motion, threatening to spill out of his mouth, but he choked it back, waited for the pain to subside. He turned his face to the lights at the end of the pier and immediately, the pain was forgotten.

"Good Lord," he breathed.

"It's like stars," she said. "Stars and snowflakes, or the fireworks after a special speech. Right pretty, it is."

"She is so very beautiful…"

"Right pretty."

"The prettiest flower... In a wildflower meadow..."

For the last thing he saw was the face of Jane Penteny of Eccelston, smiling down on him.

***

It was Jane Penteny of Eccelston.

Ivy recognized her immediately from the photochromes. She was a vision of light, her blonde hair free and radiant, her smile warm, eyes dancing. Standing beside her eldest son, the resemblance was uncanny. She turned her face to Ivy now, reached up into the air and a shape began to form in the palm of her hand. It seemed to be a woman with a young child and Ivy felt her throat tighten as Jane blew across the shapes, separating them. Ivy knew that, no matter what happened down here in this damp dungeon of a room, her mother would be fine and whole once again.

Jane opened her mouth wide next, inhaled a deep breath and the child, Tobias, disappeared into her with the rest of the universe.

Now, Jane turned to Christien. He looked like a little boy, standing so still in the center of the room. In fact, he looked as though he himself might shatter at any moment and she reached out her hand again, this time to caress his cheek, trace the tears that were spilling from his lashes. Reached her other hand up to cup his face and slowly, they way a potter works wet clay, she began to pull another face from his, the face of her husband, Renaud.

Ivy could not tear her eyes away as slowly, deliberately she split her son in two, one of flesh and the other of spirit. Ivy could see the difference in their features but when the woman leaned into the ghostly face for a kiss, the image grew distorted. Winds picked up, whipping hair and clothing and the debris from the shattered door and it was accompanied by the now familiar roar of banshees. Renaud's face began to dissolve, first the skin and hair, shewing the muscles and then the bones beneath until he was but a skeleton, clasped in his wife's deadly embrace and even that too dissolved like a cube of sugar in hot tea. Christien staggered backwards, knees buckling as his mother turned away from him toward her eldest son.

When she looked back on it, Ivy was firmly convinced that time indeed had changed for, as Jane reached for Sebastien, the machine-works ran faster than ever and Christien sank slowly to his knees. As he did so, the engine's whipping belt caught the tip of the ringed finger and it was enough to pull him off his feet and into the machine.

Slowly, heavily, as if she were made of lead, Ivy lunged forward, catching the young physician under the arms, preventing him from being pulled in entirely. She swung her good leg under her, bracing against the machine as the flywheel ground his left hand in a mash of flesh, blood and bone.

"Sebastien!"

Her voice could barely be heard over the roaring of the machines and the wailing of the spirits and she threw a look over her shoulder. Lady Jane Penteny was still reaching out toward him and his attention was riveted on her alone. The flywheel groaned as it strained against Christien's forearm, the bones acting like a wedge and they began to splinter like eggshells. His eyes wide, she thought him in shock but he had added his own feet beside hers, bracing against the constant pull of the steam engine.

"Get the knife," he hissed. "Cut it off."

"Sebastien!!" she screamed, but he was reaching for his mother and in a flash of light, Ivy saw, not the face of a beautiful woman, but rather a skull and she knew that both sons would die tonight if she didn't stop it somehow. The wheel lurched again, drawing Christien even closer and the bones crunched up to the elbow joint. He gagged with the pain.

"Cut it off, Ivy! *Please!"*

She kicked off with her good foot, swung with one arm but the blade was several yards away. She would have to release him to get it, but she knew that he could not hold out against the unstoppable force of the machine. If it pulled him to the shoulder, there would be nothing to prevent the crushing of his head and neck. He was already too close, the thundering wheel no more than inches from his face and the pistons that worked beneath the wheel still strained, snatching at his shirt and buttons and towncoat.

She turned her head and filled her lungs one last time.

"Laury!"

In spite of the whipping roaring winds, the wailing banshees and the locket's hypnotic lights, the Mad Lord inclined his head, a dog hearing a far-away sound.

"Damn it, Laury!" she bellowed, her Welsh accent strong and true. "Get yor arse over here now!"

The figure of Jane Penteny raised both arms now, pleading with him but his star-eyed gaze had turned to Ivy. He took a step toward her when the woman wailed and laid her hands around the locket and the entire room thundered with sound. The locket had him fast, drawing him with a force that seemed to suck all light into it as well. She could see him fight against it like a horse bracing against the rein. Slowly, he reached back and snapped the chain, leaving it to hover for a moment before it too flew into the central pulsing light that was the woman.

The floor, walls and machine all throbbed like a great heartbeat as Sebastien scrambled toward her.

"Get the knife!!" Ivy yelled. "Bring it here, Bastien! Bring it here!"

He did not. When he reached her side, he did, however, turn his palms upward, setting the frost circling within.

She closed her eyes. It was hopeless. He was set on talking to ghosts, while his brother was slowly becoming one.

The room throbbed again, and again, and steam began to hiss as suddenly, the temperature in the room dropped like a stone. She opened her eyes, could see the breath in front of her face. He was studying the machine, the belts and the massive flywheel, the pistons and the drums and before she could say anything, he leaned forward and laid both hands on the belt. Frost began to travel up and down its length.

The machine-works shuddered as the newly-silver collector cracked, spilling steam out into the air. This steam froze immediately, sending hailstones pelting in all directions, pinging off the engines like tiny arrows. The entire room was vibrating now, shaking itself apart and the great gears, golden now from the locket's alchemy, rolled just a little bit more, crushing the widest part of the elbow like paper. Christien grew still in her arms.

"It's all right, Ivy," he whispered. "Let me go."

"No," she growled and she braced her injured foot now, using the pain to keep her sharp. "I'll not let go, *fy ddyn da*. And neither will you."

The belt squealed with tension, and she watched Sebastien's lips moving with phrases in Latin. *Such an odd sight*, she thought to herself. Truly, life was terrible strange.

And finally, when she thought she couldn't hold out any longer, the frozen belt snapped, sending the Mad Lord reeling backwards with the force of it. Pieces of it flew off to be caught up in the second engine and the screeching of metal on metal redoubled. The first machine finally came to a grinding halt, however and she released her grip to throw herself upon the blade and drag it back across the floor.

"Christien, what do I do?"

His eyes were closed, and so she shook him.

"Christien? I have the knife. Tell me what to do."

Slowly and with great difficulty, he opened his lids. Tiny blood vessels had burst in the whites of his eyes and his lips were blue. Still, she thought he was the most beautiful man she had ever seen.

"Here," he gestured weakly with his right hand. "Cut down at an angle… through the muscle and tendons…"

His breathing was shallow so words were difficult. He gestured again. "Here. Don't stop until it's done."

She swallowed, glanced around the room. The Mad Lord was pushing himself to his knees, a red welt across his cheek from the snapping of the belt. There was no woman in the middle of the room only Ghostlight, spinning like a tiny sun, drawing light into herself and causing the entire room to shudder and warp. The second engine was running wildly out of balance and water sprayed in through cracks in the stone.

With a deep breath, she wrapped her fingers around the black-hilted blade and began to saw. The blood was more than she had reckoned for and she found her hands slipping as she cut through the flesh of his upper arm, just at the point where it joined at the elbow. The flesh was simple compared to the hacking of cartilage and she found it required everything in her to continue as the blade snagged in the rounded mounds of the joint.

Finally, the arm came free and he fell back with a splash onto the floor.

As she tugged at the laces in the back of her corset, she glanced around the engine-works room. Water was spraying in from cracks in the walls and there was already a good two inches spread evenly across the floor. The walls themselves were shifting, bending inward toward the locket that was slowly sinking to the water, causing ripples to pulse out, causing great rumbles as it beat like a heart. It was as if she was in a carnival house of mirrors—nothing seemed real anymore.

Sebastien was kneeling in the water beside the locket, eyes starry skies as he tried vainly to contain it in his palms to no avail. A radiating field of light was pushing his hands away and she could see the skin puckering and red.

"Quickly, now, Miss Savage," he murmured. His voice was hollow, echoing. "I can't hold it much longer..."

The lace came loose in her hand and she bent to tie off Christien's arm above the elbow. He moaned and she tried to rouse him.

"Christien, can you walk? Christien?"

"My hand hurts... Did that damned ring finally come off?"

She glanced at the stump. He had no ring. He had no hand. It was a crushed, pulpy mess under the flywheel of the steam engine.

"Can you stand? We need to get out of here."

The walls rumbled now and she realized that the engine house, like all the strange, surreal places she had visited in these last few months, was underground. But what was more, it was underwater of the Thames and the basins of St. Katharine's Docks. Hundreds of thousands of gallons of water on all sides and they had just effectively destroyed the engines that held that water in check.

Without waiting for a response, she slipped her arm beneath his and lifted the young physician to his feet. He was very heavy, for the water on the floor had soaked through his clothing and it took several moments before he was able to stand.

Light from the locket flashed like a beacon, but now, with each pulse, the walls, floor and ceiling stretched further inward. A piston from the dead engine had worked its way loose and flew across the room, disappearing with a flare into the center of the locket. A bolt of chain followed suit. Ivy swallowed and began to move a little quicker.

"It's physics, Ivy," Christien mumbled as they sloshed across the floor. "All physics."

It was hard going, moving through the rising water on an injured ankle and half dragging a grown man but she continued, nonetheless. The floor, however, was bending and sliding beneath their feet and she could feel colder water running up from cracks in the stone.

"The gold is from the antimony, the ghosts merely illusions from the radiation. We could all explode at any time, you know. Any time at all..."

He was delirious, she knew it. From the effects of the amputation, from the effects of the locket, from the possession of his father. She couldn't tell which was worse, but she needed to get him out of this shrinking room and into the fresh air of morning.

It had to be morning, she told herself. This night simply could not go on forever.

Finally, they made it to the base of the iron stair. It was being pulled like taffy toward the pulsing of the locket. Already, the bolts that held it in place were shaking loose.

"Sebastien!" she shouted over the roar. "Are you coming?"

"Soon, Miss Savage," he called up from his position on the floor. He looked more skeleton than man and it broke her heart to see him this way. He had been so robust, back in Lasingstoke. "Once you are both safely up above."

"But you are coming? There is nothing more to be done down here, surely!"

"Soon."

She didn't believe him.

"But if I don't," he called up as the waters rose up over the locket, causing steam to hiss and the water to boil in whirlpools all around his kneeling form. "You will take care of him, yes?"

She felt those tears, one last time. "I will do my best."

He smiled, but it was a shadow of the sun.

She turned and dragged the insensate form of Christien Jeremie St. John de Lacey up the winding metal stair and into the first breaking light of dawn.

Chapter 47

Of Mary Jane Kelly, Mushroom Clouds and a Conversation in an Eight-Wheeled Steamcar

The Steam Times (London)
November 9, 1888
East End Doubly Shocked

The District of Whitechapel was awakened once again to perhaps its most horrendous murder to date. Mary Jane Kelly, a woman of low occupation, was found brutally butchered in her common lodging house in Miller's Court, Dorset Street. The atrocities committed against this poor woman have heretofore had no equal in the history of the city of London and she was found to be unrecognizable due to severe mutilations of her face and body. Police have asked for any witnesses to come forward at this time.

In an unrelated event, the engine-works house of St. Katharine's Docks, previously a marvel of Scottish engineering, collapsed this morning in a most shocking manner. Witnesses at the scene report shots being fired, flashing lights from the engine-works house and finally, a strange mushroom cloud as the house collapsed in on itself, sinking both it and the adjoining locks to the bottom of the Thames. The basins themselves have drained into the river and all shipping has been suspended until the canal can be repaired.

While we have no reported casualties at the present time, due to the severity of the news on both fronts, the Lord Mayor has postponed his procession as a declaration of support for the people of Whitechapel and Wapping.

Police are continuing to investigate.

***

It was raining now, but the streets were still crowded with carriages, coaches and pedestrians, and umbrellas bobbed along the walks like bumps on the back of a sea serpent. It was bleak but she was tired and her imagination simply got the better of her at times like this.

Heads turned as they drove past and she watched them through the windows of an eight-wheeled steamcar. Nearly twice as long as the four-wheeled variety, its chassis was wide and set low to the ground and the eight wheels hugged the cobblestones like rails. The ride was totally different, as most steamcars chugged and bounced their way through the streets, while this car's powerful engine alternately purred and roared like a great cat. There was enough room in the cab for a host of passengers, but she was sharing the cab with only one.

Edward, Prince of Wales, sat like a regal bear, hands draped across the hilt of an ebony cane, looking every inch a monarch in waiting. And here he was, taking her in his luxurious steamcar to her little rowhouse in Stepney.

Yes, simply remarkable the things she was taking in stride.

He noticed her look, grinned beneath his great moustache.

"It will all be fine, little *Cymry,*" and he reached forward to pat her knee. His prosthetic was gloved, but she could hear the gears whining within. "We've got our own Seargeant-Surgeon on this, Sir Prescott Gardener Hewett, Baronet. Ahem. He will affix our Remy's arm same as mine, my dear, just the same. Well, not completely the same, eh wot, given that the boy's a leftwing! Ah ha! Ah ha!"

And he guffawed at his own joke.

"He'll never be a surgeon again, true enough but there's a shit-load of surgeons in the Club. They won't let him go to waste, no sir. Not someone as fine as our young Remy!'

She smiled weakly. "Thank you, sir.

"Can't say the same for old Sinjin, wot?" He shook his bear-like head and frowned. "Mum's sent the papers for a clockwork heart. If the old bludger can hang on 'til we get it, then he'll be right as rain. The Scourge of Lasingstoke will have a heart after all! Ha ha!"

Rupert had been as good as dead by the time she had pulled Christien out of the engine-works house. She had little hope for his survival. Then again, life was proving to be wondrous strange and hope was a notorious thing to kill.

"He's found himself a tough little wench, wot? French, is she? Madeleine? Marie Antoinette?"

"Marie Jeanette," she corrected. "A cousin to some friends of mine up north."

She'd read the papers this morning, seen the error in the reports. She didn't even know the poor girl's name.

"Figured he'd pick a Frenchie, damn 'em all to hell. Sounds like a Mick to me, but still, she's a pretty thing and if he's happy with this one, then God be with 'em. Deserves some fun, old Sinjin does."

"Indeed, sir."

The steamcar purred around a sharp corner, sending water spraying across the pedestrians on the walk.

"Any word on Laury?"

"No, sir. Not yet, sir."

He sat back, draped his hands across the hilt of the stick once again. "Not to worry, little *Cymry*. That boy has been dead more often than not. It just don't stick."

She stared out the window once again, remembering morning on the river, the skies low, dark and red. There had been a crowd gathered on the docks, police as well, and as soon as she had handed Christien over, she had bolted back to the canal. The engine-works house was crumbling in on itself, light slicing through in beams from deep underground. The water of the lock, the basins and the river were freezing and boiling at the same time. Ships along the quay lifted with the ice and the red sky was alive with fireworks.

The gangwalk was gone, upended in the swell, leaving only a section of railing protruding from the quay, but even if it had been intact, she doubted she could have crossed. Hands had fallen onto her shoulders as a bobbie hauled her back. It was Constable Pleasant Poole and he pulled her to the ground, covering her with his body as the engine-works house gave one last heave and fell into the lock, sending stones flying and leaving a massive pit in the earth as it went. Immediately water had begun to surge in its wake.

A sound she would never forget—a boom louder than anything she had ever heard—sent a cloud of steam rushing up into the early morning sky. It was an oddly-shaped cloud, almost like the shape of a mushroom, billowing in then out, hanging low in the sky for several moments before finally dissipating over the docks in the form of cold rain.

She had pulled herself out from under the Constable and crawled to the edge of the quay. They were more like the white cliffs of Dover now and she had knelt to wait, watching for a sign of life from the water. Chunks of ice floated and steam bubbles hissed across the surface. At one point, she spied the head of the automaton partially trapped in a block of ice and she could have sworn she saw a flash of a massive golden gear reflecting the sunlight as it sank to the bottom of the lock. Finally, her eye was attracted to a very small something moving through the waters and she steeled her jaw. Ghostlight, quiet and as beautiful as a star. It bobbed a little as the current carried it through the ice until it was lost amid the floes and broken ships of the Thames.

Of the Mad Lord of Lasingstoke, there had been no sign.

"That's why the Clubbers want him something terrible," the Prince of Wales was saying. "They'd pull him inside out to find out what makes the boy tick. But he gives 'em a go for it, don't he? Outfoxes 'em all! Ah ha! Ah ha!"

He reached forward to clap her knee once again. He had not remarked on her choice of clothing, the breeches and the corset, the boots and the bowler. He was the figurehead of the Royal Navy, after all. Surely, he had seen worse.

"Oh yes, little *Cymry,* he's got more lives than a cat. He's always been a ruffian, that boy. Why, didn't he give me old mum sass last month? She's half a mind to toss him out a window herself! But he turns the girl's heads, he does. Bloody shame he's so strange..."

She'd had no idea how Edward had been notified so quickly. Perhaps it had been the police, perhaps the Ghost Club. They had been on their way to the Royal when the St. John Ambulance Corps carriage was diverted en route and taken to a private surgery off St. James' Square near Buckingham. After that, it was a bit of a blur, for someone had slipped her some chloroform, and she had awoken several hours later, her wounds tended, her clothes mended and with news of Christien's imminent surgery.

She looked over at the Prince. "I have a question, sir, if I may…"

"Go ahead, little *Cymry*," he said.

"The rings…"

He looked at her now and she could see the intelligence in his eyes. He did seem to try so desperately to hide it behind all his bluster and she wondered if it were something they were trained to do as babes in the Royal nursery.

"Christien, Dr. Williams and the Duke had them," she said. "I can't help but think they had something to do with all this."

Once again, she deliberately kept Mary Jane out of the conversation. As far as the city of London knew, Mary Jane Kelly was dead, murdered by the butcher of Whitechapel in her own bed. Somehow, it just seemed best to leave it that way.

"Damnation," he muttered under his breath. "I'd forgotten your dad was a Peeler."

The steamcar purred around another corner and she recognized the neighbourhood now. They were passing the Tower on Hill Road and he sighed, letting his eyes drift to the sights out the window.

"Having a child is a weighty thing, girl," he said after a while. "You live like you have never lived before. You love like you have never loved, you pray like you have never prayed, and you weep like you have never wept. There is nothing like the disappointment of a child to cut you to the very quick, and sometimes, they are so much like you that it is painful to behold. Yes, parenthood is a very messy business…"

She waited patiently. There was little else to do.

"My son likes his pleasures far too much. In that, he is like me. I gave my folks a run for the money, by God I did. Me mum has never forgiven me to this day for breaking my own father's heart. Ah yes, my Eddy does like his pleasures…"

He thumped the cane on the floor a little and she wondered if it was nerves. It was hard to imagine the most powerful man in the world nervous in front of anyone, let alone a calamity like herself.

"What I mean to say, *Cymry*, is that my son likes his whores. By God he likes 'em. He has no discretion when it comes to his pleasures. It makes no difference to him age or class, looks or even sex if you believe the papers. He just can't see that what he does matters, what he does has consequences, that he has been fated to live for something larger, better than himself..."

He removed the glove, tapped his clockwork elbow and a cigarette slipped out into his hand. It had only been a matter of time and she had to give him credit for lasting this long.

He lit up with the flint and took a long deep puff, holding it inside his mouth as if he could make time stop in that simple act. He turned his sharp eyes back on her.

"He knocked one up, you see. One of those East End girls that he fancied so much. At least, she said he did, claimed we needed to pay her to keep quiet. And so we did. A goodly sum, I might add. Paid for Williams to give her an abortion too, just in case. No one would believe an East End whore, but still, facts are not required in the presses these days and scandal follows Eddy like a terrier on a rat. So before you know it, there's another one saying he's done her good and she's got three rings as proof. I pay her off as well, but she doesn't want an abortion, this one. Of course that won't do, not with those damned rings. So one night, Williams has his boys get her drunk, and they run a clinic and do her while she's out. Remy, I think, was the one who did it. Poor boy. Jack should have known, with Remy's history. The boy couldn't handle it, carved her up like a ham and didn't remember a thing the next morning."

"But it wasn't Christien's 'history', was it, sir," she said. "That's far too simple an explanation. I know both the locket and the Ghost Club were involved in some way."

"Well, off the record, m'dear, I will say that Jack had his eye on our Remy for years, given that he was a de Lacey and all that. With the sort of things Renaud was working on, it only stood to reason that something of the gift would be passed on."

"But the rings belonged to Annie Chapman. Why would Williams gave Christien the ring of a woman he had murdered? That's horrible."

"All in the name of science, dear girl. The Club believes that life goes on after the body is long dead. They keep trying to prove it using scientific methods, but I think they may have stepped in a little too deep with the de Lacey boys."

"And Christien paid the price for it," she said.

"Someone always does."

"And the locket, then? Did they use Ghostlight to contact Renaud in some way? To release him?"

"I can't say, little *Cymry*. Perhaps Ghostlight used the Club for that purpose. I think that damned locket had a mind of it's own, wot?"

Ghostlight, a siren calling men to their deaths. She thought of Christien, clinical and driven, seeking answers but losing himself in the process. She thought of Sebastien, hollow and gaunt, sitting on the floor of the airship, snowflakes circling in his hands. Ghostlight was an opiate—a dark, dangerous, giddy addiction. Perhaps it was for the best that she was gone, lost in the crush of the Thames.

"No wonder it drives them all mad."

She looked out the window, at the bleak streets streaked with rain.

"So Dr. Williams knew."

"Knew?"

"Knew that Remy was killing those women. Knew that it wasn't his fault, that it was because of what the Ghost Club was doing, or what the locket was doing, I don't know. But *he* knew. He must have known."

"Entirely possible, little *Cymry*. But Jackie is a man of principles, never forget that. He loves Remy like a son and a father will do anything to protect his son."

"But the truth and the lies and the secrets, it's almost criminal. It is like a conspiracy, sir."

"It *is* a conspiracy, little *Cymry*," said Edward. "But a conspiracy of brilliant men working out their ideals, to the exclusion of all else. It is a crime of arrogance, nothing more."

"I have it on good authority that the dead women don't agree."

Edward blew a thin line of smoke out through his whiskers and narrowed his eyes.

"Welcome to the world of civilized men."

"But Tillie Barton, Clara Clements—"

"—With regards to any other crimes, I have no knowledge and I will deny any accusation to the contrary. In fact, I think you know more than I at this point, wot, little *Cymry?* Perhaps I would like to keep it that way."

She kept her gaze fixed now on the streets, the houses, the rain until finally the dark stacks of *Fermier's Fish and Crab* down the row.

The steamcar purred to a halt.

"Yes, I think I would very much like to keep it that way."

She said nothing. There was little else to say.

"Take this, little *Cymry*. You can return it to me at Sandringham once you are healed."

As he gave her the cane, he pressed it into her hand but he held fast for a long moment. She swallowed, unsure whether his grip was affection or a threat. With a man like this, it was perhaps a little of both.

"Thank you for the ride, sir."

The door was held open for her and she limped out of the steamcar and into the night.

***

The house was dark as she let herself in, and she set her bowler on the hook by the door. Stepped out of the boots, grateful that they were strong leather. Between them and the bandages, her ankle was only barely swollen.

"Tad?" she called and the cane tapped as she stepped forward into the foyer. There was a splash and she noticed a puddle of water on the floor.

She glanced up to the ceiling, expecting to see a dark circle but there was nothing.

"Tad?" she called again into the dark house and her heart thudded once in her chest.

Slowly, she moved into the kitchen, peering into each door as she went. There was no sound, save the sound of the rain on the windows.

There was no water in the kitchen. Clutching the cane like a cudgel, she investigated each room downstairs, the dining room, the sitting room and her father's study. No sign of water anywhere and she began to

446

breathe a little easier until she spied a puddle at the foot of the stair.

Yes, she was certain of it. There was a watery trail that led up to the second floor.

"Tad?" she called up again, suddenly filled with memories of Seventh House and Lonsdale Abbey and Lasingstoke Hall. Death everywhere she went. Death and ghosts and madness and blood.

She gripped the cane a little tighter and began to climb the stair.

A puddle outside the door of her bedroom, and she took a deep breath, heart thudding in her chest. Slowly, quietly pushed the door open.

Through the moonlight, she could see a strange shape in the middle of the room underneath her floral bedspread.

"It was the bearded woman," came the voice from under the cover. "She said you wouldn't mind."

She smiled, lifted a corner and slipped underneath.

***

"I'm so glad you've come out of it in one piece, my girl!" guffawed her father, Chief Inspector Charles Dreadful. "That was a tricky bit of deduction!"

"And a supernatural amount of good luck!" sang Penny, but she laid a hand on her father's sleeve. "But father, my dear Julian? Whatever is to become of him?"

"Not to worry, darling! The Specter Society will help him now. It wasn't his fault, after all!"

"No, not at all," she mused.

"Now, if only we could find that rascal Dunn!"

Penny Dreadful, Girl Criminologist, smiled to herself, for some secrets were best kept—as they say—like the dead.

The End of "Penny Dreadful and the Terror of Whitechapel"

Epilogue

Dr. John Williams sighed and tossed his cigarette into the fire. The last of his guests had finally left and the parlour still smelled of perfume and smoke, but the whist had been good. Fotheringham was a shark, he knew it, but he had given the bastard a run for his money. He made certain to lose, however. Patrons rarely returned when their charities bled them dry.

He reached for his Scotch, swirled it in the glass. They had raised ten thousand tonight. Ten thousand for the Library. He would have it, by God. A National Library filled with all things Welsh.

There was a knock on the front door and he rolled his eyes. Likely one of the guests, forgetting something or other. With great wealth came greater senselessness and he heard his wife's voice, speaking kindly to someone. She was a fine woman, he knew that full well. It was a shame she was barren.

He sipped the Scotch in silence until he heard her footfall, her singsong voice.

"Jack?"

"Liz?"

"It's a package, Jack. For you."

He frowned, set the tumbler down as she swished into the room. A package, wrapped in string and brown paper.

"Who's it from, then?"

"He didn't say. And there's no return address on the paper."

"Odd. Fetch me a pen knife, dear."

She did and he slit the strings, carefully unfolded the wrapper, let it drop to the floor like an autumn leaf. There was a note and he lifted it to the light of the fire.

"Dear Boss," it read. *"I fond this in the River n thot you'd like it well*

enuf. Haha. You n yer boys'll know wat to do. Signed Yor frend, Jack"

His wife was staring at him and he laid the note on the table to examine the package. It was a book, an old book but not a very old book, with a parchment cover and inked illustration. A first edition most likely, and he studied the print. It was in French.

Vingt Mille Lieues sous Les Mers, par Jules Verne.

20,000 Leagues Under the Sea.

"Did you purchase this book, Jack?" asked his wife and he shook his head.

"No, dear. I admit to reading it as a boy, but honestly, I..."

It made a soft thump in his hands.

He frowned yet again, carefully lifted the cover, turned the frontispiece to the first page which began to glow and hum. His heart thudded once in his chest, for in truth, there was no first page. There were no pages. The book was empty, hollowed out as a receptacle, no more, and his fingers trembled as he lifted the tissue covering to reveal two pouches, one of satin, one of leather. Carefully, he reached in, lifted the satin pouch, emptied the contents into his palm.

His heart stopped.

It was a locket. A clockwork locket fashioned from brass, copper, silver and gold, each tiny gear a different metal, spinning in connected but opposing directions like a watch. It was housed in a polished glass globe, again with brass, copper, silver and gold circlets ringing the globe and at the bottom apex, a pin.

"Oh, Jack. That's beautiful."

He swallowed, slipped it back into the pouch, hardly daring to breathe as he lifted the leather one now, turned it upside down. It stuck and he needed to give it a good shake before its contents dropped into his palm.

It was a human heart.

The End of
COLD STONE & IVY: The Ghost Club

Other Books by H. Leighton Dickson

The Rise of the Upper Kingdom
To Journey in the Year of the Tiger
To Walk in the Way of Lions
Songs in the Year of the Cat
Swallowtail & Sword
Snow in the Year of the Dragon

The Dragons of Solunas
Dragon of Ash & Stars
Dragon of Sand & Storm

The Empire of Steam
Cold Stone & Ivy: The Ghost Club
Cold Stone & Ivy 2: The Crown Prince
Cold Stone & Ivy 3: The Seventh House

Coming Soon
Ship of Spells
To Fall from the Roof of the World
Dragon of Salt & Bone

ABOUT THE AUTHOR

H. Leighton Dickson grew up in the wilds of the Canadian Shield, where her neighbours were wolves, moose, perennial-eating deer and the occasional lynx. She studied zoology at the University of Guelph and worked in the Edinburgh Zoological Gardens, where she fed Polar Bears medicine via baby bottles was chased by lions and wrestled deaf tigers.

Heather is currently repped by Desiree Wilson of Looking Glass Literary.

Continue the Ghostly Conversation!

Join the zoo at www.hleightondickson.com or on
Facebook at
https://www.facebook.com/HLeightonDickson.

.

www.ingramcontent.com/pod-product-compliance
Lightning Source LLC
Chambersburg PA
CBHW071959110726
47910CB00005B/1594